ONE LUCKY FOOL

TOM POINTER

ISBN-13: 978-0615917832
ISBN-10: 0615917836
Library of Congress Control Number: 2014904838
Tom Pointer, Austin, TX

In memory of
Fred,
whose own struggles
inspired
the main character
of this book.

Dedicated With Love
To My Mother

1

Rooster Brown paced back and forth in the darkness along the edge of the parking lot, furiously smoking a cigarette.

"Damn her," he muttered. "Damn that bitch."

He tossed the cigarette to the ground and crushed it under the toe of his cowboy boot, then promptly lit another. Even in the shadow of night, the pain was clearly etched upon his face. He had made the mistake of falling in love with the prettiest waitress at the only truck stop in a town with three red lights. She had barely given him the time of day since he moved there, and last night she all but laughed in his face when he finally got the nerve to ask her out, but tonight would be different.

The lights on the big neon sign flickered and buzzed. Crickets, many dead or dying, were scattered across the parking lot. The crickets had come into season unusually early that year, causing some to speculate that it was an omen.

He looked at his watch. Her shift would be over soon, and she would come out that door to her car parked in the darkness, beyond the reach of the neon sign.

A brand new 1956 Chevy sedan rolled slowly through the parking lot, crickets crackling under its wheels. Rooster stepped behind a pickup and watched it go by. Then he stepped back into the light of the flickering sign, reached down into his boot, and pulled out the old .38 revolver. He spun the cylinder, satisfied that each chamber contained a round.

"That's okay," he said softly to himself. "You won't laugh tonight."

Rooster looked at his watch again. It was eleven o'clock straight up. Jeanine should be coming out that door any second now. He reached for another cigarette, but stopped as headlights flashed across his eyes, and a car pulled off the highway and into the parking lot. It was a police squad car. It passed slowly by the front entrance of the truck stop and then pulled around to the side where it was dark and stopped. Rooster stepped back behind the pickup and crouched nervously in the darkness. No more than a minute later Jeanine walked out the front door. He could hear her talking as she left.

"Okay, good night. See ya'll tomorrow."

Rooster took a deep breath and stiffened, but she didn't go to her car. Instead, she walked to where the police car was parked. She looked around as she opened the passenger door and got in. Rooster could make out their shapes in the dim light of the car as they leaned together and kissed.

He stood and watched as the patrol car took off and turned out onto the highway. It peeled out on the asphalt and sped down the road on the way out of town. Not knowing what else to do, he sat down on the back of an old flatbed truck.

"You idiot!" he said aloud. "Damn it!"

He had gone over it in his mind a hundred times, planned for every possibility, except this one. Now it made sense. No wonder she had been cool to his attempts at flirting. He felt so stupid. He berated himself for not knowing better, yet there were many things he didn't know for he was a stranger in town. He had only been there for a couple of months, and he had spent most of that time out on the ranch where he worked and lived. It had been a lonely time for him, more so than usual. Over four years ago he had buried his father in the plot next to his mother, just before leaving for boot camp. He had no other family. He was alone and poor with no real hope of things ever getting better. It seemed life had been kicking him a little harder than usual lately.

Then a couple of weeks ago he happened to go into Mel's Truck Stop and saw an angel in a blue apron. Rooster had been without the company of a woman for a long time, something he had been feeling strongly since arriving at the ranch, the rancher's wrinkled old wife being the only female there. So he was smitten hard by Cupid when she sauntered to his booth for the first time and tossed the menu on the table in front of him.

However, he was awkward, clumsy, and sometimes lacking in social skills. He had always been a little ill at ease around women. He never knew exactly what to do, or what to say. His mother had died in childbirth, and with no sisters he lacked any day-to-day experience with females. He had managed to have a couple of sweethearts before, but each time they had dumped him for someone else. The idea of a romance gave him hope for the first time in a long while.

So two or three days each week he would use precious gasoline to drive into town, gambling that he might be able to strike up a relationship. He would show up at the truck stop in his best shirt and jeans, his hair slicked back. He could only afford coffee, and maybe sometimes a slice of pie. She would politely talk to him when he tried to start a conversation, but she remained aloof, and being a waitress she was never able to spend very long at his table before she had to tend to someone else. Finally, last night, his heart pounding, he waved her over to his table and awkwardly asked her out.

In hindsight, it was probably poor timing. She was rushing about with a tray full of dirty dishes, a shock of hair dangling across her forehead. She didn't even answer him, just gave a short disdainful laugh and walked away. To make things even worse several people had witnessed his humiliation.

He pulled the old gun from his boot and looked at it in disbelief and horror, the craziness of everything beginning to register for the first time. It frightened him. Sure, every now and then he would drink too much and raise a little hell. Back in the army fistfights were not unheard of, but never had he done anything like this. He didn't consider himself a violent man, not like his grandfather anyway. Yet he had put that gun in his boot in a fit of despair, his mind taken over by a raging hopelessness. He suddenly felt the crushing realization of how low his life had really sunk.

That old gun. Perhaps his father had been right, maybe it should have been destroyed long ago. The gun had once belonged to Rooster's outlaw grandfather. He was the one who had carved the four notches in the handle. After Granddaddy was killed the gun was passed on to Rooster's father, but his father had chosen a different path in life. He became a preacher and the old gun had lain in a pine box, hidden away for many years. After Rooster's father died he found the old gun while going through his belongings. He had only seen it once before when he was a child, but had overheard his father talk about it a few times.

He turned it around in his hand, running his finger over the notches. He felt numb and empty. Slowly he raised the gun and put the barrel to his head, his finger lightly caressing the trigger. He imagined how it would be when they found him, how it might be written up in the local newspaper, and how nobody would really miss him.

He had almost summoned the courage to pull the trigger when another car turned in off the highway going very fast. It screeched to a stop a few feet from the front entrance of the truck stop and two men leapt out. Rooster could see they each were carrying a pistol, and they appeared to be wearing bandanas over their faces. They rushed in the front door, he heard shouts, and then two shots were fired.

He ducked down and crept between the parked cars closer to the front windows where he could see what was going on inside. The men were gathering everyone together with their hands up. They were shouting and waving their pistols at the people, although he couldn't make out exactly what they were saying. There was an older man who didn't respond fast enough to their commands and one of the robbers began pistol whipping him. The robber knocked him down and kicked him as he lay on the floor trying his best to protect himself. A woman, apparently the man's wife, screamed and rushed to his side. The robber struck her across the face and she crumpled to the floor. Rooster felt a surge of rage flush his cheeks. The men began herding everyone into the kitchen, dragging the old couple by their clothing across the floor. Rooster ran around to the side entrance as they disappeared through the kitchen door and he quietly entered and crept behind the dining counter. From where he was crouched he could hear what was happening through the kitchen service window. Everyone was ordered on their knees. While one of the gunmen kept watch over them, the other forced one of the waitresses back out into the main dining area and to the cash register where she emptied it into a paper bag. Rooster was out of sight below the lunch counter, but he could hear them clearly.

"Bitch, if you're holding anything back I'm gonna blow your fucking brains out," the gunman snarled at the terrified waitress.

Rooster was stunned. He recognized the voice. It was Dwayne, one of the Blackwell brothers. Dwayne and his brother Hank were a couple of local troublemakers who had done some brush clearing at the ranch where Rooster worked. They had both served time in prison, and they were widely known for the beatings they inflicted on anyone who crossed them. Rooster had heard stories about the two of them that made his blood boil.

Dwayne and the waitress went back into the kitchen with the others. Rooster crept in around the dining counter and crouched below the service window. The Blackwell brothers were discussing what to do next.

"What you reckon we ought to do with these fine folks?" Dwayne asked.

"Shit, we ought to kill 'em, but let's just have us a little fun instead," said Hank.

"You!" Hank shouted. "Yeah, you bitch, get over here!"

Rooster couldn't see who he was yelling at, but he heard a female voice cry weakly, "Oh God. Please no."

Rooster slowly rose to where he could peep around the corner of the service window. A terrified young woman was being dragged across the floor by Hank. She wore the stained white apron of a cook and she had a smudge of flour on her cheek. She looked very young. Rooster had never seen her before. There were tears running down her cheeks and she seemed to be praying. Hank dragged her out to the middle of the floor and pointed the gun at her head.

"You sure are pretty, honey," Hank said. "Don't you think she's pretty, Dwayne?"

"Oh yeah, she's real pretty," said Dwayne, smiling.

Hank rubbed his crotch, then unzipped his pants, "Come here, honey, show us what you can do."

The young woman, by now becoming almost hysterical, began to sob loudly.

Rooster stood and fired. The bullet entered the outside corner of Hank's right eye and exited the left side of his head, spattering gore on the wall several feet away. Dwayne spun around, his eyes wide, caught completely off guard. Rooster fired again, but with Dwayne jumping about his aim was off the mark. The bullet grazed deeply into Dwayne's cheek and took off part of his left ear as he fell to the floor, the gun flying from his hand. Rooster charged through the kitchen double doors as Dwayne scrambled to reach his gun. Rooster aimed and fired, hitting him squarely in the side of the head. Dwayne dropped to the floor, jerked a few times, and was still.

Suddenly it was very quiet. No one moved. No one spoke. The only sound was the humming of the deep fryer. Hank's body made a gurgling noise. Rooster walked over to where the Blackwell boys lay. Pools of blood were beginning to spread over the floor. Bits of brain and skull were splattered about. He nudged one, then the other, with his foot. Then he walked slowly back into the dining area, leaned over, put his hands on his knees and retched.

In the first few moments after the shooting everyone in the café sat very still, unsure of what to expect next. Some of the women wept and the old man who had been pistol-whipped moaned softly. The first person to stir was Fred, the night manager of the truck stop. He crept from the kitchen, into the dining area, and over to the phone by the cash register. Rooster was sitting at a table on the other end of the room, his gun lying on the table. Fred squatted behind the cashier's stand with the phone and quietly told the operator to ring the police department.

Deputy Harvey Wells answered the call. Fred whispered shakily into the receiver and Harvey almost dropped the phone. When he finished talking, Fred set the receiver down, peeked over the counter, and slowly stood. Rooster was still sitting exactly as he had been before. Fred tiptoed back into the kitchen to help comfort those in need of it and he stayed there until he heard the siren a few minutes later.

Rooster sat staring dumbly at the jukebox. He thought briefly about trying to run. He was dimly aware that someone had come in and called the police. Time seemed to stand still.

When Harvey arrived in a screech of tires, Fred ran out the side door to meet him. Rooster sat at his table watching them talk in the parking lot, a faint mirror image of himself in the window was superimposed over the two men standing outside. He could only hear bits and snatches of what they were saying: "...thought for sure we were all dead...Laurie Tucker was about one second from being raped...saved everyone..." They both turned and looked at him. He heard the manager say, "I've seen him around, but I don't know who he is."

From the parking lot they watched him through the window, and after Fred had filled in the deputy, they both walked cautiously through the front door. Rooster made no attempt to rise, or to turn around and look at them. Harvey, his hand on his revolver, slowly approached Rooster.

"Don't move, mister," he said.

Rooster didn't move. Harvey pulled out a handkerchief and picked up Rooster's pistol.

"Don't go anywhere, wait right here," he told Rooster.

Then he walked over to the kitchen door and peeked in.

"Oh Lord," he said.

Harvey looked back at Rooster, then turned to Fred.

"Don't let him go nowhere."

Harvey went into the kitchen, leaving Rooster and Fred alone. Fred began to relax a bit now that Rooster was unarmed and seemingly calm. He sat down on a stool at the dining counter and lit a cigarette. He offered the pack to Rooster.

"Smoke?"

Rooster paused, then took a cigarette from the pack. Fred lit it for him.

"Thanks," Rooster said quietly.

Fred studied Rooster as he smoked the cigarette. He was tall, lanky, and broad shouldered, and he seemed much younger now. He looked frightened and worried.

"Those sorry bastards probably would have killed somebody before it was all over with," Fred said. "I was pretty damn scared."

"I thought they was gonna hurt that girl. I had to stop 'em somehow," Rooster said dully.

"Shit, as far as I'm concerned you saved all our asses. I told the deputy the same thing, and I'll testify to it in court if need be." Then Fred leaned over and whispered, "If they would've had their way with poor Laurie it would've just plumb killed her. She would've never got over it."

Harvey leaned in from the dining area to make sure Rooster was still there, then disappeared back into the kitchen. As Rooster and Fred sat smoking their cigarettes, Wanda, the oldest waitress at the truck stop, came into the dining area and timidly approached Rooster.

"I don't know how I can ever thank you enough," she said, her voice wavering. "You saved us all. God bless you."

Rooster just stared back at her dumbly. He had been sitting there all along expecting to be arrested and promptly executed for murder. He had come to kill someone that night, and in fact had killed two men. It hadn't yet occurred to him that he had just rescued close to a dozen people from armed robbers.

"The whole time those men were here I prayed and prayed for the Lord to send an angel to protect us, and he did," she said, weeping softly. "An angel in flesh and bone," she said patting his shoulder as if to confirm that he was actually human.

Harvey came back into the dining area shaking his head.

"Well, everybody in there says he saved their lives," he said, nodding toward Rooster. "Said he just came out of nowhere."

Just then, another police car with flashing lights and siren wailing sped into the parking lot and stopped. Rooster could see the word SHERIFF in large letters on the door. The door flung open and a tall, lanky man stepped out of the car. His shirttail was partially out and he had the rumpled appearance of someone who had hastily dressed. He put on a cowboy hat and strode toward the front door of the truck stop. Harvey met him at the door.

"Where's the shooter?" he asked Harvey gruffly.

Harvey pointed toward Rooster still sitting quietly at the table.

"Goddamn it, Harvey! Why isn't he in handcuffs?" he exploded at the deputy.

"He's not going anywhere, Bill. He was sitting there just like that when I got here. They all say he's the one that saved everybody. The Blackwell boys were robbing the place and they said that fellow was the only thing that kept Laurie Tucker from getting raped."

"Two people are dead, and until we get things straightened out he goes in the cuffs." The sheriff took out his own handcuffs and put them on Rooster. "Put him in the back of my car," he told Harvey.

Harvey pulled Rooster up by his arm and took him to the backseat of the sheriff's car. As he was putting Rooster in the car Harvey spoke softly to him, "Don't worry, mister. Everybody says you're a hero. You won't be in cuffs for long. Most people around here would say you deserve a medal for shooting the Blackwell boys."

Rooster sat in the car and watched as a small crowd of eight or ten people formed along the perimeter of the parking lot. Apparently there were still a few souls up at that time of night. A cool breeze wafted in through the open windows of the car. Rooster's mind started to clear and he began to assess his situation. He was realizing that he probably would not go the electric chair, and if he was lucky, he might not even go to prison. The waitress and the manager had called him a hero, and even the deputy had said he deserved a medal. If he played it right, and gave the right answers, he might just be able to make it seem like he really was a hero. No one knew him, and certainly no one knew that he had come there that night with cold-blooded murder in his heart, or that thirty minutes ago he was seconds from killing himself. He began to think very hard.

As Rooster sat planning his alibi another police car raced into the parking lot. Rooster watched as this deputy jumped out of his car and hustled into the truck stop. He realized that this was the one who had left with Jeanine, the one whose appearance had changed his plans, and more than he understood at that moment, his life.

The sheriff, Bill Hickey, was known as a by-the-book kind of lawman, so when his other deputy, Wayne Bates, ran into the diner in a rumpled shirt and his fly open, Bill glared at him. Wayne hung his head and walked over to him.

"I had a hellacious attack of diarrhea. I was in a ditch five miles outside of town when I heard the call."

"You mean you were in a bitch five miles outside of town. If we'd had to depend on you tonight no telling how many people might be dead. Now get over there and help Harvey. I'll deal with you later."

An ambulance came to take the old couple to the hospital and everyone else gave statements to Harvey and Wayne. The sheriff called Mel Tucker, the owner of the truck stop.

"Mel? This is Bill Hickey. Sorry to wake you, but there was an attempted robbery at the truck stop tonight...no, they didn't get away with anything...Laurie's okay, just a little shaken up...it was the Blackwell boys, some stranger came in and shot both of them... no, they're dead...yeah, I feel the same way...okay, I'm taking the boy that shot them down to the station...see you in a little bit."

Sheriff Hickey hung up the phone and watched as Harvey and Wayne, each with a note pad, went from person to person. Then he walked back into the kitchen where the bodies of the Blackwell boys lay in pools of blood. He smiled slightly, and spoke softly so that no one in the next room would hear.

"They say you shouldn't look a gift horse in the mouth."

He strolled slowly around the bodies, stooping to lift the bandanas that still partially covered their faces. One of Hank's eyes was half-closed, and the other seemed to stare at a calendar on the wall. Dwayne's eyes were shut and his face frozen into a grimace. The sheriff squatted and studied them from head to toe. Finally, he got up and walked into the dining area where the deputies had just finished taking statements from the witnesses. Harvey walked over to him amiably.

"Well, Bill, I guess we don't have too much reason to hold the guy," Harvey said. "Everybody says he saved them."

The sheriff just looked at Harvey. He was an idiot, and sometimes he despised him, but he was the grandson of Henry Wells, the president of the Merky Bank, to whom the sheriff was deeply indebted.

"Harvey, you don't just turn somebody loose that killed two people. We'll take him in and have a little talk with him and figure out if any charges need to be filed, whether it's murder or disturbing the peace. Then he has to go before a judge who'll decide if he has to post bail. Most likely they'll put it before a grand jury who'll decide whether it goes to trial or not."

Harvey, knowing he had said something stupid, cast his eyes down and nodded. The sheriff spoke with Wayne, and satisfied that things were mostly wrapped up, walked out to his car where Rooster sat waiting. A hearse arrived to pick up the bodies and Harvey stayed behind to help clean up the crime scene. Wayne went to his car to follow the sheriff back to the station.

It was a short ride to the police station, which was on the first floor of the courthouse. Neither Rooster nor the sheriff said anything. Rooster mostly stared out the window at the full moon shining over the tree tops. A cool breeze rushed in from the front window, blowing across his forehead and refreshing him.

The town square was almost empty when they arrived, not surprising for so early on a Friday morning. They pulled up in front of the courthouse and parked underneath a couple of large trees. Rooster peered out from the car window at the front entrance of the courthouse.

Above the main doors in large letters was the county name—Loma Grande.

The small town of Merky was the county seat of Loma Grande County and the only community of any consequence in the two-thousand square miles that the county covered. It was eighty miles from the main border crossing in that part of Texas, and had grown up around a spring that eventually fed into the Rio Grande River. It was truly an oasis in a vast nothingness, surrounded by miles and miles of hilly, rocky terrain. Several miles south of Merky there was a small army base that had been established in Pancho Villa's heyday. During World War II it had been used as a training site for soldiers heading to Northern Africa, but now it only had a few hundred soldiers stationed there. It was kept in operation largely at the request of the local congressman. That was how Rooster wound up in Merky. When he came back from Germany he was hoping to get stationed at Fort Bliss, but had to settle for Fort Taylor (which everyone referred to as Fort Tamale), where he spent the last few months of his hitch. Having no place else to go, he decided to try his luck in Merky.

Wayne pulled in next to the sheriff and they both got out of their cars. The sheriff opened the back door of his car, took Rooster by the arm, and helped him from the back seat. A cattle truck rumbled through the town square, leaving an odorous wake of diesel fumes and cow manure. No one spoke as they all three walked into the courthouse and into the lobby of the sheriff's office. The night watchman and the jailer were waiting for them, both of them carefully scrutinizing Rooster. Wayne laid Rooster's old pistol on a desk, still wrapped in the handkerchief, and they sat him in a wooden desk chair. The sheriff looked at the jailer and the night watchman and nodded toward the office door. They took the hint and silently left, closing the door behind them. The sheriff studied Rooster for a moment.

"Take the cuffs off him," he told Wayne.

Wayne took the handcuffs off. Rooster rubbed his wrists, looking from one man to the other.

"What's your name, son?" the sheriff asked as he sat on the edge of another desk.

"Roo...I mean William Brown."

The sheriff frowned. "Don't go trying to change your name on me, son. We'll find out who you are."

"My name is William Thomas Brown, but I've been called Rooster for as long as I can remember."

The sheriff smiled slightly. "Rooster, eh? You don't look like a rooster to me."

"I did when I was a little kid, that's what my daddy told me anyway. He said my hair was almost red and it stuck straight up. Somebody thought I looked like a little banty rooster and that's what I've been called ever since."

Rooster unsnapped the top buttons of his shirt and pulled it back to reveal a colorful tattoo of an Asian gamecock on his chest.

The sheriff's smile faded, and he studied Rooster again.

"Where you from, Rooster?"

"I was born in Sonora, but my daddy was a preacher so we moved around a lot. I went to high school in Uvalde and that's where I was when I got drafted, right after I buried my daddy."

"What were you doing at the truck stop tonight? You just happened to be there with a gun?"

Rooster felt his gut tighten, and he tried to keep his face from showing it.

"I just come into town for some pie. I hadn't even barely got out of my truck yet when those two fellows pulled up and started shooting. I keep the gun in my truck for coyotes and rattlers."

"Just come to get some pie did you?" The sheriff glanced at his watch. "Must have been about eleven o'clock. Where do you work son?"

"Out on Cecil Jones' ranch."

"You work hard?"

"Damn right."

"Get up early every day?"

Rooster could see where the sheriff was leading him.

"Yes, I get up early and work hard every day, but I'm used to it, and sometimes I just can't sleep. Sometimes I get tired of being out there, and sometimes I just want to come get a piece of pie, even if it is eleven o'clock at night."

Wayne carefully unwrapped the handkerchief from the old gun as Rooster was talking. He leaned in to examine it closer, then flinched in surprise.

"Sheriff, this gun's got four notches carved in the handle."

The sheriff got up and strode over to the where the gun lay. He leaned forward and looked closely, then straightened up and looked back at Rooster. Before he could say anything, Rooster spoke.

"The gun was my granddaddy's, he's the one who cut the notches in it."

"Your granddaddy killed four people?" the sheriff frowned.

"He killed ten altogether, but four of 'em were lawmen," Rooster said.

The sheriff's face was beginning to flush.

"Who the hell was your granddaddy?"

"Devin Brown."

The sheriff turned back to study the pistol.

Devin Brown..." he said softly to himself.

His eyes widened and he turned back rapidly toward Rooster.

"Devin Brown...you mean Devil Brown!?" he said loudly. "Are you trying to tell me your granddaddy was Devil Brown?"

"Yes, sir," Rooster said softly.

The sheriff just stood and stared at Rooster for a moment, then he turned to the deputy. "Go ahead and fingerprint him and take his picture. I'm going to charge him with murder."

Rooster was fingerprinted and photographed. He was advised that he would go before the judge in the morning, and then he was taken to jail and put in a cell. It wasn't the first time he had been locked up. Twice, while he was in the army, he had been hauled in for drunk and disorderly conduct, but this time it felt different. He wasn't sure that he would get out the next morning, and when he heard the main door clank shut and the jailer's footsteps fading away he felt very alone.

Rooster sat down and looked around, taking note of his surroundings. There were two other cells, one on either side of his. One was empty and the other contained a sleeping man, who was snoring softly. There was an open window somewhere and it was chilly inside the cell. Rooster pulled the wool blanket back and took off his boots. It must have been well after 1:30, and even as tired as he was, he knew it was unlikely that he would sleep. Rooster looked back to make sure that the man in the other cell was still asleep, then he got up from the bed and got down on his knees by the bedside. He put his hands together, closed his eyes, and started to pray.

"Heavenly Father..." he began, then stopped. He put his head down upon his clasped hands. "I don't know what to say...just...please...help me. Amen."

Rooster climbed back onto the bed and pulled the blanket over him. As he lay there staring up at the overhead bunk he heard footsteps coming from the stairwell. The door clanked open and the old jailer and a short, chubby, bald man came in. The man appeared to be in his forties or fifties and was dressed in dark slacks and a white shirt which was neatly tucked in.

"There he is," said the jailer.

Rooster sat up on the bed. The man walked up to the cell and rested his hands on the bars.

"You're younger than I expected," he said.

Rooster said nothing.

"But years aren't always what make a man. It's what a man does that defines him. It's his actions that give him his name."

The man smiled at Rooster. "You're wondering who the hell who I am."

Rooster nodded.

"My name is Mel Tucker. I own the truck stop, and that was my daughter you saved. Don't you worry son, you won't be here long. I'll be here with my lawyer when you go before the judge in the morning. Whatever your bail is, I'll post it."

"I...I appreciate that."

"You get some rest now and don't you worry none. You got Mel Tucker on your side."

Mel turned to leave, then paused. "I almost forgot. Thank you. Thank you very much, Rooster."

Rooster nodded silently. The door clanked shut, and he listened as Mel and the jailer's footsteps faded away down the stairs. He lay back down on the bunk and pulled the wool blanket over himself.

"You're welcome," he said softly.

2

Sunlight had been shining in the jailhouse windows for almost an hour when a new jailer brought up coffee and breakfast. This one appeared to be younger than Rooster. The jailer smiled as he passed a tray of food through the slot in the bars.

"You must be the one that shot the Blackwell boys."

"I guess."

"Mister, you're the most popular man in town right now. You could walk out of here and get elected mayor of this town just like that," said the jailer, snapping his fingers.

"If this is where the mayor lives then I don't want the job, but I guess this is probably better than prison."

"Ain't no jury in this county ever gonna send you to prison for killing the Blackwell boys. Fact is, it wouldn't surprise me none if they gave you a medal for it. You want cream with your coffee?"

"No thanks. What do you know about Mel Tucker?"

"Mel? He ain't hurting for much. He owns the truck stop, the Western Auto, the picture show, and a big house out in the country. He's a pretty good ol' boy, but don't get between him and a dollar though. You met Mel yet?"

"Last night, he's supposed to come bail me out this morning."

The jailer's eyes widened and he let out a low whistle as Rooster sipped his coffee and buttered his toast. After Rooster finished his breakfast he splashed some water on his face and slicked his hair down. He was looking a bit rumpled after his night in the jail, but all in all he felt good and was even feeling a bit hopeful and positive about how things had turned out. He felt no more remorse about killing the Blackwell brothers than he did about killing gooks in Korea. He had heard stories about the cruelty of the Blackwell boys, and so far everyone had impressed upon him that he had done a good thing. The main thing was that he hadn't killed that waitress or himself, and that he might at least get to go back to working on the ranch, which by now was looking pretty good. He was sitting patiently on the bunk when the young jailer came to get him.

The jailer handed Rooster over to Deputy Bates, who cuffed him and put him in the back of the squad car for the short ride to the courthouse. Neither of them spoke. Rooster was escorted into the courtroom where Mel Tucker, his wife Shirley, son Kenneth, and daughter Laurie were all sitting on the right side of the room with Mel's attorney.

The Tucker family stood up when Rooster entered into the room. Mel grinned broadly and said good morning while Shirley and Kenneth both smiled and nodded approvingly at him. Laurie's deep blue eyes met his and she smiled almost adoringly at him. Rooster felt his heart flutter for a second and he smiled awkwardly before averting his eyes to the floor. Laurie didn't look anything like the terrified young girl in an apron he had seen the night before. She was wearing a crisply starched blue dress with a bow in the back and her brown hair hung in a neat sheen down to her shoulders. She was wearing lipstick and held a small ornate handbag in both hands in front of her as she stood. To Rooster she looked like a movie star. A court bailiff took Rooster to the front of the courtroom and told him to sit down and wait for the judge to arrive.

Mel and another man came up to where Rooster was sitting.

"Rooster, this is my attorney Addis Thigpen. With your permission we would like for him to represent you."

Addis thrust his hand forward to Rooster who raised both of his, which were still handcuffed together, and shook his hand.

"Pleased to meet you sir. I appreciate any help you can give me," said Rooster.

"Rooster, I'm pleased to meet you. By all accounts, you prevented a tragedy from unfolding last night, and we intend to do everything in our power to see that justice is served. Considering the circumstances, and the fact that there are so many witnesses willing to testify on your behalf, I cannot foresee any reason that this will not simply be seen for what it is—an act of heroism by a private citizen."

The court bailiff approached them. "Gentlemen, please return to your seats."

"Sir, I am this man's attorney, and as such, I have the right to counsel my client," Addis stated firmly to the bailiff.

"Fine, but Mr. Tucker, you must return to your seat."

Mel patted Rooster on the shoulder and went back to sit with his family. Rooster turned to watch him go, and once again his eyes met Laurie's.

Rooster couldn't help but wonder where Laurie had been all this time and why he had never seen her before. Then he began to look more closely at the rest of the family. Shirley was a pleasant-looking woman, not exactly beautiful but not ugly either. Whereas Mel was built like a fireplug, Shirley was more like a twig. She was slender and about as tall as Mel and appeared even more so with her hair pulled up into a modest beehive.

Kenneth resembled his mother. He also had a thick shock of dark hair and had the same dark eyes and plain face. He appeared to be a simple, likeable young kid, maybe around sixteen or so. Laurie took after Mel, shorter and slightly big-boned. She had Mel's deep blue eyes and a rounded, pleasant face. She had full, straight brownish hair. Rooster thought she looked like one of the girls from the shampoo ads he had seen in magazines.

The back door of the courtroom opened and in walked Fred, Wanda, and several of the customers who were at the truck stop last night. They all smiled and waved when they saw Rooster who nodded back at them. Addis instructed Rooster to remain silent when the judge arrived and let him speak for him. As they were waiting a man and woman entered cautiously through the back door. They appeared hesitant and acted unsure of themselves. Their whole demeanor spoke of a life of hardship. They were poorly dressed in worn work clothes and their faces had years of toil and disappointment etched into them. They walked halfway up the opposite side of the courtroom, where there were the fewest people, and sat off to themselves. Something about the beaten aura that enveloped them touched Rooster.

"Addis, who is that old couple?" Rooster asked.

"That's Joe and Betty Blackwell. They're the parents of the two men who were killed last night. It's sad. They're just poor, hardworking folk. They've never really had much, but as far as I know they are decent people. How they turned out two sons like Dwayne and Hank is a mystery to me."

For the first time since the shooting Rooster felt a pang of sadness. He hadn't even considered that the Blackwell boys might have a family and that someone might actually be grieving over their deaths. Rooster knew how it felt to be an outsider, how it was to be on the fringe of normal everyday life, and out of all the people in the room at that moment, he probably could relate more to the parents of the men he had killed than anyone else.

Sheriff Hickey and District Attorney Joe Grundy entered through a side entrance and sat on the opposite side of the courtroom with Deputy Bates. Then the bailiff shouted, "All rise!"

Judge Wilmer Kitchens entered the courtroom and sat behind the bench. After everyone else sat back down the judge briefly looked over some papers. Next, he heard statements from the district attorney and the sheriff. He then called upon Addis who gave a brief defense of Rooster. Then the witnesses were called upon to testify, and many of them, Wanda in particular, gave moving testimony to Rooster's heroism. After all the witnesses had spoken the judge looked about the room and his eyes settled on Joe and Betty Blackwell.

"Mr. and Mrs. Blackwell, would you like to address the court at this time?"

Joe fidgeted for a moment while Betty just looked downward. Then he stood and began to speak.

"Thank you Your Honor. I have heard the testimony here today and it pains me. I reckon that everybody loves their young 'uns, no matter what anybody else thinks of them. My wife and me loved our boys, and we are heartbroken to lose them. Our boys did their best to help take care of us, and I'd be lying if I said we won't miss them because they was our own flesh and blood. If I could do anything to make things right, I would. If what was said here today is true, then I reckon they brought this upon themselves, and I'll leave it up to the court and to God to judge them."

Joe sat down. The judge looked about the courtroom one more time.

"Before I consider the evidence any further, does anyone else have something to say?"

"Yes, sir, I do," said Sheriff Hickey. "While the statements given here today would indicate this to be a justified killing, I would like to ask the court to allow me time to gather evidence to present to a grand jury for possible charges against the defendant."

The courtroom suddenly was abuzz with gasps and exclamations. Mel stood up in disbelief, his jaw agape. The judge pounded his gavel and called for order.

"Sheriff Hickey, if you have evidence the court has not yet heard then please share it with us now."

"Your Honor, Mr. Brown was carrying a handgun with a notched handle that, by his own admission, has been used in at least ten killings. He told me that his grandfather was none other than the old outlaw Devin Brown and that was who had notched the gun. I find it unusual that a hard-working ranch hand just happened to be out for coffee and pie at that time of night. I also heard from a couple of witnesses who indicated that Mr. Brown had shown an unusual interest in one of the waitresses at the truck stop. If it is true that Mr. Brown had no malicious intent and that he just happened to be there, then that will come out in the investigation. I just want to be sure that there is no other motive before I close the books on this case."

The courtroom erupted into total pandemonium with people shouting and crying and cursing in anger and disbelief. Wanda and Laurie burst into tears and Rooster turned a deep crimson. Mel was beside himself and shaking with anger.

The judge again pounded his gavel and shouted until everyone calmed down.

"In light of the testimony, I think it is unlikely that you will uncover anything else sir, but I will grant you time to conduct your investigation. In the meantime, is there anyone here who is willing to post bail for the defendant?"

Mel stood up. "I will Your Honor."

"Very well Mr. Tucker. Then I set bail for Mr. Brown at $500.00. Mr. Thigpen, please make sure your client understands that he is not to leave the area until the investigation is complete."

With that, it was over, at least for the time being.

After the hearing, the Tucker family, Addis, and Rooster all gathered together in front of the courthouse. Rooster figured that he would go straight back out to the Jones ranch and try to put in a day's work, but this would not be the case.

"Rooster, would you please come have supper with us tomorrow evening?" asked Shirley. "We are so grateful, and we would love to get to know you better."

"I appreciate that ma'am, but I'm not sure if I'll be able to. I need to find out what chores Cecil has lined out for me first, that is if I still have a job," said Rooster.

"Psh!" said Mel. "Don't you worry about that son. I'll go out there and personally talk to Cecil Jones. That won't be any problem at all. In fact, before you go back, why don't you let me and Addis take you out for breakfast?"

"Thanks Mel, but I already ate breakfast at the jail."

"What, bread and water? That's no fit breakfast for a hero. Come on son, let Mel take care of you."

With that, it was agreed that Rooster would come to the Tucker home the next day for supper, and Mel, Addis, and Rooster headed for Mel's Cadillac. As they were about to get in the car, Rooster noticed a little restaurant just across the street called the Dinner Bell.

"What about that place? It's just right across the street," asked Rooster.

Mel scowled. "You mean Benedict Arnold's joint? That belongs to the son of a bitch that thinks you're a criminal, and I'll be damned if he's ever going to get another penny of mine."

Addis explained that the Dinner Bell was, in fact, owned by Sheriff Bill Hickey, and Rooster quickly understood that it would now be considered enemy territory. So they got into the car and made the ride back to Mel's Truck Stop on the edge of town. As they pulled into the parking lot, Rooster was relieved to see his truck still sitting out front. The patrons inside watched them pull up and when they entered the front door everyone in the place stood and cheered. Men that Rooster had never seen before came up and shook his hand, while women wept and children stared in wide-eyed wonder. Everyone gathered around him as if he had just hit the winning run in the World Series. All through breakfast, people came up to the booth they were sitting in and offered their thanks and congratulations. It made Rooster a bit uncomfortable, but he gamely and graciously accepted each and every compliment. Mel watched carefully and with growing interest as each person made their way to praise the conquering hero.

After breakfast, Mel insisted on following Rooster out to the Jones ranch so he could explain to Cecil why Rooster didn't make it home last night. Rooster watched him in the rearview mirror as they wound their way down a dusty winding caliche road and through the cattle guard to the Jones ranch. Cecil was working on a tractor out by the main barn when they drove up. Before Rooster had a chance to say much of anything Mel was regaling Cecil with a tale of heroism that could rival anything in the movies that played at Mel's movie theater. Old Cecil's eyes grew wider with each passing word, and by the end of it he could only shake his head in wonder.

"I guess it don't surprise me none," said Cecil. "He sure knows how to handle the most ornery critters out here, and I reckon it makes sense that he knows how to handle ornery men too."

"He's a pretty good hand, is he?" Mel asked.

"He ain't afraid of hard work, I'll tell you that," said Cecil.

"Well, that's good to know," said Mel, "real good to know. I might just steal him from you if you're not careful."

Before leaving, Mel made sure that Rooster was to get half a day off the following afternoon, which was Saturday, in order to come into town early enough to visit awhile before supper. As Rooster went about his chores he noticed a not so subtle change in the other ranch hands and particularly in Cecil. Whereas they had always treated him as just another hand, he now was being given an extra degree of respect that had not been present before. Cecil now deferred to him in a way that almost made Rooster a bit uncomfortable. Now, instead of merely commanding Rooster to do something, Cecil would preface his orders with something like "if you don't mind" or "what do you think" and so forth. The other hands averted their eyes and in some ways it was as if he had received some type of unspoken promotion. Rooster was now offered the easier jobs instead of those which required brute strength. This was something he wasn't used to, for Rooster, in spite of a gentle, if not almost fearful nature, was a big strapping brute of a man. He literally did not know his own strength and at times would break things by accident. Once in the army, when he was drunk, he actually pulled a barracks door off its hinges. Yet for all his physical strength, he seemed to be unaware of his own power and was docile and malleable to the wishes of others. Throughout his life he had allowed others much less stronger than he to order him around, even though for the most part he could have snapped them like twigs. On occasion he would show some backbone and rebel against his superiors, but at other times he was almost bovine in his capacity to be led about by other smaller and physically weaker creatures. Now that he was being treated like a leader instead of a follower he found it to be perplexing and uncomfortable.

At supper that night, Cecil's wife Mildred made sure that Rooster got the biggest steak and an extra-large slice of pie. By nightfall that evening, his previous night's adventures were catching up to him and he turned in early. He slept soundly and for once, no one poked at him when he snored.

The next morning he rose early, feeling fresh and rested. He lit out early and finished his chores before noon. Afterward, he drew himself a hot bath in the bunkhouse tub and groaned in pleasure as he soaked in the steaming water. After bathing, he lathered up his face and shaved carefully in front of the rusty, old mirror. He did not have a thick beard so shaving was easy for him. He looked at the reflection staring back at him. He was not a handsome man, not in the classic sense. He did not have a square jaw or rugged features, instead in a funny way he looked rather like a large bird, which may have been another reason he got stuck with the moniker Rooster. Once, when he grew a mustache in the army, it made him look rodent-like and a few of the guys started calling him Ratso, but that didn't last long because that was one of the rare times that he stuck up for himself and put a stop to it. He had also occasionally been referred to as Frankenstein, but that was mostly behind his back.

He put on his best pair of blue jeans and a new western shirt. He dusted off his boots and polished them as best he could. As he was about to leave he started to put on his hat, but then realized it was too dirty for a formal occasion. Probably better not to wear a hat anyway, he thought, since he seemed to recall hearing that was impolite. He looked in the mirror one last time and grinned at the big goof staring back at him. In spite of his shortcomings, he was still relatively confident and comfortable in his own skin and he was ready to get out and socialize. He hopped into his old pickup truck, turned the key, stomped the gas pedal, and took off in a puff of smoke.

When he got into town, he pulled out the directions Mel had drawn for him. Most of his forays into Merky were to the truck stop, or the shops around the town square. Today he passed through the square and drove out of town on the road that eventually wound its way to Mexico. He went about two miles past town then turned off onto a caliche road and drove for another mile or so until he spotted a large gate with a welded sign atop it that said TUCKER. Rooster passed over the cattle guard, drove through a stand of mesquite trees, rounded a bend, and there it was. He felt his stomach drop a bit when he first spotted the house. It looked like a cross between a European castle and a Mexican whorehouse and appeared to him more like a grand hotel than a house. Up until then he had been feeling happy and confident, but now he was starting to feel out of his league. Here he was just a lowly ranch hand and he was about to rub elbows with rich people. He slowed the truck down and briefly thought about turning around and going back, but he knew that was not really an option. He chugged up to the house and parked under a large oak tree alongside a Ford pickup and a Chevy sedan.

A couple of old dogs trotted up, wagging their tails and woofing half-heartedly at him. Rooster stepped out of the truck and extended his hand to allow both of the old mongrels to sniff him. As he walked toward the house he noticed two matching Cadillacs, one gold and one pink, inside the garage off to the side of the main house. The house had a somewhat Spanish style to it with a tile roof and stucco finish but incorporated elements of a southern mansion as well. It had two large columns on either side of the front door and a large veranda that wrapped around to the side. Rooster walked up to the front door and rang the bell. He could hear some muffled voices from inside and footsteps approaching. The door swung open and Mel grinned broadly at him and extended his hand.

"Come on in, Rooster."

Rooster stepped inside to a cavernous space. Toward the back of the room, a grand sweeping staircase with an ornate banister of polished wood led up and around to the second floor. Off to the right was a fireplace and stone hearth with the mounted head of a buck on either side of it. In front of the fireplace, spread out over a wide rug, two sofas and a reclining chair encircled a coffee table. Along all the walls were various family photos and an oil painting of cattle grazing in a field of bluebonnets. As Rooster stood taking it all in, Shirley and Laurie came in from the kitchen where they had been preparing the meal. They both were wearing aprons spattered with stains, which caused Rooster to think back to that night at the truck stop and wonder at how different today was from then. After the initial greetings were over the women went back to the kitchen and Mel took Rooster on a tour of his home. Mel explained that his property was a little over one hundred acres and that he kept a few cattle and did a little farming in addition to his businesses. After they had seen the inside, they wandered outside to the back of the house and Mel showed Rooster his favorite place on the property. No more than one hundred and fifty feet from the back of the house was a bluff that overlooked Butcher Creek, a pleasant little spring-fed stream that passed through

Merky and eventually made its way to the Rio Grande some eighty miles away. Here, Mel had built a nice stone cooking pit and picnic table. He spent many an afternoon here, listening to the trickle of the stream below as it spilled over its rocky bed.

"What do you think, Rooster? Not bad for a fellow who nobody thought would ever amount to a hill of beans, eh?"

"It's nice, Mel, real nice. It's the nicest house I've ever set foot in."

"I still have some other things I want to show you, Rooster. The food won't be ready for a while, so let's go take a ride. We'll come down here after supper and have a drink or two."

They went and got in Mel's gold Cadillac and headed into town.

"Rooster, tell me about yourself," Mel asked as he eased the big Caddy out toward the main road.

"Well, I guess there ain't too much to tell. I was born in Sonora, and we moved around a bunch because my daddy was a preacher. My momma died when I was just a baby. I finished high school in Uvalde, and then my daddy died. I got drafted and did two hitches in the army, went to Korea and Germany. When I got out of the army I was at Fort Tamale, and I decided to stick around this area."

"You see any action in Korea?"

"Hell yes, I thought I wasn't gonna make it home more than once."

"How'd you like Germany?"

"It beat the hell out of Korea. That was like a vacation after Korea. I enjoyed Germany, but I was still ready to come back home. Ain't no place like home I guess."

"You've already done a lot in your short life, Rooster. I admire that."

"I didn't have much choice. When Uncle Sam comes calling you got to answer."

"Uncle Sam didn't have anything to do with what you did the other night. That was your true character showing itself."

Rooster squirmed slightly. If Mel knew what had really been in his heart that night he would have thought quite differently of him.

They cruised into the city limits and on to the town square. Mel pointed out the Western Auto store that he owned, and then he turned off onto a side street and pointed out the Merky Movie Theater, which was also his. They pulled into the Texaco station and two uniformed men ran out to the car and began servicing it.

"This is mine too, Rooster. Of course, the truck stop is mine, and I own a dozen or so rent houses around town. Now I guess you're probably thinking I'm just showing you all this so I can brag about how rich I am, but that's not the case. You see, Rooster, I started out poor as a church mouse myself, and I know what it is to struggle and not have anything. The only reason that I have accomplished what I have is partly hard work and partly pure luck. When I married Shirley, her daddy saw in me something I didn't even see in myself, and he loaned me enough money to buy this gas station. I worked my ass off here every day. I hardly ever had time off for anything, but I made sure that I gave the best service for the best price and that my customers were always satisfied. When I got this place going strong, then I started buying up other places around town. It took a lot of hard work but it was worth it. I guess my point is, sometimes life kicks you in the ass, and sometimes it lifts you up by the seat of your pants, and you got to be ready for either one."

They pulled away from the service station and Mel turned off down a side road and drove for a block or so before pulling over and parking. He pointed to a tiny house set back from the street.

"That's one of mine right there. It's small but solid, and really it's one of my favorites. What do you think, Rooster?"

Rooster gazed at the house. It was a tidy little frame house, perhaps no more than four rooms altogether, but it was cute and sat on a large lot away from the street surrounded by large trees. It looked like a little cabin in the woods and it appealed to him immensely.

"Damn. That's nice. I like it. I don't know why, but I like it."

"It's empty right now. I'll be looking for a new tenant soon."

Rooster briefly imagined himself living in the little house. It was all a man needed, but before he indulged his fantasy too much, he brought himself back to reality. He was a ranch hand and he had to live on the ranch where the work was, and he knew he couldn't afford to rent a house on his wages.

"Well, I hope you find somebody that appreciates it," said Rooster a bit wistfully.

"I usually get good tenants," said Mel.

So, with the tour of the Tucker Empire finished, they headed back to Mel's house.

They drove back out to Mel's place and when they got there, supper was almost ready. Laurie and Kenneth set the table and Shirley brought out the pot roast. It was the best spread that Rooster had seen in some time, even better than what Mildred prepared for the ranch hands. Rooster wolfed down a plateful and then sat politely, not wanting to appear too greedy or too desperate.

Shirley, noticing this, encouraged him to eat more. "Rooster, there is more than enough for everybody here. Please get yourself another plate and eat as much as you like. Just be sure to save room for some pie."

Rooster did not need any more prodding and he loaded up his plate with another helping of everything. He could eat just about anybody under the table without even trying. After his second plate, he was starting to feel full, but knew he could eat at least two pieces of pie. He poured himself another glass of tea and waited as the rest of them finished their meals. After everyone had eaten, Laurie gathered the empty plates and carried them into the kitchen. She brought back a chocolate pie with a tall swirling meringue and set it on the table.

"That looks good," said Rooster.

"Laurie made it," said Shirley. "She's a real chef when it comes to desserts."

Laurie cut a large slice and put it on a saucer for Rooster. She seemed to have come down with a case of shyness since their lingering glances at the courthouse, and Rooster also was suddenly overcome with awkwardness in the midst of her family. Everyone had a slice of pie and they all made a fuss over it of course, much to Laurie's annoyance.

"Shirley, when are you going learn to cook like Laurie?" Mel said, grinning slightly, his eyes half closed and rubbing his sated belly.

"I reckon when I find a good man to cook for," replied Shirley.

Mel just chuckled, and that signaled the end of supper. The women began clearing the table. Rooster offered to help, but they just shushed him and told him to go away lest they really put him to work.

Mel, Rooster, and Kenneth went to the living area and sank down into the plush sofas.

"Hey, Rooster, you want to play Monopoly?" asked Kenneth.

"I don't know how," said Rooster.

"It's easy. We'll show you," said Kenneth as he jumped up and ran upstairs to get the game.

"Well, I'm going to pass on the game," said Mel. "I play Monopoly every day in the real world." And with that he excused himself and told Rooster he would return in a bit.

Rooster sat on the sofa gazing at the photos that hung on the walls. There were family portraits, photos of Laurie and Kenneth as young children, and pictures of people that Rooster assumed were Mel and Shirley's parents. The furnishings were nice but not overly ostentatious. The fireplace was darkened with soot, but looked as if it had not been used in some time. On one wall, a gun rack held two deer rifles and two shotguns. The two buck heads that hung on either side of the fireplace stared dolefully and unblinking ahead. As he was looking about, Rooster happened to see out one of the windows and noticed Mel's gold Cadillac slowly easing down the long drive and out toward the road into town.

Shirley and Laurie came out of the kitchen, and Shirley sat on the sofa next to Rooster while Laurie went upstairs. As they sat together, Shirley glanced around to make sure that they were alone.

"Rooster, I don't know how we can ever thank you enough," she said softly. "I heard what those boys were about to do my Laurie. If you hadn't stopped them, she would have never got over it. I don't know what we would have done. Her life would have been ruined, just ruined."

Shirley's eyes misted with emotion. "You saved her life, Rooster. You absolutely saved her life."

A door upstairs slammed shut and footsteps came toward the stairs. Shirley quickly changed the subject. "I hear your father was a minister, Rooster. What church do you belong to?"

Rooster fidgeted ever so slightly.

"Well, ma'am, I really haven't been to church much in a while. It's shameful, I know."

"Well, you've been away from home for a long time. If you don't have a regular church to go to, it's easy to get out of the habit. What denomination do you belong to?"

"Well, ma'am, we didn't exactly belong to any big churches. We went to a lot of different ones. My daddy usually preached in the small country churches."

Laurie came down the stairs. She had freshened up her makeup and changed into a pair of slacks so that she could sit on the floor and play Monopoly without compromising her modesty. Kenneth was a couple of steps behind her, carrying the box containing the game pieces.

"I think I will let you young people play among yourselves," Shirley said as she rose from the sofa. "I have some sewing to catch up on."

Kenneth opened the box and laid out the game pieces on the coffee table.

"I can't believe you've never played Monopoly," said Kenneth, chuckling. "Did you grow up in a cave or something?"

"Kenneth!" Laurie scolded. "I'm sorry, Rooster. My little brother is the one who acts like he grew up in a cave."

Kenneth curled his arms underneath, puckered his lips, and began mimicking an ape.

Laurie laid out the game pieces, patiently explaining to Rooster how they would proceed. She handed him the dice and told him to roll them.

With her parents away, Laurie seemed to loosen up a bit and her deep blue eyes met Rooster's once again. Rooster felt himself start to perk up. He began to talk directly to Laurie, something he hadn't really been able to do yet. It turned out that Laurie had just finished high school and was considering moving off to attend college, something Rooster was troubled to hear.

"I've been thinking about becoming a teacher. I would have to move to either San Angelo or San Antonio to go to school, and I would be gone for four years. That's a long time to be away from home," said Laurie. "I'm still trying to make up my mind, so Daddy said I can work for him until I decide."

"That's if she don't get married," said Kenneth. "There's a couple of boys in town that want to take her out."

Rooster fidgeted a bit. "I reckon that don't surprise me none."

"Daddy wouldn't let me date anyone until I finished high school," sighed Laurie. "He's so old fashioned."

As they were playing, the telephone rang, and Laurie jumped up to answer it. Rooster and Kenneth sat back and waited for her to return. As they waited, Rooster listened with one ear to Kenneth prattling on, and with the other to Laurie talking on the telephone. From the sound of her voice, he decided that she was talking to one of the boys that wanted to date her. She chatted with the person a few minutes, keeping her voice low. A couple of times she stifled a giggle.

"We have company. I have to go now," she said and hung up the phone.

She came back into the living room and took her place back on the rug.

"Who was that?" Kenneth wanted to know, as did Rooster, who kept silent, but was grateful for little brother asking.

"It was Billy Watson, if you must know," said Laurie curtly.

"Daddy will be fit to be tied if he finds out you're talking to one of the Watson boys," said Kenneth.

"*He* called me," said Laurie. "I was only being polite."

Rooster squirmed some more. "Who's turn is it?" he asked with just a hint of agitation.

"It's yours, silly," said Laurie, handing him the dice.

Rooster shook the dice vigorously and rolled two sixes, and with that they were off in earnest. It didn't take long for Rooster to learn the game, and before long, he started playing aggressively. As they played along, he and Kenneth were soon on the floor with Laurie, all of them engrossed in the game. Rooster was relaxed now and alternated between joking around with Kenneth and flirting slightly with Laurie. After a while, their knees were touching slightly beneath the coffee table. They had been playing for about an hour or so when Mel returned, by which time Rooster had amassed a nice pile of cash and several properties.

"Well, lookee there. It looks like Rooster may have a talent for business. Not too bad for a fellow who never played the game before," Mel said. "So who won?

"Nobody has won yet," said Laurie, "but Rooster has the biggest pile of money and the most property."

"Then I declare Rooster the winner," said Mel. "This damn game could go on all night, and I want to talk to him out by the creek before he leaves."

"Daddy!" said Laurie. "You know you're not supposed to curse in this house."

"Oh damn, I guess I forgot," Mel grinned.

Laurie and Kenneth both stood up. Both seemed disappointed that the game was over.

"Good night, Rooster," said Laurie. "I had fun." She looked at Rooster with those deep baby blue eyes and made his heart go aflutter once again.

"Me too, Rooster," said Kenneth. "I hope you can come back sometime."

"It was fun for me too," said Rooster. "If I'd a known Monopoly was that much fun, I would have come out of my cave a long time ago."

Mel led Rooster out the back door, where it was now dark, and a string of light bulbs led the way down to the picnic area. Sitting on the stone picnic table was a paper sack. Mel pointed for Rooster to sit down, and he lifted a fruit jar from the sack and a pack of Swisher Sweets Cigars. Mel opened the jar and sniffed at it. He turned his face away with a grimace and handed the bottle to Rooster to sniff as well. Rooster took a whiff, then closed his eyes and scrunched up his face.

"Damn! What is that?"

"Whiskey."

"I never smelled any whiskey like that," said Rooster.

"Try a taste."

Rooster took a small sip and gagged slightly.

Mel chuckled. "You don't have to drink it if you don't want to. Here's something a little tamer."

Mel reached into the bag and pulled out several bottles of beer, along with a bottle opener or "church key," as some folks called it, and opened two bottles. He then poured a bit of whiskey into two small glasses. Then he opened the pack of cigars and handed Rooster one and took one for himself. He reached into his pants pocket and pulled out a Zippo lighter, clanked it open and sparked a flame. He lit Rooster's cigar first, then his own, and leaned back and blew out a puff of aromatic smoke.

"Rooster, what are your plans?"

"Plans?"

"For life. For the future. What do you want to do with yourself?"

Rooster thought for a moment. "Survive, I guess."

Mel studied him closely.

"Then that's all you will do, just survive, but only for so long. I guess they can put that on your headstone. 'Rooster Brown—he survived, but only until he died.'"

Rooster said nothing.

"I think you can do better than that, Rooster. I think you've got more potential than you're willing to admit. You fought in a war. You saved my daughter and a dozen or so other people from God knows what.

Cecil Jones says you're a hard worker, and you just played Monopoly for the first time ever and won. You're selling yourself way too short, son."

Rooster still didn't know what to say, so he remained silent.

"Rooster, remember what I told you about Shirley's father seeing something in me that I didn't see in myself? Well, now it's my turn to see something in a young man who doesn't even realize his own potential. I probably would have done all right, even without the guidance and help of that old man, but it made a big difference, a huge difference. And now here I am, looking back, grateful for what was done for me, and knowing what a guiding hand can do for a young fellow who needs it. I want to make you an offer, Rooster. I need a good man at my gas station, somebody who is not afraid of hard work."

Rooster looked up at Mel, who was pacing back and forth. "I...I don't know what to say."

Rooster's mind was racing. If he took the job, then he wouldn't be able to stay at the ranch. He would have to find a place to live and he didn't know if he could afford that. The thought of working in town, pumping gas, and doing mechanic work excited him, but it also frightened him just a bit.

"Hell, son, just say yes."

"Okay, Mel. I just wasn't expecting anything like that. I'll have to tell Cecil and find a place to stay."

"You've got a place to stay, Rooster. I showed it to you today, that little house just around the corner from the gas station."

Rooster's jaw dropped.

"We'll work out a deal to make it part of your salary, at least at first. Once we get you going on the job, then you can start paying rent."

Rooster's mind was spinning, partly from what he had just been told, and partly because the alcohol was starting to kick in.

"Mel, I...I...thank you...thank you. I just wasn't expecting so much."

"This isn't a free ride, son. You've already earned the opportunity, but you'll have to prove yourself to keep the job and the house. If I didn't have confidence that you're up to it then I wouldn't have offered it. Do we have a deal?"

"Yes, yes, we have a deal."

With that, Mel extended his hand and the two men shook on it, sealing the deal. They then clinked their jars of whiskey and drank a toast. This was one of the few times that Rooster had drunk alcohol since leaving Germany. One of the reasons he had decided to stick around Merky was because Loma Grande was a dry county, and presumably one would be unable to buy alcohol. He wondered where Mel got the booze, but he didn't ask, for tonight he was on top of the world.

3

When Rooster woke up the next morning, he didn't remember how he got home. He had a headache and was nauseous, and for a brief second, he thought he was on a troop ship off the coast of Korea. When the other hands came and tried to rouse him for breakfast, he just groaned and pulled the covers over his head. Rooster's absence at the breakfast table was quickly noticed by Cecil and Mildred who were constantly amazed at how much food the strapping young man could consume in a single sitting. Cecil often joked that it would be cheaper to pay Rooster overtime rather than feeding him. Finally, Cecil went to the bunkhouse to see what the problem was. Rooster sat up in bed, smacking his lips and blinking his eyes like some lizard that had just crawled from underneath a rock into the sunlight. He told Cecil that something he ate the night before must have made him sick. Cecil only had to sniff the air around Rooster to figure out what was really the problem. Cecil did not approve of drinking, but Rooster was still enjoying the benefits of his hero status, so his story was not challenged. Fortunately, it was Sunday, and little was required of the ranch hands. A few mandatory chores had to be done, but for the most part, it was a day of rest for everyone. Rooster stayed in bed till almost noon before he finally got up and pulled on his pants and stumbled outside and sat shirtless and barefooted on the stoop of the bunkhouse to smoke a cigarette. After a few puffs he felt better. Then a wave of nausea hit him hard and he leaned off the stoop and threw up. Afterward, he hobbled over to a spigot in the yard to rinse his mouth and clear his sinuses of the taste of vomit. He splashed water in his face and ran it over the back of his head. He was starting to feel better now that he had purged himself, and he was grateful it was Sunday. Dinner was always served late on Sundays because Cecil and Mildred went to church in town.

As Rooster's recollection of the night before began to return to him, he was faced with a new dilemma. He remembered that Mel had offered him a job and a place to stay, however, he couldn't remember exactly when this new job was supposed to begin. This posed a bit of a problem. It was going to be awkward enough telling Cecil that he was quitting, but if he left too soon he would not have any place to go to in the meantime. It would be embarrassing to have to call Mel and ask when he was supposed to start his new job, and would not exactly be positive testimony to his competence. However, it would turn out to be a moot point, for Cecil and Mildred had already spoken to Mel after church and learned the news from him. As everyone was gathered around the dinner table, Cecil made the announcement himself.

"Boys, I just learned today that Rooster will be leaving us. He is moving on to bigger and better things and is going to go to work for Mel Tucker. Today will be his last day with us, so let's all wish him well."

Everyone started congratulating Rooster and patting him on the back and shaking his hand.

"Mel said you can move into the house anytime this afternoon and to be ready for work first thing tomorrow morning," Cecil told Rooster.

Rooster was relieved to have his instructions laid out for him without having to call Mel or going through the awkwardness of informing Cecil that he was leaving the ranch. He was amazed at how everything had simply fallen into place for him with almost no effort on his part. It was as if God or some divine force was leading him down a path to something he would not have even dared hope for himself. One of the ranch hands remarked that it was his reward for saving everyone and that a good heart always gets its just desserts. Rooster nodded his head but said little. For even though everyone thought he was a hero, and there seemed to be little danger of anyone ever learning the truth of what had truly been in his heart that night, he was still uneasy. He was not yet completely confident that he was clear of any repercussions of the darkness that had clouded his mind, or that he was deserving of any of what was being given to him. He felt like a hypocrite but knew better than to ever confess to what his true intentions had been that night. If he was an undeserving lout then so be it, he had known plenty of scoundrels who seemed to live charmed lives.

As everyone was congratulating him for his good fortune, Rooster also sensed that they were relieved to see him go. Ever since word of his heroism had reached the ranch, the other men seemed a bit uncomfortable around him, as if he were no longer a mere human being. It wasn't just the ranch hands either, even Cecil and Mildred seemed confused about how to act around Rooster. They no longer treated him as just another pair of hands and a strong back. They knew that he had earned an extra degree of respect, but didn't know how to convey it, and almost resented that they had to acknowledge it. Now that he would be leaving, everything would revert to its natural order and all would be well with the world. Everyone would know their place, and that was how they liked it, even the lowest one in the pecking order.

Everyone offered to help him pack and load up his belongings, which was completely unnecessary for all his worldly belongings fit into an army duffel bag. When he loaded his truck to leave, everyone gathered around to send him off. They all waved until he passed the barn, and then they watched as his old truck kicked up a cloud of dust on its way to the main road. Everyone heaved a collective sigh of relief now that balance had been restored to the ranch.

As Rooster drove toward town, he marveled at how things had turned around for him. From the lowest point in his life, he now seemed to have a relatively bright future, and all in just a matter of days. Perhaps what his father had always said was true—that it's darkest before the dawn. And now it seemed he had finally reached that dawn of a new day.

He hadn't even thought about what the new job entailed, but now he was playing it out in his head. He would no doubt be pumping gas, doing some mechanical work, fixing flats and cashiering. He had no idea what kind of hours he would be working, and he didn't care. Now he would be in the middle of town, where there was at least some semblance of civilization, where people congregated and did business, and where at last, he might finally become a part of a community. Rooster knew that Mel expected much of him, and he intended to do his best to live up to those expectations. Rooster knew that, in essence, his life and his potential for the future rested upon how well he satisfied Mel Tucker. He also knew that he had already made an excellent first step by saving Mel's daughter from what would have no doubt been permanent emotional scarring. Rooster's thoughts also kept returning to Laurie, whose blue eyes, brown hair, and pretty smile had completely captivated him the night before.

As he drove into town, he passed Mel's Truck Stop, a place that would always have deep significance for him from now on. He drove to the town square and circled the courthouse, taking in the feel of a town that now seemed to him to be a friendlier and more welcoming place. He drove past the Texaco station, which was closed because it was Sunday. He imagined it open and with customers and himself pumping gas and looking under the hoods of cars. For a brief moment, he had a vision of himself in a uniform with a star on his chest, a new man with a new life.

He drove slowly past the station and turned off onto the side street where he would be living. He smiled to himself when he turned into the long driveway, which led to the tiny house set beneath the large trees. He pulled in and parked, and for a moment, he just sat in the truck and looked at the house in wonder. Then he got out, walked up onto the small front porch, and looked inside one of the windows. It was neat and modestly furnished. Rooster turned the doorknob and stepped inside.

It had been cleaned recently and smelled fresh, in spite of the fact that it appeared to have been vacant for a while. The living room had a small sofa and two chairs. A radio sat on a table next to one of the chairs. He ran his hand along the arm of the sofa and walked into the next room, which was the kitchen. In the center of the kitchen was a small table and two chairs. Along one wall was the refrigerator and across the room was the stove. A well-used and blackened coffee pot sat atop the stove, ready for brewing. Off to his left was the bedroom, which had a bed that was covered with a cotton bedspread. A chest of drawers set next to the bed and a mirror hung on the wall. The closet door stood open, beckoning for clothes.

Rooster walked back through the kitchen and looked into the bathroom. A sink and a claw foot bathtub gleamed in the light coming through the window, both having been recently scrubbed clean. He opened the medicine cabinet, saw that it was empty, then shut it. Rooster went back into the kitchen, opened the back door of the house, and saw that he had a pleasant, shady backyard. An old, stone well house was on the left side of the yard and on the right side an aging buggy shed stood tilting, slightly askew. Humble as it all was in the grand scheme of things, it may as well have been Buckingham Palace as far as Rooster Brown was concerned. It was the first time in his adult life that he had ever had any place just to himself. He walked from room to room, sitting on all the chairs and lying on the bed.

Then, Rooster's thoughts turned to where they inevitably always turned: food. He panicked a tiny bit. He hadn't had to cook or shop for himself in years. He had lived quite happily on meals courtesy of the US Army for some time and recently was the benefactor of Mildred Jones' culinary skills. Rooster jumped up from the chair he was sitting in and ran into the kitchen. He had very little money and hadn't thought about where his next meal was going to come from. His eyes bugged out when he pulled open the kitchen cabinets and saw that they had been stocked with supplies. There were canned goods, coffee, sugar, flour, salt, pepper, and a loaf of bread in the pantry. In the refrigerator, there were a couple dozen eggs, butter, bacon, and a bottle of milk. All in all, there were enough odds and ends that even a bachelor like himself could survive comfortably for several days. And, on the top shelf of the refrigerator, he saw something that stopped him in his tracks. It was a piece of the chocolate pie that Laurie had made the day before. Rooster then realized that probably the entire Tucker family had come over to prepare the place for him. He was astounded, and deeply touched. He couldn't believe what he was seeing. He struggled not to cry. Clasping his hands together beneath his chin, he closed his eyes and fought back the tears that were starting to well up and run down his cheek.

Rooster wiped his eyes on his shirt sleeve and then decided to go out and explore the backyard. He pulled open the half-rotten door to the well house and looked in. Rusty water had stained the concrete base of the pump, and spider webs and dust filled practically every available space, but otherwise it looked as if everything was in order. Rooster walked over to the shed. A car path led up to and into it, so it was obvious that someone had once parked a vehicle there. The shed had the stale smell of dust and moldering motor oil and decay and disuse. On either side of it were shelves that held an assortment of buckets, jars, and various old cans. Along the back of the lot flowed the small creek that ran through town. It was running nicely now because of recent spring rains, but during the heat of summer it usually dwindled down to a series of brackish water puddles.

As he was walking about the backyard, Rooster heard a car door slam from in front of the house. Thinking that it was probably Mel, he turned and ran back to the house to greet him. Rooster was happy and grateful and eager to thank Mel for his incredible generosity. He strode through the back door, went through the kitchen, and entered the sitting room just as Sheriff Bill Hickey was walking through the front door.

Rooster froze in his steps. Sheriff Hickey's eyes met his. Neither man said anything at first. Then, Sheriff Hickey smiled slightly.

"Weren't expecting company, were you?" said the sheriff.

"Not until I unpacked anyway," said Rooster.

"You plan on living here, I take it?"

"As long as Mel Tucker says so."

"Well, I guess whatever Mel Tucker says is what goes. At least, that's what Mel thinks."

The sheriff ambled over to one of the chairs and sat down.

"Where is Mel?" asked the sheriff.

"I don't know. Home, I guess."

"Well, I'll have to have a talk with Mel and make sure you didn't misunderstand him."

"You do that."

"Oh I will."

"I've been talking to a lot of folks lately. I heard you were hanging around that truck stop quite a bit."

"I reckon that ain't no crime."

"Well, I don't know. Depends on why you were hanging around. Word is you were taken up with one of the waitresses there, except she wasn't too taken up with you."

Rooster said nothing.

"In fact, some folks say she turned you down just a couple of days before the shooting."

"Some folks are full of shit."

The sheriff looked at Rooster sternly.

"Well, it seems curious to me that a man who got turned down was up there right when the gal gets off work, and it sure is curious why that same man was carrying around a pistol. Don't that strike you as curious, Rooster?"

Again, Rooster said nothing.

"So what were you going to pay for your coffee with that night, Rooster? Your good looks? You didn't have a red cent on you when we took you in."

Rooster flinched slightly. "I guess I would have been doing dishes. You gonna tell me you ain't never forgot to take any money with you."

"You're going to tell me you forgot your money but remembered your gun?"

"The gun was in my truck. That's where I keep it, and I want it back."

"Once this investigation is through, you'll get it back. That is, if you aren't in jail."

"In jail for what? Doing your job for you?" Rooster retorted, his anger rising.

The sheriff flushed. "I do my job just fine. I damn sure don't need any help from the grandson of some bastard outlaw."

Just then, they both heard a car coming up the driveway, and both men looked out the window to see Mel's gold Cadillac pulling up next to the sheriff's squad car. As soon as it came to a stop, Mel hopped out and began walking quickly toward the house. The passenger door opened, and Laurie got out somewhat hesitantly. The sheriff stood up and waited for them to enter.

Mel came in first, looking agitated.

"Now what, Hickey? You on the trail of some escaped jaywalker or something?"

"Just looking after your property, Mel. I saw this man's truck outside and figured I better make sure everything was all right. I wouldn't want you to get cheated out of any rent. Mr. Brown says he's your tenant now."

"That's right, my tenant and my employee. Is that all right with you?"

"I guess it doesn't matter if it is or not. It's a free country. I'm sure he needs the money."

No one said anything for a few seconds. Then, Hickey spoke.

"Well, it looks like everything here is all right. I guess I'll be on my way."

The sheriff paused in the doorway and turned to look at Rooster. "We'll be talking again soon, Rooster."

The screen door slammed shut, and Mel glared at Sheriff Hickey as he headed toward his squad car.

Mel scowled and shook his head in anger then turned toward Rooster and smiled, extending his hand in greeting.

"I wasn't expecting to see Wyatt Earp here. What did he say to you, Rooster?"

Just then, Laurie entered the room. She seemed unsure of what to expect.

"Hi, Rooster." She smiled at him, looking slightly concerned.

Rooster smiled and said hello.

"What did Bill Hickey want, Rooster? Why was he here?" Mel asked again, a bit impatiently.

Rooster hesitated. He didn't want to say anything about the waitress while Laurie was around.

"He just wanted to know why I was here," said Rooster.

"I heard he's been going all over town asking about you. Stupid son of a bitch, I don't know why he can't just accept that you're a hero," said Mel.

Rooster cleared his throat. "I saw all that food in the pantry and the refrigerator, Mel. I can't thank you enough. I really don't know what to say."

Rooster noticed a slight trace of disappointment flash across Laurie's face.

"And I can't wait to eat that piece of pie, Laurie. How did you know that chocolate pie is my favorite?"

Laurie brightened up. "I don't know anyone who doesn't like chocolate."

"Okay, look-a-here, Rooster. We don't want to impose on you before you've even unpacked your bags, so we won't stay long. Show up at the station tomorrow morning at seven o'clock and be ready to work. Ask for Joe, he'll explain what you will be doing and get you measured for a uniform. I'll be by later in the day to see how things are going."

"Yes, sir, boss!" Rooster snapped to attention and saluted just like in his army days. Laurie giggled, and Mel nodded his head approvingly.

Rooster watched them from the front porch as they drove away. After they had disappeared, he walked out to his pickup and lifted his duffle bag from the back. He took it into the bedroom and put his socks and underwear into one drawer. He hung his jeans and shirts in the closet and placed his few other belongings here and there. Then, he took the last thing from his bag and unwrapped it tenderly. It was his father's Bible. It was the only thing he had from his daddy, except the old gun that Sheriff Hickey was still keeping as evidence. Inside the Bible was an old black and white portrait of his mother and father, taken before Rooster was born. It was the only picture he had of his mother, one of the few he had ever seen of her. Rooster placed the Bible on the nightstand as if he might actually read it. He propped up the photo of his parents next to it and sat on the bed looking at both of them. He smiled to himself. He was home.

4

After Rooster unpacked and explored the place thoroughly there was little else he could do to entertain himself. He was still excited and happy to have his own place, but now it just reminded him that he had no one to share his excitement with, and the loneliness that had haunted him most of his life once again settled in.

Rooster always looked forward to eating, but this evening he was especially happy when suppertime rolled around for that would also give him something to do. He decided to listen to some music while cooking and turned on the radio and found a few faint signals that crackled with static. Finally, he came across the local Merky station, which was the only one that came in strong enough so that he could walk away from the radio without the signal fading out. It was a country station, which was common in that part of Texas, and that suited him just fine. He turned the volume up and went into the kitchen to see what he could make for supper. He mostly just knew how to cook breakfast, so he wound up making that. Unfortunately, that only took a little while to make and even less time to eat.

However, he still had the prized piece of chocolate pie, and he sat it upon the table and admired it for a few minutes before devouring it in just a few bites. Even though it was cold, it was still delicious, and it made Rooster think of Laurie. She was pretty and nice, and damn he wished he would have met her before that bitch Jeanine. He was becoming a bit smitten with her, but he also knew that would be treading into potentially dangerous territory. He didn't know how Mel would like that, and deep inside he knew he wasn't good enough for her. He was just a working man, and he doubted that a gas-pumping grease monkey was what Mel Tucker wanted for his daughter. For now Rooster had to focus on pleasing Mel, so he tried not to think about Laurie.

He took a bath, leisurely soaking in the warm water for as long as he wanted, a rare luxury for a man accustomed to living in barracks and bunkhouses. He picked a pair of work clothes for the next day and lay them across the dresser in the bedroom. It was almost 9:00 p.m., and Rooster was still not showing any signs of sleepiness. He was too excited by the sudden changes in his life. He decided to go take a spin around town just to see what it was like on a Sunday night. He drove to the town square, which was all but abandoned. On Friday and Saturday nights, many people, mostly teenagers and young adults, parked their cars around the courthouse square and gathered to sit and talk. Rooster parked his truck on the square and watched as a few cars and a couple of trucks passed by. The most excitement was when two dogs trotted by him and disappeared around the corner.

After ten or fifteen minutes, he was about to leave when a police patrol car drove slowly past him, the driver looking over toward him.

"Aw shit," Rooster muttered to himself. He should have just stayed at home. He knew it was a bad idea to pull out and leave since that would look suspicious, so he sat in the truck and looked around to see if the police car was coming back. He spotted it in his side mirror coming slowly around the courthouse and heading toward him. He wasn't doing anything and had nothing to hide, so he resigned himself to another confrontation with Sheriff Hickey. The squad car pulled up behind him, stopped and backed in next to him, so that the driver's window was next to his. Rooster looked over as the window rolled down and the grinning face of Deputy Harvey Wells looked up at him.

"Howdy, Rooster," Harvey said.

Rooster was relieved to see that it wasn't the sheriff. He had not seen Harvey since the night of the incident.

"Howdy," said Rooster.

"What are you doing out here tonight?"

"Just taking in all the excitement of downtown Merky."

Harvey laughed. "Yeah, it is pretty dead tonight. Usually not much happens on Sunday nights. I didn't expect to see you here. I figured you'd be out at the ranch."

Rooster realized that Harvey didn't know he was now living in town.

"I just moved into town today. I start work at the Texaco station tomorrow."

"Dang, how'd that happen?"

"Mel offered me a job and a place to stay."

"Well, I guess that doesn't surprise me, after what you did for him and his daughter."

"Your boss don't think I did much. He thinks I'm the criminal."

Harvey smiled. "Bill takes his job seriously. That's why a lot of people around here don't like him. I guess he came by it honest. His daddy was a lawman too. I don't know why he's acting this way, but once his investigation is over with he'll leave you alone."

Rooster wanted to ask Harvey what he knew about the investigation but decided it was best to say nothing about it. As they chatted, it became apparent to Rooster that Harvey was just a simple country bumpkin, a little slow perhaps, but good-natured. Rooster found it easy to talk to Harvey, and he decided that he liked the easygoing, young deputy. He learned that Harvey worked the night shift, which usually just involved a bit of patrolling, keeping a chair warm in the sheriff's office, and taking the rare call for help. It was mostly just going through the motions of a boring routine day in and day out. They talked for a while, and then Harvey had to leave.

"Hey, Rooster, you want to go fishing sometime?"

Rooster was a bit surprised but pleased. "Yeah, sure. That sounds real good."

"All right then. We'll talk to you later," Harvey said as he drove off.

Rooster shook his head and smiled to himself. He started his truck and drove back home. He was even more awake now after talking to Harvey, so he tried reading his father's Bible, and as usual, abandoned the effort after a few minutes. When it got to be 11:00 p.m. Rooster decided to turn in. He knew that morning would come soon enough, and he wanted to be as well-rested as possible before starting his new job. However, sleep would not come, and he tossed and turned and fidgeted until late into the night. He finally drifted off into a light sleep and jolted awake when the wind-up alarm clock began dinging at 5:00 a.m.

He jumped out of bed, hurriedly dressed, and went into the kitchen to put on a pot of coffee. While the coffee was brewing, he got the bacon and eggs from the refrigerator and started cooking breakfast.

He made a mental note to cook something for supper besides breakfast. As he ate breakfast, he listened to the crowing of various roosters around the neighborhood and watched the blackness of night fade slowly into the dawn of a new day, perhaps the new day his daddy had always told him would come.

He had gotten up very early considering he only had to go a couple of blocks to the Texaco station. After he ate and cleaned up the kitchen, he sat in the sitting room, listening to the radio and trying to calm his nerves. Each morning, the DJ read the local news and weather and made various announcements. Rooster almost fell out of his chair when he heard this:

"Folks, Mel Tucker invites everyone to come on by the Tucker Texaco Station on Main Street and welcome his new employee and local hero, Rooster Brown, on his first day on the job."

Rooster jumped up from his chair. He couldn't believe what he'd just heard. He felt a bit of panic, then anger, and then he just shook his head and laughed. If Mel wanted to cash in on him, then who's to say that was so bad. If it brought in business then that would make him look good, and it would also be a good way to meet some of the local folks. Rooster was glad he heard it on the radio so he knew what to expect.

Rooster was really nervous now, and he paced around the tiny sitting room until it was a quarter till 7:00 and time for him to go to work. He put on his hat, went out to his truck and started the engine, and after letting it idle for a couple of minutes, headed down the long driveway and off to work. He pulled into a spot behind the station and got out. He tried to straighten the wrinkles in his shirt, and then headed to the office. Inside were two men, Joe Tatum and Billy Babbitt. Joe had been working at the station for a while and was the one who ran it and that Mel relied on the most. Billy was a young man who had recently received his draft notice and so was about to leave for the army. They both stood up when Rooster entered and shook his hand.

"Pleased to meet you, Rooster," Joe said. "Mel has told me all about you."

Joe introduced Rooster to Billy and explained that he would be training him until he left. Both Joe and Billy were tall, handsome men, and Rooster felt a bit intimidated at first. They had barely made their introductions when the first customer rolled across the air hose that rang the attendant bell. Billy ran out to greet the customer, and Joe explained the routine to Rooster.

"The first thing is you go up to the driver and greet them. Ask them if they want a fill up. Some people never fill up and will always just buy a set amount. You'll get to know them after a while and won't even have to ask anymore. Check the air in the tires, wash the windows, and ask them if they want their oil checked. That's about it. Just be sure not to run over on the gas pump, or it will come out of your check."

Then, Joe told him to follow Billy's lead for a while and they would show him more later on. Joe was about to measure Rooster for a uniform when Billy came back inside.

"Mr. Hedgepeth wants Rooster to come out and wait on him," said Billy, grinning.

Rooster looked at Joe, who just shrugged and motioned for him to go outside.

Rooster walked up to an older model sedan and leaned over to the driver's window. A grizzled old man with a few days' worth of stubbly gray beard flashed a tobacco stained smile at him.

"So you're the hero," he said cheerily.

Rooster grimaced. "I don't know about that. Just in the right place at the right time."

"You're too modest. Let me tell you something, young fellow, everybody likes to see the bullies get what's coming to them," laughed the old man.

Rooster pumped the gas, took the money, and went back inside. He had no more handed the coins to Joe when another car pulled in. Billy waved at them from the driver's window, motioning for Rooster to come. And that was the way it was all day long. A couple of times, there were even lines backed up, waiting to get in. It got to the point where Rooster would just stand by the driver's window and talk to the customers while Joe and Billy did all the work. About midafternoon, Laurie rode up in her car with one of her girlfriends. Both girls giggled and acted silly while Rooster stood by the car door talking to them. He clowned around with them and swaggered a bit, and by the time they left, he was feeling like the king of Merky.

Shortly before closing time, Mel pulled up in his gold Cadillac. He went into the office where Joe was trying to keep all the money from spilling out of the cash register. Mel's eyes widened at the sight of the overflowing tills.

"There's more in the safe," said Joe. "This is just the afternoon receipts."

There were few things in this world that Mel liked better than gazing upon piles of money. He just looked at it and shook his head, a big smile spread across his face.

"Damn!" was all he could say.

Rooster came in from the garage, drying his hands with a red shop rag. "Okay, Joe, we're ready to close her down."

"Rooster, looks like you've been working hard," said Mel. "I knew you were going to make a good hand."

"I didn't get to learn much today, Mel. We were real busy, and I just mostly talked to people, but I'll get the hang of things real soon."

"Oh, you're doing a fine job already, Rooster, a fine job," said Mel, chuckling.

The next day was busy also, but a little less than the first day, and the same with the third, fourth, and so on. By the end of the first week, Rooster had met virtually every person in town. The other gas stations had seen a serious dent in their profits, and Mel's had risen considerably. Around the end of the second week, Rooster received his new uniform. All the Texaco uniforms looked a bit like police or military uniforms and a star was stitched on the chest. Upon seeing Rooster in his uniform, old Mr. Hedgepeth started calling Rooster "Sheriff." It didn't take long before everyone else picked up on this, and soon many people were calling him Sheriff, much to Rooster's chagrin.

Soon, Rooster learned the ins and outs of running a gas station, and his brute strength came in handy for fixing flats and loosening up rusted bolts. After Billy left for the army, it was mostly just him and Joe on duty. The station was open from 7:00 to 7:00 Monday through Friday, till noon on Saturday, and closed on Sundays. They tried to arrange their shifts so that they would both be there during the busy times, but often it was just one of them on duty. Mel also had a couple of old men, Kermit and Obie, who worked part time and filled in when somebody wanted off, and Kenneth worked there part time as well. There was also a mechanic who leased one of the garage bays and he would occasionally pitch in at the pumps when mechanic work was slow.

After the first week or so, the public's fascination with Rooster waned, and things returned more or less to normal. Mel still saw an increase in business as more people started buying their gas at his station, and there was an increase in soda and candy sales as some of the locals would come and kill time by hanging out with the "Sheriff." Joe started referring to these people jokingly as the "Posse." The Posse was mostly old men and young boys, and although Rooster enjoyed the attention, he found it difficult to really befriend many of them. It seemed most of the young men his own age were married and preoccupied with their families, so it was difficult to find friends he could really relate to. Mel came by often, and sometimes he brought Laurie or Kenneth or Shirley with him. They had all gotten to know each other better during this time and kidded around with each other in an easygoing way. Rooster and Laurie had taken to playfully flirting with each other, but it had not gone beyond that stage, much to the frustration of both of them.

As things began to settle into a routine, Rooster was once again invited to Mel's for Sunday dinner. A tender pot roast was served, and once again, Laurie's chocolate pie was the dessert. Rooster and Laurie teased each other throughout the meal and stole glances at each other under the watchful eye of Mel. Afterward, Mel and Rooster sat out by the bluff overlooking Butcher Creek.

"Rooster, I'm real pleased with how you've been doing at the station. You've proven yourself to be a good worker and good for business."

"I appreciate all you've done for me, Mel. I'm real grateful."

"I've always just managed my businesses myself. That's the way I like it. I can keep track of things and make sure nobody's stealing from me. But I've been thinking lately that maybe it's time to make some changes."

"What kind of changes, Mel?"

"I want you to be the manager of the Texaco station."

Rooster was flabbergasted.

"I...I...don't know what to say."

Mel grinned, "Hell, son, haven't we had this conversation before? Just say yes."

For a brief moment, Rooster pictured himself in a white shirt, hands on hips, jaw jutting forth, standing atop the Texaco station, surveying the mere mortals toiling beneath him. Then, he thought about Joe, who had worked at the station for over three years.

"What about Joe? He's already worked there for a lot longer than me, and he knows the place backwards and forwards."

"Joe is a good man, but I want you for manager, Rooster."

"What would I be doing?"

"You'll be keeping the books, planning the purchases, and stocking merchandise. You'll keep track of hours worked and the hiring and firing too. I'm going to let you run it like it was yours."

Now Rooster was starting to feel a little worried. He was just getting the hang of being a grease monkey and cashier, and now this? He was afraid that it might be more than he could handle, and he fretted about how Joe would take the news. In spite of their friendly work relationship, Joe was an imposing figure and often quick to anger.

"Mel, I really appreciate it, but I'm not sure if I'm ready for that, and I feel bad about passing over Joe."

Mel turned a slight shade of red. "I say you are ready, Rooster. Damn it, where's that hero that didn't have to think twice about killing the two son of a bitches that were about to rape my daughter? Don't worry about Joe, I'll handle it. That's life, Rooster, if you go around worrying about hurting everybody's feelings, then you'll never get anywhere. You want to go back to working on the ranch?"

That jolted Rooster. He certainly did not want to go back to working on the ranch. Although working at the station could be dirty, and sometimes stressful when dealing with many customers, he was enjoying being in town and being around people. He understood that there was a subtle threat implied.

"Okay, Mel, I'm sorry. I'm grateful for all you've done for me, and I don't mean to sound like I'm not. I'll do whatever you want me to do."

Mel smiled, and the redness faded. "I understand, Rooster. You're a good man, that's what I like about you. Don't worry, everything will be all right."

There was a moment of silence as they listened to the gurgling stream below them. Mel cleared his throat and began to speak somewhat hesitantly.

"You know, Rooster...Laurie...she's a pretty young woman, and she's the apple of my eye...I mean, every father wants to protect his daughter, and I will never be able to thank you enough. Of course, I want what's best for her..."

Just then, Shirley called from the house, "Mel! Telephone!"

"Oh hell, excuse me, Rooster."

Rooster had been hanging on every word Mel was saying, not sure where it was leading and fearing what he might say. He felt like he just got slammed in the gut.

"Damn it," he said softly to himself.

After a few minutes, Mel came back out. "Rooster I have to run into town. There's a problem with the projector at the picture show. I'll talk to you later."

Rooster couldn't believe it. He was dying to know what Mel was about to say, and now he might never find out. Rooster sat there for a few more minutes until he heard Mel's car heading down the drive out to the main road. Then he got up and ambled back to the house. He went in through the back door, which opened into the kitchen. Laurie was standing at the sink washing dishes.

She turned and looked at Rooster and smiled.

"Just like Daddy to eat and run," she said.

"I guess that's why he's a good businessman. He takes care of things."

Rooster walked up to the sink and picked up a towel and began drying dishes.

"So, you still thinking about going off to college?"

"Thinking about it. I need to make up my mind soon."

"If you didn't go, what would you do?"

"I don't know. I can always work for Daddy. I don't like to just sit around and do nothing. I could probably get married too, there's a couple of boys that want to take me out."

Rooster felt himself flush. "Yes, I reckon you could do that, if you wanted to marry a boy."

"I don't particularly want to marry anybody right now. But I can't wait too long or else I might be an old maid."

"You won't be an old maid. You're too pretty for that."

"Pretty isn't all there is to it. Look at Miss Jenny the school teacher. She was beautiful when she was young, and even now she's still pretty, but she never got married."

"Maybe it was because she was a teacher. I wouldn't want to marry a teacher."

Laurie looked surprised. "Why is that, Rooster?"

Rooster shrugged. "I don't know, I guess because teachers were mean to me when I was in school."

"Why were they mean?"

"I don't know, because I was poor, I guess."

"If I was a teacher, I wouldn't be that way."

"That's because you're nice, especially for a rich girl, you're real nice."

Laurie laughed. "I'm not rich. I'm just lucky to have a daddy that takes good care of his family."

"That's what I call rich," said Rooster.

Just then, Shirley walked in. Seeing Rooster and Laurie doing the dishes, she acted like she was just coming in for a glass of water and left.

When the dishes were done, Laurie and Kenneth got out the checkerboard, and they all took turns playing each other until midafternoon. Rooster won the most games and so was declared the champ by Laurie with Kenneth grudgingly calling for a rematch the next time.

Although he really didn't want to leave, he knew it was time to go, and Shirley was giving subtle signals by asking Laurie and Kenneth to do various chores. Rooster thanked them all, and Laurie walked with him out to his truck.

"Thank you for coming. We always have so much fun when you come to visit."

Rooster looked down at the ground. "I'm the one who should be doing the thanking. I really like your family. I mean, I've met a lot of people now, and it's not like I'm a stranger any more, but when you live by yourself you get kind of lonely sometimes. I never had a family, so it's a real treat for me to come here."

Rooster met Laurie's gaze. Neither of them said anything. Laurie jumped up and hugged Rooster's neck, then turned and ran back toward the house. She stopped on the porch and smiled and waved at Rooster, whose heart was beating a mile a minute.

Rooster drove home with images of Laurie swimming through his head and the lingering question of what Mel was trying to tell him before he left.

5

The next morning, Rooster showed up for work nervously wondering whether Mel had told Joe about his impending promotion. When Rooster walked in the door, Joe was already counting out the till to start the day.

"Morning, chief." Joe grinned at Rooster.

"Morning, Joe," Rooster replied.

Joe was acting as though nothing was out of the ordinary, so Rooster figured he hadn't spoken to Mel yet. Rooster was relieved for the time being, but he dreaded the moment that Joe did learn about Mel's plans.

Rooster was out hosing down the driveway when he saw Mel's Cadillac come around the corner. His heart started racing, and he nervously glanced back inside the office where Joe was still preparing to begin the day.

Mel pulled up into the driveway and waved Rooster over to his car.

"Rooster, I need you to go to San Antonio with Laurie today."

Rooster's jaw dropped. "San Antone? What's going on, Mel?"

"The projector at the picture show broke last night and the part we need is in San Antonio. We can't show tonight's movie without it. I have to stay here and receive a shipment at the Western Auto. Laurie knows how to get to the supply house. I would have sent Kenneth with her, but he's got a baseball game today, and Shirley doesn't want her going alone. I'll try to get one of the part-timers to come in and help Joe. Why don't you go on home and change into some regular clothes, and I'll send Laurie over to get you."

Rooster ran inside the station and told Joe what was going on. Joe was not too happy to hear that he was probably going to be on his own today, but there was little he could do about it. Rooster rushed back home and changed into jeans and a western shirt and waited somewhat nervously by the front window. This was the last thing he had expected to do today. He didn't mind going to San Antonio, in fact, it would be nice to get out and see something new. What was bothering him was that he was going to be alone with Laurie for several hours, and he still had no idea what Mel was about to tell him by the creek yesterday.

Finally, he saw Laurie's Chevy sedan pull into the drive, so he stood up and put on his hat and stepped outside to meet her. Her car crunched over the rocky driveway, and she pulled up underneath one of the trees. She smiled and waved at Rooster as he stood on the porch waiting. Rooster waved back and stepped down from the porch and walked over to the passenger's side and got in.

"I guess you weren't expecting to see me again so soon," Laurie said, smiling.

"I guess you're right, but I'm not complaining," said Rooster. "I hope you know where we're going."

"I do, but honestly it's been a while, so Daddy wrote down the directions for me. I'm not used to driving in city traffic, so you may have to take over once we get to San Antonio."

"I reckon that's no problem. I used to drive trucks all over Germany, and let me tell you, those people are crazy."

"I think that is so wonderful that you got to go to Europe."

"Well, I was in the army, so it wasn't no vacation. It's funny, I didn't much care for it while I was over there, but now that I'm back, it seems more fun."

"I've only ever been to San Antonio and over to Mexico a couple of times."

"I still ain't never been to Mexico. I guess I ought to go some time."

"It can't be as nice as Germany," Laurie sighed.

As they passed by the station, Rooster leaned over to see Joe waiting on a customer. It still weighed on his mind that Joe would hate him after Mel promoted him, but he had no control over it, and he figured he shouldn't look one more gift horse in the mouth. They drove past the city limits and out through a landscape of rocky rolling hills and clear flowing streams. San Antonio was approximately one hundred miles away, and it would take them over two hours to make the drive because of the small roads over most of the route. Rooster sat back and relaxed, he was enjoying the ride. It was early summer and still not too hot yet. It was a beautiful day. He was in the company of a pretty young woman in a nice car and headed for the big city. At that moment, life seemed pretty damn good. Once they got past the hilly region around Merky, the drive went faster. About halfway through the trip, they stopped at a gas station that was also a hamburger stand and bought sodas and used the restrooms. They walked around and stretched their legs a bit and sat at a picnic table underneath a tree next to the station, drinking their sodas.

They sat listening to the birds chirp and the occasional truck go by, neither of them saying much, and neither of them feeling as if they had to say anything. Finally, Rooster broke the silence.

"This sure beats the heck out of working."

Laurie smiled. "I'm glad you came. I probably would have been scared out on the road by myself."

"What's there to be scared of?" asked Rooster.

Laurie paused, a shadow crossed her face. "I've been a lot more scared than I used to, ever since that night. I never thought anything like that could happen to me, especially in my daddy's truck stop. It makes you think, you know, that anything can happen to anybody, and there's nothing you can do about it."

"That's pretty much what I figured out in Korea. When it's your time to go, there's nothing you can do about it, and there doesn't seem to be any rhyme or reason as to why. I swear, the sorriest son of a guns would get out without a scratch, but the good ones would get blown to pieces. I never could figure it out, and I just quit worrying about it."

"Did you see a lot of people get killed?" asked Laurie, a tinge of alarm in her voice.

"A bunch of 'em. It used to tear me up at first, but then you do kind of get used to it. You always wonder why it was them and not you."

"Oh, Rooster, that's so sad. I'm so sorry you had to go through that."

"Let me tell you what, it sure makes life seem sweeter when it's all over. A day like this seems like a gift from heaven."

"I guess it is, isn't it?"

"I reckon so," said Rooster. He was thinking that if the good days are gifts from heaven, then what about the bad days? But he didn't want to spoil the moment by getting into a religious discussion.

They finished their sodas and got back into the car to make the last part of the drive to San Antonio. They reached the city limits around 10:30 and then had to try to find the movie theater supply house. They drove around for another thirty minutes or so before they found it. When they entered the supply house, the man behind the counter seemed surprised to see them. When Laurie handed him the broken part and explained what they were there for he seemed to remember, but told them he would need to have the part machine tooled and it wouldn't be ready until after lunch. He asked them to come back around 3:00 to pick it up. Rooster and Laurie had not expected to have to wait. This would mean that they had at least four hours to kill.

Rooster, as usual, was dominated by his stomach and asked the man if he knew of any good places to eat. The man named off a couple of places and advised them of an area nearby where there were several restaurants. Laurie asked Rooster to drive, so they got into Laurie's car and drove up and down the street looking at the various choices. It soon became apparent that these were fancier restaurants than either of them were used to.

"Dang, Laurie, I can't even pronounce the names of some of these places. It might cost a week's wages for a meal here."

"I've been here before with Daddy. He says this is close to a rich neighborhood and that's why these kinds of restaurants are here. We've eaten over there before, it's good food and not too snobby," Laurie said, pointing at a steak house.

Rooster was feeling a little uncomfortable, but pulled into the parking lot anyway. They got out and walked to the front of the restaurant just as a couple of businessmen in suits came out. Suddenly, Rooster became aware of how he was dressed and who he was, and the old feelings of inadequacy welled up inside him. He wanted to turn around and leave, but that would only make him look bad, so he kept going.

They walked into one of the nicest restaurants that Rooster had ever been in, which, in spite of his worldliness, was not saying much. They were greeted by a man in a suit who led them to a table near the kitchen. He set menus in front of each of them and left. Rooster looked around and saw that most of the other men were wearing suits. He thought back to that morning and was grateful that Mel had told him to go home and change, or he probably would have just worn his Texaco uniform. It occurred to him that he could really be clueless at times.

A pretty waitress in a uniform came to the table and asked them if they were ready to order. Rooster stared at the menu, realizing he had been reading it over and over and still didn't know what was on it.

He looked at Laurie. "You've been here before. What do you think I should get?"

Laurie skimmed the menu. "I think we should both get the grilled steak."

They chatted quietly while waiting for their food. When it finally came, Rooster was pleased to see a large slab of meat, along with mashed potatoes and vegetables, piled on his plate. He eagerly dug in and began demolishing the steak bite by bite. By the time he cleaned his plate and pushed it away, Laurie had barely eaten half of hers, so he sat back and took in his surroundings. The inside of the restaurant was dimly lit with plush carpeting and paneled walls. A couple of mounted bucks' heads stared out from one wall. He listened to some of the other patrons' conversations. A couple of men at a nearby table were discussing business matters while, at another table, a man and a woman sat chewing their food, seemingly oblivious to each other. Laurie finally set down her fork. She had only eaten about half of her meal but could not finish it.

"Rooster, would you like the rest of my steak?" she asked.

Rooster was fairly sated, but he could almost always hold more, so he let Laurie move it onto his plate. With a few bites, he finished the rest of steak, and they were ready to pay and leave. When they left the restaurant, they still had almost three hours to kill. Rooster wondered aloud where the Alamo was, and Laurie confessed that she wasn't sure. Across the street, Rooster noticed a movie theater.

"It looks like they have a matinee over there. You want to go see what's showing?"

"Sure," said Laurie.

They walked across the street and saw that the featured matinee was *Forever My Darling*, a low budget romance about War World II. Rooster shifted about on his feet, not sure what to do next.

Laurie piped up cheerfully, "Do you want to go see this?"

"Um, okay."

"Are you sure?"

"Sure."

They paid for their tickets and entered the dark, dank theater. There was a concession stand off to the left. They had just eaten, so they did not buy any popcorn. They passed through a thick velvet curtain into the main auditorium. There was no one else there, not too surprising since it was a Monday. They stood in the aisle for a minute, trying to decide where to sit. Finally, they agreed on two seats in the middle of a row toward the back of the theater. They sat down and looked around at the ornately decorated walls while waiting for the movie to begin.

"It's cold in here," said Laurie.

"Feels good to me," said Rooster.

"You've got a long sleeve shirt on, and I'm wearing a dress."

Rooster reached over and put his arm across her shoulders.

"Is this any better?"

Laurie snuggled up closer to his chest. "Yes."

Rooster couldn't believe what he had just done. Without even thinking about it, he just put his arm around her, and she didn't push him away. He smiled to himself and relaxed. He knew now that he had it made. Then, the house lights went down, and the movie began.

They sat together like that for a long time until it started getting uncomfortable. As Rooster began to fidget, Laurie pulled his hand into her lap and grasped it with hers. They both sat up straight up in their seats but kept their fingers intertwined. About halfway through the movie, Rooster looked around and saw that there was still no one else there. Deciding the time was right, he reached over and gently took Laurie's chin in his hand and pulled her face toward his. Their lips met, and they kissed gently for a few seconds before

Laurie pulled away. She leaned over against Rooster, laying her head against his shoulder. Rooster's heart was pounding, and he was starting to get a bit of a hard-on, so he had to shift about in his seat so that his growing erection had room to expand without hurting him or being too obvious. On the screen, the hero was in a foxhole firing a machine gun as bombs exploded all around him, causing a strobe light effect in the theater. For a brief moment, Rooster had the illusion of everything moving in slow motion, and then it was over. They both settled back in their seats and became absorbed in what was happening on the screen. After a boring part came back on, Rooster started getting antsy and decided to try to kiss Laurie again. Once again, he pulled Laurie toward him and kissed her. This time, they kissed a little bit longer until Laurie turned away again. Rooster knew she was only shy because they were in a movie theater, even if it was empty. Laurie grasped his hand and squeezed it with both of hers.

Finally, the movie was over, and it was a real tearjerker at the end. Laurie was sniffling and wiping her eyes, and Rooster was doing his best to blink back his own tears. He shook it off quickly and acted as if he were unaffected. They looked at each other somewhat sheepishly, both of them unable to stop smiling. They held hands as they walked out of the theater and into the bright light.

It was not yet 3:00, and they still had some time to kill. There was a drug store with a soda fountain next to the theater, and by now, they were ready for something to drink. They went to the back of the store to where the soda fountain was and sat in a booth and both ordered Cokes.

"Did you like the movie, Rooster?"

"I liked it okay. I liked what we were doing better."

Laurie blushed and smiled. "I liked it too."

"What do you think Mel would say?"

"I don't know. He likes you."

"He likes me as an employee and as the fellow that saved his daughter. He might not like it to be more than that."

Laurie frowned. "Why do you say that, Rooster?"

"I'm not from the same kind of people as y'all. I'm just a working man."

"Daddy was a working man too. He was poor when he was young. He doesn't put on airs."

"I know he doesn't, but he may want more than a grease monkey for his daughter."

"You don't always have to be a grease monkey, Rooster. He likes you. Don't worry."

Rooster let the subject drop, and they sat for a while without saying anything. Then, Laurie broke the silence.

"Is that what war is really like?" Laurie asked.

"Kind of, except a lot more scary."

"Were you afraid you might get killed?"

"If you're smart, you'll be afraid. Being afraid is probably what kept me alive."

They finished their sodas and drove back to the shop to pick up the part even though it was still a bit early. When they got there, the man had it ready for them. Laurie paid him, and they got in the car and headed out of town to make the long drive back to Merky. Rooster was driving, and he knew Mel would be upset if they didn't get there in time for the evening matinee, so he put the pedal to the metal. They stopped at the same gas station on the way back and ordered a couple of hamburgers and Cokes to take with them. They rolled into Merky a little after 5:00 and went straight to the theater where the projectionist was waiting for them. It was a simple task to replace the part, so the projector was up and running just in time for that evening's movie.

Once they had delivered the projector part, their mission and their reason for spending the day together was over. It began to dawn on them that they would soon have to leave each other, and neither of them was ready for that. Rooster thought they should find Mel, so they could tell him they had made it back in time to get the projector fixed, so they drove out to the ranch to see if he was there. They bounced over the cattle guard and past a stand of dusty prickly pear cactus alongside the road to the house. As the house came in sight, they saw Mel's Cadillac in the garage.

When they walked into the living room, Mel was waiting for them.

"Well, it took y'all long enough."

"We had to wait for them to make the part, Daddy."

"What did you do all that time?"

"We had dinner and went to a movie."

"Did you now? What movie did you see?"

"It was called *Forever My Darling*. It was about the war."

Mel sat silently, looking them both over, as Rooster tried not to fidget.

"Did you like the movie, Rooster?" Mel asked.

"Yes, sir, it was real good. We just went because we had to wait four hours for the part to be ready."

Mel sat quietly again, studying the both of them. Finally, he smiled. "Well, you did real good to make it back in time."

"We just wanted to come by and tell you that we made it back and that everything's all right," said Rooster.

"I appreciate that, Rooster, that's why I hired you. You're a good man. You're conscientious. I appreciate what you did."

"I still have to take Rooster home, Daddy. We just wanted to tell you that we made it back in time."

Mel glanced at the clock on the wall. "Well, then you better get going so you can get home before it's too late."

As they were driving back to town, Rooster was worried.

"Do you think he was mad?"

"No, if he was mad, he would have really tore into us."

"Then why was he acting that way?"

Laurie smiled. "Rooster, you just took his daughter to the big city all alone and the fact that he didn't skin you alive as soon as we walked in that door tells me a lot."

"You sure?"

"I'm sure."

They drove into Merky, by the mostly empty town square, and past the Texaco station, which was now closed. Laurie drove up the driveway to Rooster's darkened house and stopped. They sat there with the motor idling.

"I had a real good time, Laurie."

"Me too, Rooster. It was so much fun."

"I don't want to stop being with you just 'cause we're back home. I don't want to make Mel mad either, but I want to see you again. I want to spend time together like we did today."

"We will, Rooster. We just have to take it easy at first and let Daddy get used to the idea."

Rooster mumbled something and reached for the door handle.

Laurie grabbed his hand. Their eyes met, and they slowly leaned toward each other until their lips met. They began to kiss softly and slowly at first, and then with more passion. They put their arms around each other and kissed with more urgency, their tongues caressing. The only sounds were the motor running and their breathing as they hugged each other tighter and kissed with increasing ardor. After several minutes, Laurie pulled away.

"I have to go, Rooster."

"I know. Good night, Laurie."

"Good night, Rooster."

He got out of the car and watched as she backed up and turned around and then drove toward the street. He watched until her car disappeared around the corner.

"Hot damn," he said to himself and then turned to go inside.

When he got to the front door, he was surprised to see a note attached to the screen door. He pulled the note off and took it inside. He turned the lights on and opened the note. It said:

"Come to the sheriff's office. I want to talk to you—Bill Hickey."

"Aw shit," he muttered to himself.

6

The next morning, the alarm rang just as it seemed he was finally drifting off to sleep. He had tossed and turned much of the night before, partly from excitement and worry about his emerging romance with Laurie, and partly because he didn't know why Sheriff Hickey wanted to speak with him. He dragged out of bed and got dressed and started making breakfast. He followed the routine that he had been going through every morning since he started working at the station, and when the clock said exactly fifteen minutes to 7:00, he walked out the door and started up his old truck.

He pulled up behind the station and walked around front and into the office. Joe was already there and counting out money for the till.

"Morning, Joe."

"Morning, Rooster."

Rooster could tell right away that Mel had talked to Joe.

"How did it go yesterday?" asked Rooster.

"Oh, not too bad. Could've been worse." Joe stopped counting the money. "I guess I should be letting you do this, *boss*."

Rooster cringed. "That was Mel's idea, Joe. I didn't want it, but you know how Mel is."

"Yes, I reckon I do know how Mel is. I guess I know how life is too."

Rooster just nodded his head, not knowing what else to say.

"Well, what do you want me to do, boss?" asked Joe.

"There ain't nothing gonna be different, Joe. You're still the one that knows how to run this place. We'll just keep doing like we've been doing and let Mel think what he wants to think."

"No, Rooster, things are going to be different. They have to be different. If you're the boss, then I'm going to just take orders from you, and you have to decide what it is I'm supposed to be doing."

Joe handed Rooster the till and went outside. Soon, a car pulled in, and Joe started pumping gas and checking tires. Rooster counted out the money. He knew basically what to do, just start out with a certain number of bills and coins in the register and make it all balance out at the end of the day. Once he had the register taken care of, he started thinking about what needed to be done next. He walked through the mechanic's bay, looking around and taking a mental inventory of the daily tasks that he had learned so far. It looked like he was going to have to be manager whether he wanted to or not, and he decided that he had better try to do as good a job as possible.

Throughout the day, it became obvious that Joe was not going to help Rooster any more than he absolutely had to. During a couple of busy spells, Rooster had to call Joe out to help, something he would never have had to do before. By the end of the day, Rooster was frustrated, but he didn't say anything because he knew Joe had every right to be angry. At quitting time, Rooster asked Joe if there was anything else they needed to do before closing up for the night. Joe just shrugged and slipped out the door, and he was gone. Rooster sat down at the desk and wrote down what he knew needed to be done and things that he wasn't sure of. He was almost ready to leave when he realized that he didn't know the combination to the safe, and he still needed to put away the day's receipts. He pounded his fist on the desk. Now he was really starting to get angry. It wasn't his fault that Mel picked him for manager, and Joe should know that and shouldn't be taking it out on him. He wasn't going to go looking for Joe, and he didn't want to call Mel and ask him for the combination. He thought about it for a minute and then decided to just take the money home with him and keep it hidden under his mattress. It would just be for tonight, and tomorrow he would get the combination from Joe. Rooster put all the cash in the bank bag and stuffed it in his boot. He was starting to feel like the manager now, and he knew he could handle it. To hell with Joe.

Rooster went home, hid the bank bag underneath the mattress, and started cooking supper. Soon, he heard a car pull into the driveway. He went and looked out to see Mel's Cadillac pulling up in front. Mel came rushing inside.

"Rooster, I just checked the safe! Where's the money!?"

"It's in there, Mel." Rooster pointed to his bedroom. He went and pulled the bag out from the mattress and handed it to Mel. "I didn't know the combination to the safe, and Joe had already left, so I brought it home so I could keep an eye on it."

Mel looked at Rooster, his cheeks flushing. "The money always goes in the safe, Rooster, always. You don't ever take it home or anywhere else, understand?"

"I...I'm sorry, Mel. I didn't want to just leave it unlocked."

"Next time you're unsure about something you call me, okay?"

"Okay, okay, Mel, I will."

Rooster smelled something burning and ran to turn off the burner. He wanted to just keep running and leave, but he knew he couldn't do that. He felt a little surge of anger welling up.

"Damn it, Mel, I'm sorry. I know it was stupid now. That son of a bitch Joe wouldn't help me at all, and I didn't want it to get stolen."

"Okay, Rooster. I shouldn't be so hard on you. You're right. You had a lot put on you all at once, and I believe that you were trying to protect my property. I appreciate that, Rooster. I'm sorry I got mad at you."

That made Rooster feel better, and so both men calmed down and sat down at the kitchen table.

"I may need some help figuring things out at first, Mel, but once I've got it down you won't have to worry about a thing."

"I know that, Rooster. That's why I picked you."

They went over the opening and closing tasks that had to be done every day, and then the ones that had to be done weekly, and finally the monthly chores. By the time they were through, Rooster's head was hurting.

"Don't worry, Rooster. You'll get the hang of it, and then it won't seem like anything at all. Well, look, I need to go. Say did you hear about Henry Wells today?"

"No, who's he?"

"He was the president of the Merky Bank. He just died today."

"Oh, I'm sorry to hear that. Was he a friend of yours?"

Mel chuckled, "Bankers don't have friends, Rooster, just customers."

Rooster figured that meant that he wasn't a friend and let it drop. Mel took the bank bag and went back to the station to put it away. Rooster looked at his watch, it was almost 8:00 p.m., and his food was cold. For once, he wasn't that hungry anyway. He was love-struck and had been thinking of Laurie all day. He was also wondering what the sheriff wanted with him. He decided to go down to the sheriff's office and see if anyone was there. It was unlikely, but not unheard of, that Bill Hickey would still be there. For some reason Rooster decided to go. He drove down to the courthouse and parked in front. He walked up the concrete steps and through the imposing front doors. It was mostly empty, although he could hear some voices echoing in the hallway. The voices sounded as if they were coming from the sheriff's office, so he walked toward them. As he got closer, he could hear laughter and discern the voices better. It was Sheriff Hickey and Deputy Bates. Rooster braced himself and strode purposely into the office. Both men abruptly stopped speaking and turned toward Rooster. The sheriff got up from the desk he was sitting on. He glared at Rooster and then slowly began to smile.

"Mr. Brown, do come in. We've been waiting for you." Sheriff Hickey pointed to a wooden desk chair. "Have a seat."

Rooster sat in the chair and looked at the sheriff expectantly.

"We hear you got a promotion already," the sheriff smirked.

"Maybe so, what's it to you?"

"Oh, well, we just have an interest in your well-being, Rooster. You being a hero and all, we think that's just wonderful. You sure did learn fast to move ahead of a man that's been working there and running the place for over three years."

"That was Mel's decision. I didn't have nothing to do with it."

"Oh, I believe you. You and Mel got tight pretty quick."

Rooster was silent for a moment. He looked at both men. The sheriff was grinning, but Deputy Bates was staring at Rooster intently.

"You know, Wayne here is good friends with that waitress Jeanine. She says you were hanging around a bunch up there, said you asked her out a couple of nights before the shooting."

Rooster said nothing. Sheriff Hickey stopped smiling and turned to the deputy.

"Wayne, what do you think about that?"

Deputy Bates stood directly across from Rooster, his hands on his hips.

"I think it sounds like somebody up to no good."

"You better have something besides just what you think," said Rooster.

Wayne stepped up closer to Rooster, his hand on his revolver.

"I've got something all right, something that'll take care of you for good."

Rooster watched nervously as Deputy Bates' hand rested across the handle of his gun.

"You gonna shoot me? How you gonna explain you shot a man everybody says is a hero?"

"That won't be hard. You confessed to planning a robbery. You tried to fight. I had to shoot you."

Rooster was getting more nervous. He figured that, in fact, they probably could shoot him and get away with it. Just then, he heard a door slam down the hall and the sound of footsteps approaching. The footsteps got closer and closer and then in walked Harvey.

"Hi, Bill. I just left the funeral parlor, and I didn't feel like going home, so I came on in," Harvey said.

Sheriff Hickey and Deputy Bates looked at each other, neither of them knowing exactly what to say or do. Rooster saw his opening.

"Well, howdy there, Harvey. You're just the man I was looking for. We need to talk about this fishing trip we got planned," Rooster said as he stood up and shook Harvey's hand.

"Well, yeah," replied Harvey excitedly. "That sounds real good, Rooster. How about this weekend?"

"Perfect. That's just what I was thinking," responded Rooster. From the corner of his eye, he was watching the sheriff and the deputy closely. Sheriff Hickey's face was reddening and the deputy just looked disgusted. "Well, I was just about to leave. Why don't you come by the station tomorrow and we'll start making plans?" said Rooster as he started inching toward the door.

"I'll do that," said Harvey happily. "I'll see you tomorrow."

Rooster took off and made a beeline for the front doors. He heard the office door slam shut behind him, and just as he was stepping outside the front door, he could hear Sheriff Hickey starting to yell at Harvey. He was shaking as he walked out the door. He felt bad for Harvey, but if he hadn't shown up when he did, Rooster wasn't sure what would have happened. He knew that from then on he would have to be careful about when and where he met up with the sheriff and the deputy.

He went straight to his truck and headed for home. As he was rounding the final turn to his house, he thought he saw someone pulling out of his driveway. It looked like Laurie's car. His heart racing, Rooster stomped the gas pedal to catch up to the car. The car turned down a side street. As Rooster gunned his truck to try to catch up, a large dog ran into the street, and Rooster slammed on the brakes, narrowly missing the dog.

"Shit!" he yelled.

The truck stalled. Rooster turned the key and pumped the gas, but the carburetor was flooded, and it would not start. Rooster kept trying to start the truck until finally he gave up. He knew it would have to sit so that the gas could evaporate. He pounded his fist on the steering wheel. That damn dog, he should have just run over it. He sat there for ten minutes, and when he turned the key, the truck started up. Rooster put it in gear and took off in the direction he'd last seen the car. He pulled onto the main highway through town and drove up and down the main drag a couple of times, but eventually he gave up and went home. What would Laurie think? That he was out carousing or something? He was worried and frustrated that he had wasted the evening talking to those assholes and missed a chance to be with Laurie. He pulled up into his driveway and walked up to the door in the dark. He opened the front door, turned on the lights, and went into the kitchen where his supper sat coldly on the table. He slammed his fist into a wall and cursed under his breath. He had a sudden powerful urge for a shot of alcohol. He wondered where Mel got his booze, but he wasn't going to call him and ask. Eventually, his stomach got the best of him, and he turned on the stove to reheat his food. He sat glumly in the small kitchen, picking at his food. It would be hard to sleep that night.

After another night of tossing and turning, Rooster arose the next morning and put on a pot of coffee. He wasn't looking forward to another day of being around Joe, whose bitterness was quickly becoming unbearable. He was longing to connect with Laurie, and he was worried about what Bill Hickey and his deputy might try to do. He got into his truck and drove the short distance to the station. He was the one who was now responsible for opening up and taking care of the business operations.

Rooster unlocked the door and began turning on the lights. He went into the mechanic's bay and turned on the generator for the air compressor. He went back to the cash register and counted out the till for the day. Then, he went outside, unlocked the gas pumps and started hosing down the driveway. As he was squirting water on the drive, he was surprised to see Kermit pull up to the station in his old Studebaker. Rooster watched as he pulled around back and parked. Kermit was grinning as he came around the corner.

"Howdy doo, Rooster," he said cheerfully.

"Kermit, what the heck you doing up here this time of day?"

"I'm filling in for Joe. He came by late last night and said he had something to take care of today."

Rooster grumbled to himself, "That son of a bitch didn't bother to tell me anything."

In spite of his annoyance, Rooster was relieved that he wouldn't have to be around Joe's sulking today. He handed the hose to Kermit and went back inside to finish opening up. Before long customers started coming in and they were fairly busy. It was almost noon before Rooster realized it, so he told Kermit to go take his lunch break, and he would cover the pumps.

While he was standing by the door, having a smoke, he saw Joe's car pulling into the drive. Instead of going around back, Joe pulled right up to the pumps and sat there, waiting. Rooster just stood, watching to see what he was going to do. Joe didn't get out of his car; instead, he started honking the horn. Rooster swore under his breath angrily. If that damn fool thought he was going to pump his gas for him, he was seriously mistaken. Joe kept honking until finally Rooster stomped over to his window. He was about to let loose on Joe but stopped short when he noticed what he wearing. He looked closer, not sure if he could trust his own eyes. As it sank in, he couldn't believe what he was seeing. Joe saw the expression on his face and smirked.

"Hey there, boy. Check the air in my tires."

"Say what?"

"You heard me, grease monkey. Check my tires."

"What the hell is going on, Joe?"

"I want my tires checked."

"Then do it yourself."

"You expect customers to check their own air? What kind of service is that?"

"I expect employees to wait on themselves."

"Well, that's where the problem is, you see. I'm not your employee any more. I got me a better job." Joe reached up to his chest and tugged on his badge so that Rooster could see it clearly.

"I'm a deputy now," Joe laughed.

"How the hell did that happen?"

"Ask your fishing buddy."

Rooster felt himself flush as he realized that Sheriff Hickey must have fired Harvey. He remembered the sheriff asking him about his promotion, so Joe had obviously been talking to him. Rooster knew that the sheriff didn't like Harvey, and when he brought up the fishing trip last night, he figured that the sheriff must have fired him. And now this son of a bitch who hated him because of Mel was going to bully him around.

"Now check my damn tires, boy," Joe said forcefully.

Rooster shook his head and grumbled underneath his breath as he went around checking all the tires on Joe's car.

"They're all fine. How much gas you want?"

"Wash my windshield."

Rooster's face was burning red as he grabbed the squeegee and cleaned Joe's windows.

"All right, now how much gas?"

"Oh, I don't need any gas. Wouldn't buy it at this piece of shit anyway," Joe said as he started up his car. He revved his engine, peeled out on the driveway, and sped out onto the highway.

Rooster stared in disbelief as he left. "Shit," he muttered under his breath.

Kermit came up to him. "What the devil was that all about?"

Rooster shook his head and groaned slightly. He turned and walked back to the office, staring at the ground the whole way. He sat down at the desk, put his head in his hands and rubbed his eyes. He couldn't believe what had just happened. Not only did he lose the man who knew the most about running the station, but now that same man hated him and was working with two other SOBs who hated him. He looked out the window at Kermit who was happily smoking a cigarette as he filled the tank on a Chevy. It seemed like Kermit always had a lit cigarette, smoked halfway down and with a half-inch long ash on the end of it, dangling from his mouth. The first time Rooster saw Kermit smoking while pumping gas he told him to put it out or he was going to blow everybody up, but Kermit and Obie just laughed at him and called him a titty baby, so he never mentioned it again. Still, he didn't like it when Kermit smoked around the pumps, and now it looked like he was going to be stuck with him even more.

Just then, Mel pulled up to the pumps, dinging the pneumatic bells. Laurie was riding on the passenger side. Rooster jumped up and ran outside to meet them. Laurie glanced sideways at him and caught his eye. She winked ever so slightly, and Rooster felt his heart well up. He smiled at her but went around to Mel's side.

"Well, Rooster, I hear we're one man down now," Mel said.

"Yes, sir. Joe quit and joined the police force."

Mel grinned. "That's just what you need, another friend on the police force."

Rooster shook his head. "Joe hates me now. He was just here. He hates me for sure."

Mel's grin faded. "I'm sorry, Rooster. That's my fault, but I'm still happy with the choice I made. Joe will get over it, and Hickey will get over whatever his problem is. It will be all right. Just stay out of their way for a while."

"I don't have anything to hide, but that don't mean they won't try to frame me or something, Mel. Hickey left a note on my door, so I went to go see them at the courthouse last night. They were talking like they might kill me and make it look I was trying to fight them or something."

Rooster looked from Mel to Laurie and back again. Mel was beginning to turn red, his brow furrowed in thought. Laurie looked scared.

Mel shook his head. "You need to watch yourself, Rooster. I don't think they'll do anything, but they could if you provoke them. You need to lay low and not give them any excuses to mess with you, at least until this investigation is over." Rooster frowned and let out a sigh. Mel rubbed his chin thoughtfully. "We've got to make sure there is somebody with you as much as possible. Maybe you ought to stay out at our place for a while. We have a small bunkhouse you can stay in."

"I appreciate that, Mel, but I hate to put you out any more than what I already have."

"You're not putting us out. I don't think those blowhards will really do anything, but it's better to be safe than sorry. Just get your things and come on out after work. We'll feed you supper and get you set up in the bunkhouse. In the meantime, I'm going to go over and talk to Addis about this and see what he thinks. We need to have it on record somewhere that they threatened you."

"Okay, Mel. Thank you."

Rooster's eyes met Laurie's, and she smiled at him sweetly, making his heart flutter a bit.

Rooster shook his head and muttered to himself as he watched them drive away. Things seemed to be moving awfully fast.

Rooster went back to pumping gas, but he could barely concentrate on anything. Sweet images of Laurie were swimming through his head along with stark and jolting visions of being killed by Hickey and Bates. Rooster would be melancholy one moment and giddy with happiness the next. Try as he might to conceal his constantly changing emotions, Kermit noticed something strange about him.

"Rooster, you sure seem a might took up with something today."

"Yeah, Kermit, I got a lot of things on my mind. I got to run this station, and we're going to be short-handed for a while."

"Well, I guess that would be enough to tear a fellow up, but if I didn't know better, I'd say there's a woman somewhere in the picture."

Rooster stared at Kermit. He hadn't said a word to anyone about him and Laurie. He wondered if the old man knew something or if he was just smarter than he looked. Rooster decided not to take the bait and went on about his business. At quitting time, he and Kermit went about shutting everything down. After Kermit left, Rooster locked the money in the safe just as Mel had shown him. He went home, bathed, put on some clean clothes, and packed up enough things to get him through a couple of days. He could always come by to pick up anything else he might need later.

Daylight was fading when he pulled up in front of Mel's house. He parked under the trees out front and walked past the old dogs who barely paid him any attention any more. He rang the doorbell and waited as he heard the footsteps of someone running to the door. The knob turned, and the door swung open. Laurie smiled at him.

"Come in, Rooster."

"Howdy," said Rooster as he tipped his hat and stepped through the doorway. "You look nice tonight."

"Thank you. Come on in and have a seat. We've already eaten, so we're just going to heat up a plate for you."

"Where's Mel?"

"I don't know where Daddy is. He called and said he was going to be late."

Rooster hung his hat on a rack and sat down on the sofa as Laurie disappeared into the kitchen. He looked around at the things that were becoming familiar to him now. He saw a newspaper lying on the coffee table and he picked it up and began browsing through it. He rarely read the news, didn't care much about it anyway, but he was just looking for something to do. He flipped the pages of the paper about, looking for something that might interest him, but found nothing and set the paper back on the coffee table. Soon, supper was ready, and Shirley called him into the dining room. Shirley was annoyed that Mel still hadn't made it home.

"We shouldn't wait for your father, there's no telling when he might come in."

"I'll fix him a plate when he gets here," said Laurie.

"So, Rooster, how do you like working at the gas station?" Shirley asked.

"I like it real well, ma'am. I really do."

"Well, that's wonderful, we love having you there," said Shirley smiling.

"Who do you think you might hire to take Joe's place?" asked Laurie.

"I don't have any idea. Maybe Kenneth can work more hours until we find somebody."

Kenneth started silently squirming in his chair. Although he worked at all of Mel's businesses, he preferred the movie theater most of all, especially during the summer when he could stay up late to watch the movies during the middle of the week. He got to see many of his classmates there, and it was also a way to get in good with girls he discovered.

"Did you hear that, Kenneth? We may need you to work at the station more," said Shirley.

Kenneth nodded his head and grunted slightly.

Shirley smiled. "Don't you worry, Rooster, we'll get you some help."

After supper, Rooster helped Shirley and Laurie wash the dishes, and then it was time for him to go to his bunk.

"Kenneth will take you to the bunkhouse," said Shirley.

Kenneth hopped in their old farm truck and spun the wheels, kicking up a small cloud of dust. He stuck his arm out the window and waved for Rooster to follow him. Rooster pulled in behind him, and they drove a few hundred feet to a barn that Rooster had barely noticed before. Kenneth went around to the side, opened a door and turned on the lights. Inside was a small bunk area with two bunk beds and a kitchenette and bathroom.

"There's not any hot water, so if you want to take a bath you have to boil the water on the stove," said Kenneth.

Rooster decided that he would just take his baths at his little house in town, which he was already missing. At one time, he would have been happy to have a bunkhouse all to himself, but now he was spoiled, and accustomed to having his own house. Then he remembered that Laurie was just a few hundred feet away, and that made it seem better to him.

"What did Mel build this for?" asked Rooster. "Do y'all keep ranch hands out here?"

"No, not regular ranch hands, but sometimes wetbacks," said Kenneth. "Mostly it stays empty."

"Wetbacks? I didn't know Mel was a rancher too," mused Rooster.

"Oh, he's not really. Dad likes to keep a little livestock, but that's about it. There's always something that needs to be done, so he just brings them out here every now and then."

"Hmm," Rooster grunted affirmatively.

Kenneth paused for a minute. "And sometimes a guy brings wetbacks out here for a night or two, on their way somewhere else. Mom doesn't like it, so Dad doesn't do it too often, but the guy pays him for it."

"I guess that don't surprise me too much. Mel's a smart man when it comes to making money."

"Yeah, and sometimes we don't know what he's doing out here," chuckled Kenneth. Rooster still marveled at all of Mel's wealth. This barn, which would have been a palace to Rooster many times during his life, was just an afterthought for Mel, a place to store a wetback.

"Hey, Rooster, here's a housewarming present for you." Kenneth cut a fart and then ran out the door, giggling.

"You little shit!" Rooster shouted as he ran a couple of steps after Kenneth and then stopped. Rooster chuckled to himself and waved his hat to dissipate the fumes.

"Well, hell," he sighed softly and began unpacking his bag.

It was a tidy, little bunkhouse. Except for not having warm water, it was cozy. Rooster wondered why Mel didn't just hook up a hot water heater, and then he realized that by having only cold water, it was something of an incentive for people to move on. He looked at his watch. It was almost 9:00 p.m. He wound the stem on the watch and set it next to the bed. He wasn't too concerned about oversleeping, but he needed the watch so he would know when to leave for work. He paced about. He was restless and a little out of sorts being in a new place again, but he did feel safe out there, so that made it all worth it. He knew he wouldn't be ready for sleep for a while, so he stepped outside and pulled up an old cane bottom chair that was sitting on the porch. He lit up a cigarette and looked up at the stars. Just a few hundred feet away, the windows of Mel's house glowed in the darkness. One by one, they went dark until just the porch light and the light in the main room remained on.

Rooster was leaning back in the chair, blowing smoke rings, when suddenly he thought he heard something. He sat up straight in his chair and peered into the darkness. He sat motionless, listening intently. He could clearly hear the sound of someone walking up the car path toward him. One of the old dogs trotted up to him, wagging its tail. Then, from the darkness, he heard a voice.

"Rooster, it's me, Laurie."

Rooster stood up and watched as Laurie walked into the light.

"I brought you something for breakfast," she said, lifting up a grocery bag.

Rooster took the bag and looked in it.

"It's just some coffee, bread, and eggs," said Laurie.

"I hadn't even thought about breakfast," mumbled Rooster.

"Well, I better get back."

"Wait, Laurie, let me walk you back."

"Um, I don't know. Momma doesn't know I came over here. You have to be very quiet."

Rooster set the bag on the chair and took Laurie's hand. "I'll be quiet, let's go."

"Thank you," Rooster whispered.

"That's okay," Laurie smiled.

"I'm glad you came. I've been wanting to see you again, even if it is just for a few minutes."

"I know. Me too. That's why I brought you the food."

"When can we see each other again?"

"I can come by the station tomorrow."

"I mean, when can we see each other alone?"

"I don't know. We need to think of something."

"Maybe I should go and break the projector at the picture show."

"Daddy would have a heart attack. We'll have to think of something else, but I will still come by the station tomorrow, okay?"

"Okay."

Laurie glanced nervously toward the house and then turned toward Rooster. He leaned down to her, and they kissed gently for several seconds before Laurie broke away.

"I have to go. Good night."

"Good night," he said as she faded away in the shadows. He waited until he heard the screen door creak, and then he turned toward the house. Out of the corner of his eyes, he saw headlights coming down the drive from the main road. Rooster figured it was Mel, and he took off running back to the bunkhouse before he saw him.

7

Rooster tossed and turned throughout most of the night until he finally managed to doze off in the early morning hours. Then, he slept late and awoke with a start at the sunlight streaming in the window. He rushed about making breakfast and gulped down his coffee before it could cool, burning his mouth in the process. He hopped in his truck and spun out in a cloud of dust. When he got to the station, Kermit was calmly sitting out front, smoking a cigarette. Rooster jumped out of his truck before it stopped rolling and ran to the front of the station. The clock inside said it was 7:20.

"That's all right, Rooster. It ain't bothered me one bit to sit here and wait on you."

"Did any customers come by?"

"Oh, one or two drove by like they was looking to see if we was open."

"Shit," mumbled Rooster. If Mel found out about this, he would have his ass.

Rooster unlocked the doors and began turning on the lights. He told Kermit to go and open up the mechanic's bay and unlock the gas pumps.

Rooster counted out the till for the cash register, and within just a few minutes, they were ready for business and waiting for customers.

And they waited and waited, yet no one came in. Most surprisingly, none of Rooster's Posse came by, and that was very unusual.

"Damn, what's going on? Is this a holiday or something?" Rooster asked to no one in particular.

Finally, old Mr. Hedgepeth pulled into the driveway. He grinned at Rooster and Kermit.

"Howdy, boys."

"Morning, Mr. Hedgepeth," said Rooster glumly.

"I figured I better come by and give you boys a little business. Word is you won't be getting much anymore," Mr. Hedgepeth chuckled.

"What do you mean?" asked Rooster.

"Well, from what I been hearing, the entire Merky Sheriff's Department is out to get you."

"What do you mean 'out to get me'?" asked Rooster.

"Deputy Bates has been telling people if they want to avoid trouble that it might be a good idea to buy their gas somewhere else."

"Pshhh! What the hell they gonna do? Arrest people for buying gas here?"

"Oh, I don't know about that, but they can give you tickets for just about anything they want, and it's your word against theirs. They got power, and they know it."

"Jesus Christ. What have I ever done to these assholes? Why are they out to get me?"

"Sheriff Hickey is a strange man. Who knows why he does anything. As far as the deputy is concerned, Bill's enemy is his enemy."

"Do they think they can just shut down this business because they don't like me? They ain't just messing with me; they're messing with Mel, and Mel's got enough clout around here to put a stop to this type of bullshit."

"Oh, I don't reckon they're doing anything but giving you a hard time, Rooster. I suspect it will all blow over and things will get back to normal. Maybe you ought to try and find out what's got them so tore up."

"I ain't going to talk to them son of a bitches at all if I can help it. They acted like they was going to take me out and shoot me the other night."

Mr. Hedgepeth looked at Rooster intently, perhaps for the first time realizing how the serious the situation might be.

"Well, I didn't know anything like that was going on. Yeah, maybe you best just try to stay out of their way. But there's still ways to find out what the hell got him so riled up. Ask that deputy that just got fired, he probably knows a bunch of dirt on Bill Hickey."

Rooster realized that Mr. Hedgepeth had a good point. Harvey probably did have some insight into the workings of Bill Hickey's mind, and it might be easy to get him to talk.

"You know what, Mr. Hedgepeth? That's not a bad idea."

By noon, a few customers had trickled in, apparently unaware that doing so might invoke the wrath of the sheriff's department. Rooster spent the day mulling over the various developments in his life, one minute being happy, the next being sad, and the next being angry, often mumbling to himself. Kermit watched him bemusedly but said nothing other than what was necessary to get through the day. By closing time, business had picked up somewhat, and Rooster was feeling better about things and not so worried about what the sheriff might be up to. As they were locking the place down for the evening, Rooster asked Kermit about Harvey.

"Hey, Kermit, where does Harvey live?"

"Harvey Wells? He lives with his mother in his grandfather's house over on King Street. At least he did. Now that his grandfather's dead, I don't know what's going to happen to those two."

"What happened to his grandfather?"

"Nothing much, just old age and orneriness. It was his time to go I reckon. He was a banker, so he probably didn't have too strong a heart, but at least he looked after his family. If it hadn't been for old Henry, then Harvey never would have got that job with the sheriff's department."

"What did his grandpa have to do with it?"

"Henry's bank held the note that Bill Hickey took out to open that little restaurant on the square. From what I heard, that was the main reason Bill got the loan, because he promised to take Harvey on as a deputy."

"Well, what's wrong with that?"

"Oh, nothing really, Harvey's as good a fellow as you would ever want to know. He's just...well, I guess he just never really grew up mentally, you know? He's not exactly retarded or anything, but he's always been kind of like a little boy, even after he became a man."

"Hmm. Yeah, I guess maybe so. I haven't really been around him much, but now that you mention it, I guess he is kind of that way."

"Oh, listen, everybody around here loves Harvey. He's as good as gold. Anybody messes around with Harvey will get beat up by half the town."

"I guess Bill Hickey must belong to the other half."

Kermit shook his head sadly. "I guess, in a way, you can't blame Bill. He pretty much had Harvey forced on him, and really you want somebody with some brains on the police department. Poor Harvey, I know he must be hurt, but he'll find something else to do."

Rooster was finally beginning to understand the situation a little better now that Kermit was filling in the details for him. He realized that when he set Harvey up that night in the sheriff's office that Bill Hickey had probably just been waiting for such an opportunity now that the old man was dead. Still, he felt bad. He kind of liked the affable young deputy, and Harvey had been one of the first people in Merky to show him any genuine friendliness. He actually thought the idea of going fishing sounded like fun, and at that moment he resolved to go find Harvey and take him fishing.

"Where exactly on King Street does Harvey live?" Rooster asked.

"Oh, you can't miss it. It's at the end of the street and the biggest house in town."

After they finished locking up the station, Rooster decided to risk being pulled over by the sheriff and go take a look at Harvey's house. He followed the directions Kermit gave him to King Street and was at once impressed by what he saw. Clearly, this was the part of town where the rich folks lived. These houses were in Mel's league, and a few of them surpassed his. When he saw the Well's house, his jaw dropped. It was one of the grandest mansions he had ever seen. It reminded him of some of the old castles he had seen in Germany. He was shocked that he had been here for all this time, and he had no clue that such a thing existed in humble, little Merky. The road dead-ended at the house, so he had to back his truck into another driveway in order to turn around. He suddenly became aware of the old heap he was driving and felt out of place. He looked around one last time at the house as he was pulling away. Any thoughts he had of just walking up to the door and ringing the bell were fading away. He still wanted to talk to Harvey, but he would wait for another day.

He drove the rough and dusty back roads along the edge of Merky to get back to the main highway that led to Mel's house. He was feeling a little nervous and carefully looked all around and didn't relax until he turned onto the long driveway to Mel's house. He rounded the bend and saw Laurie's car parked in its usual spot under the shade of the trees. Shirley's car was in the garage, but Mel's car was gone. Rooster felt strangely relieved that Mel wasn't home. He wished he could have Laurie all to himself for a whole evening. He still didn't know whether Mel would approve of them seeing each other, and he also knew that it would be hard, if not impossible, to turn back now.

Rooster parked next to Laurie's car and walked past the old dogs who barely even raised their heads at him anymore. He knocked on the door and waited until he heard someone yell, "Come in!" He pushed the door open and saw Kenneth lying on the floor, reading a comic book.

"Well, lookee there. Somebody done left a mess in the middle of the floor," said Rooster.

Kenneth paused reading long enough to stick out his tongue at him.

"Hi, Rooster," said Shirley from the kitchen. "Have a seat. Supper is almost ready."

"Okay, Shirley," said Rooster, straining his ear to tell if anyone else was in the kitchen, and disappointed that Laurie seemed to be somewhere else.

"Is that what school books look like these days?" Rooster said as he nudged Kenneth with his boot. "I bet you'll get a good education from that book."

"I bet your school books were made out of rock since you're so old," said Kenneth.

"I wish we would've had rocks. We didn't have nothing but dirt."

Rooster sat down on the couch and looked around, listening to see if he could hear Laurie in some other part of the house.

"Where's your sister?"

"She went into town with Daddy."

"Oh, okay."

Shirley called from the kitchen. "Rooster, can you come get the lid off this jar of green beans?"

Rooster got up and sauntered into the kitchen. Shirley handed him a quart mason jar of green beans. Rooster took it and twisted it off easily.

"You're so strong," said Shirley as she wiped her forehead with the back of hand.

"I've always worked hard," said Rooster, shrugging off the compliment.

"Mel tells me you're doing real well at the station, says you've pretty much learned everything."

"I'm feeling more comfortable with everything. I think I've got it down now."

"I think Mel wants to talk to you tonight."

Rooster furrowed his brow. "Okay, what about?"

"I'm not real sure, but I know he mentioned something about it."

Rooster started worrying about what Mel wanted to talk to him about. He wondered if he had somehow messed up at the station. That got him to going over everything in his mind. He felt certain that all the cash was accounted for, and that he hadn't forgotten anything else. Then, he started wondering if it had anything to do with him and Laurie, or if it somehow concerned the sheriff. Rooster's mind was racing ninety to nothing when Mel and Laurie came in through the garage.

"All right, the head dishwasher is here. I guess we can eat," said Mel as he slapped Rooster on the back.

"Dishes? I thought I was the jar opener."

"That too," said Mel.

Laurie and Rooster stole glances at each other as everyone got ready to eat. Kenneth set the table, and Shirley started bringing out the food. Once they were seated, everyone dug in and started eating. Little was said as everyone concentrated on their food. One by one everyone finished eating and then sat back, sipping their water or picking their teeth or engaging in idle chitchat.

"Well, Rooster, I guess Laurie doesn't like us anymore. She didn't make a pie this time," said Mel.

"I know, my feelings are hurt," said Rooster teasingly to Laurie.

"I don't want y'all to think you are going to have pie every day. I'm not going to spoil you," said Laurie, going along with the joke.

"I bet when you get married you'll bake pies everyday if that's what your husband wants," said Kenneth.

"If my husband wants pies every day, he can learn how to make them himself," Laurie declared defiantly.

"Then I guess you're going to be an old maid," laughed Kenneth.

"I'd rather be an old maid than marry somebody like you," Laurie shot back.

"Rooster, I guess we ought to leave before we get caught in the cross-fire betwixt these two," Mel said while using a toothpick to dislodge a piece of meat from between his teeth.

"I ought to help with the dishes," said Rooster.

"Nah, Shirley and Laurie can take care of that. I want to talk for a bit. Let's go out by the creek."

Rooster thanked Shirley for the meal and managed to steal a wink at Laurie before getting up to go.

Mel groaned and rubbed his belly as they strolled out the back door to his perch above Butcher Creek. He veered off to the garage and told Rooster to go on and he would meet him there. Rooster sat down and listened to the creek burbling below. After a couple of minutes, Mel came along carrying a paper sack much like he had the first time they came here. Mel put the sack on the stone picnic table and took out some bottles of beer.

"I thought I'd go easy on you tonight, so no hard liquor, just beer," said Mel.

"Where do you get this stuff?" asked Rooster. "I thought Merky was dry."

Mel grinned. "It is. But where there's a will, there's a way."

"I guess I wish I had your will."

"Most people wish they had my will. I'm surprised nobody's told you where to get booze around here. There's a fellow out in Bug Town that brings in beer from Mexico and makes home brew too."

In fact, Rooster had heard plenty of people joking around about going to Bug Town for booze, and he was often tempted by the thought, but he decided it was best to just leave it alone. Bug Town was a small settlement on a hillside past the Merky city limits. The town, such as it was, consisted of, perhaps, a couple dozen houses and a small general store. The residents were mostly poor whites, but there were a few Mexicans thrown in for good measure. The Blackwell boys were from Bug Town. Most respectable people in Merky rarely ventured into Bug Town, and those who did only went to go buy booze. Usually, whenever the sheriff had to go break up a fight or arrest somebody, it was out in Bug Town. The community itself had no real official name, but people had been calling it Bug Town for years. Depending on who you asked, it was called that either because it was small like a bug, or because it was unclean and infested with insects.

"I'll take you out there soon and introduce you to the man who can fix you up with something to drink," said Mel.

"Okay," said Rooster.

"Now," said Mel, "have a drink."

Rooster took the church key and opened a bottle of beer. It was warm, but otherwise it tasted good. He took a couple of sips and then set the bottle down and waited for Mel to say what was on his mind. Mel took a long swig before setting his bottle down and looking directly at Rooster.

"Well, I don't how to say this, so I'll just say it anyway," said Mel. "Is there anything going on between you and Laurie?"

Rooster knew it was coming, but it still shook him up a little. He paused for a few seconds.

"Yes, Mel. Yes, there is."

Mel frowned. "How far has it gone?"

"Just a little hugging and kissing."

"Are you sure?"

"I promise."

Mel seemed to relax a bit and took another sip from his beer as did Rooster.

"Well, I could kind of tell something was a little different between you two. How long has this been going on?"

"Not long, just since you sent us to San Antonio."

Mel nodded his head, as if confirming his own suspicions to himself.

"I like you, Rooster. I owe you a debt that can never be repaid. At the same time, I want what's best for my daughter. I expect you to treat her with respect, and if I ever hear otherwise, then you and me will have some problems."

Mel shifted about and took another sip of beer.

"If this were to get very serious it could lead to something. I don't think I would object too much, but the man who gets my daughter has to amount to something. I think you have the potential to be more than you are, and I am willing to help you get there. But for now, I just want you to be straightforward with me about what's going on. If it works out, fine. If it doesn't, fine. I appreciate you not lying to me about it."

"I'm glad you brought it up, Mel. I've been worried about what you might say. I would never do anything to hurt Laurie. I...I've been real lonely for a while. I never even knew Laurie existed until that night at the truck stop, and now I can't stop thinking about her. I really care about her, Mel. I would never do anything bad to her."

"I know you wouldn't, Rooster. It's just that she's my daughter, and she'll always be my little girl."

Mel extended his hand to Rooster, and they both shook firmly. Then, with that out of the way, they relaxed and finished off their beers.

They spent the rest of the evening talking about the station, about what needed to be done to this or that, and how such and such could be improved. Mel said that he would make Kenneth fill in whenever necessary and that they would try to hire someone as soon as possible. They finished off the beers, and Rooster walked back to the bunkhouse happily, if not a bit unsteadily. The cat was out of the bag about him and Laurie and so far so good. He looked up at the light shining from Laurie's room and smiled. Life was pretty good after all.

8

Rooster slept soundly that night and woke up feeling rested and refreshed. He fixed himself breakfast and left for work early. He arrived at the station fifteen minutes earlier than usual and just stood out in the driveway, taking in the morning air. There was hardly anyone up and about, and the town seemed still and quiet. He could hear several roosters crowing nearby. He broke into a grin and glanced around quickly before leaning his head back and letting loose his best impression of a rooster crowing. He could do it fairly well too; you don't go through life being called Rooster without learning how to make chicken sounds. Then, he clucked to himself like a laying hen and whistled as he began opening the station for the day's work. Step by step, he unlocked the office, filled the cash register, turned on the compressors, and opened the mechanic's bays. Preparing the station was a bit like dressing a sleeping child. You did it one part at a time until it was ready to go. He was hosing down the driveway and smoking a cigarette when Kermit and Obie came riding up together in Kermit's old heap.

Kermit and Obie were close friends but were very different from each other. Kermit had dark hair and was quiet and soft-spoken, whereas Obie was a wiry, little, gray-haired ball of energy. While Obie was running around ninety to nothing, Kermit would barely rouse enough to flick the ash off his cigarettes. Yet it was Kermit who did the most work. Perhaps because he was methodical and efficient, he could get a lot done without appearing to have worked hard at all. Between the two of them, they were constantly joking and playing tricks on each other and any one else who happened to be nearby, which was now mainly Rooster. And now these two amiable old farts were Rooster's crew. Rooster would wind up working a lot harder now that he was the boss and had to take up the slack of two old men, but he felt at ease with them, so he didn't mind too much. He was finally starting to feel like the captain of the ship.

This was the day they buried Harvey's grandfather, the banker Henry Wells. It was a fairly large and impressive service attended by many from the community. Rooster watched from the driveway of the gas station as the funeral procession drove past to the cemetery. A black hearse was followed by a procession of cars, all with their headlights on. It was easy to tell by the size of the procession that someone important was being buried. At one time Henry Wells had been the richest man in the county. At the height of his wealth and influence, he had built his mansion in the finest part of town for his wife and child. His wife died soon after their son got married, and later his son was shipped out to the beaches of Normandy and never returned, leaving behind a widow and young son. Henry took them in, and they had lived with him ever since. He was the only father figure that Harvey had ever known.

As the funeral procession passed by, Rooster noticed Mel's Cadillac in the line of cars, and the whole family waved at him as they drove by. It reminded him that he was still somewhat an outsider, and he felt a little sad as they drove past him. After work, he drove out to the ranch and went to his little bunkhouse. He had stocked the pantry so that he could cook himself simple meals, but he was starting to miss his little house in town. It was the first place he had ever had to call his own, and he had even been thinking of asking Mel to sell it to him, but he knew it was too soon to do that. After he made himself supper, he sat outside by the front door smoking a cigarette. He wished he could go over and talk to Laurie and was trying to think up some plausible excuse for going over to Mel's house to see her. Before he could come up with something, Kenneth came walking up.

"Hey, Rooster!" Kenneth shouted at him.

"Hey, what?" Rooster shouted back.

"Dad wants to talk to you."

Rooster tossed the cigarette butt and jumped up from his chair. He walked out to where Kenneth stood waiting for him.

"What's he want?"

"I don't know. He just said to come get you."

They walked up the dusty path to Mel's house and in through the back door. Mel was sitting at the dinner table, poring over some papers.

"Hey, Rooster, I just wanted to let you know that I talked to Addis about your problem with the sheriff and his deputy. He filed a formal complaint with the district attorney and is threatening to notify the Texas Rangers if the harassment doesn't stop right now. He also had a private discussion with Deputy Bates and reminded him that his wife might not be too pleased to hear about his waitress friend up at the truck stop, so I think you don't have to worry about those SOBs bothering you anymore. Go ahead and stay out here until Sunday and then you can move back into your place."

Rooster exhaled in relief. "Thanks, Mel. Thank you so much."

"No problem. You look after me, and I'll look after you."

"Yes, sir."

"Oh, and also, I wanted to know how it's going with Kermit and Obie."

"Oh, not too bad. They'll be all right till we can hire another full-time hand."

"Well, I'm going to leave that all up to you."

"Okay," Rooster said a bit hesitantly.

"You can put an ad in the paper if you like, just tell them to charge it to me, but usually just putting a sign up in the window and getting the word out will work just as well."

Rooster nodded and mumbled something about getting right on it. Mel went back to poring over his papers while Rooster just stood there, unsure of whether to stay or leave. It seemed that Mel had nothing else to say, so Rooster quietly turned and left. As he stepped out the back door, he saw Laurie feeding the dogs.

"Hi, Rooster," she smiled at him.

"Hi, Laurie. How was the funeral?"

"It was nice. There were a lot of people, and the preacher gave a good eulogy."

"Did you know Mr. Wells?"

"Oh, everybody knows everybody around here. I didn't know him real well, but he has been around for as long as I can remember. He used to give me lollipops and gum whenever Daddy would take me to the bank with him."

Rooster walked over to where Laurie was scraping a pan into the dog's bowls. He lowered his voice, "Me and Mel had a talk the other night."

Laurie looked up and met his gaze. "About what?"

"Oh, about things, but mostly about...you know...me and you."

Laurie stood up straight. "What did he say?"

"He didn't say that we couldn't see each other. He just wanted me to be honest and let him know what was going on. He said if I ever did you wrong, he'd skin me alive or something to that effect."

"Really, he said it was okay?"

"Pretty much."

Laurie smiled. "You want to go sit on the front porch with me for a while?"

"You know I would."

"Go on around, and I'll meet you there."

Laurie took the pans back into the kitchen and set them in the sink to soak for a while. She ran some hot water over them and then dried her hands on a dish towel before heading to the front porch. She walked past Mel, who was engrossed in his paperwork and past the sitting room where Shirley was stitching a new dress from a pattern and listening to the radio. Laurie went through the front door and out onto to the porch where Rooster was sitting on the swing, waiting for her. She sat down next to him, and they sat together, gently swaying back and forth, neither of them saying anything for a few seconds. Rooster cleared his throat.

"You want to go see a movie this weekend?"

"That would be nice. You need to ask Daddy, though."

"Oh...um...yeah, I guess I ought to go do that...I guess...now. I'll be right back."

Rooster got up and gently opened the front door and stepped inside. Shirley looked up from her sewing and smiled but went right back to work. Rooster walked softly into the dining room where Mel was sorting papers.

Rooster went over to Mel and stood quietly before clearing his throat. Mel looked up at him expectantly.

"Uh, Mel...um...I need to ask you something."

"Well, go ahead."

"You think...I mean...would it be all right if I took Laurie to see a movie this Saturday?"

Mel laid his pen down and leaned back in his chair.

"What movie do you want to see?"

"Um, uh, I'm not sure. Whatever is showing this weekend."

Mel smiled slightly. "I guess it doesn't matter too much, does it?"

"No, sir."

"All right, Rooster. Have her back home no later than 11:00. Got it?"

"Yes, sir. Thank you, Mel."

Rooster turned and walked softly back through the sitting room where Shirley once again looked up at Rooster and smiled as he passed by.

Rooster sat back on the porch swing with Laurie.

"We got us a date," he said as he reached over and squeezed her hand.

She squeezed his hand back, and they sat there holding hands until they thought they heard somebody coming. They sat on the porch, gently swaying back and forth and talking quietly in the cool night air. It was almost the end of May, and before long the cool spring nights would give way to the heat of summer. When it was time for him to go, Laurie walked him to the edge of the yard where the porch light began to fade into darkness.

"Good night," Rooster said, squinting into the night to see if anyone was looking. Laurie glanced over her shoulder, and then they leaned toward each other and kissed. This time she was different, she grabbed his arms with her hands and leaned into him, pushing her breasts against him. She kissed him with more passion than before, running her tongue into his mouth, exciting him so that he squirmed about, trying to suppress his suddenly growing erection. Suddenly she pulled away, looked at him coquettishly, winked, and then turned back to walk to the house.

He stood there for a few seconds, his heart pounding and his breathing heavy. He watched as she ran into the house without turning and looking back. He exhaled deeply and turned to head back to the bunkhouse. Although he still missed the little house in town, he was enjoying the benefit of being near Laurie. He clucked and cackled like a strutting rooster all the way back to the bunkhouse.

Saturday arrived, and Rooster was excited about his date with Laurie. He was in a good mood all day at work, and when they closed the station down, he went to his little house in town to bathe and get ready.

He filled the tub with hot steaming water and eased slowly into it, groaning in pleasure as the water warmed and relaxed his body. He scrubbed himself extra hard and washed his hair three times so as to be sure and get rid of the smell of oil and gasoline that inevitably clung to anybody who worked at the station. He put on his best shirt and newest jeans and even splashed on some cologne he had bought in Germany. He looked in the mirror as he carefully parted and re-parted his hair four times. Finally, it was time to go, and he hopped into his old truck and spun the wheels in the dirt driveway, kicking up a cloud of dust. He whistled cheerfully on the way to Mel's place, waving at everyone he encountered. Soon, he was standing on the front porch and calmly knocking on the door. Mel opened the door and greeted him.

"Come on in, Rooster. Have a seat."

Rooster sat down on one of the sofas. Mel handed him a set of car keys.

"Take my car tonight. Drive the speed limit, and you won't have any problems."

Rooster took the keys. "I'll have her back by 11:00."

"If you don't, I'll come looking for you."

"You won't have to do that."

"Have a nice evening. Enjoy the movie."

When they showed up at the movie theater in Mel's car, obviously on a date, everyone took notice. People gawked and whispered to each other as they walked past. They went and got popcorn and sodas first and then went to find seats. The houselights were still on in the theater, which was about half full. They walked slowly down the aisle, looking about to find just the right seats. Those already seated saw them come in together, which set off a whole new round of whispering. If their blossoming relationship had been a secret up until now, it would soon practically be front-page news all over town. In a way, this was their coming out party and the point of no return. From this point on, they would be considered a courting couple, and linked together in the public mind.

Rooster felt the eyes of every single person in the theater locked upon them, and he knew there would be no kissing in the theater this time. Still, he felt relaxed and confident. He intuitively knew that if everyone else began to think of them as a couple, that would in some way help to make it so. As the lights dimmed and the previews came on, he and Laurie settled into their seats and began munching on their popcorn. After they had finished their popcorn and soda, Rooster waited until the theater grew dark and furtively reached over and took Laurie's hand. She took his hand and interlocked fingers with him. Occasionally, one of their arms would go to sleep or become uncomfortable, and they would have to move, but they always found a way to maintain physical contact throughout the whole movie.

After the movie was over and the lights came on, everyone in the theater rose and began to walk out. Rooster, being mindful of appearances, let go of Laurie's hand, and they scooted sideways along the row of seats out to aisle. Rooster waited for her, and when she joined him in the aisle, she placed her hand in his once again. Rooster took her hand and held it as they walked out into the lobby, fully aware that everyone else was taking note of this as well. He was proud and happy, and for the first time in his life, felt what it might be like to be one-half of a couple. He knew in his heart, that at long last, he had found the love of his life.

They walked up the sloping floor to the lobby and through the heavy curtains that kept the light from coming in. As they entered into the lobby, Rooster saw the waitress Jeanine coming in from the opposite aisle with a tall, lanky cowboy on one arm. Their eyes met. Jeanine quickly looked away but managed a short smile and hello to Laurie as she passed by them. Laurie smiled and returned the hello. Rooster nodded politely without saying anything. Laurie looked up at Rooster.

"That was Jeanine. You know her, right? She used to work at the truck stop."

"Oh, right." Rooster relaxed a bit upon hearing that Jeanine was no longer at the truck stop. "I didn't know she quit."

"She didn't. Daddy fired her."

"For what?"

"I don't know. Sometimes, he doesn't need a reason."

That both relieved and worried Rooster. He could now go to the truck stop without worrying about running into Jeanine, but if Mel could just shit-can her out of the blue, then he could do the same thing to him.

Laurie sensed Rooster's discomfort but neither of them said anything as they walked outside into the night air. Rooster was a bit shaken by the encounter. He kept thinking how tonight Jeanine looked cheap and harsh, and he wondered how he'd ever found her attractive. He realized that he was lucky to have wound up with Laurie instead of her. Then, he thought back to that night, that dark night, when he had murder in his heart and how close he had come to doing something incredibly foolish and evil. He wondered why it had turned out the way it did, why he was seemingly being rewarded for an act that had been more reflex than heroism, and he worried just a little whether the true reckoning had yet to be accounted for.

As they walked back to the car Laurie looked up at him with a funny expression on her face.

"Did you like Jeanine?"

"I hardly knew her."

"Did you find her attractive?"

"She was okay."

Laurie looked down at their feet marching below them.

"I heard you asked her out."

Rooster felt himself flush. He had been dreading this ever since he met Laurie. He didn't know what to say, but he knew better than to lie.

"It's true."

Laurie smiled wryly and let out a breath. "I knew you did. I'm glad you didn't lie to me."

"I wish I hadn't. I was just thinking how rough and...and kind of trashy she looked just then. I was just lonely. I didn't know anyone here. If I had met you first, I wouldn't have given her a second look."

"That's okay. I went to the prom with a boy I thought I liked, and he turned out to be a real sorry person."

Rooster felt a pang of jealousy.

"How many other boys have you gone out with?"

Laurie sensed his hurt. "I've never really dated anyone before, just little things for school mainly."

Rooster was growing uncomfortable with the way the conversation was going. "Look, I'm sorry that I ever asked Jeanine out, real sorry, because now I know she wasn't worth it. The only person I want to be with is you, so let's talk about something else. Okay?"

Laurie smiled. "Okay."

It was only a little after 10:00 p.m., so they had almost an hour before Laurie had to be back. Rooster was very aware that Mel would be watching the clock and that to bring her home late would be tantamount to an outright challenge, and Rooster wasn't about to let that happen, but he wasn't ready for the evening to end either.

"We still have some time. You want to go to the truck stop and get a soda?" he asked.

"We can...," said Laurie, "or we can go to the Dairy Delite."

The Dairy Delite was a hamburger joint and soda fountain that was the main teenage hangout in Merky. Rooster had driven by it many times but never stopped in. It reminded him of his high school days, and it made him uncomfortable. He really didn't want to go, but he didn't want to disappoint Laurie either.

"Okay, sure," he said.

They got in Mel's Cadillac and drove to the Dairy Delite, and pulled in under the canopy out front. He shut off the engine, and they could hear the din of the jukebox and laughter coming from inside. Rooster put on a brave face, and got out and took Laurie by the hand. As soon as they walked in, everyone noticed them. Several girls called out to Laurie and ran up to greet them. Rooster stood there awkwardly, towering over them, as Laurie and the girls giggled and carried on among themselves. Laurie introduced Rooster to everyone, and then they went and sat at a table. Rooster said little as Laurie and the girls did most of the talking. He looked around at the young faces. He wasn't all that much older than most of them, yet he felt like the only adult in the room. He had fought in a war, been to Europe and Asia, had consorted with prostitutes, was tattooed, and he had killed men. And yet now he was doing well just to hold his own with a room full of teenagers. He began to wonder if he should be with Laurie at all.

Soon, a couple of young men came to the table and introduced themselves to Rooster. They appeared to be around seventeen or eighteen and looked to be football players as they were somewhat larger than most of the rest of the boys there. They congratulated Rooster for his heroic rescue of Laurie and the others at the truck stop that night. They seemed especially interested in hearing that he had been in the army as they had just finished high school themselves. They chatted for several minutes while Laurie and the girls carried on their own conversation. By the time they were finished talking, Rooster felt more relaxed and at ease, and he realized that everyone else there was not much different than him, just a bunch of good natured country kids. When the young men left, Rooster leaned in and joined Laurie and the girls' conversation, and soon he was joking around and laughing with them. He was enjoying himself so much that he forgot to check the time until it was almost 11:00. When he realized how late it was, he stood up suddenly and told Laurie that they had to go quickly. Laurie was disappointed at having to end her evening before she was ready, but she understood that Rooster did not want to offend Mel, so they hopped in the car and raced back out to the ranch. It was a few minutes after 11:00 when they pulled up in front of the house. Rooster looked up at the bedroom windows nervously to see if anyone was looking outside, but it appeared that everyone was already in bed. He walked Laurie up to the front door. She stood by the door and looked up at him, beaming.

"Oh, Rooster, I had such a good time. Thank you so much."

"Thank you, Laurie. You're the one that makes it fun. I want to do this again."

"Me, too."

Laurie looked around to make sure no one was watching and took Rooster's hands. He leaned down to her and kissed her, gently and slowly at first, and then with more passion. They kissed for a few more minutes, and then Laurie pulled away, smiling up at him and telling him good night before she slipped through the door and into the house.

Rooster stood there for a few seconds and then turned to walk away. He walked down the steps and past the Cadillac and off through the darkness to the bunkhouse. He would stay there one more night, and then tomorrow he would move back into the little house in town. He looked up at the stars and the moon as he walked. He was in love. He was a lucky man.

9

The next morning, Rooster pitched his bag in the back of his truck and headed into town. He was eager to get back to his little house even though it had worked out exceedingly well for him to stay at Mel's for a few days. He knew that he had won Laurie's heart, and barring something totally unforeseen, she was his. He was also aware that this would elevate him to a social standing that he had never experienced nor ever even dreamed of attaining. This also worried him, for Mel had made it clear that he would have to prove himself worthy of her, and it was unlikely that he would be able to do that pumping gas for the rest of his life.

Rooster had something else on his mind that morning. He was going to find the former deputy Harvey Wells and invite him to go fishing. He wanted to learn what he could about Sheriff Hickey, and truthfully, he kind of liked Harvey and was in need of a friend. Not that he hadn't become popular since bursting into the Merky consciousness as a hero, but most everyone he met was just riding his coattails, eager to be seen with the big man in town. Rooster despised sycophants, and he sensed that Harvey liked him for who he was and not for what he did. Also, Harvey was different enough to never really fit in, something Rooster identified with. His plans were to unpack and settle back in his house and then go by Harvey's house later that day after everyone returned from church.

He pulled up into the driveway of the little house and rolled to a stop underneath the shade of the ancient trees. He got out and noticed that the morning air seemed especially fresh and crisp that morning, and the birds were singing particularly sweetly. He grabbed his bag from the back of the truck and pushed the front door open. Everything was as he had left it, but the air was a bit stale from the house being closed up. He opened the doors to let the place air out and put on a pot of coffee. He had enough fixings to make breakfast, and he ate at the kitchen table while looking out the back door at the squirrels chasing each other around the backyard.

He couldn't quite get over how things had turned out. He wondered how it was that just when he was at his lowest moment and on the verge of evil, things could change so profoundly for him. It made him a bit suspicious and a bit worried. If God knew what was in his heart that night, then why was he seemingly being rewarded? Had Deputy Bates not shown up when he did, he would likely be on death row. And if the Blackwell boys not shown up when they did, he would be dead. His father had always said that the Lord works in mysterious ways and that sure seemed to be the case now. All he could do was shake his head in wonder and enjoy that which had been bestowed upon him. Perhaps, he wasn't a bad person after all.

It was midmorning and time for all good and decent folk to be getting ready for church. However, church had no appeal to Rooster, so he decided to do laundry instead. He filled an old tin tub with soapy water and began to wash his jeans on a rub board. He washed enough to get him through a few days and hung them on the line in the backyard. He thought how it would be nice to have a woman do his wash for him, a luxury he had never had. After he hung all the clothes, he sat in the shade and smoked a cigarette, and watched the water drip from his wet laundry into the cool green grass. He counted his change and decided he could afford a hamburger and a slice of pie, so he hopped into his truck and chugged noisily to Mel's Truck Stop. He was always given a hero's welcome whenever he went there, he often got all or part of his meal for free, and today was no exception. He walked in and sat down at his favorite booth, and Wanda came up and hugged his neck.

"What'll you have today, Rooster?"

"Oh, I reckon a hamburger, ice tea, and a slice of pecan pie."

"So how was the movie last night?" Wanda smiled slyly.

Rooster looked up at her and grinned. "News travels fast around here, don't it?"

"Sugar, it's old news already. You can't keep secrets around here. The whole town knew by nine o'clock last night. I just think it's wonderful."

Rooster nodded. "So far, so good."

"Well, I hope it works out. You really do make a nice couple."

Rooster sat sipping his tea and thinking about what Wanda said about keeping secrets. It made him uncomfortable, and once again, he thought back to that night at the truck stop. He wondered if he had ever said anything that might have indicated he wanted to hurt Jeanine. He thought back very carefully over the events preceding that night, and he felt reasonably assured that he had not spoken of it to anyone, yet he was still not entirely comfortable. That was another reason to talk to Harvey, to find out if he knew anything. Rooster felt that he could probably coax information out of simple Harvey without arousing any suspicions.

When he was finished eating, Wanda refused to let him pay, so he pocketed his money and headed back home. He rummaged around in the shed and found a few rusty, old fishing hooks, some string, and a bit of cork, and then began cutting a pole from some saplings that grew along the creek at the back of the yard. When he figured it was late enough for everyone to be back from church and to have had their Sunday dinner, he headed out to find Harvey.

Rooster drove back to the fine mansion he had discovered not long ago and once again, he felt awed and diminished by it. In spite of his painful self-awareness, he parked his dusty, old truck out front, went through the gate and up to the porch and rang the bell. He could hear it tolling deeply from inside the cavernous depths of the grand old home, and he stepped back a few feet from the door and waited. Soon, he heard footsteps approaching, and the door swung open and Harvey stood there, still dressed in his Sunday best, his mouth agape.

"Rooster!"

"Hello, Harvey. I thought I'd take you up on that fishing offer if you don't have nothing else to do."

Harvey's eyes widened, and he broke into a huge grin. "You betcha! Let me go tell my mother, and I'll be right back."

Harvey turned and ran back into the dimly lit interior of the house, disappearing from view, while shouting for his mother. Rooster leaned forward and peered into the house. It was unlike anything he had ever seen, it made even Mel's house look puny by comparison. He could see overstuffed chairs and polished tables covered with doilies and a large painted portrait of a woman that he imagined must have been Harvey's grandmother. He could hear Harvey running about and stomping up a flight of stairs. As he stood there, a woman came to the door. She was slender and frail. Although she was probably about the same age as Shirley, there was something about her that made her appear older, even though her skin was smooth and youthful. She was wearing clothes that were somewhat old and out of style. She eyed Rooster suspiciously.

"May I help you?" she asked cautiously.

"Oh, no, ma'am. I just came to see if Harvey wanted to go fishing."

"And who are you?"

"My name is William Brown, but everybody calls me Rooster."

"So you're the famous Rooster Brown."

"I don't know about the famous part, but I am Rooster Brown."

"Why do you want to go fishing with my son?"

"He invited me a while back, and it sounded like fun. It's a nice day, and I thought this was as good a time as any."

Harvey's mother just stood silently for several seconds until Rooster started to fidget.

"Where are you going?"

Rooster hadn't thought about that yet.

"Um...I don't know. I figured Harvey must know where all the good fishing holes are."

"I'm sure he does."

Just then, Harvey came running to the door carrying an expensive fishing rod and a tackle box.

"Harvey!" she scolded him. "You are not going fishing in those clothes. You go upstairs and change right now."

Harvey suddenly realized that he was still wearing his Sunday church clothes. He threw the rod and tackle box to the floor, and ran back into the house.

"I'll be right back, Rooster!" he shouted. "Don't leave without me!"

Mrs. Wells looked at Rooster suspiciously. "My son is a good boy, but sometimes he doesn't think things out. He needs to be watched over. Normally, I wouldn't let him go with a stranger, but I have heard about you. You look after him, you hear?"

"Yes, ma'am. I will."

Mrs. Wells turned and faded into the shadows and left Rooster standing there by himself.

A couple of minutes later, Harvey came bounding to the front door. This time he was dressed in jeans and a faded shirt. He picked up his fishing rod and tackle box.

"Okay, I'm ready," he said breathlessly.

They walked back to Rooster's truck, and Harvey put his fishing gear in the bed of the truck.

"Okay, where are we going?" Harvey asked cheerfully.

"I don't know, I thought you had some place you wanted to go."

"I hardly ever go fishing."

"Then why did you ask me if I wanted to go fishing?" Rooster asked with a hint of exasperation.

"What else is there to do? I like to fish, I just don't get to do it much."

"Hmm," Rooster mumbled to himself. He figured that it wouldn't be too hard to find a fishing hole somewhere. Some people just pulled off the road next to a bridge and sunk their lines. The problem with that was that most land in the state of Texas was private property, and some landowners didn't take kindly to trespassers. He didn't want to give anyone a reason to call Sheriff Hickey, so he decided against that.

"Where does everybody else go fishing?" he asked Harvey.

"There's a city lake here, but it's mostly just for drinking water. Some people fish in town at Butcher Creek, but the best spots are mostly out on farms and such."

Rooster thought about the creek at Mel's place. It had a few nice holes and was easy to get to. He could go out there and ask permission to fish, and it would give him an excuse to see Laurie too. He sort of hated to bother the Tuckers on a Sunday afternoon, but figured that it probably wouldn't be a problem.

"Well, let's just head out to Mel's and see if he'll let us fish out there," said Rooster.

"All right then," said Harvey.

They chugged slowly out past the city limits and on to Mel's place. As they neared the house, they could see Mel sitting on the porch. Rooster cut the motor off and coasted underneath the trees.

Mel watched as they both got out of the truck and walked to the porch.

"Now there's two dangerous characters," Mel said.

Rooster sensed that Mel seemed to be in a bad mood, and he wished they had gone somewhere else, but it was too late now.

"Hey, Mel, I'm sorry to bother you, but me and Harvey decided to go fishing and then figured out we don't have any place to go to. Would it be all right if we fished in your creek over by the bunkhouse?"

Mel studied them both silently, as Rooster began to fidget.

After what seemed like an awfully long time to Rooster, Mel finally replied. "Why don't y'all go down to the north end instead, there's not any good fishing holes by the bunkhouse."

That puzzled Rooster because he had heard Kenneth say that he had caught several good size catfish there, then he remembered what Kenneth said about Mel keeping wetbacks in the bunkhouse.

"Just follow the fence line up that way, when you get to the cross fence go down to the creek, you'll find a nice hole there."

"Okay, Mel, thank you," said Rooster.

"Thanks, Mel," said Harvey.

They drove the truck as far as they could and then parked and got out and walked the rest of the way. When they got to the cross fence, they followed it down to a steep embankment which dropped off to a nice rock shoal. It was shaded by cypress and willow trees, and sure enough, just as Mel had said, there was a nice deep hole that looked like it might have some fish. They lay down their poles and went to look for bait. Rooster caught a couple of grasshoppers and gave one to

Harvey, and they both stabbed them onto the hooks and tossed their lines into the green water.

"It's nice out here," said Harvey.

"Yeah, Mel's got it made. He's got everything a man could want."

"I guess he's got what you want."

"What does that mean?"

"I heard you want to marry Laurie."

Rooster shook his head. "Ain't nobody said nothing about getting married."

"Laurie's pretty."

"Yes, she is."

"You think you'll get married?"

"Damn, Harvey, I've only been on one date with her."

"How many does it take?"

"I don't know, more than one, that's for sure."

"I think my mother and father only had one date before they got married."

Rooster looked over at Harvey to see if he was serious.

"Are you kidding me?"

Harvey laughed.

"You little shit," Rooster chuckled.

They sat there quietly for a few minutes before Rooster's cork went under the water and he jerked on the line. He could tell the fish was hooked, so he started pulling in the string and soon dragged a gar out of the water.

"Shit!" he exclaimed loudly.

"Ha! There's your supper," laughed Harvey.

Rooster unhooked the gar, being careful not to get bit, and tossed it back in.

"At least, I can catch something."

Just then, Harvey got a bite, and he began reeling it in. Soon, he pulled ashore a nice catfish.

"Just let me know if you want me to teach you how to fish, Rooster," Harvey said.

"That'll be a cold day in hell," snorted Rooster.

They ran a line through the catfish's gills and tied it to a large branch on the shoal. Then, they both fell silent for several minutes as they watched their corks float on the surface of the water.

Finally, Rooster spoke, "Sorry to hear about your grandpa."

Harvey exhaled deeply and nodded his head silently. Neither of them said anything for several seconds.

"I got fired too."

"I heard."

"Momma said that Bill was just waiting for my grandpa to die."

"He's a son of a bitch."

Harvey shook his head, still pained by the recent trauma to his life. Rooster figured this was his opening.

"Did Hickey ever say why he hates me?"

"No, but he sure has something against you."

"But what? Damn it, I never even saw him before that night at the truck stop."

"I don't know. Bill always seems like he's a little mad about something."

"What do you know about him?"

"He came to live here when he was in grade school. Something happened in his family, and he came to live with his grandparents."

"What happened to his family?"

Harvey furrowed his brow, trying to remember. "I think his daddy got killed. I've heard him talk about it a couple of times. I'm pretty sure that's what it was."

"Did he get killed in an accident or something?"

"No...oh, I remember now. His daddy was a lawman too, and somebody shot him. That's what it was."

"Where did this happen? Can you remember?"

"Um, it was somewhere north of here."

"Where, Harvey? Try to remember."

Harvey furrowed his brow even more. "I think it was around Sonora or somewhere like that."

Rooster took off his hat and rubbed his forehead oblivious to the cork that was bobbing up and down in the creek. A dreadful realization was slowly settling in. He understood why the sheriff had reacted so strongly when he saw the notches on his gun and learned who his grandfather was. One of those notches was Bill Hickey's father.

"Rooster! You got a bite!" yelled Harvey.

Rooster saw his cork bobbing up and down in the water and yanked his pole, but the hook didn't set.

"Well, it's a good thing I know how to catch fish," laughed Harvey. "I'll catch enough for both of us."

Rooster didn't care about any fish at that moment. He was still in shock at what had just settled in his mind. He suddenly felt ashamed. His father had often commented that sons sometimes pay for the sins of their fathers. He knew his father was burdened by the deeds of Devil Brown, and sometimes Rooster had experienced those feelings as a child, except Rooster was dually embarrassed. Not only did he have a cold-blooded murderous drunk for a grandfather, he also had a Holy Roller preacher for a father, and in some ways that was almost worse. He felt an emotional numbness wash over him and he barely heard anything Harvey said as he prattled on about fish.

Harvey fell silent again, mesmerized by his floating bobber, as they sat on the rocky shoal listening to various birds chirping and the occasional mournful lowing of someone's cows. Rooster leaned back against a log and tried to clear his mind of his troubles and just enjoy the moment. Suddenly, his cork went under water again, and this time he yanked on his pole at just the right moment and he pulled in a large catfish.

"Well, here's poppa fish looking for his little baby that you caught," said Rooster drolly.

"Dad gum!" Harvey exclaimed loudly. "We'll be having fish for supper tonight."

It suddenly dawned on Rooster that he would indeed have a supper of his own freshly caught fish tonight and he mentally began thinking about what he could use to round out the meal.

"You want to come over and eat fish tonight?"

"You betcha," Harvey said breathlessly. Then he thought of his mother alone in that big house and he seemed to deflate just a bit.

"I probably ought to go home and eat with my mother," he said sadly.

"Hell, can't you eat two meals? We'll cook up the fish at my place, and then you can go on home and eat with your mama."

"Okay, sure. I can eat enough for two men anyway," Harvey said, smiling.

"Well, let's fish a little more and then go back into town and cook these critters up."

They caught a couple more grasshoppers and cast their lines into the water. The fish must have been in the mood for grasshoppers, for within fifteen minutes they both caught another fish and were ready to pack it up and head back into town. When they drove past Mel's house, Rooster decided to pull in and show Mel what they had caught. He went up to the front door and knocked, hoping that Laurie would answer. And she did, and Rooster could tell right away that she was perturbed about something.

"Hi, Laurie. We just came by to show Mel our fish."

"Daddy's not here. He went in to town," she replied curtly.

"Well, do you want to see them?"

"I suppose."

Rooster turned and shouted at Harvey, "Hey, Harvey! Hold up the fish for her!"

Harvey reached into the back of the truck and pulled the stringer of four fish from a bucket of water. He held them aloft for Laurie to see.

"Not bad, huh?"

"I guess they're okay, if you like fish."

"I know what I like better."

Laurie said nothing, but Rooster could tell she was trying to suppress a smile.

"Are you mad at me or something?"

"I just thought if you came by here you would have at least said hello or something before heading off down the creek," Laurie said softly.

"I wanted to, but Mel was acting kind of prickly, so I thought it was best if we just headed on down to the creek. The whole time on the way out here I was thinking about you and hoping I would get to see you."

"You shouldn't worry about how Daddy is acting. That's just the way he is."

"I know, but he's also my boss...and the father of my girl."

Laurie looked up at Rooster. "Am I your girl?"

"I want you to be."

"Me, too."

"Well, then you are. When can I see my girl again?"

"You can come out and sit on the swing after work if you want."

"I would like that, but what about another date?"

"Ask Daddy."

"When can I stop asking Daddy and just ask you?"

"Oh, I think soon. Just give it a little more time. He likes you."

"I know, and I don't want to make him mad either. I owe him a lot, but I want to see you more."

"You will, you just have to go by his rules for now."

"Okay. Well, me and Harvey are going to go cook up those fish so he can eat before he goes home for supper."

"Those fish aren't even enough to feed you," Laurie giggled.

"Yeah, I'm gonna have to cook some beans or something too."

"Bye, Rooster."

"Bye, Laurie. I'll come by after work tomorrow, if that's all right?"

"You know it is."

Rooster turned and got into the truck and off they went bouncing down the drive to the main road.

"So you and Laurie are sweethearts, huh, Rooster?" Harvey asked.

"I'm working on it, brother, I'm working on it," Rooster said as he watched Mel's house growing smaller in the rearview mirror.

10

The next day, Rooster showed up at the station bright and early and still in a happy mood from yesterday's fishing expedition. He and Harvey had cooked up the fish and some potatoes in a fire pit in the backyard of his little house, and it was the most fun he had had in a long time, aside from his dates with Laurie. He hadn't really had a best friend in a long time, and it felt good to have a buddy to hang out with and talk to. Harvey was a bit slow but not retarded by any means. Rooster decided he was probably smarter than most people thought. He was mostly just different. He knew that people always judged each other for how they appeared to be, not how they really were, and he knew how it felt to be judged in that way.

The station was open and ready for business when Kermit and Obie showed up. They had initially been somewhat grateful for the extra hours and a chance to make a little more money, but they were also retired old men who mostly wanted to do as little as possible. Kermit had taken to dropping hints around Rooster that he should hire somebody soon. Rooster had placed a sign in the window and a couple of people had inquired about it, but they didn't pursue it and neither did he. He didn't want to make a mistake and hire somebody that was just going to goof off, or worse, steal. He decided that if someone didn't come along by the end of the week he would run an ad in the paper like Mel had suggested. He almost asked Harvey if he would be interested but felt like it would be too lowly a position for a man who had just been deputy and who lived in a mansion.

The town was slow to wake up that day and they all sat around smoking cigarettes and enjoying the cool morning air. Kermit had his usual half inch of ash hanging from the cigarette that seemed to perch perpetually on his lip. Obie smoked like he did everything else—fast. He would blow smoke rings and let the smoke curl up from his mouth and into his nostrils, and then after a few hard drags the cigarette was finished. They were enjoying being lazy this particular morning and were disappointed when a customer finally rolled in. Rooster decided to let the old men have their morning tranquility a little longer and got up to go wait on the customer. It was old Mr. Hedgepeth, smiling his tobacco-stained grin.

"Well, howdy do, Sheriff. Looks like y'all ain't making Mel Tucker much money this morning," Mr. Hedgepeth joked.

"Yeah, it's kinda slow this morning. I 'spect it'll pick up later, it usually does."

"So you found anybody to hire yet?"

"Naw, sir. You know anybody?"

"I know lots of people, but ain't none of 'em worth a damn."

"That don't surprise none. You know what they say about birds of a feather."

"I sure do," said Mr. Hedgepeth, grinning. "Just look at that crew of yours."

Rooster turned and looked at the two old timers practically napping in their chairs. He just shook his head and smiled. He finished pumping Mr. Hedgepeth's gas and took the money to the cash register. Kermit and Obie both tried to rouse themselves, and Obie got up to go putter around in the mechanic's bay.

"Well, Rooster Brown, the old men ain't what they used to be, and probably never was what they thought they were in the first place," said Kermit.

Rooster looked at Kermit and grinned, "Okay, Kermit, I get it. I know y'all are ready for me to hire somebody, and I will. I know I need to do something soon. I just haven't found the right person yet."

"I guess a person could spend a mighty long time trying to find just the right man, but I know you'll get somebody before too long."

Rooster went out to the front of the station and stood by the door, waiting for a customer to show up. He started to think very hard about what he was going to do. He knew that if he didn't find somebody fairly soon Mel would begin to question his ability to run the station. He tried to think up an ad to run in The Merky Magpie, but he had never been very good at writing and was having trouble thinking of how to word it. He decided that he would go and sit down at the desk and try to write it out, but every time he thought of something a car would pull in or he would have to wait on someone. Finally, he grew frustrated and wadded up the paper he had been writing on and threw it in the trash can.

About noon, Harvey showed up at the station in his grandfather's old Cadillac. It was several years old but still in very good shape. Rooster went out to pump the gas and wash the windshield. As Rooster was checking the air in the tires, Harvey got out and opened the hood to check the oil.

"Hey! That's our job, Harvey. Get back in the car, and I'll take care of it for you."

"Oh, I don't mind. I always helped Grandpa look after his car. It wouldn't feel right to let somebody else do it."

"It don't look right for a customer to be servicing his own car, especially if Mel Tucker sees it," said Rooster, as he looked around nervously just in case Mel happened to be driving by.

"Oh..." said Harvey slowly, "Oh, all right. I don't want to get you in trouble or anything."

On the other side of the pumps, Obie was looking under the hood of an old Chevy and scratching his head.

"I don't know what to tell you," he shouted over the sound of the roughly running engine, "but something ain't right. You best bring it back when the mechanic is on duty."

Harvey, hearing him, walked over to side of the car and stuck his head underneath the hood. He cocked his head one way and then the other, listening carefully.

"You got a screwdriver?" he asked Obie.

Obie reached into his back pocket and pulled out a medium-sized screwdriver.

Harvey took it and started adjusting a couple of screws on the carburetor. The engine slowed almost to a stop and then he began turning it back the other way. When he got it running better, he looked around and spotted a spark plug wire that was not on tightly, and when he pushed it on, the engine started running even better. He turned the screws on the carburetor some more until the engine was idling smoothly.

"That ought to do it," he said, handing the screwdriver back to Obie.

Obie laughed. "Well, I guess you can always find work as a mechanic."

"You know anybody that's looking?" Harvey asked with interest.

"I don't know anybody that needs a mechanic, but we need some general help around here."

"You do?" Harvey asked as he looked over at Rooster, who was wiping off the dipstick and putting it back into its slot. "You need help here, Rooster?"

"Yes, of course we do. Joe took your old job."

Somehow Harvey hadn't quite made the connection that Joe taking his old job left the station short-handed.

"Well, dang, Rooster. What's wrong with me?" Harvey asked, a hurt look on his face.

"Nothing's wrong with you. I just didn't think you'd be interested."

"Why wouldn't I be interested?"

"Well, hell," Rooster sputtered. "You was a deputy, and your grandpa owned a bank."

"My grandpa didn't own the whole bank. He was mostly just the president."

"Then how'd he build that big, fine mansion?"

"With the money he inherited from great-grandpa."

Rooster looked at Harvey incredulously. He had rarely had two coins to rub together for much of his life, and here was this young man who had grown up in a family of rich bankers, and who seemed to think nothing of it.

"Well, what about a job? I'm real good with mechanical stuff, and I need to work."

"Wuh...uh...okay, all right. When can you start?"

"Right now!"

Rooster couldn't believe what he was hearing.

"Well, okay, but you better go home and change clothes and tell your mother."

"Yes, sir!" Harvey said as he hopped in the car and peeled out into the street.

Obie looked at Rooster. "Did he pay for that gas?"

Rooster suddenly realized that Harvey had not paid for the gas. His shoulders drooped, and he slowly shook his head.

"Write down how much he bought, and we'll take it out of his pay-check," Rooster told Obie.

Kermit came out of the mechanic's bay to see what all the tire squealing was about. Obie nodded toward the rapidly receding tail fins of

Henry Well's Cadillac and said with a certain degree of satisfaction, "The new help."

"The sheriff's got himself a deputy now," Kermit said, laughing.

Rooster felt relieved and a little concerned over whether he had made the right choice, but like many things in his life lately, it had just dropped in his lap, so he decided to just go with it and not worry. It would work out one way or the other he figured, and things seemed to be working out pretty well for him much to his amazement.

About thirty minutes later, Harvey came careening around the corner and parked the big old Cadillac behind the station. He was wearing the same clothes he went fishing in yesterday.

"Okay, boss, here I am. What do you want me to do?"

Rooster thought for a second. "Just start waiting on cars, and if you have any questions, ask somebody."

Harvey ran up to the next car that pulled in and thus began his career as a gas station attendant. He had a natural ability to put people at ease, as Rooster had learned, and this was a definite asset for this line of work. In spite of his reputation for being slow, he would learn all the duties of running a gas station in a matter of days. However, just as Rooster would begin to think Harvey was perfectly normal, he would do something completely stupid, so Rooster soon figured out that he had to keep a close eye on him and could probably not leave him on his own for very long. In spite of this shortcoming, Harvey was a good worker and definitely took much of the burden off the others. It was determined that Rooster and Harvey could carry most of the day to day operations of running the station with back up from Kermit, Obie, or Kenneth. Within a week, they had it down, and things were running smoothly once again.

As things settled into a comfortable routine at the gas station, Rooster relaxed and concentrated on spending every spare moment he could find with Laurie. As the relationship blossomed and grew stronger, Mel gradually relinquished control of his daughter and allowed them to see each other whenever they wanted. In the eyes of the towns-people, Rooster and Laurie had become established as a couple, and soon talk turned to whether they might get married. Rooster was entirely aware of this, as it seemed every time he turned around some local rube would ask him point-blank when the wedding would take place. Even though the romance was still in its fledgling stage, everyone in town already had it in their minds that the two of them belonged together, and it was understandable that they would think so. When Rooster burst into that kitchen with guns blazing he perma-nently etched himself into the local lore as a hero. He was the dash-ing commoner who had saved a princess and was now himself ready to ascend some throne yet to be determined. All this was not lost on Rooster, who in spite of his own inner knowledge to the contrary, was willing to be that hero and to assume the role that the town of Merky, Texas was handing him. He was still a bit uncomfortable about how this had come about, but as each day passed he gradually let go of those reservations and became more and more confident, allowing the memory of his original intent to become buried underneath the mantle of hero.

A few weeks after Harvey was hired, they had an unexpected guest at the station. A police car rolled over the air hoses, ringing the bell, and stopped in front of the office. Since police cars fueled up at the town depot, no one got up to wait on it, and instead waited to see what was about to unfold. Joe got out of the cruiser, hitched up his pants and put on his hat. He walked into the office where Rooster and Harvey sat, watching him silently.

"Afternoon, Rooster, Harvey," said Joe curtly.

"Hello, Joe," said Rooster cautiously.

Harvey just nodded his head and said nothing.

"The sheriff sent me over here. He asked me to tell you that the investigation is over and you can come get your gun."

Rooster frowned suspiciously. "Why didn't he just bring it himself, or let you bring it?"

"I don't know. I guess you have to sign something when he releases it to you. It was considered evidence."

Rooster remembered all too well what happened the last time he went to the sheriff's office, and he wasn't eager to repeat the experience.

"Maybe I'll have Mel go get it."

"He didn't ask me to go talk to Mel."

"All right. I'll come by tomorrow."

"I'll let the sheriff know. Good day, gents."

As soon as Joe left, Rooster picked up the phone and called Mel at his office in the back of the Western Auto.

"Mel? This is Rooster. Joe just came by and told me I can pick up my gun."

"Hot damn! That must mean that bullshit investigation is over. Congratulations, Rooster. Looks like you're finally a free man."

"I don't want to go there by myself, Mel. Those bastards threatened to shoot me the last time I went there on my own. Will you go with me tomorrow?"

"Oh, hell yes. I'd love to go over there and hear that SOB finally admit you're innocent."

Mel's mischievous tone concerned Rooster. He just wanted to get his gun, and he didn't want to cause any more trouble. Especially since he figured out that his grandfather had shot and killed the sheriff's father. He had not told anyone of this, not even Harvey, but he knew now that he had to tell Mel.

"There's something I need to talk to you about before we go get the gun," said Rooster haltingly.

There was a pause at the other end of the line. "And what is that, Rooster?"

"Can I tell you tonight? I was going to come out to see Laurie anyway."

Mel chuckled. "Just come on out in time for supper. We need to celebrate anyway."

"Okay, Mel. Thanks."

Rooster went home after work to clean up and then headed out to Mel's. Laurie greeted him at the door and gave him a hug as the rest of the family applauded. Shirley hugged him too, and Mel and Kenneth shook his hand.

"We're so happy for you, Rooster. Finally, your name is cleared once and for all," said Shirley.

"Thanks, Shirley. Now I just got to get my property back, and hopefully that's the last I'll have to do with the sheriff from now on."

They had a nice supper, and afterward Rooster and Mel went out to Mel's spot above Butcher Creek.

"What is it that you wanted to tell me, Rooster?"

Rooster exhaled deeply before speaking.

"That day I took Harvey fishing out here I started asking him about Sheriff Hickey, about why he's such a prick. I found out that his daddy was a lawman too, and he was shot and killed when Hickey was just a little boy."

"Yeah...I had kind of forgotten, but now that you mention it, I do recall that."

"Well, I kept asking Harvey what he knew about it, and I found out that his daddy was killed up in Sonora."

"Okay...and..."

"That's where my granddaddy did some of his bank robbing. It was where he got into a big gunfight right before he was killed."

Mel just looked at Rooster without saying anything.

"I think my granddaddy killed Hickey's daddy."

Mel let out a breath, his eyes wide. "Do you know that for sure?"

"I know it in my heart. He acted real strange when I told him who my granddaddy was. He got real upset. That's when he said he was going to charge me with murder."

Mel let out a whistle. "Damn, son. Now I can see why he acted the way that he did. I mean, it's not your fault. You didn't do anything, but seeing the gun that probably killed his father must have been hard on him."

"Yeah, I mean, I still don't like the son of a bitch, but I feel bad about what happened."

"Well, damn, even though it had to have upset him, he still didn't have any right to take it out on you. He can't blame you for what your granddaddy did."

"I been carrying blame for my granddaddy all my life. My daddy used to say that the sins of the fathers stick to the sons, and I believe him."

"Psh. You didn't do anything. You never even met your granddaddy, did you?"

"No, he was killed before I was born."

"And your daddy was a preacher too. You don't have any blame in what your granddaddy did."

"I know, but I still want you to come to the sheriff's office with me. I just thought you ought to know about this."

Mel nodded his head in agreement.

"I guess that does change things a little, but it still didn't give him any right to act the way he did, and it damn sure didn't give that asshole deputy the right to do all the crap he did. But don't worry, Rooster. We'll go get the gun, and it'll be all right."

With that settled, they went back to the house to spend the evening with the rest of the family.

11

About midmorning the next day, Mel, Addis, and Kenneth pulled into the driveway of the gas station in Mel's Cadillac. Kenneth hopped out, dressed in his Texaco uniform, and waved Rooster to the car.

"Get in, Rooster. Let's go get your property back," grinned Mel from behind the wheel.

Rooster was relieved to know that he would be accompanied by two of Merky's most upstanding citizens when he went to get his gun. Surely, Bill Hickey wouldn't try to pull any crap around those two.

"Congratulations, Rooster," said Addis from the front passenger seat. "It looks like you're finally off the hook."

"I sure hope so, Addis, but I won't believe it until I hear it from Hickey himself."

"We're going to make sure he says it too. We want this crap over with once and for all," said Mel, grinning mischievously.

Mel looked up into the rearview mirror and saw Rooster's worried face in the back. "But don't you worry, Rooster. We're going to be real respectful. No sense in making a man look like a fool when everybody already knows he is one."

That made Rooster feel a little better, but he was still nervous, and he somehow felt guilty about what his grandfather had done. He really couldn't blame Sheriff Hickey for hating him, he would have felt the same way if the shoe had been on the other foot.

They pulled into a parking spot underneath the shade of the ancient trees that ringed the courthouse and they all got out. They stood there for a moment, stretching and yawning as if they had just driven a thousand miles instead of just a few blocks.

Mel winked at Rooster. "Let's go get your gun."

The sun was shining brightly, and it was starting to get warm outside. Rooster noticed that he was sweating. He took out his handkerchief and wiped his brow, and off they marched into the courthouse.

They walked through the large wooden doors of the main entrance and down the hallway to the sheriff's office, their footsteps echoing down the long corridor. They got to the sheriff's office, and Addis opened the door and walked in, followed by Mel and Rooster.

The sheriff was sitting in a desk chair, his boots propped up on the desk. When they all entered the office, he quickly took his feet off the desk and sat up straight.

"Well, I wasn't expecting to have such distinguished visitors today," Hickey said, trying to conceal his surprise.

"It must be your lucky day," Mel replied.

"I guess so."

"My client is here to collect his property, and we are here as witnesses and to provide legal counsel if that should be necessary," said Addis.

"I see."

Hickey stood up and walked to the back of the office and unlocked a wooden desk. He reached into the top drawer and pulled out Rooster's old revolver.

"I guess this is what you are here for," he said to Rooster.

"Yes, sir," said Rooster.

"So does this mean your investigation is over?" asked Mel.

"I reckon it does."

Sheriff Hickey held the gun in his hand for a moment and looked at it intently, as if memorizing its features.

"Here it is," he said, handing it to Rooster.

"Is that it?" asked Rooster.

"That's it."

"I don't have to sign anything?"

"That's probably not necessary since you've got two of Merky's finest as witnesses."

"If you have a release form, let him sign it anyway," said Addis. "Just so there's no misunderstanding later."

"Whatever you say, Mister Attorney Man."

Sheriff Hickey rustled around in his desk until he found a release affidavit and handed it to Rooster along with a pen.

Addis took the release form from Rooster and read over it, then handed it back to him.

"It looks okay to me. You can go ahead and sign it," said Addis.

Rooster took the pen and wrote his name in large cursive script at the bottom of the letter.

"Anything else I can help you gentlemen with today?"

Addis looked at Rooster, who shook his head.

"That will be all, sheriff. Thank you very much."

And with that it was over, and they all began to leave. As they were passing through the door, Rooster paused.

"Do y'all mind waiting out here for minute? I want to talk to the sheriff...in private, I mean."

Mel and Addis looked at each puzzled.

"It won't take long. I just need to talk to him for a minute."

"Rooster..." said Mel.

"It's okay, Mel, really."

Mel and Addis hesitated and then acquiesced to Rooster. As the door closed behind them, Sheriff Hickey waited, curiosity etched across his face.

Rooster looked at him silently for a few seconds and then spoke.

"I think I know why you acted the way you did that night."

"What do you mean?"

"The night you arrested me and put me in jail."

"I arrested you because you had just killed two men, and we needed to get the facts straight before turning you loose."

"I talked to Harvey, and he told me your daddy was a lawman and that he got shot and killed."

Sheriff Hickey's face turned red.

"So what about it?"

"I figured out that it must have been my grandfather that did it...with this gun."

Sheriff Hickey said nothing but just stood there, breathing heavily.

"I'm sorry for what happened, but I didn't have nothing to do with it. You can't blame me for what my grandfather did before I was even born."

"I don't blame you for that, Rooster. I never blamed you for that. But I know that sometimes the apple doesn't fall far from the tree either."

"Well, my daddy was a preacher. How do you explain that?"

"Sometimes, there ain't a hell of a lot difference between an outlaw and a preacher. The one acts on his instincts, and the other tries to hide them behind a Bible. I've known a few preachers that were just as sorry, if not more so, than anybody else. In fact, sometimes it's the religious ones that make me the most suspicious."

"I don't know nothing about all that. All I know is I didn't kill your daddy, and I'm sorry it happened. That's all."

"Well, it did happen, and I don't buy all this talk about you being a hero. I know you were up to no good that night, and right now, I just can't prove it. It doesn't mean I won't be able to prove it later or find something else to hang you with. You may not be my enemy, but you're not my friend either. You'll show your true colors someday, and when you do, I'll be waiting, Rooster. I'll be waiting."

Rooster felt his own face flush red, and he turned without saying anything else. He was angry with himself for trying to talk to Hickey and angry that he apologized for something he didn't do. He was embarrassed for trying to make amends, and he wished he had just left when he had the chance. He stepped out into the hallway and spotted Mel and Addis sitting on a bench near the front doors. They stood up as he stomped toward them.

"What was that all about?" Mel asked. "What did you say to him?"

"I told him he's a son of a bitch," growled Rooster. "Now let's go."

When they got to the car, nobody said much of anything. It was the first time that Mel had seen Rooster angry, and he sensed it was best not to push him about what was said in Hickey's office. They dropped Rooster off at the station and went about their business. Rooster went into the office and plopped down and put his feet up on the desk. He held the old gun in his hands, turning it over and examining it closely. It appeared unchanged since the last time he had seen it. As he ran his fingers over it, he felt both a sense of relief at having one of his few worldly possessions back and a low-grade feeling of disgust welling up from deep inside. He looked at it as if seeing it for the first time. He had never really thought about what each of those notches meant. They had always been just simple symbols to him. He had never thought how each one of those little cuts resonated in people's lives and how even to this day resonated in the life of Sheriff Bill Hickey. Rooster thought about how his own father had to carry the legacy of Devil Brown upon his shoulders. Even now, those notches were extending their influence to Rooster, reaching out like the tendrils of some fast growing weed, threatening to choke off the new life he had carved out for himself. Yet it was the gun that also gave him this new life, for if he had not been carrying it that night, he is certain he would not have had the courage to stop the atrocity that was about to occur. Rooster knew that gun was both his ticket to something better and the iron ball attached to his ankle that would always impede his progress. He shook his head, put the gun into a drawer of the desk, and got up and went outside to wait on a customer.

Later that night, he went to see Laurie. They saw each other just about every day and the entire town was certain that they were destined to be married. Rooster also had determined that this was his destiny. He was secure in his job, he felt secure in his relationship with Mel, and Laurie adored him. Now that the investigation was over, he knew that he could move on. It was something that he had thought about almost since the beginning, but the cloud of suspicion that hung over him kept it out of reach, and now it seemed that obstacle had been removed. It had only been a few months since he burst into the truck stop that night, yet it seemed as if it could have been a year. So much had happened, and so much had changed, that it was hard for him to fathom. He knew that his life had turned in ways he could never have dreamed of, and he was confident that it was not a dream and that he was going to claim what the divine intelligence seemed to have dropped in his lap. He knew better than to worry too much about how and why. It didn't matter. It just was, and that was all that counted.

When he greeted Laurie, he took her in his arms in a forceful and confident way that he had never done before. Laurie noticed this immediately and sensed that something had changed.

She looked at him searchingly.

"I'm no longer a suspect. I can go on and live my life the way I want and with who I want. I've been set free."

Laurie said nothing, not sure what was coming next.

"Laurie, we've only known each for a few months now, but I feel like I've always known you, like I've always loved you. I know what I want, and I don't see any sense in waiting much longer."

Rooster dropped to his knee and held Laurie's hand in his. He gazed into her wide blue eyes intently.

"Laurie Tucker, I love you. Will you marry me?"

Laurie burst into a tearful smile. "Yes, Rooster. Yes, I will marry you."

Rooster stood and drew her close to him. He leaned down and tenderly kissed her lips, and then they hugged each other tightly.

From the living room window, Mel stood watching them from behind the drapes. I think this is it, he thought. He pushed the curtain back and went and sat in his chair and waited for them to come inside. In a different room, Shirley was also looking outside a window, and like Mel, she also sensed what was happening, so when the couple turned to enter the house she ran toward the living room, then stopped short and entered casually. She sat down on the sofa just as the front door opened and Rooster and Laurie came in.

Both Mel and Shirley tried to act like nothing special was happening. Laurie and Rooster stopped and stood just inside the doorway and Rooster cleared his throat. He had it all worked out in his mind how he was going to announce this to them, had rehearsed it in his mind many times how he would eloquently express his love and devotion for their daughter. But, as he stood there, his mind went blank and the best he could do was to just blurt it out.

"We're gittin' married."

Shirley and Mel both leapt up from their seats and ran over to hug and kiss and congratulate them. Mel shook Rooster's hand firmly, holding his hand in his for several seconds. Rooster couldn't believe that he was now going to have a family, a real family, for the first time in his life. They all talked and carried on excitedly for several minutes, and then they began to separate. Laurie and Shirley went up to one of the upstairs bedrooms to find Shirley's wedding dress and to start planning.

Rooster and Mel slowly drifted out to Mel's overlook. Rooster waited as Mel went into his garage and returned with a paper sack containing a fruit jar of whiskey, a couple of bottles of beer, and two drinking glasses. He had two cigars in his shirt pocket. He set the glasses down and began pouring. They raised their glasses together and drank the bitter liquid.

"Damn! I'm happy, Rooster. I had a feeling this was coming. I'm proud to have you in my family."

Rooster smiled. "I'm honored to be part of this family, Mel. I promise to do my best to make y'all proud."

"You already have, son. You already have."

They sat there silently, neither feeling the need to talk, and smoked cigars and drank whiskey and listened to the crickets chirp and the creek gurgle as the sun went down.

12

In no time, word spread all over town that the local princess and her knight in shining armor were engaged. It was the talk of the town, and the place fairly buzzed with excitement. The first couple of days, Rooster couldn't go anywhere without somebody slapping his back and shaking his hand. Laurie was on cloud nine, floating about in a dreamy haze, indulging in every little girl wedding fantasy that she'd ever had.

The first thing to be decided was the date. It was already almost July, and if they wanted a June wedding that would have meant waiting another year. Rooster made it clear that he didn't want to wait that long. For the past couple of months he had limped around trying to conceal the spontaneous erections that were prone to strike at just about any time of day or night. He was in love, no doubt about it, but he was ready to fuck too, and he wasn't just about to wait another year. So they decided on September. That seemed to make everybody happy. It was still three months away and gave them plenty of time to plan it all out. The weather would be cooler too, a definite bonus for a formal church wedding. Although Rooster wouldn't have to wait too terribly much longer to deflower his bride, it still seemed like an eternity to him. He was so horny he was about to burst.

It wouldn't be his first time though. Like many a young soldier, he had paid for the services of prostitutes on occasion. He struggled with his desires mightily. His father had firmly implanted the idea that sex was only acceptable in marriage and that masturbation was almost as bad as fornication. So he resisted as much as possible, but it was terribly hard, and on those occasions when he had been weak and sought out the ladies of the night he almost always felt bad about it soon afterward. But that would no longer be a problem for him. He would be married, and he could have sex whenever he wanted and without guilt. He wondered briefly whether he should tell Laurie about his dealings with the whores of Europe and Asia and then decided that this was probably one time when honesty wasn't the best policy.

But before they could get married, they had to undergo premarital counseling from the Methodist preacher who would be performing the ceremony. Rooster didn't care for this at all and balked at first, but eventually he knew had no other choice. He knew in his heart that if he wanted to get married he would often have do things he didn't want to and he might as well start getting used to it.

They went to the minister's office one afternoon and met with Reverend Darwin Glover. He was a friendly, gray-haired man of about sixty, and Rooster felt at ease with him right away, much to his surprise. Reverend Glover welcomed them into his office, which was decorated with objects he had collected as a missionary in Africa. They chitchatted politely for a few minutes before easing into the subject at hand.

"The union of a man and woman in holy matrimony is one of the most beautiful things in God's creation," the reverend said as he leaned back in his chair and folded his hands across his stomach, "but it requires an effort on the part of both parties to be successful."

Rooster found himself looking around at the objects in the room as the preacher spoke. One African mask in particular caught his eye, and Reverend Glover noticed him looking at it.

"It is rather captivating, isn't it?" he smiled. "I got that in a very remote region of the Congo on my first mission to Africa."

Rooster, embarrassed that he was already caught not paying attention, sat up straight and nodded his head.

With the reverend's gentle nudge, they were back on track, and this time Rooster made sure that he paid attention to what was being said. The old preacher spoke about the importance of respect and honor and that this was a commitment not to be taken lightly and so forth. Rooster listened intently for as long as could, and then he noticed how Laurie's dress lay across her legs, and he realized he was about to be visited by another unwanted erection if he didn't get his mind on something else, so he turned his focus to what the preacher was saying.

"You must take seriously the vow of fidelity," he said sternly. "Adultery is a serious sin, and many marriages do not recover from it."

That was the last thing Rooster was worried about. Ever since he had met Laurie, he had thought of no one else, and he knew that she would always be true to him.

Then, Reverend Glover talked about children and how they were both a blessing and a burden and how they would change their lives. Finally he was through, and he asked them if they had any questions or concerns they would like to talk about.

Rooster shook his head. He was ready to leave.

Laurie hesitated, as if she wanted to ask something but then stopped.

"Yes, Laurie. You have something you want to ask?"

Laurie blushed. "No...no, I guess not."

"Are you sure?"

"Well...I just wondered if...I mean...how do we...you know, control our desires until our wedding night?"

Rooster could not believe what he was hearing. If anybody was having a problem with self-control, it was him. She had always pushed back when he became too aggressive, except for that night outside the bunkhouse at Mel's when she had thrust herself against him suggestively. It hadn't occurred to him that she might be struggling with those feelings herself. Suddenly, Rooster's old friend Hard Dick was trying to enter the picture once again, and Rooster squirmed around in his chair, trying to put his mind on something else.

The minister smiled. "Just remember that the best thing you can do is to save yourself for your wedding night. If that doesn't work, then you may want to try reading scripture. I find that often helps to focus the mind."

With that, it was pretty much over. The good Reverend Glover offered his services any time they felt the need to talk to him, but he also said he thought they were both well balanced individuals and that he could see no reason for them not to be married.

Rooster and Laurie walked out to the car holding hands. Rooster escorted her to the passenger side and opened the door for her. She turned and looked up at him, and he leaned in and gave her a gentle kiss. Once they were in the car, Rooster turned and looked at her quizzically.

"Are you having trouble...you know...um...controlling your desires?"

Laurie blushed again. "Yes, Rooster. I love you, and I want to be with you. It's very hard for me sometimes. I have never felt like this before. Don't you feel urges too?"

"Shit! I can barely keep my mind off it. Off you, I mean. I swear, Laurie, sometimes I don't know if I can even wait until the wedding. It just about drives me crazy."

"Oh, I know. Me too. That first night you stayed at the bunkhouse, I wanted so bad to be with you, but I knew I couldn't."

Rooster's blood was running hot. He wanted to throw her down and fuck the shit out of her right there in the front seat of her car. He took a deep breath and wiped his forehead, which was beginning to bead with sweat.

"Oh, Lord, it's gonna be a long three months," he groaned.

Rooster dropped Laurie off at Mel and Shirley's and got in his old truck and drove back into town to help Harvey close up the station. He got there just before closing time, and Harvey was having a heated discussion with a customer.

"I'm telling you that I gave you the right change. You gave me a five dollar bill, and that's your correct change."

"Damn it, grease monkey, I know I gave you a ten, and I want my money."

"What's the problem?" asked Rooster.

"Your attendant here can't count. That's the problem," said the man.

"Look, Rooster, he bought $2.00 worth of gas, a pack of cigarettes, and a Coke. With tax, that's $2.48. He gave me $5.00, and I gave him back $2.52."

"I gave you $10.00, dang it. I had a ten dollar bill when I came in here, and now I don't," said the man, holding out his wallet to show that there was nothing in it.

"Did you put the customer's money on top of the register until you made change like I asked you to?" said Rooster.

Harvey hung his head. "No."

Rooster was frustrated and angry. He had told Harvey many times to always take the bill the customer paid with and lay it on top of the register until he had counted out the change. That way, if the customer tried to claim he paid with a larger bill, you had the proof sitting right there. He knew that Harvey was good at counting out change and that the till always balanced at the end of the day. He felt that Harvey was correct, but there was no way for him to prove it. He knew if he gave the man the extra change back and it was wrong then the till would be short.

"I don't have any reason to doubt you, sir, but Harvey is always right on with his transactions."

"Oh, I see how it is. You're in on it too."

"No, sir, nobody's in on anything. But there ain't no way for me to prove this one way or another."

"Well, I think y'all are a bunch of thieves, and I'll make sure that everybody in town knows it too."

Rooster was beginning to think that probably the best thing would be to just give the man the money and be done with it. Once they balanced out the till, they would know who was right. If necessary, he would just take the difference out of Harvey's pay. It would teach him a lesson for not laying the customer's bill out on top of the register like he was told to.

"All right, sir. I still don't think that Harvey cheated you, either on purpose or by accident, but this time we'll give you the benefit of the doubt," Rooster said as he started to open the cash drawer.

"Wait, Rooster. I can prove I'm right," said Harvey.

"How are you going to do that, little man?" smirked the customer.

There's exactly $108.74 in the cash register. We started the till with $25.00 and sales receipts for the day are $83.74, counting what he just bought."

"Says you," said the customer, "how do I know any of that is true?"

"I write everything down. We know how much we started with and we got a ledger with all the sales in it," said Harvey, pointing at the sales register lying on the desk.

"Hell, Harvey, that'll take an hour to figure out," said Rooster. Balancing the books at the end of the day was the task that Rooster hated the most, it almost always took him three tries to get the numbers to add up.

"No it won't. I can do it in less than a minute."

"How the hell can you do that in less than a minute?" asked Rooster impatiently.

"I'm good at math, just watch and see."

"I'm not going to wait all night," the customer said angrily.

"Just watch," said Harvey.

He opened the cash drawer and quickly counted out the till aloud and then wrote down the amount. Then, he scanned the sales register and wrote down a number at the bottom of the page.

"See there. Here's what we started with, and there's the sales totals. There's what's left. It balances out."

"What the hell?" snapped the customer. "There's no way he just added all that up."

Rooster looked at Harvey. "How could you have added that up already? You didn't even look at it more than a couple of seconds."

"I told you, I'm good at math. Check it, you'll see that I'm right."

"It'll take me at least thirty minutes. Let's just give the man his money and be done with it."

Now the customer balked. "Oh, hell no. Let's add it up and check Mr. Einstein's math. I've got time to watch a man make a fool of himself."

So Rooster got a piece of scratch paper and a pencil and he began going through the sales register. He did it twice and came up with the same total, which matched Harvey's count.

"Wait a minute," growled the customer, "let me check that."

The customer sat down and took a clean piece of scratch paper and he added them up twice and he came up with the same amount as Harvey too.

"Damn it! This is some kind of trick. I don't know that this register is right. You probably forgot to write something down."

Rooster knew that was unlikely since Mel insisted on having all sales written down so there was no chance of pilfering.

"Mister, I believe that our records are correct, but I'm not going to argue about it all night either. I'll give you your damn change this time, but from now on we'll make sure that we know what you gave us."

The man smiled and reached into his shirt pocket to get a cigarette. He felt something different and looked down and pulled out a ten dollar bill.

"What the...?" The man looked at both of them in astonishment.

"Is that the ten dollar bill you couldn't account for?" asked Rooster.

"I...I guess it is...damn, how'd it get in there?" the man said, scratching his head. He looked at the both of them sheepishly. "I guess I'm the one that was wrong."

"My apologies, gentlemen," the man said, shaking his head. Then, he turned and left.

Rooster looked at Harvey. "How the hell can you cipher like that?"

Harvey shrugged. "Like I said, I'm good with numbers."

Rooster went and got a stack of sales ledgers that he had already totaled up. He took one from the top of the stack, covered the total with his thumb, and showed it to Harvey.

"What do these add up to?"

Harvey barely glanced at the sheet of paper. "Ninety-eight dollars and twelve cents," he said.

Rooster lifted his thumb and stared at the total he had written himself—$98.12.

"What the hell?" he exclaimed.

He took the next sheet and again showed it to Harvey with his thumb covering the total.

"Try this one."

"One hundred three dollars and thirty-one cents."

"Shit!"

And he continued until he had shown Harvey the entire month's receipts and he was correct on every one. There was no way that he could have memorized it. Rooster was incredulous; he almost felt faint.

"I ain't never seen nothing like this. This is scary."

"I'm sorry, Rooster. I won't do it anymore."

"The hell you won't. Balancing the books is going to be your job from now on. I just can't believe anybody can add in their head like that. It don't seem possible."

"Yeah, that's what some people say."

"Why the hell didn't you work in the bank if you can cipher like that?"

Harvey hung his head. "I'm good with numbers, it's other stuff that I have problems with."

Rooster would learn later that Harvey had been caught going into the vault to get money for one of the Blackwell brothers who had come into the bank and jokingly asked for a loan. It was because of this type of behavior that Rooster rarely left Harvey unattended for very long.

"Well, now you're the official bookkeeper here, okay?"

Harvey grinned, "Okay!"

13

The next few weeks were hell for Rooster and Laurie. Once they had confessed the extent of their lust for one another, it made it so much more difficult to ignore. Their hugs had become more sensual and lingering, their kisses deeper and wetter. They had taken to exploring each other's bodies with their hands, and clothing became less attached with each encounter until it seemed they would both spontaneously combust with pent up passion. Rooster was jacking off regularly just to let off steam, and still he dripped with lust. There was one thing for certain, their honeymoon night, if they made it until then, would be a night to remember.

Things were running smoothly at the station too. Since Rooster had discovered Harvey's amazing math skills, balancing the books at the end of the day was a breeze. It turned out that Harvey could tell you the exact amount of money in the cash register at any time of day, no matter how many transactions had transpired. Rooster made good use of this talent by playing tricks on Kermit and Obie. He would have Harvey whisper to him the amount of money in the cash register and then bet one of them that he could tell the exact amount of change in the till just by looking into the cash drawer. Kermit, especially, was taken in by this. Kermit sometimes had a tendency to wager on just about anything, so he went double or nothing and lost twenty dollars before Rooster let him in on the joke and gave him back his money.

As the wedding day got closer and plans were beginning to gel, a bridal shower was planned for Laurie, and Mel decided to throw a bachelor party out on the back part of the ranch for Rooster. It was still late summer and stifling hot during the day, so Mel picked out a nice spot of bottomland near a deep pool in Butcher Creek where they would make camp. Besides being near a good fishing hole, it was also prone to be cooler at night.

Mel invited quite a few people, some that Rooster didn't know or didn't know very well, such as Oliver Ruggles, the new president of the bank, and Arlen Moore, the owner and editor of the local newspaper The Merky Magpie. Rooster had been interviewed by Arlen soon after he rescued Laurie and the others when the whole episode was written up in the paper, but that was the extent of their relationship. Addis was there, as well as Harvey, Kermit, Obie, and a hodgepodge of locals from the high and low end of Merky society. Some of them would go home after the main cookout was over, but many were staying the night, some in tents and others sleeping out in the backs of pickups or the backseats of cars.

They made camp a couple of hours before dark and built a big campfire and set up a camp kitchen. Mel had a calf slaughtered for the occasion, and he brought a huge kettle for cooking beans, as well as a Dutch oven for biscuits. Soon, smoke was billowing from the fire pit, and the smell of barbecuing meat set everyone's mouths to watering. And to top it all off, Mel brought enough beer to float a battleship. Rooster couldn't get over it.

"Where the hell did you get this much beer?" asked Rooster.

Addis looked at Mel in astonishment. "Damn, Mel, haven't you introduced your future son-in-law to Cletus yet?"

Mel shook his head in mock shame. "It's disgraceful, I know. I'm going to have to rectify that situation real soon."

Mel looked over at Rooster. "It's about time you met, Cletus. I'll take you over there soon."

Rooster had heard about the local bootlegger, Cletus Gross, more times than he could count, but he was trying to be on his best behavior and do a good job for Mel, so he always tactfully avoided invitations to meet Cletus. Also, whenever he did find himself in a drinking situation, somebody else always provided the booze, so he was content to leave things be. But tonight he was ready to cut loose and drink, and this was the first time he has seen so much beer in one place in Merky.

Mel was the camp cook, and he was good at it. Before long, everyone was gnawing on choice cuts of meat and washing it down with beer. After the booze started flowing, the laughter got louder as night fell. Soon, they were all gathered around the glowing embers of the fire. With their bellies full and their mouths loosened from the alcohol, they were all having a grand, old time.

Eventually they got around to the inevitable topic of women, and it turned into a contest as to who had traveled the farthest to get laid. Just about everyone had been to Mexico at least once to the red-light district, or perhaps, a trip to a nearby town, but a few had gone a little further.

"Well," said Arlen, the newspaperman, "I once drove all the way to San Antone to get me some pussy."

"That better have been good," said Kermit.

"It wasn't too bad. The old gal was kind of good-looking, except she had this enlarged eyeball, and Lord have mercy did her pussy ever stink, but all in all, it was pretty good."

"Damn. If you drove all the way to San Antone for that, then I'd hate to see what you wound up with around here," laughed Mel.

As the evening grew late, the ones who weren't staying the night slowly trickled away. As it got later, men started seeking out their various bedrolls until it was just Mel, Addis, Rooster and Harvey still up and about. Rooster and Harvey were running a trotline down at the fishing hole, and they decided to check the lines one last time before calling it a night. Mel and Addis sat around the embers of the fire, nursing their beers and talking in the lazy relaxed manner that late night campfires and alcohol tend to evoke.

"Well, it looks like we've got another four years of Sheriff Bill Hickey to look forward to," said Addis.

"How so?" asked Mel.

"I was at the courthouse today just as he was filing to run for reelection. As of yet, he is unopposed."

"Damn! That makes me sick. Nobody likes that son of a bitch, if anybody ran against him that would be it. Surely, there's got to be somebody around here that's interested in the job."

"What about you, Mel?"

"Ha! That's a good one. I'm too busy just running my businesses although I have to admit it has crossed my mind before."

"Well, then I guess you can't complain too much."

"I can still complain, but there's not much point in it."

At that moment, they heard Rooster and Harvey laughing from down at the fishing hole.

Addis chuckled. "We ought to get Rooster to run. He's already got a gun and a deputy."

Mel froze for a second, then suddenly sat up straight, his eyes flashing. He looked at Addis excitedly.

"That's it!"

"What?"

"Rooster! Why can't he run for sheriff? The way he took care of those Blackwell boys, everybody already thinks he's a hero. Everybody loves Rooster. Everybody would vote for him."

"Do you think he would do it?" asked Addis.

Mel rubbed his chin thoughtfully. "I think it could probably be arranged. I just need to talk to him, get him used to the idea. I sign his paycheck. He lives in my rent house, and he's about to marry my daughter. Sheriff Rooster Brown. I like the sound of that. Now, there's a fitting job for the man that's going to be my son-in-law."

Mel and Addis, now wide awake, threw a couple of sticks of firewood onto the campfire and began talking quietly yet intently in the flickering light of the flames. Mel was especially excited by the prospect, but he knew he had to play it just right to keep Rooster from balking. They heard Rooster and Harvey talking as they came up the footpath back to the camp.

"Let me handle this," Mel whispered to Addis as Rooster and Harvey walked out of the shadows and up to the campfire. Rooster and Harvey were still giggling about some silliness, and it was obvious that they were both drunk.

"Are the fish biting tonight?" Mel asked.

"Sure are. They just ain't biting our hooks," Rooster laughed.

"You fellows ready for another beer yet?"

Rooster took the beer he was carrying and put it to his mouth and tilted his head back, taking a long drink as the beer bubbled and gurgled out of the bottle and down his throat. He wiped his mouth and tossed the bottle to the ground with a grin. "I am now."

"Good, good. Here you go, young man. Drink up. It's your wedding that we're celebrating tonight and we want everybody to have a good time. What about you, Harvey, ready for another one?"

"Uh...no thanks, Mel."

"You know, Rooster, me and Addis were just talking about your friend Bill Hickey."

"What the hell for?"

"He's running for sheriff again. He just signed the papers today to make it official."

"Shit. Sorry to hear that. Hope whoever he's running against beats the hell outta him," Rooster said. He was slurring his words some, and he reeked of alcohol. He had drank many beers over the course of the evening.

"That's not too likely. You see, there's not anybody else running against him."

"Whaa?" Rooster slurred.

"That's right. If he's the only son of a bitch in town who shows up to vote, he'll still win."

"Damn. Somebody neesh to run against that sumbitch," said Rooster wobbily.

"That's what me and Addis were just saying."

"Who you gonna get?"

"Well, now that's something that needs to be thought out. You don't want just anybody running. You want somebody that's proven himself, somebody that the community respects and who will do a good job. Maybe somebody that feels he owes the town a debt of gratitude."

"Okay, Harvey can be sheriff," Rooster laughed.

Harvey was fading into a stupor and could only manage to groan, "Uuuhhhh."

Mel flinched. This was not where he was trying to lead him.

"No, not Harvey, damn it. Rooster, I'm talking about you."

"Wha?"

"That's right, you. You've already proven yourself, proven that you can handle a gun, proven that you're not scared to do what's right.

Everybody likes you. You could win, Rooster. You can be sheriff, and I can help you make it happen."

Rooster was stone drunk, and he just wobbled back and forth and blinked at Mel.

"Merky has been good to you hasn't it, Rooster?"

"Uhh..."

"And what better way to pay the town back than by becoming a public servant? That's what we're really talking about here. This is not some bullshit to be taken lightly. This is a noble calling, and it shouldn't be entrusted to just any old prick. That's how we wound up with Hickey. Merky needs you, Rooster. We need you to step up and serve your community."

Rooster stared at Mel stupidly for a few seconds before he slowly tilted over and passed out.

Addis smiled. "I've got to hand it to you, Mel; you know how to pick them."

Mel sighed and shook his head.

The next morning, Rooster awoke in a fog of confusion. He was still lying where he had keeled over the night before. Someone had covered him with an old army blanket. Dirt and sticks were stuck to his arms and face, and he was itching with what felt like a thousand bug bites. He tried to roll over onto his back but was stopped by something. He raised his head and looked over his shoulder to see Harvey laid out on the ground next to him. His mouth was parched, and he smacked his lips dryly. He laid his head back down and moaned softly. He heard someone laughing and raised his head once again to see Mel sitting on the tailgate of a pickup truck.

"Some fun, huh, Rooster?" Mel chuckled.

"Uhhh," Rooster moaned, and then he drifted back to sleep. He woke up again a short time later to the sound of pots and pans clanging and the smell of bacon cooking. He groaned and sat up, twigs and leaves dropping from his hair. He stood up shakily. He spotted a jar of water and wobbled over to it, unscrewed the lid, and chugged down half of it in two swallows. He stood there for a moment before he felt a wave of nausea, and he staggered off to the edge of the campsite. He vomited until there was nothing left. He was now dripping with sweat, which ran down his dirty arms in brown rivulets. He went to the ice tub, which was now full of warm water and the remaining beers. He pulled out a bottle, nudged the top off against the bumper of pickup, and swigged down half of it in one swallow. He just stood there weakly, his chest heaving and the sweat dripping, until he began to feel a bit of relief. He downed the rest of the beer, went back to the tub, and splashed water on his face and over his head. He made it over to where Mel was cooking breakfast and poured himself some coffee from the blackened coffee pot. He sat on the tailgate of a pickup truck.

"Well, reckon you're ready to get married now?" asked Mel.

"I don't think I'm up for it right this minute, but I will be when the time comes," Rooster said quietly.

"Good, good. Hungry yet?"

"Let me finish this coffee and I will be."

"Damn, son. I must say, you can flat put away the beer."

"Yeah, it's been a while, but I can still knock a few back."

"I don't think I've ever seen anybody drink that much in one sitting."

"I guess I got it from my granddaddy. He was a big drinker, a drunk really. You should have seen me in the army. I could drink anybody, and I mean anybody, under the table."

"I believe it."

"But that was when I drank almost every night. I guess I'm out of practice now."

"Well, we like to see young men have a good time, especially before they get married. Getting hitched puts a stop to a lot of shenanigans."

"I reckon that might be a good thing."

"I reckon it is."

Mel scooped up a big plateful of scrambled eggs, added a few pieces of bacon, topped it off with gravy and biscuits, and handed it to Rooster who greedily wolfed it down, showing no signs that he had just thrown up not five minutes before. Once he had swallowed the last bite, he set the plate down and leaned back against the side of the truck. He was feeling better, but he knew he would suffer the effects of the hangover for most of the day. At that moment he just wanted to go home and soak in the tub and try to get a nap. Tomorrow he would have to go back to work.

Mel seemed to sense what he was thinking.

"Why don't you take tomorrow off? I'll get Kenneth to go in and take your place."

"You sure?"

"Yeah, I'm sure. Obie went home fairly early last night. I'll get him to go in case Harvey's not up to it either."

Harvey was sitting up, looking about as if he just woke from a long coma. He had never really drank much before and he had tried his best to keep up with the others. His mother would dress him down good when he got home, but it was worth it to be one of the boys for one night of his life. If drinking was what it took, then so be it.

Mel was studying Rooster closely, watching him as he emerged from his stupor and regained his senses. He chitchatted casually but in a way so that he could question him and find out what he remembered about the night before.

"You were flying like a kite there last night, Rooster. You remember much of what you did?" Mel asked as he cracked a new batch of eggs.

"I remember drinking a shit load, and I sort of remember checking the trot lines," Rooster said quietly, trolling his memory while sipping another cup of coffee, "but that's about it."

Mel chuckled softly. "Yeah, that ol' booze will steal your memory of the good time you had."

Rooster grunted in agreement.

"What about you, Harvey?"

"I don't remember anything either," said Harvey proudly.

"Is that right?"

"Yep, at least, I think I don't. I'll have to study about it a spell."

"You do that, Harvey, you do that."

Mel was not a man to make the same mistake twice. He had wasted a good sales pitch on Rooster the night before, and he wasn't going to let that happen again. He would bide his time until the moment was right, and he would make sure that the right moment was not too far off.

"You know, since you're going to be off work tomorrow you ought to come and have lunch up at the truck stop with me and Addis. Then, maybe we can go over to Bug Town, and I'll introduce you to Cletus."

"Oh, okay, sure," Rooster said, but he could have done without the lunch. He liked Addis, who had always been friendly and kind to him, but he still always felt out of his league around him and Mel. He couldn't help but feel like the hired hand, which in reality he was, and not their equals. He remembered that Mel told him he needed to strive to do better, and he felt it strongly at that moment. He was about to marry into a higher class than he was accustomed to, and he realized that, whether he wanted to or not, he needed to find some way to climb the ladder and join them.

By now, everyone was rousing from their various states of slumber, and the campsite was coming to life. Smoke wafted this way and that, and the sound of eggs and bacon sizzling over the campfire was drowned out by the voices of men being brought back to life by Mel's black coffee. Soon everyone was joking and laughing, and before long, it was time to pack it all up and head home. Rooster was feeling almost back to normal and he was happy that his bachelor party had turned out so well. As the last of the revelers were about to leave, he walked over to Mel and extended his hand.

"Thank you, Mel. Thank you very much. I had a real good time."

Mel took his hand and shook it firmly. "I'm proud to do it, Rooster, proud to do it."

"I'm grateful for all that you've done for me. I'm indebted to you," said Rooster.

"Oh, you're not indebted to me, Rooster. You saved my daughter."

"I'm still very grateful, Mel."

Mel watched as Rooster got into his truck and slowly drove off with Harvey riding shotgun.

"I guess we'll see just how grateful you are," Mel said softly to himself.

14

When Rooster got home that day after dropping Harvey off, he thought something seemed different. Then he realized that someone had been in his house. He had nothing of value except his personal belongings, which really only were valuable to him, but still he ran around looking to make sure that everything was accounted for. The first thing he did was look in the top drawer of the chest and make sure that his gun and his Bible were still there. Once he had confirmed that everything was in its place, he realized that there was a small package sitting on his kitchen table. He picked it up. It had his name written on it. He tore off the paper and was astounded to see that it was a very elegant shaving kit. There was a note in the box. It said *"To my darling Rooster, Love, Laurie."* Rooster, then realized that the house had been cleaned while he was away. He opened the refrigerator and sure enough there was a freshly baked chocolate pie. Rooster felt his heart sing a little song of love and joy that he had never experienced before. Someone loved him and cared for him, and that was the best gift in the whole world.

He made himself another breakfast for lunch and finished it off with a piece of chocolate pie. It was a little after noon, and he decided to clean up after his night of sleeping in the dirt. He drew a bath and soaked in the hot water. Afterward, he took out the fine shaving kit, filled the cup with lather, and used the brush to dab it on his face. He took the razor and carefully scraped his face with it until the lather was almost all gone and his face was soft and smooth. He took a towel and dabbed the little bit of blood that was seeping out in a couple of places. He was lying across the bed in his underwear when he looked out the window and saw Laurie's car turn into the driveway. He jumped up and hastily put on a pair of pants and a shirt. He went out onto the porch in his bare feet and waited for Laurie to get out of her car.

When she stepped out, Rooster felt his heart surge for she was wearing a pretty red dress that he had never seen before and she had on lipstick. If he wasn't careful his, old friend Hard Dick would likely make an appearance.

"Good morning, beautiful. Thank you for the razor. I've already used it."

"I was hoping so. You look very handsome," Laurie said as she stepped up onto the porch. She reached up and gently caressed his face.

"Mmmm, it feels good too," she purred.

Rooster sensed something different about her, but he said nothing.

"Come on in," he said.

Laurie entered the door and turned to embrace him.

"Did you have fun last night?"

"Oh, heck yes. We all got pretty tore up."

"I could tell. Daddy came home and went straight to bed. I could hear him snoring when I left."

"I hope Shirley wasn't too mad at him."

"I don't think so. Mama went to church and then off to a bake sale."

Laurie ran her arms around Rooster's waist and looked up at him with her luscious blue eyes. Rooster put his arms around her and drew her close. Their lips met, gently at first, and then more urgently, then with tongues darting in and out. Laurie pushed her hips toward Rooster and rubbed against him. He pushed back, grinding his pelvis against her. She stuck her hand up his shirt and ran her fingers over his back and sides. Rooster ran his hands over her buttocks and up to her breasts. She kissed him even more passionately. Rooster reached around, found the zipper on the back of her dress, and pulled it down.

Laurie pulled back, and he thought she was going to stop him, but instead she closed the front door.

"Let's go in there," she said, pointing to the bedroom.

Laurie took his hand and led him into the bedroom, where they stood by the bed, kissing and fondling each other. Rooster gently pulled her down onto to the bed and kissed her. He slowly began removing her dress while she lay back gazing up at him. She pulled the snaps on his shirt open, exposing his chest and rubbing her hands across it, tracing the outline of his tattoo with her finger. Soon her dress was lying on the floor next to Rooster's shirt. She unbuttoned Rooster's pants, and he wiggled out of them. They both lay on the bed in their underwear, caressing each other. Rooster reached around and clumsily unhooked her bra, allowing him to gaze upon her breasts for the very first time. He ran his hands across them softly and then began kissing and sucking on them. Laurie lay back and closed her eyes. Rooster continued to suckle them as he reached down and pulled her panties down, exposing her pubic hairs. Laurie helped him pull them off until she was completely naked. Rooster still had his underwear on and his penis, which was raging hard by now, was sticking out of the top of them. Laurie pulled his underwear down and took it in her hand, running it through her fingers. Rooster reached down and began to fondle her vagina, working the folds of the labia until she was moist. He continued to fondle her until she was wet, then he rolled over on top of her and positioned himself to enter her. Laurie lay back and grimaced as he penetrated her for the first time, grabbing a fold of the skin on his back and squeezing it into her fists. Rooster slowly and gently pushed until he was completely inside her. He started to push back and forth, slowly and easily at first, until she was used to it. He stuck his tongue inside her mouth, and they began to rock back and forth together. Once he felt that she was over the initial discomfort, he began to pump with more enthusiasm, slowly building up until they were both rocking together with abandon, and the bedsprings were creaking, and the headboard was banging against the wall. They kept on and on for what seemed like a long time, building with intensity and passion, until finally Rooster could hold back no more, and he groaned and let loose a spasm of sperm into her. He continued to pump until he was empty, and slowly they wound down until they were both lying there, naked and covered in sweat. They laid there for several minutes, eyes closed, until their heartbeats slowed down and their breathing returned to normal. Rooster gently rolled off of her, letting his flaccid penis slowly come out of her. He laid his arm across her belly and put his chin on her shoulder. Laurie put her hand over his.

"I love you, Rooster."

"I love you, Laurie. I love you so much."

Eventually, they got up, somewhat sheepish at seeing each other naked for the first time. Laurie went and splashed around in the bathroom, and Rooster dusted off her dress, which had fallen onto the floor. Once they were dressed, Rooster walked Laurie out to her car.

"I love you, Laurie, like I have never loved anyone."

"Me, too," said Laurie. "I mean, I feel the same way."

They kissed one more time, and Laurie left as Rooster stood on the porch and watched her drive away. He felt good. He felt like a man. He would sleep well that night.

The next morning, Rooster slept in, something he had not done in a long time. It felt good to lay there in the soft bed in the cool morning air listening to the birds chirping outside his window. He lay in bed until his stomach started growling, and then he got up to make coffee and breakfast. Afterward, he sat on the front porch, trimming his toenails with a large pair of scissors. When that was done, he popped the hood of his old truck and checked the oil. By midmorning, he was already bored and glad that he was going to have lunch with Mel and Addis. When Mel finally turned into the driveway a little before noon, Rooster was sitting on the porch ready to go.

When they got to the truck stop, Mel led him into a small room that was usually closed off and only used for private dinners. Rooster was surprised to see not only Addis, but also Arlen the newspaperman. Rooster had the feeling he had just walked into a trap or something. He was polite and greeted each man, but he also said little else until he could figure out what was going on. At first, it was just idle chit-chat, which continued while they ate their meals. It was only after the waitress removed the last dirty dish that Mel spoke.

"Rooster, we brought you here for a reason today."

Rooster nodded his head. "I thought something seemed kind of fishy."

"You're a smart young man," Mel chuckled. "That's what we like about you."

Rooster said nothing and waited to hear what Mel had to say.

"Rooster, many people around these parts consider you a hero. You stopped a crime in progress and rid this town of a couple of its worst criminals. You acted decisively when the situation called for it. You have proven yourself capable as a manager of my station, and many people in this community like and respect you."

Rooster looked around as Mel was talking, the others were watching him intently.

"In other words, son, you are an asset to this community, and everyone knows it, and now we have a proposal for you," Mel said, pausing to look at the others before continuing.

"We want you to run for sheriff."

Rooster wasn't sure he heard Mel correctly.

"You want me to do what?"

"We want you to run for sheriff."

Rooster was flummoxed. Never in a million years would he have considered such a thing. He struggled to find the words for what he was feeling.

"Whu...I...uh."

This time Addis spoke. "Rooster, the only reason that Bill Hickey is sheriff of this county is that he ran against a lamebrain in the last election. Now he is going to run again, and there is no one at all opposing him this time. We feel this town deserves better, and we think you are just the man for the job."

"But...but...I don't know nothing about being a sheriff."

"What the hell is there to know?" asked Mel. "Look at the knuckle-head that's in there now. He tried to pin some bullshit charges on you, and for what? Just to make himself look good? It takes more than some dumb ass with a badge to be a good sheriff. It takes somebody who knows when to play hard and when to back off. In other words, it takes somebody who knows how to deal with people, and that some-body is you."

Arlen chimed in, "You don't have to be a legal expert. You just have to win an election. You can learn the law after you're in office."

"I looked up the statutes," said Addis. "The only requirements are that you be a legal adult of sound mind. There is a residency requirement, but there's a special exemption for military veterans who served over-seas within the last two years. There is no reason you couldn't run."

"But...but...I just don't know."

"The county needs a good man, Rooster," said Arlen. "Not many peo-ple like Bill Hickey, and most would love to get rid of him."

"We need a good man as sheriff," said Addis, "and we think you're that man."

Rooster just sat there, shaking his head. There was absolutely no way in hell they were going to talk him into running for sheriff.

Mel leaned in and locked his gaze upon Rooster. "If you don't want to serve the community that has taken you in and welcomed you as one of its own, I guess that's up to you. I had hoped you would aspire to something other than pumping gas, but if that's all you want to do, then I guess Laurie will still love you anyway."

Those words stung Rooster. He knew what Mel was trying to do, and yet it had the desired effect.

"I don't know. I need to think about this."

"Well, that's fine. It's a big decision, but we need an answer soon because the filing deadline is next week," said Addis.

"Damn it, son," said Mel, "where's that young man who charged in guns ablazing? This is a hell of an opportunity for you. This is not just any old job we're talking about. This is a chance for you to really be somebody and a chance for you to provide a good living for your wife. What about when you have children of your own? You want them to have a daddy who's the sheriff or a daddy who pumps gas for grandpa? You need to think about the future."

Rooster looked at all of them staring at him. Mel's words had hit him hard. He had just been thinking about how he was not up to their standards, and now here they were practically begging him to actually run for sheriff. He knew that Mel was right, people did like him, and he knew that he probably had a pretty good chance of winning an election. In that moment, he pushed away the doubts that had always plagued him, and he decided that they were right.

"All right," said Rooster. "I'll do it."

The others let out a whoop and got up and started slapping his back and shaking his hand. There was no turning back now.

Then, they got down to business. It was obvious that Addis and Arlen had come prepared to wage a campaign. They soon had the table covered with various papers and were scribbling away at them. Addis would handle getting the proper documents ready to be filed, and Arlen was jotting notes for a newspaper article and advertisements. Mel would pay the costs of the campaign. Rooster's main job was to just show up and do what he was told. There was electricity in the air as everyone realized that they just might make this thing happen. In fact, it never entered their mind that it wouldn't happen. Even Rooster, the most negative one in the bunch, understood that they were about to turn Merky on its head.

After the initial groundwork had been laid, the men all shook hands and left. Mel and Rooster left in Mel's Cadillac and headed to Bug Town just as Mel had promised at the campout.

"Damn, Rooster! I'm excited about this," Mel said, pounding the steering wheel as they passed through town.

"Me too, Mel, and it's making me kind of shaky, but I reckon that'll pass."

"That's adrenaline, son. You ever hear of that?"

"Not that I can recollect."

"It's something in your blood, and it tells your body when to stand up and fight or haul ass and run. It's a survival mechanism."

"Yeah, I felt that in Korea, but that was life and death. I don't know why I'm so shaky now."

"It's the same thing. This is going to be a fight, and your body knows it whether your brain does or not."

They passed the Merky city limits and went over a hill and soon they were at the turnoff to Bug Town. Although Rooster had passed by the Bug Town turnoff many times before, he had never taken the time to explore it. Mel turned off the highway and down the main road leading to the tiny settlement. About a quarter of a mile from the highway was the center of the community, which consisted of one crummy general store, and across from that, a large vacant patch of grass with a mossy, old horse trough and a few old chairs. Ramshackle houses lined the dirt road on either side of the general store and along another dirt road that intersected the main road at the general store. Most of the houses were either unpainted or in need of paint, and the yards were grown up with scraggly weeds which even the goats and chickens that roamed freely didn't appear to want to eat. People sat on their porches or stood around in their yards. Clotheslines, laden with ratty pants and faded dresses, flapped in the breeze. A few children with dirty faces stared blankly at them as they drove by. Rooster tapped his fingers on the armrest as they passed through the forlorn village. They passed the small community quickly, and after a few hundred yards, turned off through a gate and drove a couple hundred more yards up a gentle sloping hill to a couple of small shacks that sat in a grove of trees. Several chickens were scratching about, and a couple of mangy dogs jumped up and started barking at them. Mel pulled over and parked in the shade near one of the shacks. He had barely shut off the motor when someone came out of the shack. A short, squat figure wearing overalls and boots came striding toward them purposely. He was bald, and the grayish hair along the back and sides of his head was scruffy and in need of a trim and he hadn't shaved in days. In a funny way, he could have passed as Mel's sloppy brother. He walked up to Rooster's side of the car which was closest to him.

"Afternoon, Mel," he said, looking at Rooster curiously.

"Cletus, this is my future son-in-law Rooster Brown. Rooster, this is Cletus Gross."

Cletus's eyes grew wide. "You mean this is the famous Rooster Brown? Why I'm right proud to meet you."

Cletus stuck his hand in the window, and Rooster took it and shook it firmly.

"I'm pleased to meet you, Cletus. I've heard a lot about you."

"Yeah, I reckon that's true, but don't believe all you hear. Y'all get out and sit a spell."

Rooster and Mel got out of the car and waded through the sniffing dogs and sat on a couple of chairs in the shady spot between the shacks. Bits of trash and debris were scattered all over the place as if a garbage can had exploded. A few goats grazed nearby, and the smell of a pigsty floated in on the breeze.

"You fellows like a beer?"

"Why sure," said Mel.

Cletus turned and shouted toward one of the shacks.

"Alice, venga!"

A Mexican woman appeared in the doorway.

"Tres cervezas pronto!"

The woman disappeared for a few moments and then came back carrying three bottles of warm Mexican beer.

"Here," she said gruffly.

Cletus took the bottles and handed one each to Rooster and Mel. He reached into his pocket and pulled out a church key then handed it to Mel.

Alice went back to the shack and sat on the stoop.

"Does she speak English?" asked Rooster.

"Hell yes I speek English. Yoo speek Spanish?" said Alice harshly.

Rooster flinched as if he was surprised that she could actually talk.

"Well...yoo speek Spanish?" Alice asked again.

"No, I don't."

"Okay then. Why you worry I speek English?"

"I...I...was just asking. I didn't mean nothing."

"Okay then."

Alice unsettled Rooster in many ways. She was obviously Mexican, and her face was deeply lined from years of hard living. Once you got past her wrinkled face, you could tell that she had once been a beautiful woman. She had been born into a middle class family in Mexico, however, fate had been cruel to her. Her father died when she was a young girl, so she was sent away to be a housekeeper. She soon ran away and married a man who beat and abused her, and it went downhill from there. She went through a series of men, had a few children, and eventually became a drunk. The pretty young girl who was once known as Alicia Christina Benavides del Torres grew up to become the common law wife of Bug Town's bootleg-ger and was known to everyone as Mexican Alice (pronounced "Meskin" by most of the locals). Sometimes, even Cletus referred to her that way.

They sat there sipping their beers as Cletus happily prattled on about his goats and hogs and his garden.

"Cletus, what do you think about Bill Hickey?" asked Mel.

"Bill Hickey? I don't think much about him at all if I can help it."

"I mean, do you think he's worth a shit as sheriff?"

"Oh, hell no. I mean he's good about enforcing the law and that kind of thing but not too many people like him."

"If somebody else ran against him, do you think people would vote for that person?"

"Oh, hell yes. I think I could run my best hog against him and win. Why you ask, Mel? You thinking about running for sheriff?"

Mel was coy. "No, I've just been thinking how people might vote if somebody ran against him."

"I suspect that person would win. I got no doubt about it."

Rooster said nothing while this conversation was going on, but Mel watched him carefully from the corner of his eye. They sat there in the shade, just engaging in idle chitchat until they finished their beers. Then Mel bought a fruit jar of homebrew and they got into the car to leave.

"I'm pleased to meet you, Rooster. Any time you want a little nip, you're welcome to drop by," said Cletus.

"Thanks, Cletus, I appreciate that," said Rooster.

Mel eased his Cadillac back onto the dirt road, and they headed home.

"So that was the famous Cletus Gross," said Rooster.

"You just met the most important man in town," chuckled Mel.

I thought the sheriff was the most important man in town, mused Rooster, but he just nodded his head and said nothing.

15

Laurie was not as enthusiastic about Rooster running for sheriff as everyone else. The job was potentially dangerous, and also the campaign would detract somewhat from their impending wedding, but she mostly said little about it. In the meantime, Mel had thrown himself full tilt into the role of campaign manager. Political campaigns in Merky were usually about as exciting as watching a faucet drip, however this one would prove to be different. Mel had a bunch of campaign signs printed up and even ran some ads on the radio. He was shrewd enough to capitalize on Rooster's nickname, as well as his fame. He had the image of a rooster printed on all the campaign posters and a slogan that said "Vote for Rooster. He's no chicken." The radio ads featured the sound of a couple of bandits committing a robbery, then gunshots and a rooster crowing and a voiceover that said, "The people of Merky will have nothing to worry about with a rooster guarding their hen house."

When Sheriff Hickey first learned that Rooster was going to run for sheriff, he had a good laugh. He underestimated Rooster's hero status, and overestimated everyone else's opinion of him. Soon the laughter faded as he watched Mel placing campaign signs all over town and he realized that people were actually excited at the prospect of electing Rooster Brown as their new sheriff. The last election for sheriff had been a cakewalk, his only opponent was a local yokel with no charisma, and who was even less well liked than he was. Hickey had assumed that no one else would dare challenge him this time and that his reelection was assured. He had not given one whit of thought to a campaign of any sort, but when he saw the effort that Mel and his various cronies and minions were putting into their effort, he got worried. He immediately enlisted his two deputies, Wayne and Joe, to work on his campaign, and they had a vested interest as well, for it was all but certain if Rooster Brown were elected sheriff they would be out of a job. And to be fair, Sheriff Hickey had his supporters. In spite of himself, he tried to be fair and just to everyone. He really cared about his job, and he took it seriously, if not a little too seriously at times. It was his by-the-book attitude that often got him crossways with the citizenry of Merky. When he first got elected, he immediately set out to shut down Cletus Gross's bootlegging operation much to the consternation of most of the men in town. It took a serious tongue lashing from the mayor and many angry run-ins with various members of the community to convince him that it was in the best interest of everyone to leave Cletus alone. He learned his lesson, but he still managed to ruffle feathers occasionally when he would haul in some local big shot's kid for drinking, or something similar, that everyone else thought he should just let be. Perhaps most damning of all, he just wasn't that likeable of a guy. He managed to annoy people without trying, and that was a hard thing to get past when you have to depend on public support to keep your job. So now, faced with a real threat to his livelihood, he had to try to overcome all the baggage he had carried to his present position, and he knew in his heart that it wouldn't be easy. He also knew that his life would be very different if he lost the job that he loved.

As events in Merky began to heat up so did the weather. They were now in the dog days of summer, and everyone was suffering through the wilting heat. A few fortunate souls with the resources to do so had bought air conditioning units for their homes and offices. One of those fortunate souls, of course, was Mel Tucker, and he embraced this new technology wholeheartedly, outfitting his home and office with cooling units. The rest of the poor SOBs, such as one Rooster Brown, suffered through as best they could. By the time the workday was over, the men at the gas station were soaked with sweat. Rooster would go home and sit in a cold bath to try to cool himself down as much as possible. He even bought a small fan which helped some, but otherwise he just toughed it out. He had sometimes taken to tossing his mattress in the back of his truck and sleeping outside at night, which he found to be rather pleasant until one night when a thunderstorm blew in quickly and got him wet before he could get the mattress back inside. Even that wasn't too bad, he just flipped it over and slept on the dry side while enjoying the cool breeze brought in by the storm.

After he became a political candidate, business at the station picked up again, much to the delight of Mel. However, Rooster found it to be sometimes tiring and annoying when people just wanted to hang around and talk when he had customers waiting. Mel made Kenneth start working every day at the station so that took some of the strain off and allowed Rooster to schmooze with the potential voters. He was already getting used to the idea of being sheriff, and now that he had decided he wanted it, he worked hard at being a good candidate. He realized that he didn't want to keep pumping gas and fixing flats, especially when the weather grew too hot or too cold. He liked the idea of being sheriff. In fact, it had grown on him tremendously after he got over his initial resistance. He knew that it was his to lose, and he wasn't going to let that happen.

In the meantime, while the men were busily girding for their political battle, the women were plotting the impending march down the aisle, which was now scarcely six weeks away. Laurie and Shirley were the brains of the operation, the generals running the show. They had their battle plan in place, and now it was just a matter of getting it all done. They had the church and the preacher lined up. Shirley hired a seamstress to alter the wedding dress and a baker to make the cake. They made up a guest list, and Laurie chose her bridal party. Her bridesmaids would be two of her best friends, Janet Crump and Glenda Binkley, and the maid of honor would be her very best friend ever, Mary Ann Muckleroy, whom everyone called Molly. Initially it was going to be a simple affair until Mel got the idea of renting a hall and throwing a big bash and inviting virtually the whole town to help bolster Rooster's prospects in the election. This was where Laurie put her foot down, declaring that her precious wedding day would not be sullied by turning it into a shameless political ploy. Mel grudgingly gave in, but he made sure to include as many prominent locals on the guest list as possible on the theory that the leaders of the town would affect the lower ranks. All in all, it was shaping up to be the wedding of the year, if not the decade.

The wedding was planned for September when everyone hoped that the hot weather would have abated somewhat. Rooster picked Harvey for his best man, which thrilled Harvey to no end. He insisted on buying a new suit just for the occasion, and he wore it around the house after work, marching around and practicing taking the ring from his pocket and handing it to Rooster.

The heat blazed on, and it looked like everyone would swelter at the wedding, but the weather changed at the last moment and blew in a nice cool front a couple of days before the ceremony. A rehearsal was held two days before the wedding with a meal served afterward for the wedding party. Everyone felt rejuvenated by the cool weather, and the excitement and sense of anticipation were palpable. The change in weather was interpreted as a good omen by all. Finally, it was the big day.

The church was filled with guests, not a single person had declined their invitation. It was a nice early fall evening and not too hot nor too cold. The air was clear, the sun was bright, and the world seemed to shine like it had been cleaned and polished. Rooster, Harvey, and Mel were having a last minute smoke outside while Laurie, Janice,

Glenda, and Molly were waiting, hidden away in a side room. Shirley and Kenneth took their seats up front and began waiting for the organist to begin playing. The last minute rustling and adjusting was done and then it was time. Rooster and Harvey took their places near the altar alongside the minister, the organist began playing the wedding march, and everyone turned to watch as proud Mel Tucker walked his beautiful daughter down the aisle to be married.

To Rooster, it seemed surreal, so much so that he had to pinch himself once to make sure he wasn't dreaming the whole thing. When the minister began to speak Rooster saw his mouth moving, and he perceived the sounds reaching his ears, but it reminded him of someone speaking Korean. The preacher's words came at Rooster, and when it was his turn to speak, he mimicked what the preacher said. Then it was Laurie's turn, then the preacher spoke again, then they kissed, and then they turned and walked out the door and had rice thrown at them and that would pretty much be Rooster's recollection of it for as long as he would live.

The reception was a lively affair, with a professional band from San Antonio playing popular music. The cake was a work of art, three tiers of sugary bliss, complete with figurines atop it. A large bowl of pink punch accompanied the cake, and for those guests who were fortunate enough to be in on the secret, there was another bowl of "special" punch in the kitchen area. Kermit and Obie took turns keeping an eye on the "special" punch so that no one got any by mistake. Out in the main hall, Laurie and Rooster held court over the reception line, greeting their guests and watching as the gifts piled up.

Eventually, it was time to shut everything down and to send the newlyweds on their way. Rooster and Laurie had decided to go to Mexico for a couple of days and then head down to the coast. They changed out of their wedding garb and got into Laurie's car, which was adorned with a *Just Married* sign and had tin cans tied to the bumper. The guests, many of whom were now flying high on special punch, came out to send them off. The crowd let out a cheer as they pulled away from the church, and off to their honeymoon.

Rooster and Laurie were still charged from the excitement of the day as they sped out of town, past the city limits, and on toward the border. Laurie sat next to Rooster, who kept one hand on the wheel and the other on her knee. The past few weeks, unable to contain themselves any longer and seeing no reason to hold back since their first sexual encounter, they had been intimate on a regular basis. Even so, Rooster was still preoccupied with the idea of getting laid every chance he could. Now, he was married, a man with a license to fuck, and there would be no more reason to hide it anymore. He was deeply in love, and he was ready to make love to his wife for the first time. He was also slightly drunk from a big cup of special punch and ready to check into the first motel he saw. However, he would have to wait, the only lodging between Merky and Mexico was a fleabag motel in the miserable backwater of Pony Crossing, and Laurie made it clear she was not going to stay there no matter how horny he was.

They meandered along until finally, just after dusk, they spotted the lights of the border town of Rio Sueño. It was exciting to see those lights and know that just on the other side was another country. Rooster was eager to finally see Mexico, even though everyone had assured him that he would be disappointed after having been to Europe. However, something about the idea of the border intrigued, frightened, and beckoned him.

They pulled into town and began driving around looking for their hotel. Everyone had recommended a place called the Contessa as the classiest hotel in town, and soon enough they found it. Rooster was a bit awed when he first saw it. He had never stayed in any place so fancy in his life, but then he reminded himself of how far he had come, and where it looked like he was heading, and decided that he was good enough to stay in the Contessa Hotel in Rio Sueño, Texas.

They parked out front and walked through the lobby up to the front desk where a man in a suit sat behind the marble counter.

"May I help you?"

"Yes, sir. We'd like a room tonight."

"Please sign in here," said the man, pushing the guest book toward them.

Rooster picked up the pen and looked over the form. In the space where it asked for the guest's name, he wrote in Mr. and Mrs. William T. Brown. He glanced over at Laurie who looked up at him and smiled.

"You folks on vacation?" asked the clerk.

"We're on our honeymoon," replied Rooster.

"Indeed!" exclaimed the clerk. "You are in luck; we have a vacancy in one of our presidential suites."

"How much is that?" asked Rooster, trying not to show he was worried about the cost.

"For newlyweds, we offer it at our regular rate," said the clerk.

"Then we'll take it," declared Rooster.

The clerk instructed them where to park and told them he would send a bellhop out to assist them with their bags.

"I can get the bags," said Rooster.

"That won't be necessary," said the clerk. "It's our policy to carry our guests' bags."

"Okay," said Rooster as he silently fretted whether he was supposed to tip the bellhop.

They parked the car as instructed, and a man in a hotel uniform greeted them and took their bags from the car.

"You folks on your honeymoon?"

"Yes, sir," said Rooster.

"Well, congratulations. If there's anything we can do to make your trip more pleasurable, just let us know."

"Where do you recommend we go over in Mexico?" asked Rooster.

"We have a brochure that you can pick up at the front desk which has some useful information about that. Just don't drink the water over there."

"Why is that?"

"It will make you sick, definitely not what you want on your honeymoon."

"What's wrong with the water?"

"It's just not treated like ours is. It can make you very sick. Be careful about what you eat also."

Damn, thought Rooster, if you can't eat and drink over there, then what's the point?

When the bellhop took them to their room, he stood around expectantly. Rooster was a little miffed about having to tip somebody for carrying his bags when he could have done it just as easily, but he reached into his pocket and dropped some coins into the bellhop's hand. After the bellhop left, they walked around inspecting the room. It had a large bed and a telephone, and to Rooster's surprise, it also had a television. Rooster went to the window and pulled back the drapes. They were on the fourth floor, the very top of the hotel, and they had a nice view of the town and the road into Mexico. It was getting late, and they were hungry, so they went back down to the lobby and asked the clerk where they could eat.

"There's a very nice restaurant two blocks to your right," said the clerk and off they went.

They stepped out of the hotel lobby into the night. It was cool out, a hint of autumn in the air. There was a full moon beaming down that cast a ghostly glow upon everything. They strolled hand in hand along the sidewalk past darkened storefronts. In the street, cars rolled slowly past them, their headlights illuminating the dusty street. A nearby neon sign buzzed and flickered, and a car rolled slowly by. Then Rooster stepped on something that made a crackling noise, and suddenly he remembered that not so long ago, he was out on a similar night with murder in his heart. He hadn't thought of it in a while, what with all the excitement about the wedding and the election, but now it came back to him, and for a moment all the despair he had felt that night weighed on him anew. He looked at the beautiful young woman walking beside him, holding his hand. He hadn't even known she existed back then, had no idea how much she would mean to him. At that time, all he could see was a bitch who had insulted and crushed him, and he was ready to throw everything away to get even. He thought how different his life would be if he had succeeded that night, and he shuddered slightly.

Laurie sensed something. "What's wrong, Rooster?"

The sound of her voice snapped him out of it.

"Nothing, nothing's wrong."

Laurie didn't believe him, but she didn't ask again. They were at the restaurant, and it was time to eat. They ordered the best steaks on the menu, and Rooster happened to notice that they served wine and beer, something he was not accustomed to in the dry county of Loma Grande.

"You want something to drink?" asked Rooster.

"I'm having tea, silly."

"I meant something alcoholic. They have wine and beer."

"No, I think I'll pass, but if you want a beer, it's okay with me."

"I just thought we should drink a toast, you know, to celebrate."

"Oh, you're right. I guess I'll have a glass of wine."

Rooster ordered a glass of wine and a beer, and they clinked their glasses together.

"To us," said Rooster. "To a long and happy life together."

"To us, and babies too," said Laurie.

"Babies too."

They clinked their glasses again, and each took a sip.

"Ewww," said Laurie.

"You don't like it?"

"I've never really drank much before. Let me try your beer."

Laurie took a sip. "Ewww. You can have my wine too. I'll just drink tea."

"Okay," Rooster shrugged. He had gotten a little drunk earlier at the wedding and was in the mood to drink again.

They ate their supper and topped it off with a couple of pieces of pie. They walked around the block on the way back to the hotel. Rooster kept noticing their reflection in the storefront windows. He couldn't get over his tall, gangly self walking next to the petite and pretty young woman who was now his wife. Even though he had just spent all day getting married, it still seemed unreal to him.

They went back to their room. At last, they were alone as man and wife and in the good graces of man and God alike. Rooster turned on the television and got a fuzzy signal. He turned the knob, going through all thirteen channels quickly. A couple of American stations buzzed in and out with poor reception. Only one channel came in clearly, and it was a Mexican station and was in Spanish. He turned off the television, wondering why they would even bother to put them in their rooms if all you could get was Mexican stations.

As he lay on the bed with his boots off, he settled back against the pillows piled up against the headboard. He was tired and a little sleepy and feeling a nice glow from the two drinks at supper. Laurie was in the bathroom doing something.

"Whatcha doing in there, you cutie pie you?"

"Nothing. I'll be there in a minute."

"You better, or I'll come get you."

Soon, Laurie came out in a silk robe, with fresh makeup on, and lay next to Rooster on the bed.

"Damn, woman, you're beautiful."

"Damn and beautiful shouldn't be together in the same sentence."

"You and I probably shouldn't be together in the same room, but here we are."

"What do you mean?" Laurie sat up.

Rooster realizing he was about to make a blunder quickly recovered.

"I mean, who would have ever thought that we would wind up together? But here we are, and I think that is a damn beautiful thing."

Laurie smiled and shook her head. "I'll let you off the hook this time."

Laurie eased back down on the bed and lay against Rooster. She smelled good, she was beautiful, and the silk robe felt good against his skin. He pulled her toward him and kissed her. She reached up and caressed his face. They kissed again, each running their hand over each other's bodies.

"I guess we should turn off the lights," said Laurie.

"Take off your robe first."

Laurie blushed slightly.

"We're married now. We get to see each other naked," said Rooster. "Besides, I've seen you before."

"I know, but it still feels strange for me to take my clothes off in front of somebody. You know, like I'm being naughty or something."

"We are being naughty, but now it's allowed because we're married."

"You take off your clothes first."

Rooster got up from the bed, took off his shirt and laid it across a chair. Then, he unbuckled his belt and let his trousers drop to the floor. He was starting to get a hard-on, and his penis was pushing out on his underwear. He pulled off his socks, then his underwear, and stood there with nothing on. Laurie smiled shyly.

"It's big, isn't it?"

"I had the biggest dick in the barracks," Rooster said proudly.

Laurie untied the sash around her waist and let the robe slide off her shoulders. She was wearing a sheer nightgown with a bra and panties underneath.

Rooster's dick began to stiffen even more. "You can take off the rest," he said.

Laurie slipped off the gown and laid it across a chair. She reached around and unfastened her bra, then turned her back to Rooster as she took off her bra and panties. She turned back around and smiled at him, then got into bed under the covers, and turned off the light. Rooster slid under the blankets up next to her soft, warm body. He ran his hand along her side, feeling the curve of her body, and he caressed her breasts and began to kiss her. Laurie took his penis in her hand and fondled it until he was moaning softly. Rooster put his hand over her vagina and started working the folds of her labia until it was moist and he could get his finger inside of her. Once he had his finger in, he began to work it around until she was wet and ready for him. He got on top and eased inside of her, slowly working up speed and rhythm, until they were both thrusting back and forth in unison. He held back for a long time until he couldn't hold it any longer, and he let loose with a spasm into her vagina, humping until he was empty, and then they slowly wound down. They kissed a little more, and Rooster pulled out of her and rolled over. He got up to get a glass of water and brought it to the bed, so Laurie could have a sip. They finished their water, curled up together, and drifted into a nice dreamy sleep, as man and wife.

Rooster woke up first the next morning, accustomed as he was to rising early anyway. While Laurie slept, he got up and looked out the window. It was just becoming light outside. The streetlights were still on, and everything had a golden tint to it as the sun rose above the horizon. He watched as a few cars poked along lazily around the downtown area. The border crossing was on the edge of town, and he could see it faintly from where he stood. He realized that just beyond it lie Mexico. Something about that excited him, aroused something primal from deep within. He didn't know what it was that stirred him so, but at that moment he felt the presence of his grandfather, as if he were in the room with them. It was so strong that he looked around behind him just to be sure there wasn't a ghost in the room with them. All he saw was Laurie sleeping softly in the middle of the bed. The sight of her lying there caused him to get aroused again, so he went to the bathroom and emptied his bladder before crawling into bed with her. He slid up against her gently but firmly enough to wake her. Laurie moaned softly and moved her hand across the pillow. Rooster spooned up against her backside, enjoying the warmth and softness of her skin.

"What time is it?" Laurie asked sleepily.

"A little after seven. You don't have to get up yet if you don't want to," said Rooster.

"Oh, that's okay. I don't need to sleep all day."

Laurie pulled back the covers and suddenly realized she was naked.

"Oh," she said, still half asleep. She got out of bed and stumbled into the bathroom. After she was finished peeing, she padded softly across the carpet and got back into bed, quickly pulling the blankets back over her.

"What do you want to do today?" she asked Rooster.

"Oh, I guess go over to Mexico and do a little looking around."

Rooster ran his hand along her hips, "But I'm in no hurry to get up, at least no hurry to get out of bed."

Laurie smiled and snuggled up next to his chest. She put her hand on his chest, tracing out the tattoo of the Asian cock and then moved it down to his belly and past his waist where his hard dick was waiting. She fondled him as he ran his hand over her breasts. Soon, he was inside her again, groaning in pleasure as he thrust back and forth. This time he finished quickly, and they lay there together as the room began to get lighter. Eventually, their stomachs started growling and they got up to go find breakfast. By the time they stepped out onto the street, it was almost nine. It was a lazy Sunday morning and little seemed to be happening. The fine restaurant they ate at the night before was closed, but they found a diner not much farther away and went in and ordered coffee and breakfast. Rooster picked up a local paper to see what might be going on. He soon became excited.

"Hey, there's a bullfight over there tonight," he said.

"Oh, I think those are bloody. Don't they kill the bull?"

"I guess it wouldn't be much of a fight if there wasn't blood."

Laurie seemed unimpressed and showed little interest, so Rooster let it drop. For some reason he wanted to go, even though he didn't normally care for hunting and blood sports. After breakfast, they walked around the downtown of Rio Sueño, looking in the windows of the mostly closed storefronts. They walked past an ornate Catholic church where some of the parishioners were lazing about on the lawn even though the morning mass was over and the noon mass was yet to begin. A few vendors were also there selling tacos and religious icons from carts.

"That's such a strange religion. I never really understood much about it," said Laurie.

"Me either. I barely understood regular, old Christianity," said Rooster.

"You never said much about the church you went to," said Laurie, looking up at him inquiringly.

"Not much to say. Daddy preached and I slept, and that was about it."

"What kind of church was it?"

"Why does it matter?"

"It just does. We're married now. I want to know about things like that."

Rooster looked away, as if searching for the answer.

"My daddy was a Holy Roller preacher," he finally said a little angrily.

"You mean like a Pentecostal?"

"Yeah."

"Oh."

"I got laughed at and made fun of because of it."

Laurie said nothing.

"I got picked on up until about sixth grade. Then I just got sick and tired of being the butt of everybody's joke, and I was mad because my mother died and my daddy was real strict with me. That's when I started acting up and telling everybody that my granddaddy was Devil Brown. That's about the time I started growing a lot too. Pretty soon, I was bigger than everybody else, and after I whipped a couple of kids' asses, the teasing stopped, at least to my face."

"I'm so sorry, Rooster, but the kind of church you go to doesn't matter, as long as you believe in God."

"I don't know what I believe."

"Rooster!"

"Well, if you like church so much, let's go take a look around inside this one."

"I don't know..."

"Why not? It's the same God, ain't it?"

"I don't know about that either. I think they worship the Pope or Mary."

"See there. That's another reason I don't know what to believe. They're supposed to be Christians too, but my daddy said they're all going to hell. He would have said you're going to hell too because you're a Methodist. You're the last person what ought to go to hell as far I'm concerned."

"Well, I don't want to go in there. Let's go somewhere else."

They walked on, and soon they figured out that most of the town was closed and there wasn't that much to do. They went back to the hotel and lay on the bed for a while. Rooster was inclined to fuck again, but Laurie acted as if she wasn't interested, so he didn't push it. At noon, they went back out and found a quirky, little restaurant on the edge of town called Juanita's. The proprietor was a wrinkled old woman named Juanita McDonald, who made some of the best enchiladas in Texas; even the Mexicans went there to eat. Rooster and Laurie ate as Juanita regaled them with tales of the border and Mexico. Rooster didn't know whether to believe half of what she was saying, but it piqued his interest so that he was eager to cross the border and see for himself.

They left the diner and headed for the border, which was a mile past the edge of town. They rounded a curve in the road and saw a large sign that said MEXICO looming over a series of tollbooths. Cars were slowly passing through the booths from both directions. Rooster pulled in behind a truck and they waited their turn. Finally, they made it to the tollbooth and Rooster handed some coins to the toll taker. As they drove across the bridge, he looked over the edge at the brown water flowing underneath, and was surprised that it seemed smaller and more insignificant than he expected. Then they crossed over and went through another tollbooth, and they were in Mexico. The first thing Rooster noticed was that immediately it became dirtier and more colorful than just a few hundred yards behind him. The roads were rough and unpaved, and a thin haze of dust hung in the air. It seemed to be much livelier on this side of the border, and cars paraded back and forth along the dirty streets among pedestrians, burros, and mangy dogs. Music blared from a couple of bars, and men on the sidewalks whistled at the passing cars. Rooster drove around until he came to an area that seemed a bit nicer. A series of tourist shops lined the streets. He saw an empty parking spot and pulled into it.

He and Laurie got out and gawked at the row of tourist shops lining the street. The shops seemed to be mostly selling cheap, gaudy baubles that Mexicans thought Americans wanted. They held hands and walked down the street, looking at the colorful wares. Laurie saw a shop that interested her, and she went inside, while Rooster waited on the sidewalk smoking a cigarette. A little boy approached him.

"Hey, señor. You want pussy? I get you some."

Rooster couldn't believe what he had just heard. "Excuse me?"

"You want girl or lady? I take you there now."

Rooster stood looking in disbelief at this young boy standing before him.

"Hell, junior, I'm here on my honeymoon, so I guess I'll have to pass."

"Oh, you marry? Hokay. You want or no?"

The little kid stood before Rooster, grinning happily. Rooster shook his head and chuckled softly. He reached into his pocket and pulled out a few coins that he put into the young boys hand.

"Thanks anyway. Now get the hell out of here."

"Hokay, Meester. Gracias."

Laurie came out of the shop.

"What did that little boy want?"

Rooster grinned. "I guess he wanted me to meet his sister."

Laurie looked at Rooster for a few seconds, and then she understood what he meant.

"Oh, my goodness."

"Did you find anything you wanted?" Rooster asked.

"No. Did you?"

"No."

They joined hands again and resumed their promenade down the street in Mexico. Laurie laughed about the little boy at first, but then she grew quiet. She looked up at Rooster as they walked down the street.

"Did you ever go with one of those women? You know when you were in the army?"

Rooster didn't hesitate. "No. Never."

Laurie smiled. "Never? You mean it?"

"I mean it."

Laurie held his hand a little tighter and smiled as they walked down the street. Rooster silently congratulated himself on thinking fast and not saying what would have sunk him. He knew now that sometimes it was better to lie.

They shopped a while longer then decided to head back to the United States side. They went back to the hotel and flopped on the bed. They were both tired from all the excitement of the weekend and the trip to Rio Sueño and were ready to just rest for a little while. As they lay there, Laurie reached over and rubbed Rooster's belly. It felt good, and at first, he just lay back and enjoyed it. Then, he turned his head to look at her. Her eyes met his, and before long, they were both naked and going at it again. When they finished, they both curled up under the sheets and drifted off to sleep.

When they awoke later, it was getting close to suppertime. They both bathed and put on clean clothes and headed out again. They found another place to eat in town and then headed back to Mexico. They got there a little before dark. Rooster parked near a bar that was popular with tourists, and they went in and found a table. Rooster ordered a beer for himself and a Coke for Laurie. They sat there for a while watching the people come and go and then they got up to walk around. Outside, a man was wearing a sandwich sign that promoted the bullfights that evening. He saw Rooster looking at it, and he approached them.

"Beeg bullfight tonight, señor."

Rooster scratched his head. "Sounds good to me, but I don't think my wife wants to go."

"Ees at night, very special."

Laurie looked at the sandwich board. It was a colorful painting of a man waving a red cape in front of a charging bull. She looked around at the row of bars and shops and the steady flow of pedestrians milling in and out.

"Well, maybe it might be interesting. I mean, we are in Mexico."

"You sure?"

"I guess so."

The man told them how to get to the arena, so they got in the car and took off to find the place.

As they turned a corner, they saw it, and Rooster felt a surge of excitement. It was a large arena with cars parked all around. It was brightly lit, and there was an air of anticipation about the place. There was also the musky smell of cows and manure and dust enveloping the arena that somehow added to the overall atmosphere. They parked and followed the crowd to get in line. When they got to the ticket booth, Rooster handed the man some pesos and the man gave him a program in Spanish. They followed the crowd and settled in for the evening.

Soon, there was the sound of bugling and an announcement in Spanish, and the crowd let out a roar. A band played and a parade of various officials and matadors strode through the arena to the cheers of the crowd. After more announcements in Spanish, the arena was cleared.

Then, a bull came running into the ring, bellowing and pawing at the ground.

"Damn! Look at that thing!" exclaimed Rooster excitedly.

A man came out and waved a cape at the bull, testing it for the matador, and then left. Then the picadors rode out on horseback, and inserted two lances into the back of the bull, which enraged it and caused it to bellow even more.

Laurie covered her eyes. "Oh, Lord. Why did we come to this?"

When the bull was at his full fury, the matador entered the ring, and the crowd shouted loudly. Soon the dance of death began. With each pass of the bull, a shout of "ole!" echoed across the arena. Rooster, even though he winced when they lanced the bull, watched with rapt interest. Laurie would only look out from behind her fingers occasionally when a particularly loud shout echoed throughout the arena. Then, it was time for the kill. The matador ran his sword between the bull's shoulders and it was over. Rooster felt almost giddy, for he was not accustomed to such artistic acts of killing. Laurie sat next to him with tears running down her cheeks.

"Can we go now?" she asked dejectedly.

Rooster, realizing that she had been sickened by the whole spectacle, and feeling somewhat guilty about his own voyeurism, nodded sheepishly and stood up. He tried to take Laurie's hand, but she pulled back, and he followed her silently as they made their way back to the car. Once in the car, Laurie burst into tears.

"That was awful! How could you have watched that?"

"I...I...didn't know what to expect either," Rooster stammered.

"You liked watching him kill that animal like that?"

"No...no...I didn't enjoy it. It kind of made me ill too, but for some reason I couldn't turn away from it."

"Can we go home now...I mean, back to the room?"

"Don't you want to shop some more or get a drink?"

"No! I want to go back to the hotel."

Rooster felt bad. He had not intended to upset Laurie, and in truth, he had not realized how violently it would all play out. Now Laurie was angry with him and thinking that he was some kind of sadistic brute. He realized there would probably be no playing around tonight, and he was glad they had made love that afternoon. He knew he would eventually be able to smooth things over, but it might take a while, and he didn't want to let this ruin their honeymoon. As they drove over the bridge, the moon was rising in the sky, and it looked to be a beautiful evening. He didn't want to go straight back to their room where Laurie would sulk all night, so he drove around a bit, acting like he wasn't sure which was the way back.

"Where are you going? This isn't the way to the hotel."

"Oh, I must have turned the wrong way. I'm sorry. I'll get us back."

As they drove around, Rooster spotted a small carnival and headed toward it.

"Look, Laurie. It's a fair."

"I don't care," she replied sullenly.

Rooster drove up as close as he could get to the fair, and they heard the music and the voices of the people laughing and squealing.

"Let's take a look around," said Rooster.

"I don't want to," said Laurie, but she was looking out of the corner of her eye and trying not to show any interest.

"I'm sorry about the bull fight, honey. Honest. I didn't know it was going to be like that. Let's not let it spoil everything. Let's get out and have some fun. C'mon, it's our honeymoon."

Laurie didn't want to give in too easily, but she didn't want to just go back to the room either.

"Oh, okay," she said reluctantly.

They parked and got out and walked up to the admission gate. It was cooling off and turning into another pleasant fall evening. The moon was high up in the sky, and everything was glowing in the moonlight and the colored lights of the carnival rides. As they strolled along the midway, little children scampered back and forth and under their feet, giggling and squealing as they went. It was hard to be sad around happy children, and soon Laurie's mood lightened, and she let

Rooster take her hand as they walked about. The barkers kept calling out to Rooster, noticeable as he was because of his height. He spotted one that had a particularly impressive collection of teddy bears, so he went up and put his money on the counter. It was a baseball toss game, and the object was to knock down a row of Coke bottles. The man set three balls up on the counter and stepped out of the way. Rooster took the first one in his hand and stepped back. He rubbed the ball around in his hands and then took a pitcher's stance. He wound up and—Pow! He knocked the first bottle down. The carnie let out a whistle. Rooster took the next ball and repeated the ball rubbing and stance and—Pow! He knocked the second ball down. The carnie was clearly impressed as were a few onlookers. Then, he took the third ball, rubbed it in his hands, took the stance and—Pow! Down went the third ball. The onlookers burst into cheers and claps. The carnie shook his head and told Rooster to take his pick of prizes.

"Which one do you want?" he asked Laurie.

Laurie looked over the teddy bears and pointed at a pink one.

The carnie gave Rooster his prize, and he gave it to Laurie.

As they walked away, Laurie could barely contain her excitement.

"Rooster, that was amazing! How did you do that?"

Now, it was Rooster who became melancholy.

"I was always a good pitcher. I could have probably played for the pros, but my daddy wouldn't let me."

"But why?"

"Games are the playground of the devil," Rooster sighed. "At least, that's what Daddy said."

"Aww," Laurie said gently. "I'm sorry."

"Nothing to be sorry about. If I had taken that path, I might not be here with you now. Ain't no game worth losing you. Maybe the old man knew what he was talking about after all."

Laurie stopped and pulled Rooster down to her and kissed him gently on the lips.

"Thank you, Rooster. You're my hero, and you always will be."

The next day, they went back over to Mexico one more time. They went to some shops that had been closed the day before, bought a few things, and then decided to pack up and head down to the coast. They went to Corpus Christi and rented a little beach front cottage and spent the days lounging on the beach and the nights rocking the headboard against the wall. When it was finally all over and time to go home, they packed up the car and began the long drive back to Merky, back to the new life they were starting together.

16

It was a long drive back from the coast, and they were both happy to finally be nearing good, old Merky. They rounded the last curve and then went over the final hill that would take them into town. It was late in the afternoon, and they were both weary and ready to get to Rooster's little house where they would be making their home, for the time being at least. As they passed the city limits sign and entered town, they spotted a newly erected billboard. In large red letters, it said:

ROOSTER BROWN FOR SHERIFF

Courage – Integrity – Honesty – Fairness

There was, of course, an illustration of an actual rooster in the background as well as a pistol, a cowboy hat, and a badge. Rooster and Laurie drove slowly past the sign, gawking as they went, yet neither of them saying a word. They drove on into downtown and around the square and saw smaller versions of the billboard and red, white, and blue posters in shop windows all around. Mel and his crew had been busy while they were gone. With the election barely a month away, they were mounting a final push to seal the deal. It looked oddly festive, and as tired as they were, they couldn't help but feel energized by it all. They drove around the square once, taking it all in before going to the little house. They pulled up under the trees and got out of the car and stretched. Rooster just wanted to take in their bags and flop on the bed and rest for a while. They hadn't even made it up to the porch yet when Mel's Cadillac turned into the driveway and sped up to the house. Mel hopped out of the car, obviously happy to see them both.

"Howdy, young love birds!" he shouted at them.

"Hi, Daddy," Laurie said as she went up to him and kissed him on the cheek.

"Evening, Mel," said Rooster as he shook his hand.

"I'm glad to see you made it back all right. Shirley will be mighty pleased to hear that you're home."

"We just got home, Daddy, and we're really tired," said Laurie, hoping Mel would get the hint.

"All right, all right, I understand. I'll leave you be," Mel chuckled. "I'll see you tomorrow at the station, Rooster. We got lots to talk about."

"Okay, Mel. I'll see you tomorrow."

And with that, Mel got in his car and left. Rooster carried the bags in, and once they had unpacked and settled in, they took off their shoes and lay on the bed together.

"I wonder what Daddy wanted?" said Laurie.

"I'm sure it's probably about the election," said Rooster. "I think he's more excited about it than I am."

"Do you really want to be sheriff?" asked Laurie.

Rooster hesitated briefly before responding. "Yes, yes, I do. I didn't at first, but after I thought about it, I think it's a good idea. I've got a wife now, and we'll have kids, so I need to make a good living."

Laurie said nothing.

"What do you think? Wouldn't you rather be married to the sheriff than to the Texaco man?"

"I don't care what you do. I just don't want you to get hurt. Being a lawman can be dangerous."

"So can being a grease monkey. There's plenty of ways to get hurt. Ain't nothing guaranteed safe."

"I know, but grease monkeys don't usually get shot."

"Most lawmen don't get shot either, unless they come across somebody like my granddaddy."

"That's what worries me."

"No point in worrying about it. There's no backing out now."

They both became quiet and were soon dozing softly as the room grew dark as the day ended.

When the alarm went off the next morning, they were both sound asleep. Rooster usually awoke before the alarm, but after a week of sleeping as late as he wanted, and being tired from the trip, he slept later than usual. Neither of them were ready to get up, and they snuggled together under the sheets, enjoying the warmth and softness of each other's bodies. Soon, Rooster had a hard-on and, before long they were making love. After he finished, they rolled apart and lay on top of the bed, trying to cool off. Rooster got up to pee and then went into the kitchen to put on a pot of coffee. Before the coffee was finished brewing, Laurie came in and began making breakfast. This was a new luxury for Rooster who was used to doing it himself. Laurie got busy and quickly made a heaping breakfast of eggs, bacon, sausage and even a stack of pancakes, a treat that Rooster was unaccustomed to. He wolfed it down and swallowed his last drop of coffee.

"Damn, woman, that was good."

"I'm sure it would be just as good without the damn."

"I'm sorry. I'll try to watch my language from now on."

"You should, especially if you're going to be a public figure. People will be paying attention to what you say."

She paused a bit, then added softly, "And you should probably stop saying 'ain't' and try to use proper English more."

Rooster flushed, but he just nodded his head and grunted. He realized that she was right and that he did in fact need to be very careful about what he said and did these last few weeks before the election. His own father had often admonished him for his sloppy speech. Being a preacher, he had an intuitive sense of the importance of words, and how they represented you to others. However, Rooster also knew that a bit of well-placed slang could work to one's advantage too, so he made a mental note to monitor what he said and how he said it. Now that the wedding and honeymoon were over, he needed to direct his energy on winning this thing and making Mel and everybody else happy and assuming a new role for himself. He went into the bathroom and cleaned up before changing into his uniform and heading out to work.

"What are you going to do today?" he asked Laurie on his way out the door.

"Oh, there's plenty to do around here. I need to make this place a home for the both of us now."

Rooster put his arm around Laurie's neck and drew her close to him, kissing her and snuggling his nose on her neck and ear, and then he was off to work for the first time ever as a married man.

When he got there, he was surprised to see a crowd of a dozen or more people milling about the driveway of the station. The full crew was there, Harvey, Kermit, and Obie, as well as Mel and Arlen, who was carrying a camera, and various other people, mostly members of the Posse but some others as well.

When they saw him pull into the station, they all let out a cheer. Rooster stared at them as he rolled past, not sure what to think. He parked off to the side and hopped out of his truck. As he came around the corner, they all let out a cheer again.

"Wha...what's going on?" he asked, sounding a bit confused.

"Just a little welcome home celebration for you, Rooster," said Mel.

As the crowd gathered around Rooster, Arlen stepped off to the side and began snapping photos.

"What the hell?" said Rooster.

Arlen took a few more photos then slung the camera strap across his shoulder and took out a notepad and pencil.

"Rooster, how was your honeymoon?" Arlen asked.

"Wh...why it was fine."

"It...was...fine," Arlen muttered as he jotted down his notes.

Rooster looked around at the crowd surrounding him. He spotted old Mr. Hedgepeth's tobacco stained grin and many of the other regulars.

"Rooster, the campaign for sheriff is in its final stages now. Do you have anything you would like to say to the people of Merky?" asked Arlen, pencil at the ready.

"Buh...uh...huh?" Rooster stammered.

Mel jumped in. "Rooster will have an official statement for the press soon, but for now he is just focused on running the station and doing a good job as always."

Arlen scribbled furiously while everybody cheered.

Just then, a police car drove slowly by, then turned around and pulled into the station. Rooster saw, much to his dismay, that is was none other than Bill Hickey.

"Oh, crap," he said under his breath.

Hickey pulled into the driveway, forcing everyone to step aside. He parked the car and got out, carefully studying the crowd.

"Well, well," he said, "what do we have here?"

"What we have here is a hero's welcome," said Mel, "which you obviously wouldn't know anything about."

"Well, I reckon I might know more than you think," snorted Sheriff Hickey. "For example, I might know how to run a police department, and I might know about the law, and I might actually know just how to do this job."

"Yeah, you might, and you might not," snapped Mel.

Arlen stuffed his pad and pencil back in his pocket and began snapping photos of the sheriff and Mel squaring off.

"Hey! What the hell do you think you're doing?" Sheriff Hickey shouted at Arlen.

"Reporting the news, sheriff. Reporting the news."

"What damn news? A bunch of fools standing around at a gas station?"

"You see anything else more interesting going on right now?" retorted Arlen.

"Okay, Mr. William Randolph Hearst, if you want some news, here's some news for you. I challenge this fool to a debate."

"Say what?" shouted somebody from the crowd.

"I challenge Rooster Brown to a debate on the courthouse steps. If y'all think he's so smart let him prove it. The citizens of this town ought to know what kind of person they're voting for. Report that, Mr. Newsman, and if you don't, I'll make sure everybody knows about it anyway."

"We accept your challenge, Mr. Daniel Webster! Rooster's not scared of you or anybody else!" shouted Mel.

"Uh...Mel..." Rooster muttered, but nobody seemed to be paying attention to him now.

Suddenly everyone was oblivious to Rooster as Mel and Bill Hickey set about deciding the date and time of the debate. Rooster slowly slipped away from the crowd and eased into the office. He sat down at the desk and put his head in his hands. He had just wanted to come to work and get back into his routine after his honeymoon, but it was apparent that nothing would be routine until Election Day.

The ruckus continued outside for several more minutes before Sheriff Hickey left and Mel came rushing into the office, red-faced and out of breath.

"Two weeks! The debate is in going to be in two weeks!" he shouted at Rooster.

Rooster sat there in disbelief.

"Mel, are you out of your mind!?" I don't know nothing about no debates. I don't know nothing about nothing!" Rooster shouted back at Mel.

"There's nothing to it. You just get up there and flap your gums like you know what you're talking about."

"Easy for you to say! It ain't gonna be you looking like a fool!"

Rooster dropped his head back into his hands and rocked side-to-side moaning loudly.

Mel turned around and saw the crowd outside looking in at them and he realized he had to get things under control quickly.

"Look here, Rooster. Just sit up and act like everything's all right. Don't let them see you like this. Serious, boy, sit up now," Mel said firmly.

Rooster sat up and upon seeing the crowd looking in at them, grew agitated again.

"Goddamn it, Mel! Don't be doing me this way. You don't know what you just got us into."

"I didn't do it. It was that asshole Hickey. He's the one that started this shit. We didn't have any choice but what to accept. If we had turned him down it would have made you look chicken shit."

"I am chicken shit, damn it. I ain't no hero. I ain't never been no hero. I just happened to be at the truck stop when all the bullshit went down, and that's all damn it."

"Okay, all right. Just calm down. That's all you got to do for now is just calm down. Don't you worry, son. Ol' Mel ain't done you wrong yet, has he?"

Rooster winced. "Well...no...I guess not," he sighed.

Mel smiled. "That's right, damn it, and I'm not going to do you wrong this time either. Listen, we got a full crew here today, there's no need for you to stay. Just go on home and try to calm down. I'll go get a hold of Addis, and me and him will figure out what to do."

That suited Rooster just fine. He was in no mood to talk to anybody right now. He sat there for a couple of minutes working up the nerve to get up and walk past the crowd that was still outside while Mel went out and spun another yarn for them.

When Rooster finally was ready, he stood and opened the door and stepped outside. As the door swung open, he could hear Mel speaking.

"...and because of his heroics over in Korea, sometimes Rooster gets a mite worked up around crowds and excitement. It happens to a lot of vets, and it's just the price they pay for fighting our wars for us."

The crowd applauded politely when Rooster came out, now aware of his condition and apparently not wishing to upset the delicate balance of his heroic psyche.

Mel waved at him. "I'll see you in a bit, Rooster."

238

Rooster mustered a smile and waved to the crowd as he walked past. He got into his truck, gunned the motor and peeled out in the dirt behind the station, leaving behind a cloud of dust.

When he got home, Laurie was busily cleaning and rearranging things. She looked up at him in surprise when he walked through the front door.

"Rooster...what on earth?"

"Mel sent me home because I'm going to have to debate that SOB Hickey, and now I'm some kind of crazy war hero to boot."

"What...what are you talking about, Rooster?"

Rooster plopped down on the sofa and tried to compose himself. Once he calmed down, he related the story of the crowd waiting for him, Sheriff Hickey showing up unexpectedly, and that he was now supposed to debate him on the courthouse steps two weeks from now.

Laurie listened quietly throughout the whole story, and when Rooster was finished telling it, he sat glumly on the sofa. Laurie said nothing at first, but soon she began to snicker. She tried to hold it back, but she was unable, and soon she was laughing hysterically while Rooster watched in frustration, his aggravation growing with each second.

"Goddamn it, woman! This ain't funny. I ain't never got up and spoke in front of people, and now I'm supposed to debate that son of a bitch in front of the whole town."

"I'm sorry, Rooster," Laurie said, trying to stop laughing. She almost had it under control when she got another fit of the giggles, and she buried her face in her hands and tried unsuccessfully to stop.

Rooster snorted in disgust, and got up and stomped out of the house. He got back in his truck and peeled out, leaving yet another cloud of dust in his wake. He screeched his tires on the main road, stomped on the gas pedal and shot down one street after another, turning here and there until he reached the highway, and then he floored it, sailing out past the city limits. He was going nowhere in particular when he spotted the turn off to Bug Town, and he hit the brakes, screeching into a turn and headed down the bumpy road. He roared through the sleepy settlement, which fortunately was mostly deserted, and zoomed on to Cletus's homestead. He fishtailed through the gate, spinning his tires all the way up the two-track road to Cletus' shack, and slammed on the brakes, sliding to a halt in a spray of gravel, sending chickens and pigs scattering. He had barely stopped when Cletus came charging out the door of his shack in his underwear and bearing his rusty old shotgun.

Cletus raised the shotgun and pointed it at the truck. Rooster thrust his hands out the window and shouted, "Cletus! It's Rooster Brown! Don't shoot!"

Cletus was still half-asleep and scared out of his wits. He pulled the hammer back on the ancient firearm.

"Cletus, don't shoot! It's me, Rooster!"

Cletus lowered the gun slowly and stepped around to the side to get a better look. When he finally realized who it was, he lowered the gun and shook his head.

"Damn, son! Don't ever come barreling in here like that again. Next time, you might not be so lucky. I was a hair from blowing your head off."

"I'm sorry, Cletus, I won't do it again. I was just pissed off, and I didn't even know I was coming here until I turned in the gate."

"It's mighty damn early to be carrying on like that. What the hell could get a man that riled up this time of day?"

"It's a long story. You got anything to drink?"

"I always got something to drink, but first I got to shake the shit out of my drawers. Man, you done scared the hell out of us."

Alice poked her head out of the shack. "What that crazy bastard doing?"

"I'm sorry. I didn't mean nothing. It won't happen again, I promise."

Rooster eased out of the truck and sheepishly walked up to the sitting area under the trees.

"I was just mad as hell and acting stupid. I didn't mean nothing."

"Damn loco gringo," Alice muttered.

Rooster sat down in one of the chairs as Cletus and Alice rummaged around getting dressed. Cletus came outside in a pair of ratty pants held up by suspenders and an old undershirt. He was barefoot and treading lightly although his feet were dirty and heavily calloused. Alice came out in an old frock and went over to the other shack where they kept an old wood burning stove. She stirred the embers, put on some kindling and soon had a fire going. Then she took some coffee from a tin can, put it into a blackened pot and put that over the fire. Soon, the smoke from the campfire and the aroma of the coffee wafted through the air as the sun rose up higher in the sky.

"I don't get too many customers this time of day and in that big a hurry to boot. I reckon a feller might wonder what the ruckus is all about," said Cletus.

Rooster let out a big sigh. "I guess things is just getting too crazy for me, Cletus. I barely been in this town six months, and already I killed two men, been put in jail, been declared a hero, got made manager of a gas station, married a rich man's daughter, and now I'm running for sheriff."

Cletus, who was lighting his pipe with a burning stick, choked a bit, and then laughed.

"I reckon that is a lot for a feller to take on in that short a time. Hell, that's more than most folks can put in their obituaries, and you're a young 'un to boot."

"If things don't slow down, I reckon somebody might be writing my obituary soon."

"Well, let's hope not. We done got used to all the excitement you brought with you. If'n you weren't around no more I 'spect everybody would get a mite bored."

"Shit, I don't mind doing my part, but it's somebody else's turn to provide the entertainment around here."

Alice brought them each a tin cup of steaming coffee, which they sipped under the trees. No one said anything; instead, they just sat listening to the birds singing and the cattle mooing off in the distance.

"Well, what can I do for you this morning?" Cletus finally asked.

"What kind of whiskey do you have?"

"Just some home brew, but it'll kick like a mule."

"I'll take a bottle."

Cletus motioned to Alice who got up and went off to another smaller shack that Rooster hadn't noticed before and brought back a fruit jar of brownish liquid. She handed it to Cletus, who unscrewed the top and took a sniff.

"Whew! Yes, sir, this ought to do the trick," he said as he handed the jar to Rooster.

Rooster took the jar and sniffed it. He turned his head away, his nostrils burning.

"You got a beer to wash it down with?"

Alice got up again and returned with a warm bottle of beer. Rooster took the beer in one hand and the home brew in the other. He braced himself and then lifted the home brew to his mouth and tilted it back. He took as large a swallow as he could stand and then gagged. He quickly drank half the beer and then got up and walked away a few steps, feeling as if he were going to vomit. When the nausea passed, he sat back down and took another sip of the beer. As he sat there talking to Cletus, he began to feel a warm glow as the home brew did its work. He felt better, more relaxed and less worried than he had been just a few minutes ago. Soon, he worked up the courage to take another shot, this time taking down two large gulps before the gag reflex kicked in. He finished the beer and sat there as the warm glow began to envelope his body.

"You might want to hold back a bit there, Rooster. That stuff has a way of sneaking up and kicking the shit out of you."

"Thas okay," said Rooster, slightly slurring his words, "I'll juss have another beer."

Alice brought him a beer, and he was now starting to feel more than just warm, he was feeling lit up. In spite of Cletus's warning, he took another slug of the home brew, and by the time he finished the second beer he realized he was getting very drunk.

"Okay, no more," he said as he fought to sit steady in the chair. "Damn! Thas good shit."

Cletus quietly picked up the fruit jar and handed it to Alice, who carried it away.

"Thas really goot shit, Cletus...'preciate it. Gis I'm ready to run for goddamn sheriff now," Rooster laughed.

"I reckon you might want to wait a bit before you go out and start campaigning, but it does loosen up the nerves some," chuckled Cletus.

"Damn shure does."

"Next time, just try not to scare the hell out of us when you come by."

"Hah! Okay, Cletus. I'll be careful neks time. I'll be rel shmoove coming in."

"Well, all right then."

"Hah! You wanna hear sumpin funny?" Rooster slurred as he struggled to keep from falling off the chair.

"What's that, Rooster?"

"Yoo know that night I sh..shot them boys?"

"I reckon everybody knows about that."

"Hah! Thas wha you think. I was up ther gonna shoot that bitch Jeanine. Thas what I was relly gone do. I was gone shoot that bitch for fuckin' with me. She fucked wif me and I was gone fukn kill her fukn ass."

Cletus and Alice looked at each other and said nothing. Rooster was wobbling all over his chair, almost falling off of it. His eyes were deep red and looked like little buttons.

"I wash gone kill that fukn bitch and killed those fukn bastards insted," Rooster said as he finally leaned too far over and fell off the chair and onto the ground. He tried to sit up and speak, pointing his finger at Cletus before he closed his eyes and blacked out.

17

When he finally opened his eyes again, it was warmer, and he was lying in the sun, glistening in sweat and covered with dirt. The first thing he saw was Mel and Addis, sitting in two chairs, looking down at him. He moaned softly and closed his eyes. He was confused, not sure where he was, or even who he was, but then it started coming back to him. He remembered talking to Cletus and Mexican Alice and getting thoroughly drunk. He had a blurry memory of the world spinning by as he fell from the chair and of looking up at Cletus before everything went black.

He then remembered something that troubled him, something that he wasn't sure really happened, or if he'd just imagined it. He remembered talking about that night, something he never did with anyone, not even Harvey or Mel. He began to worry, thinking that he might have said something, but he wasn't sure. It was something that always lurked just beneath the surface and he often worried that he would say something in a moment of carelessness.

He turned his head the other way and opened his eyes again, this time seeing Cletus grinning down at him. He closed his eyes again and smacked his lips, which were parched with thirst.

"You all right there, Rooster?" Cletus cackled.

"Uhh..." was all Rooster could muster.

Suddenly, he was jolted by cold water being splashed in his face. He looked up again to see Mel standing over him, holding a tin cup. Mel was not smiling.

"Get up, Rooster," he said flatly.

Rooster groaned and sat up, rubbing his forehead with his eyes closed.

"Got any coffee?" Mel asked Cletus.

Cletus snapped his fingers. "Alice. Café."

"I need some water," Rooster said softly, "to drink."

Mel went to the water jug, filled the tin cup again, and handed it to Rooster. He took it with both hands and downed it in two swallows, then let the empty cup fall to the ground.

"Shit," he said.

"Yeah," said Mel.

Alice brought him a cup of coffee, and he blew on it and then took a sip. It was hot, but he took as much as he could, blowing on it between sips. Mel brought him another cup of water, and before long, he was feeling well enough to stand up. He had little to say, somehow knowing that verbalizing anything would invite a tongue-lashing. He looked at Mel who was still not smiling but whose visage had softened somewhat.

"I'm sorry, Mel," he finally muttered.

Mel didn't respond right away, but when he did speak, his words were measured.

"I was pretty pissed off when I saw you there like that, Rooster. Not how anybody wants to see their son-in-law. Not how anybody wants to see their sheriff. But I had time to think, and I realized that you've been hit with a lot in a short amount of time, a whole lot, and a man's got a right to get tore up every now and then. You might as well just go on home and rest up because tomorrow you're going to get a schooling in matters of the law, and you are going to learn how to speak. You're going to be ready for this debate, you're going to win this election, and that's that. You don't have to worry about going to work tomorrow, or maybe even the rest of the week. Now go on home and be ready tomorrow morning because me and Addis will be coming to get you bright and early."

Mel and Addis got into Mel's Cadillac and drove away. Rooster watched as they slowly bounced along the two-track road. He turned to look at Cletus and Alice, he wasn't about to ask them what he'd said while he was drunk. If it had happened, it was best to pretend it hadn't. He would go on home and try to sober up and clear his head, and then he would think about how to handle things. He quietly said thanks and goodbye to Cletus and Alice and left.

Cletus and Alice watched as he slowly drove down the gentle slope to the gate.

"You reelly think he was gone kill that woman?" asked Alice.

Cletus stroked his chin thoughtfully. "I reckon maybe so, but it's hard to say for sure. You can't convict a man on account of what he says when he's drunk. Either way, that fella's probably gonna be our next sheriff, so it's best to just leave it be."

Rooster had the windows down on his truck and was feeling somewhat revived by the wind blowing on him. The sweat had dried on his arms so that he could just brush the dry dirt away with his hands. He didn't know exactly what time it was but judged it to be around noon time. He wasn't looking forward to facing Laurie, but he had little choice, he had to go home eventually. He drove past the station and turned to look at the crew waiting on customers. He turned down the street and into the long drive to the little house. He pulled up under the trees and shut off the engine. He inhaled deeply and let it out, then opened the door and got out of the truck. He stepped up onto the porch, opened the door, and saw Laurie sitting on the sofa.

"Where did you go?" she asked curtly.

Rooster paused, "I wound up at Cletus Gross' place."

"Rooster!"

"I didn't mean to. I mean, I didn't plan it that way. I just took off, and the next thing I knew, I was there."

"You've been drinking."

"I didn't drink much."

"You're filthy...and you stink."

Rooster looked down at his uniform which was covered in dirt.

"I'm sorry."

Laurie said nothing for a few seconds and then finally, "Go clean up, and I'll start dinner."

Rooster went to the bathroom and filled the tub with water. He climbed in the steaming bath and eased down until only his knees and head were above water. He splashed water on his face and began scrubbing with soap. He scrubbed himself until his skin was red, and then he lathered up his hair and dipped his head underneath the water. When he finally felt clean, the water was getting cold, so he got out and dried off. He wrapped the towel around himself and padded into the bedroom where he got out some clean clothes and got dressed. He lingered for a while in the bedroom as he listened to Laurie cooking in the kitchen. When he finally felt ready to talk again, he braced himself and went into the kitchen.

Laurie was setting the table. She said nothing when Rooster came in.

"I'm sorry, Laurie. I had no intention of going out there and getting drunk. I just wanted to go to work today, and instead I got interviewed and photographed and talked into a damn debate and all before seven o'clock in the morning. This stuff is just happening too fast for me, I get used to one thing and then something else comes up."

"I know it's a lot, Rooster. I do. I'm sorry too that we can't just settle in and get used to being a married couple, but going out to see that awful Cletus Gross and getting drunk before noon is not going to help any."

"I didn't mean to do that, and I won't do it again."

"Okay. Let's just eat and forget about it."

They said little during their meal, and after they were finished, Rooster helped Laurie clean up and wash the dishes. Then he went into the bedroom and lay down and soon he was sleeping. When he woke up later, it was mid afternoon. He got up and drowsily went into the kitchen and put on a pot of coffee. Laurie was nowhere around. When his coffee was ready, he poured himself a cup and sat at the kitchen table staring into space. As he began to wake up, he opened the back door and sat where he could watch the squirrels chasing each other among the treetops. Soon he heard Laurie's car pull up and she came in carrying a bag of groceries. He helped her carry in the rest and they put everything away. When they were finished, Laurie suggested they go for a walk downtown. That sounded good to Rooster who was now awake and ready to get out and enjoy a little fresh air.

Even though the house was only a few blocks from downtown, he rarely ever walked there, opting to take a vehicle instead. It was a nice day, still warm but the blazing heat of summer had passed. They took a leisurely pace, holding hands and enjoying the simple pleasure of spare time, especially now that the frenzy leading up to the wedding was over. They passed by shop windows, pausing to peer inside and imagine that they could buy the goods on display.

A funny thing began to happen as they wound their way around town. Time after time, someone stopped to talk to them, congratulating them on their new life together and offering their support in the upcoming election. Virtually everywhere they went, someone came up and spoke to them. Soon it became obvious to Rooster that there was a groundswell of support for him. It touched him tremendously, and at times he had to fight the urge to tear up. He realized that he must give his all to win this election or else he would let down not just himself or Mel, but many good people in the community who had now come to see him as one of their leaders. It also made him nervous to think about debating Bill Hickey in public, so he tried not to worry about it. Mel was taking care of everything and already had a plan in place to deal with this. Rooster knew that, once again, Mel would help him when he needed it the most. He realized how very lucky he was.

By the time they walked around the square, they had spoken to numerous people, and it had taken them over an hour to make the short walk. They went home and cooked supper together, and much to Laurie's surprise and delight, she discovered that Rooster was very handy in the kitchen. That night, they sat out on the porch in the dark, listening to the sounds of children playing and dogs barking and other such mundane sounds that comprise the background noise of small towns. They went to bed early so that Rooster could rise at his usual time and be ready when Mel came to get him. Rooster made love to Laurie that night in an especially passionate and physical bought of sex that surprised both of them. Laurie sensed that he was trying to penetrate beyond simple coitus and that she might soon be with child. As they lay there in the dark she rubbed her belly while listening to Rooster's gentle snoring.

Early the next morning, they were awakened by a knock on their front door.

"Who on earth could that be?" whispered Laurie.

"I don't know," replied Rooster. The knock came again, this time louder.

"Who's there?!" shouted Rooster.

"It's Mel!" came the reply.

"What the hell...?" mumbled Rooster.

"Daddy is everything all right?!" Laurie cried out.

"Yes, everything is fine."

Rooster put on his pants and went to the door to let him in.

"I'm sorry to wake you up, but I wanted to take y'all to breakfast this morning, and I wanted to catch you before you ate," said Mel as he stepped inside.

"Well...uh...okay, Mel. Give us a minute to get dressed," said Rooster sleepily.

"Oh, it's not that big of a hurry. I'm going to go back home and get Shirley. We'll come pick you up in about half an hour."

"In a half hour...okay."

Mel left and Rooster stumbled groggily back to the bedroom.

"Did I just hear Daddy say he wants to take us to breakfast?" Laurie asked, still squinting against the bedroom light.

"Yeah, he'll be back in a half hour with your mother."

Laurie flopped back onto the bed. "Oh, good grief. Why can't I just have a normal family?"

"It's better than no family, trust me."

They got up and washed their faces, brushed their teeth and gargled, and got dressed and then sat down and waited for Mel to come back. They waited several minutes before they heard his car pulling up the driveway. They went outside to meet them and got in the back of the car.

"Children, I'm so sorry that your father has no sense," said Shirley, sounding irritated.

"I may not have any cents, but I've got plenty of dollars," retorted Mel.

They arrived at the truck stop before the morning rush, and sat in a corner booth. As Rooster sipped his coffee, he began to wake up more.

"So, Mel, what's the big deal about taking us out to breakfast this morning anyway?" he asked.

"I've been thinking, and I wanted to talk to you and do some strategizing."

"Strategizing? About what?"

"What the hell you think, fool? The election, of course."

"What's there to strategize about?"

"Well, first thing, Addis is going to be working with you the next couple of days. He's going to teach you a little about the law, but mostly just about how to bullshit people. That's real important for this damn debate."

"Daddy!" Laurie fussed at Mel for cursing so early in the morning.

Mel ignored her and continued, "I'm putting you on paid vacation till the election, and I want you to use every day to get out and campaign."

"Campaign?" Rooster groaned. "Why? Everybody I talked to says they're going to vote for me anyway."

"Well, of course they're going to tell you that. You expect them to tell you that they're not going to vote for you?"

"Well...I don't know."

"People change their minds for all kind of reasons, Rooster. Once it gets close to Election Day, they might decide that it's best to go with the man that's already in office. I don't know if that will happen, but we can't take that chance. We've only got one good shot at this thing, and we've got to make it count. We've got to make it look like you're serious and that you are up for the job."

Rooster hung his head and groaned.

"Also, you need to look the part, so we're going to get you some new clothes, a new pair of boots, and a new cowboy hat. Listen, son, quit your fretting, it's going to be fine. Just let ol' Mel take care of the details. You show up and do what I say, and everything will be okay."

Mel talked excitedly through breakfast while the rest of them ate mostly in silence. After they finished eating, Mel took Rooster and Laurie home and told them he would be back soon. Rooster went straight to the bedroom and curled up in a ball on the bed. Laurie came in and sat next to him, stroking his hair.

"I'm sorry, honey. I never guessed that it would turn out like this," she said softly, "but don't worry. Daddy is a smart man. He's not going to do anything he doesn't think is best."

Rooster said nothing. He felt like sucking his thumb, but he didn't think that was a good thing for a possible future sheriff to do. He kept his eyes closed and tried to suppress the panic that was starting to well up inside him. Laurie curled up beside him, spooning around him and laying her arm across his chest.

"I love you, Rooster Brown," she whispered.

Rooster mumbled a puny, "I love you too," and squinched up even smaller.

Laurie got up and started puttering around the house, and before Rooster knew it, he was asleep. He had a strange dream, about a white horse and a man in black, a gun was fired, and the next thing he knew, Laurie was shaking him awake.

"Honey, wake up. Daddy's here," she said softly.

Rooster sat up and rubbed his forehead before heading out the door and getting into Mel's car. Mel took him to Addis' office and dropped him off at the curb.

"Now don't worry, Rooster, just listen to Addis. He's probably the smartest fellow in the county. I'll be back later to check in and see how things are going."

Mel drove off, leaving Rooster standing in front of an office building along the main square of Merky. The plate glass window in front was painted in gold letters, it said:

ADDIS THIGPEN ATTORNEY AT LAW

Rooster stood out front, dreading going inside. He liked Addis, but also felt intimidated by him. He had never done that well in school and the notion of a crash course in law made his stomach hurt. Mostly, he was still overwhelmed by the thought of standing in front of the whole god-damn town to debate a seasoned lawman in less than two weeks. He felt like vomiting right there in front of the honorable Addis Thigpen's law office. Instead, he took a deep breath, steeled himself, and walked inside the door and up to the desk of Addis' secretary, Lacy Clark, who was busily typing away. She smiled pleasantly at Rooster.

"Good morning, Mr. Brown."

"Morning, Lacy. I'm here to see Addis."

"Go on in," she said, nodding to a large ornate door. "He's expecting you."

Rooster went to the door and knocked softly. He heard a muffled voice from inside.

"Come on in!"

He pushed the door open and stepped inside Addis' office. The first thing he noticed were the deep wood tones of the walls and the large antique desk that Addis was sitting behind. Addis' desk was covered with stacks of papers and books and the place had the look and feel of a college professor's den, not that Rooster had ever been to one, but it felt like what such a place must be like. Addis stood up and smiled at Rooster.

"Come on in, Rooster. Have a seat." He gestured to the chair opposite his desk.

"Morning, Addis. I'm sorry to be a burden for you," Rooster apologized.

"No, no, not at all. This is for the benefit of the whole community. We need a good man to be our sheriff, and I agree wholeheartedly with Mel that you are that man. Don't worry. We don't expect you to become versed in law in this short of time. We just want to teach you a few things about public speaking and, perhaps, memorize a few statutes that have particular relevance to our community."

Addis picked up a stack of papers and began thumbing through them.

"Rooster, in this community you will rarely have to deal with more than just a few key offenses, and for those few occasions when something else may come up, we have the Texas Reference of Statutes. The district attorney should be your primary legal resource, and of course, you are welcome to consult with me any time. The position of sheriff mostly entails keeping the general peace and maintaining a presence of authority, which you are more than adequately equipped to handle."

Rooster sat in the chair listening politely, but he was more interested in looking around at the rows of bookshelves and the diplomas hanging on the walls. Once again, he was starting to feel out of his league.

He noticed on one shelf an expensive looking camera and many framed photos that Addis had apparently taken himself.

"The most valuable thing we can impart to you, Rooster, is some basic debating skills, and foremost among those is the simple fact that it is not so much what you say, as how you say it. In everyday vernacular, we are going to teach you how to bullshit with the best of them."

Rooster was mildly shocked to hear Addis use such a coarse term, but it also calmed him a little bit. Addis was now speaking a language he understood.

Addis handed him a few sheets of typewritten paper. "These are the main laws I feel you should be concerned with. Don't worry about memorizing them verbatim. Just try to retain the basic intent of the law."

Rooster looked at the sheets of paper, and it was as if the letters were scrambling around on the pages like a colony of ants. He started to feel the old panic begin to well up. Addis, sensing this, tried to put him at ease.

"Just read that tonight when you get home. Again, don't try to memorize them word for word. We'll go over it tomorrow after you've had a little time to read them without distraction."

Addis sat on the corner of his desk and smiled as Rooster rustled through the sheets of paper.

"Rooster, have you ever gotten in an argument with anyone?" he asked.

"Yes, sir, many times."

"Did you ever win any of those arguments?"

"Yes, some of them."

"What do you think it was that helped you to win?"

Rooster paused and studied for a moment. "I don't know. I guess being right mostly."

"Did you ever believe something you thought was right, only to find out later it was not true."

"Yes, I suppose so."

"So it wasn't necessarily the fact that you were right or wrong, rather it was possibly that you thought you were right. Is that a fair assumption?"

"I...I guess." Rooster was becoming puzzled with the direction this was going.

"The point I'm trying to make here, Rooster, is that it isn't always how much you know, or think you know, but rather the belief you have in yourself. Personal conviction and confidence in one's self has carried the day for many a fool. It's practically a requirement to be a preacher."

Hearing mention of the word preacher, Rooster looked up intently at Addis.

"Your father was a preacher, wasn't he?"

"Yes."

"Did you ever see your father walk on water or raise the dead?"

"No."

"But he believed that it had been done or else he couldn't have gotten up in front of people and asked them to believe in it. Nobody that I know of has ever seen anyone walk on water, yet many believe it happened, and mostly because someone like your father was willing to get up in front of them and say with conviction that they believe it."

Rooster understood what Addis was trying to convey to him, but at that moment he was feeling low and not yet ready to make the leap that Addis was suggesting to him.

"Now, Rooster, I want you to get up and walk over to that lectern in the corner and tell me why you would make a good sheriff. Don't worry about anything, it's just you and me here."

Rooster got up and shuffled over to the lectern and stood behind it. He ran his hands along the edges of it and over the top, feeling the smoothness of the wood.

"Go ahead, Rooster. Just talk to me like we're having a regular conversation."

"Well...uh...I think I would make a good sheriff because...um...I ain't scared to fight...and um...I try to look out for folks and...uh...," Rooster struggled for the right words.

"Okay, that's not too bad for a start. The first thing we have to do is identify the qualities that make you the right candidate for this job," Addis said as he picked up a tablet of paper and a pencil.

"Let's start listing them right now," he said as he began scribbling on the paper.

"Number one: you're brave, and you have proven this already by stopping a robbery in progress," he said as he wrote furiously.

"Number two: you care about people and want to protect them from the misdeeds of others. You have become a member of this community which has been good to you and you want to repay them for their kindness," said Addis as continued to scribble rapidly.

"Number three: you're a veteran of war and have been tested in combat."

Rooster stood and watched dumbly as Addis continued to rattle off attributes he was only vaguely aware he possessed.

"Number four: you have common sense and know how to treat others. You know when to use force and when to use persuasion."

"Number five: you're a regular man of the people. You don't think you're better than others."

"Number six: you're smart and learn fast, as you've proven by running a gas station and managing employees."

Addis put the pen down. "Okay, we have a start. Now I want you to say in your own words what I just wrote down. You may look at my notes if you like."

Rooster took the pad and read over what Addis had written. He straightened himself up and looked intently at Addis.

"I'm not afraid of a fight. I've shown that already by stopping a robbery in progress. I care about this town, in fact I love it, and I want repay all the kindness that has been shown to me. I'm a combat veteran, and I fought in some of the fiercest battles in Korea."

Rooster could feel his confidence rising, and he continued, "I have common sense and I know how to treat people. I'm a regular person, and I won't think I'm any better than anyone else once I'm elected. I learn fast. I had never even worked at a gas station before, but when I was made manager I jumped in and worked hard and learned everything I needed to know and I have done a good job."

Addis jumped up from the desk, clapping his hands and clearly pleased.

"Rooster, that is amazing. I am impressed. I didn't expect you to improve so much that quickly. Do you realize how much better you sound just on your second try?"

"I...I...think so. It was better, huh?"

"It was much better, amazingly better."

Addis took the pad and pencil, and together they came up with a few more reasons why Rooster would make a good sheriff. Addis had Rooster give his statement two more times, and each time it was better than before. Addis was genuinely excited, and this in turn, increased Rooster's confidence.

After the second run-through, Mel came in and was delighted to see the two of them excited and confident. Addis had Rooster go through it again for Mel.

"Not bad, son, not bad," said Mel happily.

"He's made a lot of progress since his first attempt," said Addis.

"I'm feeling better about it, Mel," said Rooster with relief in his voice.

"It's almost lunch time, Rooster. Why don't you take off and meet me back here about 1:30, and we'll move on to something else."

"Okay, Addis, that sounds good," Rooster said. As he was about to walk out the door he paused, "Thank you, Addis. Thank you very much."

Neither Mel nor Addis said anything until Rooster left and they could hear his footsteps fading away.

"Well, what do you think? Be honest," asked Mel.

"I think he can do it. The first go round was pretty bad, but I wrote down some of his attributes for him and encouraged him, and the second time was a lot better. We need to get him a little bit versed in law and have him start speaking in front of other people, but I think he can do it. I think we can win this thing," replied Addis.

Mel grinned and nodded his head. "Good. That's what I like to hear."

When Rooster came back from lunch, he was surprised to see Addis, Mel, Shirley, and Kenneth all waiting for him.

"Uh, what's going on?" he asked cautiously.

"We want you to go through your routine again. This time, in front of a few people you know," replied Addis.

Rooster felt his pulse quicken and his face redden slightly.

"Uh...okay...I guess."

"There's nothing to be concerned about, Rooster. Everyone here is someone that you know and care about. This is what psychologists refer to as cognitive behavioral conditioning. In layman's terms, you will learn to feel at ease speaking in front of others simply by doing it, and we will gradually build you up to where you are completely at ease speaking in front of a large group of people."

"Large group of people..." Rooster mumbled to himself as his pulse quickened a bit more.

"You can do it, Rooster. We've got faith in you," said Shirley, smiling her pleasant smile.

Rooster was starting to feel panicked and ready to bolt for the door. Addis could see it on his face.

"But there's no hurry. Why don't you sit down and rest for a spell," Addis said in his most soothing, lawyerly voice. Rooster sat down and nervously rested his cowboy hat on his knee.

"What did you have for dinner?" asked Addis.

"Um, chicken fried steak and mashed potatoes."

"That Laurie, she's a fine cook," said Shirley proudly.

"She better be, with that bottomless pit to feed," said Kenneth, laughing.

"Where do you put it all, Rooster? In your boot? You could eat a horse and not show it," chuckled Mel.

They bantered about for several minutes until Rooster was relaxed and joking along with them. Addis, sensing that now was the time, nonchalantly handed Rooster the note pad and asked him to go through his speech just like before. Rooster stood up at the lectern and jumped right in and gave his little spiel like there was nothing to it, and they all clapped and cheered as if he had just given the greatest performance of Macbeth in the history of the world. Then they had him do it again, and then again, until he was not the least bit nervous. Addis decided that was enough of that for now and that it was time to move on to something else. At that point, everyone left, and he brought out the typewritten pages of laws, he handed it to Rooster and asked him to read them. Then he quizzed him, asking him to explain what each one meant in his own words. They did this a few times until Rooster seemed competent and then Addis called it a day.

"Okay, Rooster, come back tomorrow morning at the same time and we'll work on something else."

Rooster was relieved to be finished and decided to go to the station and finish out the day and clear his mind with a little good old-fashioned manual labor. When he got to the station, Harvey and Kermit were sitting on a couple of chairs under the canopy, enjoying a brief respite from the usual parade of customers.

"What the hell's this all about?" Rooster said jokingly. "I leave and the place goes to pot."

Kermit took it all in stride. "That's right, Rooster. I reckon this place will go out of business once you're elected sheriff."

Harvey, not sure if Rooster was joking or not, hopped up out of his chair. "We're just taking a break between customers. We've been working plenty hard."

"Oh, hell, I know that, Harvey. Relax, I'm just teasing you."

"Oh, okay."

Rooster walked around the place, inspecting it like a drill sergeant. He had to admit that it looked pretty damn good. Everything was in its place and clean.

"Well, fellows, I got to hand it to you. It looks real good," he said.

"I told you we've been working real hard," said Harvey.

Just then, a customer pulled in. "Let me get this one," said Rooster, "before I get plumb out of practice."

Rooster filled up the tank, checked the air in the tires, and washed the windshield. He took the money and went inside to make change, which he took back out to the customer.

"I hear you're going to be debating the sheriff here soon," said the customer.

"Yes, sir, I reckon so."

"Well, I suspect you got most of the town rooting for you. Good luck, young man," said the customer as he pulled away.

Rooster went over and joined Kermit and Harvey under the canopy.

"Everybody in town is all excited about that debate," said Harvey.

"That so?" replied Rooster, who by now was feeling much better about the whole thing.

"Oh, yes. They want to see you beat the pants off Sheriff Hickey."

"I don't know about that, but I reckon I better put up a good showing."

"I guess you better. Lots of folks are saying that Sheriff Hickey can debate like hell."

Rooster frowned. "Who says that?"

"Mr. Hedgepeth said he could skin a cat with his tongue and spit out a fur coat."

"How does old man Hedgepeth know that?"

"I don't know," said Harvey. "He knows a lot of things."

Now Rooster was starting to feel the old panic beginning to well up again.

"Look, fellows, I got to go home. I'll see y'all later," said Rooster, and he got in his truck and left. Now, Rooster was angry, that damn Harvey would have to go and say something like that. He just wanted to get the hell away from everybody and not have to think about anything until tomorrow. He pulled into the driveway, and the first thing he saw was Mel's Cadillac sitting in front of the house. He cursed under his breath, and for a fleeting second, he considered turning around and leaving, but he figured they would see him, so he just kept on going. He parked next to Mel's car and got out. When he got to the front porch, he could hear them talking inside.

"Daddy, I'm getting tired of all this, we can't even enjoy just being married before we have all this other stuff thrown at us."

"Please, sugar pie, just a few more weeks, and it will all be over."

Rooster paused for a second, then opened the door and went in. Mel's face lit up at the sight of him.

"Rooster, we were just talking about you."

"I reckon that's why my ears were burning."

Mel laughed, "Oh, no, we weren't talking bad about you. Listen, they're having a pot luck social at the church tonight. Why don't you and Laurie come by and visit with everybody?"

Rooster looked at Laurie, who was frowning and clearly not interested.

"Uh, well, I guess I'll leave that up to Laurie."

"I've already made supper, Daddy."

Now it was Mel's turn to frown. "Look, the election is just around the corner. Hickey's not going to be just sitting around letting opportunities to mingle with the voters slip through his fingers."

"Is Hickey going to be there?" asked Rooster.

"He's going to be somewhere. You can count on that."

Rooster had, in fact, heard that Bill Hickey was alarmed by all of Mel's campaign activities and had been out pressing the flesh and running like he had some real competition.

"How about if we just take what you cooked for supper and go and visit with everybody for a while?" Rooster asked Laurie.

Laurie sighed, "Fine."

"Okay, Mel. We'll head up there soon as we change clothes."

"Attaboy," Mel said, slapping Rooster on the back. "If you want to win this, you got to work for it."

Mel got up to leave. "I'll see y'all up there shortly."

As soon as Mel left, Laurie snapped at Rooster. "You're getting to be just as bad as Daddy. You're letting this thing take over our lives."

"I didn't even want to do this in the first place," Rooster protested, "but now that we're in it, it would be stupid to just let Hickey win."

"I don't think all this campaigning is necessary for a little town like Merky. People are either going to vote for you, or they're not, and most of them have probably already made up their minds."

"That's what I thought too, but you can't take nothing for granted. From what I hear, Hickey is starting to get worried, and he's out trying to win votes. We done put too much into this already to let him come and take it away at the last minute. Besides, it'll all be over with soon enough, and then we can get back to normal."

"It won't ever be normal," Laurie cried out, her voice cracking. "You'll be going out in the middle of the night to pull people out of wrecked cars and arresting people and maybe even getting shot. I never cared if you were sheriff or not. I was happy just being with you. There's nothing wrong with pumping gas. Besides, you could have always found another job if you wanted something better. We didn't have to go through all this."

Rooster just stood there with his mind racing. At first, he didn't want to be sheriff either, but now he did. He had gotten to like all the attention, and he liked the idea of being somebody important, and he knew if he didn't take advantage of the situation that he found himself in, he would never have another chance like this again.

"Look, Laurie, I understand that this is a lot to be going through when we're just getting started, and I didn't plan it this way. But this is important, you might not mind being married to a grease monkey now, but in a few years you're bound to want more than what that could provide, especially if we have kids. I never in a million years ever imagined anything like this for myself, and I know that if I don't do it now I'll never have another chance at it. This all happened fast, real fast, so fast I can barely understand it all. If it hadn't been for that night at the truck stop, I probably would never have met you. Even if I had, I would have never had the nerve to ask you out, and Mel wouldn't have allowed it anyway. This thing just happened, and I'm glad it did or else I'd still be working out on that ranch and all alone. I don't know why all these things happened like this, but I know that this is a once in a lifetime opportunity for someone like me, and we have to make the best of it."

Laurie just sighed, and Rooster knew he had gotten through to her.

"Then let's get ready to go," she said resignedly.

They changed into nice clothes and loaded Laurie's supper into the back of her car. When they got to the church, they could see that the parking lot was full of cars.

"Oh, man, the whole congregation must be here tonight," said Rooster nervously.

"I'm sure Daddy had something to do with that," said Laurie peevishly.

Rooster turned to Laurie. "Please, just be nice to everybody."

"Rooster, I'm always nice," Laurie snapped.

"Okay, okay."

They took all that they could carry out of the car and walked to a side door that led to the room where the social was being held. As they got closer to the door, they could hear people talking and laughing. Rooster balanced a plate of chicken in one hand and pulled open the door with the other. When it swung open, the sound of people's voices enveloped them. They heard a woman's voice call out.

"Rooster, Laurie, over here!"

It was Shirley, waving to them from the other side of the room. They passed through the doorway, and suddenly everyone was calling their names, greeting them, and slapping Rooster on the back as he tried not to drop his plate of food. They made their way to a long table and set down their platters, and then they were swallowed up by the crowd, all of whom wanted to talk to them and wish them well. Rooster was unable to break away, so Laurie found Kenneth, and together they brought in the rest of the food. To Rooster, the rest of the evening seemed as if he had been swept away on a wave, and all he could do was try to stay afloat. Before he knew it, the evening was over and it was time to leave, and once again they had to run a gauntlet of hand shakers and well wishers on the way out the door, and by the time they got to the car they were overwhelmed and exhausted. They said nothing on the way home, and as soon as they got back Laurie went to the bedroom, changed into her nightgown and went to bed. Rooster was tired too, but also too wound up to go to sleep right away, so he sat up in the living room with his boots off and his feet up on the coffee table. As he sat there, he noticed for the first time, all the changes Laurie had made to their little home. It no longer looked like the barren den of a bachelor, but now it had a woman's touch. He looked around and noticed doilies and rugs that had not been there before, as well as a vase of flowers, a small oil painting, a cute lamp and throw pillows. He couldn't believe that he had not noticed these things before because they completely changed the look and feel of the place. He realized just how busy and stressed he had been. He suddenly felt ashamed of himself. Laurie had done all this work, and he hadn't even noticed or said anything about it. He was truly a loutish oaf and undeserving of the lovely young woman he was now married to. His eyes welled up with tears, and he shook his head in dismay. What a terrible way to treat his wife. When he finally began to get drowsy, he tiptoed into the bedroom and undressed. He snuggled up next to Laurie, who was sleeping quietly. He kissed her on the cheek, then lay next to her and went to sleep.

18

The next morning, Rooster went to the station and helped open. He waited on a few customers and then went to Addis' office around nine. He expected to go through another round of speechifying just like the day before; however, this was not the case. When he arrived, the first thing he noticed was that Addis was a little less jovial than he had been the day before. He wasn't rude, but he was not as warm as he had been yesterday.

"Okay, Rooster, today we're going to try something a little different. I'm going to ask you some questions that might come up in the debate."

Rooster nodded, "Oh, okay."

Addis had Rooster stand in front of the podium same as before, and he went and sat in a chair across the room. He sat there quietly for a moment, stroking his chin, studying Rooster who began to fidget behind the podium.

"You arrest a man for stealing cattle. What do you charge him with?"

Rooster froze.

"Well?"

"I...I don't know."

"Where are your notes?"

"Uh, back at the house."

"Bring them when you come back from lunch."

"Okay, I'm sorry."

"Say you get called out to a house because somebody's beating his wife. What do you do?"

Rooster fidgeted again. He was starting to feel flustered. He could feel himself turning red.

Addis softened his tone slightly. "Just think for a moment, Rooster. Don't worry about what the law says. What would you do?"

Rooster took a breath. "I would see how bad the woman was hurt first. If she was hurt bad, I would arrest the husband and take the woman to the doctor."

"Good. Now, what if the woman wasn't hurt, but it was just an argument that got out of hand?"

"I would tell them to settle down, or they would both be going to jail. If it looked like they could do that, then I would leave them be."

"That's good. See that isn't too hard, just common sense. That's ninety percent of being sheriff in a small town like this. Okay, let's say you catch old so-and-so driving around drunk, then what?"

"Depends on how drunk he is. If it looks like he can make it home all right, then I'll just tell him to go home, maybe follow him home if it ain't too far."

"What if he's so drunk he can't see straight?"

"Then, I'd probably drive him home myself."

"You wouldn't arrest him?"

"Not unless he was up to no good."

"All right. Good answer."

And so it went for the next couple of hours until it was getting close to lunch.

"All right, Rooster. That's enough for now. Go on home and get something to eat and bring back those notes I gave you."

"Okay, Addis," said Rooster, and he headed out, happy to be free for an hour or so.

As he stepped out onto the street, he noticed that his armpits were sweaty. A grain truck groaned slowly around the square and out to the main highway. It was a nice October morning, not too hot and not too cold, the sun shone brightly, and the air was crisp and fresh. The whole town somehow seemed young and new.

It was still a bit early for lunch, so he got into his truck and headed to the gas station. Harvey and Kermit were busily working, so he just went into the office and looked around. It seemed like everything was in order so he didn't linger long. It occurred to him that it would be strange if he no longer worked here, and he wondered who Mel would replace him with. He knew Harvey was not up to it, in spite of his amazing math skills. Kermit and Obie were old men, and they just wanted to work enough to help pay their basic expenses. Kenneth could do it, but he was always talking about joining the army or the navy or going to college or running off with the circus, so he didn't seem like a likely candidate either. Rooster figured that somebody around town would be looking for a job, and that would be Mel's problem, so he quit thinking about it and went on home.

He arrived home to find a piping hot chicken fried steak with potatoes and gravy sitting on the kitchen table. He wolfed it down vigorously, and when he was done, he leaned back in his chair picking his teeth. Laurie was running around the house in an old dress that fit her a little too tight, and Rooster was starting to get horny watching her bustle around the kitchen. He rubbed her ass, but she brushed him away. After the dishes were washed, Rooster went and stretched out on the bed, and soon he dozed off. Before he knew it, Laurie was shaking him.

"Rooster. Rooster. Wake up."

"Uh...I must have fell asleep."

"Obviously, you did. It's time to get up. You have to leave soon."

Rooster went into the bathroom and splashed water on his face. This time he remembered to take the notes before walking out the door. When he got to Addis' law office, he was once again greeted by the sight of a small audience waiting for him. As the day before, Addis put him through his paces, going over the same questions they had covered that morning. Rooster was less nervous this time, and he managed to get through it fairly well. Addis was obviously pleased with his performance.

"You're making good progress, Rooster. Come back tomorrow morning, same time, and we'll hit it again."

That is how it went for the rest of the week, and by Friday, Rooster was feeling more confident than he would have ever imagined. He felt he was ready for the debate, so he was surprised when Addis told him to come back again Monday.

"Damn, Addis, what else is there to go over?"

"Oh, you've got the basics down, there's no doubt about that, but we need to put the final touches on it. I want you to work on really memorizing those laws this weekend."

Rooster sighed, "Okay."

He left the law office and briefly thought about going by the station, but then decided it was time to move forward with his life. The crew had been managing just fine without him, something that both surprised and troubled him. The station had become such a big part of his life that it seemed strange that they could get along without him, but then it occurred to him that they had gotten along just fine before he showed up. He decided to kill a little time before going home and just drive around town for a spell. He made a few laps up and down the drag, and almost every car he passed waved at him. The whole town was plastered with campaign signs for both him and Bill Hickey. It was still strange to him to see his name on signs all over town, but it also filled him with immense pride and wonder at just how far his life had come. Less than a year ago, he was a drifter, staying in a bunkhouse with others like him, working hard for his meager living, and the loneliest he had ever been in his life. Now, he was married into one of the town's prominent families, with his name on everyone's lips. Before, he was like a ghost, invisible to everyone, now he was the center of attention. He was the happiest he had ever been, in spite of the stress and worry of the election. He knew that if he lost the election he would lose something that he would never regain, so he vowed to memorize the statutes that Addis had given him and more if possible. He felt confident and positive, and he knew that unless some unforeseen calamity befell him, he was going to be the next sheriff of Loma Grande County.

The next day was Saturday and Mel had big plans. Saturday was typically a busy day for the downtown merchants. Many people came in from the nearby farms and ranches and the townspeople usually took care of much of their shopping and other business. It was also a big day for socializing and sitting around the square and sipping coffee in the handful of restaurants around town. Mel decided that he and Rooster would make the rounds, walking the square and visiting all the shops, and driving to the ones on the edge of town. Mel picked up Rooster bright and early and they had a hearty breakfast at the truck stop before embarking on their hand shaking and baby-kissing endeavor. After breakfast, they drove to the gas station and greeted a couple of customers there, and then it was on to the square. Although this sort of thing would have been unthinkable for Rooster a mere two months ago, he had now become more comfortable approaching people and talking to them. Even if he had retained his old shy ways, Mel would have carried the ball for him, and in fact, Mel did most of the talking, patting Rooster on the back and singing his praises as a hero and a man of the people. Rooster mostly just shook hands, smiled and offered a few platitudes when prompted by Mel. In fact, it may have worked out better that way for it made Rooster seem like the tall, silent hero, the man of few words who could be counted on to spring into action and save the day, guns blazing.

They made a round of the square and then got in Mel's Cadillac and drove to the various businesses on the edge of town. Mel had written "Rooster for Sheriff" on the windows of his Cadillac with shoe polish and taped banners to the doors, and he made sure not to skip any place where two or more people were gathered.

However, Hickey was not to be caught napping either, and he was pressing the flesh and asking for votes apace with Rooster and Mel.

Moreover, since he owned a diner on the square, around mid morning he posted a sign that said "Free Cookies and Coffee for Everyone" which brought in a crowd. When Rooster and Mel made it back to the square for another round of campaigning, Mel spotted the signs and the crowd right away.

"Why that bastard! He's trying to buy votes!" exclaimed Mel.

"It sure looks like he's got a crowd there," fretted Rooster.

"Ooh, that low down bastard," Mel seethed.

They drove by slowly watching the crowd of old and young alike as they happily chewed on cookies. Mel looked over at Rooster.

"Rooster, let's go get us a cookie."

"What? Mel, are you crazy?"

"Why not? It says free cookies and coffee for everyone. You and me are everyone aren't we?"

"Mel, Bill Hickey will shit if we go up there and ask for a cookie."

"Well, let's just go find out."

Rooster groaned and slid down into his seat. Just when he had gotten comfortable with one thing, Mel was throwing something completely unexpected at him. They parked and got out of the car. Rooster did not want to go and was dragging his feet as much as possible. Mel was raring for a fight and waited impatiently for him.

"Rooster! Come on, dang it."

"I'm coming."

278

They made their way along the sidewalk and approached the crowd. Someone spotted them and began nudging the others, who all turned to look, wide eyed.

"Good morning, sheriff! Mighty nice of you to provide cookies for everyone like that, don't mind if we do," said Mel loudly in a cheerful voice.

"The heck you say!" said Hickey. "These cookies are for voters only."

"Like I said, we appreciate it."

"You get away from those cookies," said Sheriff Hickey.

"You just said them cookies was for voters, and we is voters," said Mel in his best bullshitting drawl.

"Not for you, so just get away."

Mel put his hand on the shoulder of a bystander. "Mister, what's that sign say?"

"It says 'free cookies and coffee for everyone,'" the man chuckled.

"Do you see any place where it says 'for everyone but Rooster and Mel'?"

The crowd laughed at Mel's unfolding prank.

"No, sir, it doesn't say that."

"Now, folks," said Mel, addressing the crowd, "this man is the sheriff, and he ought to know about the law. Here he has posted a sign that says 'free cookies and coffee for everyone.' It doesn't say anywhere on that sign 'everyone *except* for certain people.' Now do you reckon that would hold up in a court of law?"

A few people from the crowd laughed and shouted no.

"Now, sheriff, I expect that when a man puts up a sign that says 'free cookies and coffee for everyone,' that's what it ought to mean. I think if you're going to say one thing, and then do another because the results don't suit you, then that might indicate deceitfulness."

By now, the crowd was starting to laugh loudly. Hickey, sensing that he was being made a fool of, gave in.

"All right, fine. Take a cookie and get on out of here."

"Why thank yew, sheriff. We sure nuff appreciate that," drawled Mel in his best antagonistic manner. He took a cookie from the table and handed one to Rooster.

"Them is mighty fine cookies, sheriff. We do thank you."

Mel, deciding he had gotten enough of Bill Hickey's goat, nodded at Rooster, and they began to stroll down the sidewalk away from the crowd.

Mel could hardly contain himself, "Ha! That ought to get 'em talking. That story will be all over town before noon, how Rooster Brown went up and ate one of Bill Hickey's free cookies."

"Mel, you are crazy," said Rooster, shaking his head as he slowly chewed his cookie, but he had to admit that it was a pretty good cookie.

Mel and Rooster spent the rest of the day shaking as many hands and bending as many ears as possible, and by the time they were finished, Rooster was exhausted. When Mel finally dropped him off at home, he just wanted to lie down and close his eyes for a while. The house was empty when he got there, so he went straight to the bedroom and plopped on the bed. He fell asleep quickly and later was awakened by the sound of Laurie carrying in groceries. He laid there for a few minutes, listening as she put away things in the cabinet and refrigerator. It felt good to be lying on a soft comfortable bed as his wife stocked the pantry with food. He felt safe and secure, and it was a good feeling.

He got up and walked into the kitchen. Laurie saw him and smiled.

"Hi, honey. I hear you've had a hard day campaigning."

"That's for sure. I had no idea it was such hard work running for office."

"Well, you won't have to do it much longer."

"Thank goodness for that."

"I'm making steak tonight, so just go sit down, and I'll call you when it's ready."

Rooster kissed Laurie on the cheek and sat down on the sofa in the living room and promptly went back to sleep.

They got up early the next morning and got ready for church. Rooster was rested and feeling good. There was a big crowd at church, and of course everyone wanted to talk to Rooster and wish him well and shake his hand. He knew he could count on the votes of just about everyone in his church. Although he hadn't really embraced church attendance, he did discover that he liked almost everyone in the congregation. He generally avoided thinking much about religion, having had it forced on him his whole life, but he had been welcomed into this church. He liked this church, it was calm and sedate, not like the ones he had grown up in where people were prone to jump up and dance and shout and blabber away in gibberish. This was a nice, normal, respectable church, and he wasn't embarrassed to be associated with it.

When the services were over, he and the entire Tucker clan went to the truck stop for dinner. As always, Mel and Rooster were greeted like movie stars, and it always made Rooster feel both important and uncomfortable. Wanda always lavished extra attention on Rooster, making sure that his tea glass was always full and that he never wanted for anything. She fussed over him even more than Mel. After dinner, they went home and spent the day idling about and resting up for the week to come. Rooster had another week of debate boot camp with Addis and then the actual debate was that weekend, and the election itself was just a few days later. It was almost over.

The next morning, Rooster showed up at Addis' law office. Addis was in a good mood, and he put Rooster through his paces, covering every-thing they had gone over last week. It was now to the point where Rooster was getting bored with the whole thing. When Addis turned him loose for lunch, he told him to be ready for something different when he got back. Rooster went to the station and helped out for a while and then went home and had dinner with Laurie. When he got back to Addis' office, he was surprised to see it packed full of people that he didn't know very well. They were some people he had seen around and others he had never seen at all. None of them looked very friendly. Addis told Rooster to go up and go over his routine. He had barely gotten started when the roomful of strangers began booing and catcalling him. He stopped and looked at Addis who just shrugged. Rooster started again, and the audience, once again, began interrupt-ing and booing him.

"What the hell, Addis?" Rooster asked sharply.

"Don't expect everyone to love you, Rooster. You need to be ready for whatever comes your way. Now keep going."

Rooster started over, and once again, the abuse followed. Rooster felt himself getting angrier until finally he blew up and yelled at them to shut up which only made them laugh and pick at him more. Addis stepped in and told everyone to be quiet for a minute.

"That's exactly what you don't want to do, Rooster. Once you show you're upset and flustered, they have you where they want you."

"Well, what the hell am I supposed to do?"

"You turn it back on them. You find something about one of them, maybe the way they talk, or what they're wearing, or what they're saying, and you twist it around and make them look foolish. If you can be funny while doing it, that's even better. It's best not to get too personal, but once they attack you then you can fire back at will."

"Nobody around here's going to act like that."

"For the most part, I agree with you, but it only takes one. It's just something I want you to be prepared for. Now try it again, and instead of getting angry, find something about one of them and throw it back at them. Don't get into a fight with them, just say something to throw them off and continue talking."

Rooster resumed his speechifying, and once again the abuse came. This time, he picked one of the men who was particularly loud and responded to him.

"Hey, slim, the Charles Atlas seminar is around the corner."

The man frowned. "What did you say?"

Rooster ignored the man and resumed his speech and the crowd started in on him again. He paid no attention to them until another man yelled out an insult. Rooster paused again.

"Friend, you're in the wrong place. I'm not a dentist, and there isn't anything I can do about those rotten teeth you keep flashing at me."

The man stood up and began walking intently toward the podium.

"Okay, whoa now!" Addis said firmly. "Joe, sit back down. Rooster, I told you not to make it personal. If you can't think of a good response then just ignore them. Now let's all take a break and you can try it again."

Joe and the rest then went outside for some air and to smoke and scratch while Addis and Rooster sat down and talked.

"Hecklers are the hard part, Rooster, and there's really not much I can do for you in that regard. Just do whatever it takes to stay calm, and don't let them get to you."

"That's the hard part all right. I never did take bullying too well. I'd just as soon knock the shit out of them and be done with it."

"Well, you can't do that either. Just remember, they're trying to make you slip up. If you lose your temper, then they have won. It's not so much a matter of having a good response, although it is good if you can. It's mostly just about keeping your cool. That's the main thing. Show everybody that you can handle the pressure."

Rooster sighed, "Okay, Addis. I'll do my best."

When Addis brought the boys back in again, they gave Rooster all kinds of hell, but he never lost his temper or forgot what he was saying. He just kept focused and tuned them out, and in the end, he realized that he made another big step toward winning this debate. When they finished that day, Addis told him that he didn't have to come back any more.

"Rooster, I think that we have done all that we can do to prepare you for this debate, and I think you will do well. I am confident of that. If there is anything else I can do to help you, just let me know."

Rooster was touched. He had developed something of a bond with Addis these past several days, and although he still respected him tremendously and was still somewhat in awe of him, he now felt more of a friendship with him. He was deeply grateful for he knew that without the training Addis had given him he would have gone up on that stage and flopped badly. Rooster held his hat, running his fingers along the brim as he fumbled for the words to express his gratitude.

"Addis, I don't know how to thank you enough. Without what you have done for me, I don't think I could have pulled this off, but now I feel pretty good about it. I owe you a lot."

Addis smiled. "This is for the good of the whole community, Rooster. We need a good man as our sheriff."

Rooster looked down and nodded his head, but he felt a flash of shame as that night at the truck stop suddenly entered his mind. Here this educated man had spent all this time preparing him to win something that he himself knew he didn't deserve. For the most part, Rooster had put that night out of his mind. He rarely thought about it, but sometimes it hit him when he least expected it. He turned and left the office and went to go home.

On the way back to the house, he decided to go to the station instead. It was late in the day, and it was just Harvey and Kermit on duty. Rooster pulled into the drive and stopped next to the pumps because he needed gas. Harvey came out and started washing the windshield as Rooster pumped his own gas.

"Well, boss, you ready for the big debate?" asked Harvey cheerfully.

"I reckon I'm as ready as I'm ever going to be," said Rooster.

"I suspect you'll do fine."

"I guess. I just wish I could remember some of those laws better."

"Which ones?"

"All of them but especially that one about cattle rustling. I think I got it, and then I can't pull it out of the hat. I know what it says. I just can't remember the exact statute."

"Oh, cattle rustling. That's in Chapter 31, subsection 4, under state felonies on page 233, paragraph 2. If it's less than ten head, then it's just a third degree felony, but if it's more than ten head, then that can get you in some real trouble. A third degree felony will get you anywhere from two to ten years as stated in Subchapter C subsection 12.34 and a fine of up to $1000."

"How the hell do you know that?"

"I read the law book."

"And you can remember the whole thing, even the page it's on?"

"Well, sure."

Rooster studied Harvey quietly for a moment. If it had been anyone else, he wouldn't have believed them for a minute, but this was Harvey. He had already amazed everyone with his incredible mathematical abilities, and in fact, he balanced the books at the station every day entirely in his head and dictated the final numbers to Rooster at the end of the shift.

"What's the charge for...kidnapping?"

"That's in Chapter 20, subsection 3 on page 101. That one's a third degree felony too, unless it's aggravated kidnapping, then it's a second degree felony."

"How do I know you're right?"

Harvey shrugged. "Look it up yourself."

"I wouldn't even know where to look it up."

"It's in the Texas Penal Codes. You can borrow my copy if you want."

"You have a copy of the Texas Penal Codes?" asked Rooster, a hint of irritation in his voice.

"Well, sure."

"What on earth do you have one of those for?"

"I used to be a deputy, remember?"

"I remember. You got fired."

Harvey looked at Rooster with a pained expression on his face. "I didn't do anything to deserve getting fired. I was a good deputy."

Rooster felt a twinge of shame. In spite of his funny ways, Harvey was truly his best friend and a good and pure hearted soul.

"I'm sorry, Harvey. I shouldn't have said that."

Harvey resumed cleaning the windows. "That's Okay."

"Say, why don't you bring that book to work tomorrow and show me what you know."

"Okay, sure," said Harvey excitedly. "That'll be fun."

"Yeah, it might be. It just might be," said Rooster, stroking his chin as he studied Harvey carefully.

Rooster topped off his tank and filled out a receipt to have it deducted from his pay. He got into the truck, and instead of heading the few blocks home, he took the main drag through town. He drove around in deep thought. If that damn Harvey didn't beat all, first he turned out to be a human adding machine, and now it comes out that he was a walking law encyclopedia as well. Rooster wondered if Bill Hickey was aware of Harvey's talent, and, if so, why would he fire him? Somebody with that ability would be invaluable to have on the police force. That got Rooster to thinking even more. He hadn't really given much thought to who he would hire as deputy when he was elected sheriff, other than he knew was going to clean house and get rid of both those SOBs who were wearing badges now. Harvey could be an incredible dumb fuck at times, but there was no denying that he was damn near a genius in other ways. He thought and thought, and when he was through thinking, he went on home to Laurie and a nice, hot supper.

The next morning, Rooster opened the station. He had gone in earlier than usual, before anyone else arrived, and he was enjoying the early morning solitude. It was just a few days until the debate, and he was grateful to be back at his regular routine. He liked working at the station and would have probably been content to do so from now on if he had not been prodded into this new venture. He knew that he was not ambitious, and if left to his own motivations, would probably have never amounted to much. Yet here he was, on the verge of becoming sheriff, married to the daughter of one of the richest men in town, and widely regarded as a hero. It still seemed unreal to him at times. He wondered how it could have happened to him, of all people, especially in light of what was really in his heart that night. That was the part that confused him the most, why would God reward him like this when surely he knew what his real intentions were? It made no sense. If anything, he should be sitting in a prison cell awaiting the electric chair, but instead he was the toast of the town. Although he was hardly riddled with guilt about it, the awareness of what had been in his heart never truly left him. In one sense, he would always have trouble accepting his good fortune, because the truth of who he really was would always be with him. However, at other times he almost gloated about how he had completely fooled everyone. Of course, he occasionally worried about what he might have said to Cletus and Mexican Alice that day, but he also knew they would likely never say anything, being as low in the social order as they were, and especially once he was elected sheriff.

He was completely engrossed in all this when Harvey startled him by walking into the office carrying his legal tome.

"Okay, Rooster, here it is," he said as he dropped it on the desk with a thud.

Rooster looked up at him as if awaking from a dream. He ran his hand over the leather cover of the immense tome. It must have cost an arm and a leg, and he couldn't imagine where one would even buy something like this, but Rooster was learning not to be surprised by anything that Harvey Wells was capable of.

"Damn, it's huge," muttered Rooster.

"Sure is. It's got every law you need to know to run the state of Texas," said Harvey proudly.

Rooster lifted the cover and laid it open across his desk. He looked at all the words covering the pages and then looked up at Harvey, grinning down at him.

"Go stand over there," Rooster told Harvey.

Harvey walked to the opposite side of the room. Rooster pulled the large book toward him, placing the bottom of it in his lap and with the spine resting against the edge of the desk so that Harvey couldn't see what page he was looking at. Rooster flipped through the book until he found something that caught his eye.

"Okay, tell me what criminal mischief is."

Harvey cleared his throat. "Criminal mischief, that would be in Title 7, Chapter 28, subsection 03. It states that 'a person commits an offense if, without the effective consent of the owner: (1) he intentionally or knowingly damages or destroys the tangible property of the owner; (2) he intentionally or knowingly tampers with the tangible property of the owner and causes pecuniary loss or substantial inconvenience to the owner or a third person; or (3) he intentionally or knowingly makes markings including inscriptions...'"

Rooster stared at the page in disbelief, the hairs on the back on his neck standing straight up. Harvey was not only defining the offense accurately, he was reciting it word for word exactly as it appeared on the page. Rooster held up his hand, unable to speak.

Harvey stopped and stared at him curiously. "What's wrong, Rooster?"

Rooster shook his head silently. He felt a surge of fear well up from deep within his gut. His hands were shaking. He took a deep breath and tried to speak.

"I...I...don't know what to say. I can't believe this. This has got to be a joke."

Rooster flipped through some more pages. This time he just told Harvey the page number. Again, Harvey recited word for word what was on the page that Rooster was looking at. Rooster picked another page, and once again, Harvey repeated word for word what was on the page. Rooster closed the book and slid it back onto the desk. He got up and walked outside without saying a word. He stepped outside, inhaled deeply, and then threw up on the driveway. Harvey ran out and grabbed him by the arm.

"Rooster, Rooster, are you all right?"

"I don't know, Harvey. Would you please hose off this mess before we get a customer?" Rooster gasped as he walked around to the back of the station.

Rooster's head was spinning. He couldn't believe what he had just witnessed. There was no way Harvey could have been faking it. It defied logic and reality. It was impossible, yet he had seen it with his own eyes. A few minutes later, Harvey came around looking for him.

"Okay, Rooster, I washed off the vomit."

"Good...good. Thank you, Harvey. Thank you very much. Now let's get ready for business," he said as he choked back the taste of vomit that hung in his throat.

All through the day, Rooster was distracted and out of sorts. There was an unusually high volume of customers as everyone came by to wish him well and offer him words of support. He did his best to play the part and campaign and ask for everyone's vote, but he was just going through the motions. However, few people seemed to notice. Rooster was spooked by what he had seen that morning. It just didn't seem real. On more than one occasion, he had seen Harvey get down on his knees and play marbles with a group of children. Many people regarded him as slightly retarded, and he sometimes did the stupidest things imaginable. Yet he could perform incredible feats of mathematics in his head, and he had apparently memorized an entire law book. Rooster couldn't figure out whether he was a genius or a freak of nature. Whatever he was, it was just plain damned amazing.

When they closed the station down that evening, Rooster asked Harvey to come into the office and locked the door behind him. They both sat down and began to talk, and when they were through talking, Harvey ran out so excited he could barely contain himself. Rooster called out to him as he left.

"Remember, Harvey! Don't say a word to anyone!"

19

At last, the big day arrived, and the town buzzed with excitement. Rooster did not work at the station that day, although he might have preferred to do so to keep his mind busy. Instead, he went off fishing by himself at Mel's ranch, even though he didn't really care to fish. And even though he tried his best not to, he managed to catch a few fish, which he skinned and gutted and brought in for Laurie to fry up for supper. He then bathed, shaved, and put on a suit and his best cowboy hat, and he and Laurie drove to the courthouse so he could do battle with Sheriff Hickey.

By the time they got there, a crowd had already gathered. Mel had put out the word a couple of days ahead of time for anyone who had a sociable rooster to bring it to the courthouse in support of Rooster. So there were a couple of dozen chickens squawking and scratching about and clucking and crowing to beat the band. A few rubes from the country were also doing their best rooster crow impersonations, and the place had taken on a circus-like atmosphere, complete with a couple of snack stands selling pie and sodas. Rooster was nervous but composed. He was grateful to Addis for all that he had done for him. There was little to do now but wait for the main event to begin.

Mel and Shirley were already there, and they both greeted them warmly. Harvey, Kermit, Obie and all of the various members of the Posse were there, and in fact, probably most of the town was gathered around the square. Hickey made a big show of it, driving up in his squad car with his lights flashing and his siren blaring, just to make sure that everyone knew that he was still by-god the sheriff around here. There were two podiums arranged on the east side of the court-house, and red, white, and blue banners hung from the courthouse columns behind them. The high school band was there, and they played the National Anthem and "God Bless America" with "Yankee Doodle Dandy" thrown in for good measure. There were some pre-liminary speeches by Arlen Moore and Mayor Pee Wee Jones, who were the moderators of the debate, and then the rules were explained and the battle was on.

The format was this: at the very beginning, each candidate would have three minutes to speak. This was generally the sales pitch part of it, the chance for each man to put forth why they thought they were best for the job. Then, there would be questions submitted by the audience and selected by the moderators, with each man given three minutes to respond. Halfway through there would be a short break, and then they would switch the order so that the other man got to go first. Then, after the questions had been answered, there would be one final three minute sales pitch to conclude the debate. Pee Wee Jones flipped a coin, and Rooster called heads—and heads it was! Rooster won the toss to go first which elicited a loud cheer from the crowd. He went to the podium, which had a microphone set up by the local radio station, and he cleared his throat. This echoed off the buildings around the square, which surprised him and caused him to jump slightly. The local radio announcer who had set up the microphone quickly turned it down. Rooster's heart was thumping in his chest. He walked back up to the microphone.

"Can y'all hear me all right?" he spoke into the microphone.

"Yes!" the crowd roared back at him.

"Well, all right then. My name is William Thomas Brown, but everybody calls me Rooster..." and, with that, he recited flawlessly the script that he and Addis had concocted, and he finished up right on time just before the bell rang.

The crowd roared its approval as he stepped back from the microphone to allow Hickey to begin his speech.

"I reckon most people here know who I am. My name is Bill Hickey, and I have been your sheriff for the past eight years..." and Hickey started his spiel, and he was still talking when the bell rang three minutes later which caused some of the crowd to laugh a little.

Next was the question and answer segment. Mayor Pee Wee Jones pulled a scrap of paper from a hat that held the questions they had chosen.

"What do you think is the most important quality a sheriff has to possess?"

Rooster stepped up to the microphone confidently. That was one of the potential questions that he and Addis had practiced with, so he felt good about this one.

"There are many qualities a good sheriff should have, so it's hard to just name one, but since I am limited to one, I would have to say the most important quality is good old common sense. A man with common sense will know when to play rough and when to give a fellow a break. A man with common sense will know when to use a gun or when words are the best option. A man with common sense..." and Rooster continued until he had used up his three minutes. The crowd cheered and then, once again, it was Hickey's turn.

"I have to say the most important quality is something that I have, and which my opponent does not, and that is practical experience. I have been your sheriff for eight years, and before that, I served as a deputy and as an MP in the US Army. Common sense is a mighty good thing to have, but when you're in a dangerous situation you can't beat experience..." and Hickey talked until his three minutes were up and he got a good cheer from the crowd.

Now Rooster was starting to worry a bit but trying not to show it. Hickey was doing a lot better than he had anticipated. The next question Hickey answered first, then Rooster, and so they alternated each question.

Each successive question got just a little bit harder or so it seemed to Rooster. He tried to concentrate on what Addis and Mel had told him, that it wasn't so much what you said as how you said it. So he just stood tall and tried to speak clearly. Even if he didn't really have an answer to the question, he just acted like he knew what he was talking about and filled the time with words until the bell rang. It seemed to work, and the crowd always cheered enthusiastically when he was done. Whenever he saw a familiar face in the crowd, they were smiling, cheering and clapping for him and that gave him courage.

When they reached the halfway mark, a fifteen minute recess was taken. Hickey went inside the courthouse while Rooster stepped down into the crowd and joined Laurie and the others. She ran up and kissed him on the cheek while Mel, Shirley, Addis and the others gathered around and slapped him on the back offering words of praise and encouragement. It seemed to Rooster like just a few minutes had passed before it was time to go back onto the stage for the final half of the debate.

This time, Hickey went first. Rooster watched the crowd for a bit until he started feeling nervous again, so he found a spot on a building across the street, fixed his gaze upon it and tried to think of his parents. Not looking at the crowd helped, and he found that if he just thought about something else it helped him to stay calm. When it was his turn to speak, he would bravely plunge ahead, doing his best to sound smart and keep talking.

When it was time for the final question, Pee Wee pulled the last slip of paper from the hat and read the question. When Rooster heard it, he felt his knees quake a bit. This was exactly the type of question he had dreaded.

"How well do you know the laws that you will be required to enforce?"

Hickey smiled broadly when he heard this question. He knew that this was his strength and that this might be his chance to land a lethal blow against Rooster.

"I believe that I can say to you who are gathered here tonight that I am probably the single most qualified person in this county in regard to knowledge of the law. I have studied the laws of Texas for years and have many of them committed to memory. For those rare situations that arise where I am unfamiliar with the law, I keep a copy of the Texas Penal Codes so that I can be sure of which laws have been broken and what to charge the perpetrator with..."

Hickey continued talking until his three minutes were up. He looked over smugly at Rooster after the bell rang, knowing that he would be hard to beat on this, the final question, the one that people would most likely remember.

Rooster stepped up to the microphone and smiled confidently.

"I have a pretty good boss right now, and I have learned a lot from him. One real important thing that I have learned from Mel Tucker is above all else it's important to hire good help. It's true that I don't have the knowledge of the law that Bill Hickey does. That is something that will take time to learn. But I have a secret weapon when it comes to knowing the law, something that Bill Hickey himself once had but that he got rid of. That secret weapon is something that is so amazing as to be downright scary, but it can be proven to each and every person here that this secret weapon is for real. The secret weapon I am referring to is a man who was once a deputy, and if I am elected, will once again be a deputy, and that man is Harvey Wells."

At this point, a great commotion arose from the audience, some laughter, some hooting, a lot of murmuring and mostly just a lot of confusion. Sheriff Hickey laughed out loud at the preposterousness, indeed the foolishness of what he had just heard. He couldn't have asked for any more than this. Rooster Brown was committing an out and out act of campaign suicide right there for the whole town to witness. Rooster took all this in and just grinned.

"I reckon y'all must think I'm crazy, but after this debate is over I will prove to everyone here tonight that Harvey Wells can recite every single law in the Texas Penal Code by pure memory and without mistake. I know it is hard to believe, and I wouldn't have believed it myself but for the fact I have seen it with my own eyes."

The crowd was now murmuring with confusion. Mel and Addis looked as if they had just been punched in the stomach, and Laurie and Shirley appeared to be about to cry. After all this time and effort, Rooster had gone completely crazy and was about throw away all they had worked for. Sheriff Hickey was not one to let an opportunity like this pass. He raised his hand and motioned to the moderators.

"Gentlemen, I know that you have established strict rules for this debate; however, this is highly unusual, and this type of claim should not be allowed to pass without open and honest examination. I hereby request that the formal debate be declared over and the final time remaining be used for Mr. Brown to prove this outlandish statement for all to see. No one can do what he is claiming. He is obviously lying, and now is the time to expose him for what he is."

Pee Wee Jones looked at Arlen Moore, who also was looking pale and worried. Arlen said nothing, so Pee Wee spoke.

"Mr. Brown, it is up to you. We can either continue the debate as agreed or you can accept Mr. Hickey's proposal to stop formal debate and you may have an opportunity to prove that which you have stated."

"I accept Mr. Hickey's offer, Your Honor. We will need a copy of the Texas Penal Code and for Harvey Wells to come up and join us."

Rooster squinted into the crowd. "Harvey, get your book and come up here on stage with us."

A voice rang out from the crowd. "I'll be right there, Rooster."

This really got the crowd buzzing loudly. Many people felt that Rooster had just shot himself in the foot. No one believed that anyone could do what he had just claimed, but no one was willing to leave until it had been settled.

Rooster waited calmly on stage as Hickey smiled broadly, and Mel and Addis bowed their heads in disbelief. Then Harvey ran up onto the stage, carrying the huge black leather bound volume of the Texas Penal Code.

"Give it to Arlen and Pee Wee and let Hickey look it over too," said Rooster.

Harvey set the book on the table where Pee Wee and Arlen were sitting. Rooster gestured to Bill Hickey to go over and look at the book himself. They all opened the book and flipped through the pages for a few minutes.

"Do y'all agree that that is an official copy of the Texas Penal Code?" Rooster said into the microphone.

They all nodded their heads. Pee Wee Jones spoke into his microphone, "Folks, this appears to be a standard copy of the Texas Penal Code."

"Sheriff Hickey, do you agree that is a legitimate copy of the Texas Penal Code?" asked Rooster.

Hickey was now beginning to get suspicious, so he went back and flipped through the massive tome once again, this time looking up certain laws that he was familiar with. After examining it closely for a few more minutes, he stood and announced that as far as he could tell it appeared genuine.

"Okay, Harvey, come on over here and stand by me," said Rooster. Harvey walked up next to Rooster and stood grinning before the crowd.

"Folks, get ready, you're about to witness something that defies explanation," said Rooster calmly into the microphone as the crowd watched the two of them intently. Rooster, aware that every eye was on him, stepped back from the podium and looked over the crowd before him. He put his hands on his hips and leaned his head back, his jaw protruding. Then, he spoke, slowly and deliberately.

"Sheriff, why don't you ask Harvey to tell you about a law, any law in that book?"

Hickey stared at them both sternly, his suspicions now thoroughly aroused, perhaps remembering the cookie incident and not eager to be made a fool of again. He stroked his chin thoughtfully then smiled slightly.

"I'll be easy on you. This is something Mr. Brown should be acquainted with. What's the statute concerning public intoxication?"

With that, most of the men in attendance fidgeted uncomfortably, each one feeling as if the question was about them personally.

Harvey stepped up to the microphone and cleared his throat, "That's on page 349."

Rooster put his hand on his shoulder to stop him until Arlen and Pee Wee found page 349. Once they found the page, he patted Harvey on the shoulder and softly told him to continue.

Harvey cleared his throat again and then began.

"Chapter 49, subsection 02. Public Intoxication a) A person commits an offense if the person appears in a public place while intoxicated to the degree that the person may endanger the person or another. (b) It is a defense to prosecution under this section that the alcohol or other substance was administered for therapeutic purposes and as a part of the person's professional medical treatment by a licensed physician..."

Rooster stopped Harvey again.

"Well, gentlemen. Is that correct?" Rooster asked the moderators.

Arlen and Pee Wee looked at each other in astonishment. Pee Wee addressed the crowd.

"What he just said was word for word what is in this book."

A huge gasp arose from the crowd.

"This is some kind of trick. That was too easy. Let me give him a hard one," snarled Hickey.

"Go right ahead, Sheriff," said Rooster.

Sheriff Hickey studied them for a moment, "Okay, wise guy, tell me about abuse of a corpse."

"That would be on page 322," said Harvey.

Arlen and Pee Wee flipped quickly to page 322. Once they found the page, they looked at Rooster and Harvey. Once again Rooster patted Harvey on the shoulder.

"Chapter 42, subsection 08. (a) A person commits an offense if, not authorized by law, he intentionally or knowingly: (1) disinters, disturbs, removes, dissects, in whole or in part, carries away, or treats in a seriously offensive manner a human corpse; (2) conceals a human corpse knowing it to be illegally disinterred; (3) sells or buys a human corpse or in any way traffics in a human corpse; or (4) transmits or conveys, or procures to be transmitted or conveyed, a human corpse to a place outside the state. (b) An offense under this section is a Class A misdemeanor..."

Rooster put his hand on Harvey's shoulder. "Is that correct?"

Arlen and Pee Wee were shaking their heads in disbelief. Neither of them responded.

"Well, moderators...is that correct or not?" asked Rooster again.

"It...it...it's exactly as it appears in the book," stuttered Arlen into his microphone.

This time, the crowd erupted in a cacophony of confusion and chaos.

"This is some kind of trick!" shouted Hickey angrily. "It's that book, that book is rigged somehow."

"Then explain how it could be rigged," demanded Rooster.

"I don't know. This is your trick. I just know something's not right. I have one of those books. We'll use mine instead and then see if he can still do it." Hickey summoned Joe to go into his office in the courthouse and bring out his version of the book. This worried Rooster, it occurred to him that the page numbers might not match. He took Harvey aside away from the microphone.

"Harvey, what if he has a different version of the book?"

"Shouldn't matter too much, the laws should be the same," replied Harvey calmly.

Everyone waited around nervously, the crowd was murmuring, and Rooster was beginning to wonder if this was such a good idea after all. It had certainly shaken him up when he realized what Harvey could do, and now he realized that it may have had a similar effect on everyone else. After a few minutes, Joe came rushing back with a large leather-bound book just like Harvey's. This time, Rooster protested.

"Hey wait a minute! Let me and Harvey have a look at that book just to make sure Hickey's not pulling some kind of trick."

Rooster, Harvey, Bill Hickey, Joe, Arlen, and Pee Wee all huddled around the books examining them both in detail. As far as Rooster could tell, they looked exactly the same. The moderators looked at some printing on the first few inside pages and declared that they were, in fact, the exact same book. The debaters went back to their podiums, and the questioning resumed. Each time Harvey was quizzed about a statute, he recited it exactly. Then, they just called out various page numbers, and he told them exactly what was on each page.

This seemed to affect the crowd in two distinct ways, half of them would erupt in shouts of victory and jubilation each time Harvey answered a question correctly, while the other half stood stone-faced and silent. Mel watched the crowd intently, and he sensed that at least half of them were uncomfortable with what they were witnessing, so he tried to rally the ones they were losing. He collared a couple of members of the Posse and sent them out into the crowd to lead a cheer every time Harvey answered a question correctly. This did have some effect. They were able to bring at least some of the wavering ones back into the fold while others stood quietly, trying to quell the primeval fear that was welling up inside them. With each passing question, half the crowd grew louder while the other half became quieter. When they finally stopped asking Harvey questions, half the crowd quietly drifted away. Hickey himself left without saying much. It was as if the air had been let out of the gathering, and it had to limp home like a car with a flat tire. Rooster realized that his plan had, if not exactly backfired, certainly not gone as he had imagined, and the disquieting realization that he may have blown the whole thing crept onerously into his mind. Laurie and Shirley and Mel all came rushing up to him once the event was officially declared over and hugged and patted his back and shook his hands and told him what a wonderful job he had done. Likewise, the Posse and dozens of his supporters all crowded around him calling him Sheriff Brown and predicting victory. While all the backslapping and glad-handing was going on, Addis and Arlen stood off away from the crowd talking quietly to each other as Mel watched them from the corner of his eye.

A consensus would emerge over the next couple of days, about half the town was firmly in Rooster's camp while the other half was affected much differently. For those in the latter group, it was as if a spell had been cast over them, yet no one could quite say just why. In some ways, it had just been too much for them to comprehend. Here was this person that many considered a nitwit, who had performed impossible feats of memory. Some of the preachers around town would later quietly murmur that it had been some type of witchcraft and surely the work of the devil. It left much of the town feeling hazy, queasy, and uncertain of what was and what was not. And it had tipped the momentum, at least for the time being back to a more equal footing for Hickey. While Hickey may have been an asshole, he at least had the good sense to fire a freak like Harvey Wells, and that was something that half the people of Merky could feel good about.

When they went home that night, even Laurie seemed a little embarrassed by it all and avoided talking about it. It was just some unspoken thing that hung in the air like a big noose. Rooster said little about it himself, but mentally he was kicking himself. Had he just stuck to the plan that Addis had worked out he would be sailing smoothly to victory, yet now it all seemed uncertain. The next day, Mel went out to take the pulse of the town and he sent several others out as well. By the end of the day, he was concerned that Rooster might lose after all. He went to his office and closed the door. He called Addis. The phone rang a few times. Addis answered, sounding slightly drunk.

"Addis, it's Mel...yeah, I know...I can't believe it either...the big dummy...I don't know what got into him...I know, I know..."

After they talked for several minutes Mel knew what he had to do.

"I really didn't think this would be necessary, but I think we better go to Plan B. You've got what we need, right? Good. I heard some dirt the other day that I think we can use to help this along. I'll go see what kind of deal I can cut tomorrow. Okay, Addis, good night."

Mel hung up the phone. He was agitated and nervous, but somehow he liked it that way. He always did work well under pressure. He was angry at Rooster, but at least he knew what he had to deal with. He wasn't about to let this slip out of his hands now.

20

At last, the big day arrived. It was the first week in November, and another cold snap had blown in, whipping leaves and snippets of paper down the streets and blowing the hats off men's heads. It wasn't too cold though, just about the perfect temperature for people to be out and tending to the business of electing men to office. It was a presidential election too, so a high number of people turned out to vote. There was a steady stream of customers coming through the station all day, much to the delight of Mel Tucker, who always managed to find a silver lining to just about everything. Rooster was nervous but glad that it was about to be over. He would be bitterly disappointed if he lost, but either way, he could go back to a somewhat normal life once it was over. Mel had given him the day off, but he was too nervous to just sit around, and he was tired of going out and shaking hands and kissing babies. He figured there was little more he could do at this point, so he decided to go the Texaco Station where, at least, he could stay busy. About noontime, Mel came by and told him to go do some last minute campaigning, which he did reluctantly. As he was heading to his truck, Mel hollered at him.

"Don't forget to vote, Rooster!"

Rooster stopped in his tracks. He had never given any thought to it all, but suddenly he realized that he never registered to vote. He looked back at Mel, and he almost said something, but then he thought better of it and just nodded his head and kept on going. He was really beating himself up now. What an idiot he was, what if he lost the election by one vote? His vote! If that were to happen he might as well pack it up and leave town and disappear once and for all into misery and blessed obscurity.

He went home and lay on the bed and tried to relax which was nigh impossible. Laurie was off running around town, so he had the place to himself. He looked over at the chest of drawers and a thought occurred to him. He went over and rummaged around the drawer that contained his socks and underwear until he found his Bible. He took it out and looked at it, running his fingers along the embossed lettering of the cover. He flipped through the pages, searching for something, but he had no idea what. Finally, he stopped and looked down at the page. It was Deuteronomy 23:2. It said:

"A bastard shall not enter into the congregation of the Lord; even to his tenth generation shall he not enter into the congregation of the Lord."

Rooster slammed the Bible shut angrily.

"Shit," he said to himself.

His grandfather was born illegitimate. Some folks said that was why he became an alcoholic and an outlaw. He put the Bible back in the drawer, angry at himself for reading it, but then he decided that he couldn't just leave it at that and that he would have to find a good verse. He flipped the pages again, this time he found Matthew 17:20.

"And Jesus said unto them, Because of your unbelief: for verily I say unto you, If ye have faith as a grain of mustard seed, ye shall say unto this mountain, Remove hence to yonder place; and it shall remove; and nothing shall be impossible to you."

That sounded better, although he wasn't entirely sure what it meant and he wasn't sure if being the descendant of a bastard would disqualify him from moving mountains. He sighed and put the Bible back into the drawer. If his father were here, he could explain it to him, not that he ever listened to him much when he was alive. That got him to thinking about his father. He missed him, and he missed his mother, even though he was very young when she died. He was grateful to have the Tuckers. He really felt like he had a family for the first time in his life, yet he knew that it wasn't really the same, but it would no doubt be the closest he would ever come. He wished that his father and mother could see him now, see that he at least got this far in life. He wondered if they were in heaven, looking down upon him, or if they had just faded away into the darkness. He was still thinking these thoughts when Laurie walked into the house and startled him. He usually heard her pull into the drive, but this time he was so lost in thought that he was caught completely off guard.

"Rooster! What are you doing just laying around?" she scolded him. "Daddy wants you to go to the square and campaign some more."

Rooster groaned and got up off the bed. He was sick and tired of being bossed around. Once he got to be sheriff, if he got to be sheriff, he was going to tell everybody to kiss his ass and do as he damn well pleased.

They got into Laurie's car and headed to the square, but because it was Election Day, there were many more people in town than usual. Folks had come in from the country and were making a day of it by shopping, strolling and socializing. Even the townspeople were downtown taking in the excitement of the atmosphere. For the first time that he could remember, Rooster was unable to find a parking space in downtown Merky. He muttered a curse under his breath and pulled the car into an alley behind the businesses along the west side of the square. As he made the turn, he saw something that sent a slight jolt of fear up his spine. It was a parked police car, and on the other side of the alley, he could see Deputy Wayne Bates leaning into the window of another car. His foot went for the brake then he pulled it back. It occurred to Rooster that there was no reason for him to be afraid of Deputy Bates any longer and so he put his foot back on the gas pedal and eased the car around the side of the patrol car. Deputy Bates squinted at them as they cruised slowly toward him. Recognizing the car and then finally the driver, he smiled slightly and turned his head back to who he was speaking to. As they cruised past, they both recognized the car that Deputy Bates had been talking into and the person sitting at the wheel. It was Mel. Their eyes met as they passed by, Mel neither smiling nor frowning, Rooster also expressionless, like two strangers passing in the dark. Rooster drove on past, back out to the square.

"Was that Daddy?" asked Laurie.

"It sure looked like him," said Rooster flatly.

"What on earth could he have been talking to that deputy about?" Laurie asked.

"No telling."

"That's odd," Laurie mused softly. "I'll have to ask him what it was about."

Rooster frowned. "Might be best to just let it drop."

"Why? Aren't you curious?"

"Yes, but, with Mel sometimes it best to just let things be."

Now it was Laurie frowning. "Sometimes, I don't know about either one of you."

They found a place to park a couple of blocks from the square and walked toward the courthouse. They were met by well-wishers along the way and stopped to talk several times. Some were genuine, enthusiastic supporters, while others were polite yet noncommittal and vague about their intentions in the voting booth. Rooster was starting to fret again that he may have blown the election and that he would have to put up with bullying from Hickey and his deputies for the rest of his life. When they got to the courthouse Rooster lied and told Laurie that he had already voted, so she went into the courthouse to cast hers. While Rooster waited, a small crowd of supporters gathered around to shoot the breeze. They were all joking and cutting up when Laurie emerged from inside. Rooster tipped his hat and asked everyone to vote for him if they hadn't already, and they went on their way. They walked around the square and into the shops, talking to everyone they met. Rooster shook the men's hands, tipped his hat to the ladies, and kissed all the babies. By the time the polls closed, he was ready to retire from campaigning for good.

By Merky tradition, the ballot boxes were escorted to the county jail and locked inside a cell with an armed guard posted outside. The election judges would then convene at the jail and be locked inside with the ballots, and no one could leave until all the votes were counted and a winner was announced. On elections of particular interest, a crowd would form outside the jail until the count was finished. On this particular evening, there was an especially large crowd gathered, and it was apparent that no one was going home until the count was finished. At about 7:30, a police car with flashing lights came creeping slowly through the crowd. Deputy Bates parked the car and got out. He went to the trunk and opened it, exposing four ballot boxes in the trunk. He stood guard as Joe carried the ballot boxes into the jail cell under the watchful eye of Mayor Pee Wee Jones. Inside the jail, Sheriff Hickey watched as all four ballot boxes were locked into the cell to await the final count.

When the election judges arrived, they were locked in the cell with a card table and four stools to begin their count. The first count showed that Ike had won the presidential race and some state and local elections were decided as well. When it came time to announce the sheriff's race, the judges read off the vote tallies.

"Bill Hickey—one thousand, one hundred, and seventy-five votes."

"William Brown—two thousand, one hundred, and eighty-two votes."

The crowd burst into pandemonium, and the news quickly spread. Within minutes, a crowd had gathered outside the home of Rooster and Laurie Brown, cheering and chanting. Rooster, who had been lying on the bed awaiting the final word, stepped out onto the porch to be greeted by the cheering crowd. He could hardly believe it. He was certain that he would lose, and now it seemed all but certain it was over. However, Hickey would not give up without a fight, and he demanded a recount. The ballots were counted once again, and there was a difference from the original count but it did not change the results. He demanded yet another recount. By this time, Rooster and Laurie showed up at the jail only to be informed that it had not yet been decided and that they were now counting the ballots for the third time. Hearing this, Rooster's shoulders dropped, and he fell, once again, back in the depths of gloom, fearing that fate had simply played a cruel trick on him. The third count came out exactly the same as the second, and this time there could be little doubt that Rooster had won the election. At this point, he was hoisted upon the shoulders of the crowd and carried to the courthouse like a true conquering hero. In contrast, Hickey left quietly without saying much of anything. He went home to his wife and children, soon to be a civilian once again. The festivities on the square were just getting started, and it wasn't long before someone showed up with home brew fresh from Cletus' still. The jar was passed around, and cigars were smoked, and the crowd didn't disperse until close to eleven o'clock, a late night for the people of Merky. When they finally got home, Laurie practically pulled the clothes off Rooster before pushing him onto the bed and fucking the living daylights out of him. Afterward, as he lay there in the darkness, listening to Laurie's soft breathing, he looked out the window at the moon high in the sky. He couldn't believe how his life had turned out.

On the other side of town, two figures huddled in the darkness around a small fire. Mel and Addis both sat on wooden boxes with the word "ballots" stenciled on the sides, sipping home brew and beer and tossing papers into the fire. They were both smiling and reveling in the satisfaction of a job well done. Mel picked up a piece of paper and held it up so that he could read it by the firelight.

"Another vote for Bill Hickey," he chuckled as he tossed the ballot into the fire.

"Cheers," said Addis as he raised his glass.

Eventually the papers were all burned, and the boxes as well, the liquor was drank, and two men with a dark secret went their separate ways into the night. A few hours later, well before the sun came up, two different figures crept along the deserted streets of downtown Merky. They walked cautiously along the storefronts of the square and stopped in front of the drugstore next to a large wooden storage box that was padlocked shut. This was where the Greyhound bus stopped to pick up packages and passengers. Soon the early bus would arrive; another would come from the other direction in the afternoon. The two figures stood and waited, fidgeting nervously lest someone spot them. Before long, they saw headlights coming down the main street, and they fidgeted more until they were sure it was the bus. As the bus pulled up, it illuminated the face of the waitress Jeanine, which was somewhat concealed beneath the scarf she had wrapped around her head. However, the scarf could not conceal the bulge of her belly. Next to her, Wayne Bates, in civilian clothes and wearing a cowboy hat low over his eyes, reached into his jacket pocket and pulled out the envelope that Mel had given him the day before. He ran his fingers across the money in the envelope, letting his thumb riffle across the bills, reassuring himself that there really was that much money in there.

He took out a bill to pay the driver and they both got on the bus. Once aboard, they felt safer and more relaxed, but neither of them uncovered their heads until they were past the city limits. Wayne looked out the window one last time, imagining his wife and children finding the note he'd left for them. He exhaled deeply, leaned back and closed his eyes. Jeanine loosened her scarf and took his hand. They both smiled at each other and relaxed. A long road lay ahead of them.

The sun was just starting to brighten the horizon. A new day was about to dawn for the people of Merky.

21

Wayne Bates' neighbors were awakened by the sounds of his wife's shrieks when she found his note that morning, and when Jeanine didn't show up for her job at the dime store most people figured out what had happened. This was very troubling to Bill Hickey. He was having a hard time accepting his loss and considering who he was up against, namely Mel Tucker, he was also very suspicious. He went back to the jail where the card table and ballots were still set up in the jail cell. He went through each stack recounting the ballots. Although his count agreed with the election judges, he was bothered by the way the votes were dispersed. Two of the boxes had ballots in which the counts were close. In one box he came out ahead and in the other Rooster was the winner, whereas the other two boxes were significantly in Rooster's favor. Hickey was no statistician, but he thought that the odds of the votes coming out like that were unlikely. He compared the sets of ballots to each other. They looked the same. Then, he noticed the ballot boxes. Whereas he thought they were all almost exactly alike, two of them seemed to be somewhat different from the other two. They looked similar if you weren't paying close attention, but when you examined them closely, it was clear that two of them were newer. The fact that Wayne Bates had been in charge of transporting the ballot boxes and he was now nowhere to be found was very troubling indeed. The only other person present when he picked up the ballot boxes was one of the election judges, Arlen Moore, whom Hickey also did not trust. Hickey could feel a deep burning anger welling up from inside. He couldn't prove it, and he wasn't sure if anyone would listen, but he was almost certain that the election had been stolen from him, and by the son of a bitch whose grandfather killed his father. He went to Mayor Pee Wee Jones and told him of his suspicion. Pee Wee was more sympathetic to Hickey than most, and he was no fan of Mel Tucker either, so he listened carefully as Hickey relayed his theory.

"It sounds plausible, Bill, but what proof do you have?"

"If I could find the stolen ballot boxes, that would prove it."

"Yes, it would. But where can you look? Surely, if this was a real case of fraud, whoever did it would destroy any evidence."

"I know where I should look, out on Mel Tucker's ranch, that's where."

"You've got to have more than just a hunch to go snooping around on Mel's place. Besides, if Mel did it, he's probably already destroyed the evidence."

"That son of a bitch!" Hickey fumed, as he smacked the mayor's desk with his fist.

"Sometimes, Bill, you just got to take what life delivers and move on."

"Easy for you to say."

"That's right, it is easy for me to say, but it's also the truth."

Hickey left the Mayor's office and drove around town looking for anybody or anything suspicious. He still had some time before he was officially out of office, and he damn well planned to use it to his best advantage. By chance, he saw one of Addis Thigpen's neighbors working out in the yard, so he pulled over to chat.

"Hello, Tom, how are you?"

"I'm fine, Bill. Sorry about the election."

Hickey nodded his head.

"What's your neighbor over there been up to lately?" Hickey asked, gesturing toward Addis' house.

"Ol' Mr. Lawyer Man? He don't give me much trouble. He drinks a little whiskey every now and then and makes a little racket, but otherwise he's okay. I heard him and somebody out sitting in the backyard last night drinking and sitting around a fire till late in the night."

"That right? Reckon who it was?"

"Probably Mel Tucker, seems like those two are always up to something."

"Well, maybe I better take a look around, just in case it was somebody else over there up to no good."

Hickey parked the patrol car in front of the neighbor's house and walked around to the back of Addis' yard. As he went around the side of the house, he looked about to see if anyone was watching him. He stepped quietly so as not to make any noise until a couple of cats bolted from beneath a bush, startling him and causing him to jump. He pushed open a creaky wooden gate and crept softly into the backyard. He saw a couple of chairs gathered around a pile of ashes. He took a stick and stirred the ashes. They were long cold, and there was little of any substance remaining. Hickey felt the stick catch on something, and he fished around until he pulled out a small hinge. He wiped the ash from it and held it in his hand. He fished around some more until he found another and then he pulled out a couple of small hasps. He sifted around the ashes some more until he found a couple of small scraps of charred paper. He had no doubt about what he was looking at. It was the hinges from the ballot boxes and a couple of pieces of the ballots that had been burned the night before. It was precious little, probably not enough to make a case that would stand up in court, but it satisfied him to no end that he had at least solved this for himself. He put the pieces of hardware in his shirt pocket and walked around, looking here and there for anything else that seemed suspicious. When he was satisfied there was little else of interest, he got back in his car and went to the courthouse.

Hickey tried to make his case to anyone who would listen. He spoke with Judge Wilmer Kitchens and District Attorney Joe Grundy both of whom showed some interest but were not inclined to pursue it further. He even called the Texas Rangers in Austin but they told that he would at least have to have some witnesses and more convincing evidence before they would get involved. He tried every possible thing he could think of to make a case, and when it became evident that there was nothing else to do, he finally gave up. He was stung by the whole thing and had no desire to remain in Merky as a civilian. His pride wouldn't allow that. So he put his house and the diner up for sale and moved his family to Rio Sueño. Mel decided to make an offer on the diner and sew up the restaurant business in Merky. He tried to convince Rooster to buy Hickey's house, but Rooster thought that was adding insult to injury, and so he declined. Someone else put a bid on the house, and once the deals were done, Hickey loaded up the last of his possessions and turned in his badge.

This meant that Rooster would be sworn in earlier than scheduled, something he felt strangely apprehensive about even though he'd had a slight swagger to his step ever since the election. The mayor called Mel to bring Rooster to the courthouse so that he could be sworn in. A special assembly was called midmorning soon after Hickey left, and Judge Kitchens swore Rooster in as Laurie, Mel, Shirley, Addis and several others watched proudly. Once the swearing in was over, Laurie pinned the badge to his shirt, he strapped on his grandfather's gun, and he was officially the sheriff of Loma Grande County, Texas. They all went out to eat afterward with Rooster driving Laurie, Mel and Shirley in the patrol car. He played with the siren and lights on the way and grinned like a big kid as cars pulled over to let him pass by. After the meal, Mel asked the question he had been dreading.

"What about Joe?"

Rooster frowned. "I don't know. I'll talk to him."

Mel, sensing his discomfort, let it drop.

As it turned out, Joe would take care of things himself. When Rooster went to the courthouse after the celebratory meal, he found Joe's badge, uniform, and service revolver waiting for him. The secretary, Mildred Crowe, smiled a wrinkled old smile when Rooster entered the office as sheriff for the first time. Rooster tipped his hat and sat as his desk. It was then that it hit him; he didn't have the slightest clue as to what he was supposed to do.

He decided it was better to look busy rather than do nothing, especially with Mildred around. He started looking through the desk. He found a few pennies, various pens, pencils and a couple of paper tablets. There was a set of keys, but he didn't know what they went to. He looked around and spotted a gun cabinet with a few rifles and shotguns locked away. He tried the keys and discovered that they fit the cabinet. He smiled to himself. He saw a file cabinet and started looking around in it. He saw files on Cletus and the Blackwell boys and then he saw one that said 'William 'Rooster' Brown.' He took the file to his desk, sat down and began reading through it. It detailed his arrest and noted that he had admitted that his grandfather was Devin Brown. He read on further. Hickey had written about his suspicions that Rooster had been planning a robbery or shooting when the real robbery occurred. Hickey noted in the margins of one paragraph: "I don't believe him." There were notes about the people Hickey had interviewed and the questions he had asked. It went on for page after page. Rooster was shocked at how much information there was about his case. He had not realized just how much effort Hickey had put into this investigation, and he was shaken when he realized once again just how fortunate he was. Hearing Mildred shuffling about he closed the file and put it back. He would dispose of it later. He went back to looking around and found the various logs that Hickey kept and some of the forms he might need. He was intrigued when he spotted a ticket book in one cabinet. All his life, he had been the recipient of tickets and now it dawned on him that he could actually write tickets on other people. The power that was now in his hands was starting to register for the first time. He was actually the goddamn sheriff. He was the law in Merky, Texas. He didn't have to worry about anyone arresting him. He would be doing the arresting from now on.

He went into the outer office where Mildred sat and pulled up a chair. He began to ask her about the daily routine and about anything significant that he was supposed to be aware of. Mildred, unaccustomed to being asked much of anything and flattered by Rooster's openness, began to recite the normal routine and duties of the sheriff. Rooster asked Mildred if she would help him learn all this and of course, she agreed. Rooster, sensing that this woman was indispensable, at least in the beginning, realized he would need to keep her happy in any way he could. He asked her about her family and her home life, and he got a pretty good feel for the kind of person she was. He was slightly alarmed and concerned to hear that Mildred was planning to retire in the near future, but she had not yet decided exactly when.

He continued to rummage about, acquainting himself with the office where he had once been the suspect instead of the law. Anything he found that had Bill Hickey's name on it, he either tossed or marked out his name. He pried the nameplate bearing Hickey's name from the door and threw it in the trash. Once he had inspected every-thing there was to inspect in the office, he got restless and decided to go out on patrol. He hopped in the squad car and began adjusting everything to fit him. He looked in the rearview mirror at himself and grinned. He eased the car slowly around the square and out onto the street. He pretended not to notice as the pedestrians along the square stared at him. He drove around town for a while then decided to take the car out onto the highway and see what it would do.

Once past the city limits, he turned on the lights and siren again and floored it until he was doing well over 100 mph. He sailed down the highway as everyone pulled over to let him pass. A grin spread across his face as the car roared over hill and dale. He topped one particu-larly steep hill, and as he zoomed over the crest, he spotted an old tractor chugging slowly along in his lane, and approaching from the other direction was a truck. He realized instantly that he couldn't stop and had no shoulder to go on, so he aimed for the middle. He squeezed the steering wheel, and at the last minute closed his eyes as he zoomed between the truck and the tractor, forcing both of them almost off the road. He hit the brakes and slowed the car down quickly, narrowly missing yet another car. As the car slowed to nor-mal speed, he went over a couple of more hills, his heart pounding. He turned off the lights and siren and found a spot to turn around. He waved sheepishly at the tractor driver as he passed him on the way back to town. Soon, he spotted a familiar road and turned off toward Bug Town. He rolled slowly through the sleepy settlement as everyone turned to stare and little kids ran down the dirt road fol-lowing him. Once past Bug Town, he kept on going and turned into the gate leading to Cletus' shack.

Cletus and Mexican Alice were sitting outside in the shade when they saw the police car pulling up the rough drive toward them. Rooster could see the look of concern on their faces as they watched him get-ting closer. It was apparent from the look on Alice's face that she was on the verge of running. Cletus, sensing this, grabbed her arm and waited to see what was going to happen. Rooster pulled up to them and stuck his head out the window, grinning from ear to ear. Cletus recognized him and jumped up.

"Rooster Brown, is that you?" he shouted.

"That's Sheriff Rooster Brown, Cletus."

"Well, I'll be goddamn. Is this a social call or business?" asked Cletus warily.

"Both," said Rooster as he got out of the car. "I reckon a man who just became sheriff ought to have a little nip to celebrate."

"I reckon that's exactly right, Sheriff Rooster. Come on over and have a sit."

Cletus motioned to Alice, and she disappeared into the shack where the brew was kept.

Cletus offered his hand to Rooster who shook it firmly.

"I thought you wasn't supposed to be sheriff for another month," said Cletus.

"Me, too. Turns out Hickey didn't want to stick around anymore, so he left. They swore me in this morning."

"Well, I'll be damn. I sure was relieved to see you. I thought that asshole Hickey was coming out to stir up some shit."

"You don't have to worry about him anymore."

Alice brought out a jar of home brew and a couple of beers.

"Now, go easy, sheriff. You don't want to wind up like the last time," said Cletus.

"I learned my lesson," said Rooster, "but I reckon ain't nobody gonna arrest me if I do get drunk."

"I reckon not," said Cletus.

"Yoo wife still boss," laughed Alice.

Cletus laughed, "Between Laurie and Mel, you still got plenty to worry about."

"Mel ain't the boss of me no more," said Rooster slightly perturbed.

Cletus studied Rooster for a moment. "Yeah, I guess you're right."

Rooster took a shot of the home brew and chased it with a beer. He stood up and reached into his pocket.

"How much do I owe you, Cletus?"

"This one's on the house, Rooster," said Cletus, taking the bottle of home brew. "Just remember, we're your friends."

"Oh, I remember, Cletus, I remember."

Rooster got into the car, feeling slightly drunk and headed back to town, spinning his wheels on the dirt road. He headed for the station where Obie and Kermit were on duty. He wheeled into the drive, dinging the bells as he came to a stop in front of the pumps. Obie and Kermit both stared at the car, looking slightly confused. Rooster rolled the window down.

"What's it take to get some service around here?" Rooster shouted.

"Rooster, what the hell?" asked Obie.

"Hickey decided to leave early. I'm officially the sheriff now."

Obie and Kermit both whistled and Kermit saluted.

Obie leaned in toward the window to talk and started sniffing the air.

"Had a little celebration already have you?"

Rooster was surprised. "You can smell it?"

"Hell yes, that home brew of Cletus' sticks to you like burrs on a dog's tail."

"Oh, shit, get me a pack of gum."

Obie went to get the gum, and Rooster got out of the car. He rustled around in his pocket for some change and went to the Coke machine. He pulled out a bottle of Coke and popped the top with the opener on the side of the machine. He slugged it down in a few swallows, and when Obie handed him the pack of gum, he popped two pieces in his mouth. He inhaled deeply a few times, and he was starting to feel a little more sober. He should have known better, he thought, than to go out to Cletus' the first day on the job. What if something had come up and he had to answer a call or something? He was feeling very stupid at that moment. Then, he worried that someone else might come by and figure out he had been drinking his first day on the job. He realized he needed to nip this in the bud right now.

"Look, fellows, this is just between me and you. Don't say anything to anybody about this. If anybody mentions something about me drinking the first day on the job, I'll know it came from one of you."

Obie and Kermit both swore to secrecy and Rooster decided he had better leave before somebody else showed up. He got in the car and drove around for a while with the windows down, trying to shake off the alcohol. Even though he had only had a shot and a beer it was affecting him. He needed to watch himself when it came to Cletus' home brew, it was always stronger than he anticipated. He looked at his watch. It was mid afternoon, and he didn't know what else to do. Then he realized that he didn't really have any set hours and that he was basically on duty all the time. He also realized that he didn't have a deputy and that he must bring someone on soon. He decided to go find Harvey.

He drove over to Harvey's house and parked in front. Even now, the old mansion intimidated him. He went up and rang the bell. He could hear footsteps from inside, and after a few moments, Harvey's mother answered the door. Seeing Rooster's badge and gun seemed to alarm her.

"Is there something wrong?"

"No, ma'am. I just came to see Harvey."

She closed the door and left him standing there. A few minutes later, he heard footsteps running toward the door. It swung open, and there was Harvey grinning at him.

"Howdy, Rooster. It's not time for my shift ye..." Harvey noticed the badge and gun and stopped in mid-sentence.

"There's been a slight change in plans today, Harvey. Hickey turned in his badge and left town. I'm the sheriff now, and I need a deputy."

Harvey just stood there gaping, unable to formulate a word, or perhaps even a thought.

"Harvey, did you hear me?"

"Uh...uh...yes..."

"Well, what do you say?"

"Uh...uh...okay, okay, Rooster."

"Come to the courthouse tomorrow and get your badge."

Harvey still stood there gaping and unable to speak. He nodded and closed the door in Rooster's face. Rooster shook his head; he was beginning to wonder if this was such a good idea after all. Here it was his first day as sheriff, and already he had gotten drunk on the job, almost killed a couple of innocent motorists, and hired the town idiot. He hoped tomorrow would be better.

22

The next morning, Rooster began his first full day as sheriff. He was sitting at the kitchen table eating breakfast and watching Laurie as she bustled about in the kitchen. She was wearing a housecoat that hugged her ass and made it seem even cuter and rounder than usual. In spite of what she had said about not caring whether he was a sheriff or a grease monkey she had been fucking him like a French whore ever since he won the election and had given him a particularly hearty screwing last night. He was sipping his coffee wondering whether he had time to knock off another piece of ass when he heard someone coming up the drive. He looked out the living room window and saw Mel's car coming up the drive. It occurred to him for the first time that Mel was no longer his boss. Mel parked the car, rapped on the door lightly, and walked in.

"Good Morning, Sheriff Brown," he said jovially to Rooster. Then he tipped an imaginary hat to Laurie. "Mrs. Brown," he said politely.

"Come on in, Mel. Have some coffee," Rooster said.

"Don't mind if I do."

"Daddy, what brings you here this early in the morning?" Laurie asked.

"Oh, nothing much, just thought I'd see what the sheriff has planned for today."

"I'm going to swear Harvey in this morning," said Rooster.

"Harvey?" Mel asked quizzically. "You really going to hire that boy?"

"I said I would, in the debate, remember?"

"Oh, I remember. I just didn't know if you were still planning on doing that. He still works for me, you know, and that's going to leave us short handed again."

Rooster started to squirm slightly. "I need somebody Mel, and Harvey has done the job. He knows a lot even if he is kind of different."

"Oh, he's different all right, but I guess you have a point. He probably does know some things that you need to learn. All right, dang it, I guess you can have him. I better tell Kenneth that he's going to have start working after school more."

Rooster looked over at Laurie, who just turned to wash the dishes.

"Well, Rooster, I guess I better get going. I need to work out a new schedule at the station. I might have to get out there and pump some gas myself."

Mel left and the place suddenly seemed very quiet.

"I didn't think I was stealing one of his employees," said Rooster. "I thought he knew I was going to take Harvey with me."

"Oh, Daddy will be all right. He just has to get used to idea that he's not your boss anymore," Laurie said as she walked up behind Rooster and wrapped her arms around his neck. "You're Sheriff Rooster Brown now, honey."

Rooster reached up and ran his hand along Laurie's arm. She lay her head down on his shoulder and kissed his ear. Rooster looked at the clock. He felt Mr. Hard Dick making his presence known, and he knew that he was going to be late for his first full day on the job.

When he finally did make it to the office, Mildred was sitting at her desk shuffling some papers around. She smiled when she saw Rooster coming in.

"Oh, good, Sheriff, you're just in time. I need you to sign off on the payroll."

Rooster looked at her as if she had just spoken Japanese to him. It had never occurred to him that he might be responsible for people getting paid.

"Um okay, I'll take a look at it," said Rooster.

He took the stack of papers and went to his desk. He looked at them one after another. He may as well have been looking at chicken scratch. He handed them back to Mildred.

"It looks fine to me."

Mildred looked at him funny.

"Well, then you need to sign them right here," she said, pointing to the bottom of the page.

Rooster took the papers back and signed each one, then handed them back to Mildred. He went into his office and began looking around more. He looked through some more drawers until he was satisfied that he had found everything there was to find. He leaned back and kicked his feet up on the desk. He put his hands behind his head and let the moment sink in. He was the goddamn sheriff of Loma Grande County, Texas. If he had been declared the King of England, it wouldn't have seemed any more bizarre to him. He couldn't believe how much had happened to him in such a short time. It seemed like a dream, yet no dream he had ever had could have turned out this fantastic. He wondered, what had he done to deserve all this?

He was sitting there reflecting on all this when Harvey came in wearing his old uniform and grinning to beat the band. When he saw Rooster, he snapped to attention and saluted.

"Deputy Harvey Wells reporting for duty," he said cheerfully.

Rooster smiled at the sight of him.

"Well, good, Harvey, real good. We just got to get you swore in, and then we're in business."

Rooster then realized he had no idea how to go about swearing in a deputy, so he asked Mildred, who informed him that he could basically do it however he wanted. Rooster had Harvey raise his hand and swear to uphold the law and conduct himself morally while in the employ of the Loma Grande Sheriff's Department. Once the swearing in was done, he again found himself at a loss for what to do. He sent Harvey out to patrol around town so as to establish a police presence. As he waited around, he studied Mildred. He deduced that she probably knew as much about the day-to-day operations of the sheriff's department as anybody. He called her into his office.

"Mildred, how long have you worked for this department?"

"Almost twenty years," Mildred answered proudly.

"I reckon you know just about everything there is to running this place."

"Why yes. Yes, I suppose I do."

"I think, as a testimony to your service, we need to have you write down all that you do and all that you know about keeping this place running smoothly."

Mildred looked at him incredulously. "You want me to write down everything I do here?"

"Yes, I do."

"What on earth for?"

"You said you're going to retire soon, aren't you?"

"Well, yes, but I haven't set a date."

"That's the whole point. What if you quit tomorrow? Then all that knowledge you have acquired is lost. We need some kind of guide for the next person."

Mildred looked flustered. She put her hand to her mouth. "Oh, my."

"It don't have to be real fancy, Mildred, and nobody's going to grade your spelling, but it's important that we have this information. You don't have to do it all at once. Just try to do a little bit every day so that when you leave we will have it."

Mildred went back to her desk shaking her head. Rooster was feeling pleased with himself, he had done something smart after all. He needed the information, and it would be good to have it in writing. He could always get Laurie to help him figure it out later.

He then decided to walk around the courthouse. All the county and city administrative offices were located here. As he walked down the hallways, his footsteps echoed along the corridors, and each time he passed by an open door the occupants would look to see who was there. As he made the rounds, he was greeted respectfully by the various administrators he encountered, and he was beginning to feel more comfortable in his new role. He walked around all three floors of the courthouse and returned to his office to find Mildred busily writing on sheet of paper. Harvey had returned and was awaiting further instructions. Rooster was starting to feel more in charge, and he liked it.

It was almost noon, so Rooster told Harvey to wait at the office in case anyone called, and he went home to eat. As he passed by the station he noticed Joe working the pump. For a moment, Rooster thought about pulling up to the pump and bossing Joe around, but then he decided to wait and talk to Mel first. He would not have to wait long, for Mel's car was sitting outside the house when he arrived. Rooster was hoping to see a little less of Mel after the election, but he realized it was still soon afterward, and Mel had worked hard to help him win. Rooster entered to find Mel and Laurie sitting at the kitchen table.

"How did you talk Joe into coming back?" asked Rooster.

"It wasn't hard. He needed a job, and I offered him the manager's position."

"He didn't have any hard feelings about what happened before?"

"If he did, what's he going to do about it? We had a talk. He understands that business is business. He understands why I did what I did."

"Well, I'm going to go over there and lord it over him like he did me."

"You leave Joe alone. Whatever hard feelings you got, you'll just have to get over."

Rooster clenched his jaw but didn't say anything.

"Never mind about Joe, I got more important things to discuss," said Mel.

Rooster looked over at Laurie who smiled and shrugged her shoulders, obviously playing coy.

"Now that you're the sheriff, you need a telephone," said Mel.

"A telephone?! What on earth for? I ain't never had a telephone in my life."

"You've never been the sheriff before either."

"A telephone...why?"

"Rooster, you're the sheriff. You're the man people are going to call when they need help. If somebody on the other side of town is getting robbed, they can't call time out and come over here and get you in person. They need to be able to call you right away."

"Then, they can call the courthouse."

"Okay, are you going to be there at two in the morning just in case somebody's getting killed?"

"Well, no..."

"That's what I'm talking about. You need to be accessible to the public."

"Oh, good grief..." Rooster was realizing that Mel was right, but he wasn't quite ready to give in just yet. He just sat there, shaking his head.

"We'll get the phone company up here to install it. Now that you're the sheriff, you can afford it."

Rooster sighed, knowing he was beaten once again, but Mel wasn't finished yet.

"And one other thing, Rooster, then I'll leave you alone. You need a better home for your family," said Mel, "and renting is no good either. I think you and Laurie ought to buy a house."

Rooster's jaw dropped. Of course he had thought that some day he would like to own a home, but that was still far off in his mind. He had barely been married three months and was just on the second day of his new job, and now Mel was already trying to talk him into buying a house. He felt completely flabbergasted. He also felt a small ember of resentment growing in his gut that he was still being bossed around by Mel.

"Goddamn it, Mel, let me try to digest one thing at a time. I'm still trying to get used to the idea of being a sheriff, and now you want me to buy a house after two days on the job. I'll get a telephone, you're right about that, but give me a little time to think about a house."

"Okay, Rooster, I'll give you some time."

'Some time' turned out to be less than a week. Rooster and Laurie were sitting around the house enjoying a quiet evening together when the phone rang, startling Rooster.

"Dang it. That thing makes me jump every time," he muttered softly.

Laurie got up to answer the phone.

"Hello? Oh hi, Daddy...just sitting around listening to the radio... what?...um...I thought that...okay...okay...I'll mention it to him...I will... goodnight, Daddy."

Rooster looked at Laurie. "What was that about?"

Laurie sighed. "I almost hate to mention it. You'll probably just get mad."

"Well...what is it?"

"Daddy said there's a real nice house with some land for sale next to him and Momma's place."

"Oh, jeez...I knew it...I told him I wasn't ready for that yet," Rooster fumed.

"I know, honey. I'm sorry. Don't worry, I won't let Daddy bully you into it. I don't need a big fancy house, I'm happy here...with you."

"Dang it, Laurie, of course I want to buy a house for you. I just don't want to be pushed into it, that's all."

"I know, Rooster. I know."

Rooster glared at the telephone. Ever since they had it put in, most of the calls were from Mel and Shirley or Laurie's friends. They had yet to be called for an emergency, but Laurie was obviously enjoying it, and one benefit was that now Mel could just call when he wanted something instead of coming by unannounced.

They sat around listening to the radio for a while when finally Rooster broke the silence.

"What did he say about the house?"

"He said it was real nice, on quite a few acres and near Butcher Creek. He said he thought he could get us a good deal on it."

Neither of them spoke for a while. Then, Rooster broke the silence again.

"Maybe we can go take a look at it this weekend."

Laurie smiled. "Okay."

That Sunday, Laurie and Rooster drove out to Mel and Shirley's for dinner. All through the meal Mel never said a word about the house. Rooster was determined not to mention it either. Finally, Shirley decided to bring it up.

"Did your father tell you about the house on the property next to us? It's for sale."

"Yes, he did. We thought we might like to look at it," said Laurie.

Mel smiled slightly. "Well, if you want, we can drive over later and take a look."

Rooster said little, but he was starting to feel a little excited about the whole idea now, although he was determined not to show it. After they finished eating, they got into Mel's Cadillac and drove over to look at the place. It was adjacent to Mel and Shirley's property and was almost as big. They had to open a barbed wire gate and drive down an overgrown car path to where the house sat. It had been vacant for several months since the previous owner had died, and it had the look of abandonment, but even in its overgrown and neglected state it still was an attractive house. Rooster sat up in his seat when he first glimpsed it. Mel was watching him in the rearview mirror.

"It's not too bad, eh, Rooster?" said Mel softly.

Rooster just grunted, but it was an affirmative grunt. As they got closer, he could see it was actually a fine old farmhouse, with a nice stone chimney and a gabled roof. It had a porch running the length of it, and the yard was enclosed with a crooked picket fence. It needed paint and cleaning, but it definitely had a bit of charm to it. They parked in front and waded through the weeds, which were brown and dying with the approach of winter. There was a well with a pump house off to the side, and a chicken coop in the back, and a nice barn off to the other side. There was still a faint smell of livestock lingering in the air, and a few old chicken feathers and dry cow patties lay about. They went up onto to the front porch and pushed open the door. It was stale and slightly musty inside, but the interior looked solid as well. They walked about, exploring each room, their footsteps and voices echoing in the emptiness of the place. Rooster and Mel went out back and followed a trail, which led to a bluff that overlooked Butcher Creek. It was much like Mel's spot, perhaps even a little nicer. Rooster stood on the bluff watching the creek burbling below him. It was quiet, with just a slight breeze. In the distance, a cow mooed plaintively, and the leaves rustled and fell from the trees in anticipation of old man winter. The air was crisp, as if a norther were ready to blow in. Rooster looked back toward the house, and he could see Shirley and Laurie walking about. He only had to see the look on Laurie's face to know it was already a done deal. He looked about once more, imagining it with the yard cleaned up and the house painted and maybe a child or two playing in the yard. Rooster looked at Mel, who also seemed to be deep in thought.

"How much do they want?" he asked softly, almost apologetically.

"Oh, I'm not sure, but I can find out. The old man that lived here didn't have any heirs, so it will go to auction for back taxes if nobody wants it. I suspect you could get a pretty good deal on it. I can call Addis to look up the records on it if you want."

Rooster nodded his head silently. He wanted to say something, but wasn't sure what. He was feeling ashamed of himself for being so angry when Mel first mentioned this. He realized that, once again, he didn't even know a good thing when it fell in his lap. He looked up at the clouds passing overhead and wondered once again why he was being blessed. Finally, he spoke.

"It's nice, Mel, real nice. I guess I'm just a dumb ass. I should know by now that when you come up with something, it's usually for the best. I didn't even know I wanted a house, but now that I've seen this I realize you were right. This is what I want...for Laurie...this is what she needs, and I want it for her...th...thank you, Mel."

Mel grinned broadly but wisely chose not to gloat. "It's not a done deal by any means, but I think you got a good shot at it. If need be, I'll cosign the note for you."

Rooster nodded his head again, a lump in his throat. He felt about an inch high for being so unwilling to even consider it at first. Mel clapped his hand on Rooster's shoulder, and they walked back into the house where Laurie and Shirley were already painting and decorating in their imaginations.

Of course, the next day, Mel set the wheels in motion without Rooster so much as having to lift a finger. Addis pulled the tax records and the deed, and they learned that it was to go on the auction block within a few weeks. Mel, determined that no one else should have it, went behind the scenes and pulled the necessary strings, and it was sold to Rooster and Laurie with no competing bids. And he got a good price on it and cosigned the note to boot. It was all done in a matter of days with hardly anyone in town aware of what had transpired.

As soon as he got the papers and the keys to the place (although no one ever locked their doors around Merky), Rooster started to work. He and Laurie spent all their spare time working on it, cleaning, painting and making minor repairs. They enlisted the help of Harvey and others, and of course, Mel and Shirley pitched in as well. Even Kenneth, perhaps caught up in the excitement of it all, came over and put in a fair day's work himself. When it was all done and the yard was cleaned up and the fence painted, the house just sparkled like a diamond. It was amazing to witness the transformation. Rooster could hardly believe it. It was just one more thing that had far exceeded his expectations.

Once they moved their meager belongings in, they realized how little they had. They were able to pick up some used furniture here and there and a nice old throw rug for the living room, and soon it didn't feel so empty, and it had become their home. When he took the last load of things from the little house in town, Rooster paused to look around wistfully. In a strange way, he felt a little melancholy. Although his new house was much nicer, he would always have a special fondness in his heart for the little house in the trees. In a matter of days, Mel would have it rented to someone else.

After they settled in and recovered from all the exhausting work of fixing up the place, they began to plan a housewarming party. Laurie was eager to show all her friends her new home. She also was feeling a bit overwhelmed at all the events of the past several months, but unlike Rooster, she was accustomed to good things happening to her. It was how her whole life had been, and she had no reason to think it would ever be otherwise. She especially wanted to show off for her friend Molly Muckleroy who had married into a nice family and whose husband was an up and coming officer at one of the two banks in town.

It took a little while before they were ready to throw the party. They wanted to make sure the place was as perfect as they could make it and that they could afford to buy all the food and drinks for their guests. Now that Rooster was sheriff, he was earning quite a bit more than when he worked at the station, and each payday he simply gave his check to Laurie who deposited it into the bank. It turned out that Laurie was a good manager, and she was able to provide for the house and to put money aside for little luxuries too. Mel and Shirley pitched in as well, and by the time the night of the party arrived it was after Thanksgiving.

A blue norther came in before the party, dropping temperatures significantly, so Rooster hauled in a load of firewood and built a fire in the fireplace for the party. Although he didn't tell Laurie, he had also made a run out to Cletus' to pick up drinks for the boys. He would have invited Cletus and Alice as well, but he knew Laurie would throw a fit and besides, they wouldn't fit in with all the society types that would be there.

By the night of the party, the house had undergone an amazing transformation. Whereas not long ago, it had been a faded, empty, musty and neglected hull, it was now clean and painted, gaily lit up and brightly decorated when the guests arrived. Once the party was in full swing, the house was packed with people all talking and laughing. The cream of Merky society was there, a fact not lost on Rooster. Less than a year ago, he was a nobody, in fact less than a nobody, for all intents and purposes invisible to the world. Now here he was, the toast of the town in his own fine home with the mayor and assorted dignitaries in attendance. It didn't seem real, and at times he wondered if it actually were real. However, in spite of all his apparent good fortune, a slight feeling of dread gnawed at him. He often worried that someday, when he least expected it, the world would collapse around him, that he would wake from a beautiful dream and find himself in a prison cell, having actually killed the waitress Jeanine that night at the truck stop. But, if it was a dream, then so be it, he would enjoy it until he woke up.

As the party continued through the night, the women all congregated in the living room around the fireplace where they giggled and gaggled and carried on. The men slowly all slipped away to the outside even though it was cold. Rooster had hauled some wood down to the bluff overlooking Butcher Creek and built a campfire, and the men stood around sipping home brew and beer and warming themselves by the fire. It was a cold, clear night and the stars sparkled brightly overhead. In spite of the big talk and guffawing, Rooster could still hear Butcher Creek burbling below. He watched as Mel and Addis and some others laughed and joked, and his heart filled with gratitude. He was still feeling a little chagrined for being angry with Mel for trying to talk him into buying the house. Clearly, it had been the best thing to do, and he now realized it. Although Mel pushed him into things he didn't want to do, he had to admit that Mel seemed to know more what was best for him than he did himself. He was both grateful for this and somewhat confused by it. He didn't know whether to trust his own judgment or not. However, he was a grown man, and he couldn't always let Mel make his decisions for him. He determined that he would be more open to suggestions from others and try to learn from the successful ones.

He made a conscious attempt to speak to everyone, and so walked around from group to group to engage all in conversation. As he made his way over to Mel and his group, he heard Mel mention that he had new tenants in the little house he had once called home. This piqued his interest.

"So what are the new tenants like Mel?" he asked.

"Oh, they're a nice young couple. He's an officer in the army and his wife is from Germany."

"I wonder why they rented a place in town," Rooster mused.

"Well, he's about to get stationed in Korea for a while, and I suspect he decided to move the missus into town to keep her away from all the hard dicks on base," Mel laughed.

"You think?" asked Rooster.

"If you see her, you'll probably think so too," Mel said and let out a whistle. "That woman is just about the prettiest thing I've ever laid eyes on."

Rooster began to wonder just how pretty she could be. He decided to drive by sometime and see if he could catch a glimpse of her just to satisfy his curiosity. Then the conversation took a different tack and he forgot about it.

Not surprisingly, Rooster drank more than he should have that night, and when he woke up the next morning on the living room floor, he had to contend with a pounding head and an angry wife. He was awakened by the sound of pots banging loudly in the kitchen. At first, he was confused as to where he was, but slowly it came back to him. After most of the guests had left, a few men remained drinking around the campfire until the wee hours. When the last one finally departed, Rooster stumbled back to the house. He lost his balance and fell in the living room, then passed out on the floor where he stayed all night. He was cold and stiff, and his mouth was dry. He groaned as he rolled over and sat up. Hearing him stirring about, Laurie banged a pan loudly. Rooster winced in pain. He knew he was in trouble, and for a moment he considered laying back down on the floor and pretending to be asleep. However, he knew that eventually he would have to rise and face the music, so he stood up unsteadily and pondered his next move. Before he could take another step, Laurie stomped into the living room and glared at him. She turned and left without saying a word. She didn't have to say anything, her look said everything that Rooster needed to know and then some. He knew he had fucked up, and he would have to do some serious ass kissing to fix it, but first he had to get up and get himself together. He went to the bathroom and started running a bath. He sat on the commode while letting the tub fill with water. Then, he smelled coffee brewing so he poked his head out of the bathroom to see where Laurie was. He didn't hear her anymore, so he decided to try to sneak into the kitchen and get a cup before she noticed. He made it there undetected and poured himself a cup, and was tiptoeing back to the bathroom when Laurie's voice stopped him in his tracks.

"I didn't want to marry a drunk."

"You didn't. I just had too much last night. That's all."

"Why did you have to drink in the first place?"

"It was a party. People drink at parties."

"I didn't. Momma didn't. Harvey didn't. Molly didn't. Kermit didn't..." Laurie shot back.

"Well, good for y'all. Since we're naming names, let's identify some of them that did drink, such as *Mel* and *Addis* and *Arlen* and *the mayor*..."

"I don't care!" Laurie shouted, cutting him off.

"Well, I don't care who didn't drink! It's a free country damn it!"

"Alcohol is not legal in this county. Where did it come from? Did you go out to that Cletus's place again? You're the sheriff, you know. You're supposed to act better than that."

"I don't give a damn what..." Rooster stopped and cocked his ear. He could hear the sound of water running out onto the floor.

"Shit!" he shouted and put down the coffee cup and ran to the bathroom to shut off the water. Now, he was really angry. He pulled the plug in the tub to let some of the water run out and went back for his cup of coffee. He was ready to let Laurie have it now, but she was gone by the time he got back. He took his coffee to the bathroom and sat on the commode drinking it. Once the water had receded some, he put the plug back in. He was still sitting there, sipping his coffee when Laurie leaned a mop against the door and left. When he finished his coffee, he took the mop and swabbed up the water then got into the tub and leaned back and closed his eyes.

As he lay there, he could smell bacon and eggs cooking in the kitchen. As much he wanted to just soak in the tub and avoid Laurie, he couldn't ignore the fact that his stomach was growling and he was hungry as hell. He finished bathing and got dressed. By now, his mouth was practically watering he was so hungry. He walked softly back to the kitchen, cautiously poking his head through the door before entering. There was a plate of bacon, eggs, and toast waiting for him on the kitchen table. Laurie was gone again, for which he was grateful, so he sat and wolfed down the breakfast and then poured himself another cup of coffee. He was feeling better now. The hangover was subsiding and his stomach was full. He began to feel guilty. Laurie was right. He wasn't just some ranch hand anymore. He was the sheriff of Loma Grande County, and he needed to start acting like it. He then began to wonder what the guests at the party had seen and what they thought of him now. He gathered up the dishes and set them in the sink. He was about to leave them there then thought better of it. He washed the dishes as well as the skillet and wiped down the table and the counter top and then he went to look for Laurie.

He walked softly through the living room and down the hall to where their bedroom was. He looked around the corner and saw Laurie lying on the bed facing away toward the wall. He knocked lightly on the doorjamb. She said nothing, so he walked in and sat on the bed facing her back.

"I'm sorry, honey. You're right. I shouldn't be drinking, especially now that I'm the sheriff. I just wanted to have a little fun with all my friends and family. I won't drink anymore."

Laurie still said nothing, but she sighed softly and rolled on to her back.

"I don't care if you drink a little every now and then, Rooster. What bothers me is when you get drunk like that."

"I know. I'm sorry. I won't do it anymore."

Laurie looked over at Rooster sadly. Then, she mustered a little smile.

"I think I'm pregnant."

Rooster's jaw dropped. "What?"

"I've been sick the last couple of mornings. Something's different. I just feel like that's what it is."

Rooster lay down next to her and put his arm gently across her belly. Neither of them said anything for several moments.

"Do you need to go to the doctor?" he asked softly.

"I don't know, probably not yet. I'll talk to Momma about it."

Rooster rolled over onto his back and stared at the ceiling.

"A baby," he said softly to no one in particular.

23

Rooster spent the next couple of days in a dreamy, near trance-like, state. Having a baby was the culmination of manhood. Once he became a father, he would have fulfilled all the unspoken requirements to enter the world of adulthood. Even fighting in a war had not commuted upon him the status of community elder that he would acquire simply by siring a child, and he knew that he would be regarded differently in the eyes of the town. However, Laurie had sworn him to secrecy until the pregnancy was confirmed, so he was in a state of limbo, clearly affected by this new development, yet unable to explain to anyone what was causing it. Everyone noticed that something was going on, and everyone asked what was going on, but they got nothing more than mumbled nonsense and grunts. Even Harvey, whose ability to identify social cues was lacking, was aware that something had changed, but even he could not pry the information from Rooster. Mildred just pretended nothing was different and went about her work as she began to think more about retiring. Finally, Laurie went to the doctor who put his stethoscope on her belly and did some tests. Nothing was conclusive, so he told her to monitor her periods and to come back in a month. This was torture for Rooster. He wanted to know now. He wanted to tell somebody. He wanted the world to know that he was going to be a father.

Christmas came, and it was the nicest one that Rooster ever had. He had a wife, a family, a home, and all that was missing was a child, and with any luck, that would come soon. During his own childhood, his Christmases had always been somewhat disappointing. His father would usually get him something, but it was never what he wanted, and it always felt lonely with just the two of them. Sometimes, one of his father's parishioners would get him a gift or invite them to spend Christmas with their families, but he always felt like an outsider. This year, they had a tree and gifts and a big dinner with Mel and Shirley and a few other guests. It was finally the Christmas that he always wanted.

After the holidays were over, Laurie missed her period and went back to the doctor again who did another test, and this time he was able to confirm that she was pregnant. Laurie went by the courthouse to tell Rooster, but he was not in, so she went home. She started to call Shirley, but she knew that if she didn't tell Rooster first that he would be hurt, so she set about cooking supper and waited for him to arrive.

Rooster was well aware that Laurie had an appointment with the doctor, and he was even more nervous and anxious than usual. He drove past Bug Town a couple of times and almost turned off onto the road toward Cletus' place, but he resisted and instead drove around until it was quitting time. He really didn't have to keep any set hours since he was basically on call all the time, but he liked to be seen out on patrol, and he was conditioned to work a regular schedule. Finally, the clock ticked off to five o'clock, and he went home. He pulled up in front of the house and parked. It still gave him a little thrill whenever he went home to his very own house. He could smell supper cooking as he walked up to the porch. He went into the kitchen where Laurie was turning a burner off on the stove. She turned and smiled at him. He knew right away but still had to ask just to be sure.

"Well?"

Laurie paused for just a second then smiled happily. "It came back positive. I'm pregnant."

Rooster whooped, threw his hat up in the air, and ran over to Laurie and kissed her. They put their arms around each other and just stood there, blissfully hugging each other.

"How long?" he asked.

"The doctor thinks I'm about two months along, so in about another seven months we should have a baby."

The reality of that number hit Rooster suddenly. That was not long at all. He pulled back and looked at Laurie.

"We need to get a crib and a high chair," he said wide-eyed.

Laurie laughed. "There's plenty of time for that. Besides, somebody will throw me a baby shower."

"Oh...yeah," Rooster said. He had no idea how these things worked. He picked his hat up and exhaled deeply. Suddenly, he felt weak-kneed and pulled up a chair and sat at the table.

"Damn, I think I'm going to faint. Two years in Korea didn't rattle me like this."

"You are happy, aren't you?" asked Laurie, frowning slightly.

"Oh, baby, I'm on cloud nine. I can't wait. I don't know how to explain it."

Laurie ran her fingers through his hair. "Why don't you go sit down in the living room and relax until supper is ready."

"Yeah, okay," said Rooster, and he got up and ambled to his favorite big chair and flopped down in it. He felt as if a big weight had been lifted from his shoulders. He couldn't wait to tell the world, and Laurie couldn't wait to tell her mother. As soon as she was able to take the biscuits from the oven and turn off the burners on the stove, she sat down and called Shirley. Rooster smiled as he listened to Laurie excitedly telling Shirley the big news. He could hear Shirley's voice coming through the earpiece, even from across the room. He closed his eyes and imagined himself holding a baby. He didn't even care whether it was a boy or girl. He began to think what they might name the child. Then, something occurred to him that made him sit up and open his eyes. Remembering his own lonely childhood, he silently vowed that they would have other children so that this one would have playmates. Rooster determined right then that this child would not have a similar experience to his. He thought that the worst thing he could do to this child would be to raise it alone as his father had with him. Then, he began to worry ever so slightly, what if something happened to Laurie. He shook his head as if to shake the thoughts away and scolded himself for worrying about something that would likely not ever happen.

After supper, Mel and Shirley came over to congratulate the young couple with hugs and kisses and handshakes. Mel was puffed up with pride and couldn't stop smiling. Rooster felt the happiest he had ever been in his whole life, and as he looked about at these people milling about in his house, yes *his* house, he realized just how fortunate he was. Life was truly good.

The next day, on the way to work, Rooster stopped in at the grocery store and bought a box of the finest cigars he could find. Before he went to the courthouse, he stopped at the filling station and handed out cigars to Kermit and Obie, and in a display of unusual magnanimity, even offered one to Joe, who quietly accepted it. Then he went on to the courthouse. Mildred was sitting at her desk as usual, busily scribbling away at her ongoing narrative of her day-to-day duties.

Although she had resisted this idea at first, once she began putting things down on paper she soon got caught up in it almost to the point of obsession, as if she were writing a great work of literature. Now she could scarcely do anything without putting it down on paper and had even started doing the same thing at home, noting all the things she did around the house, much to her husband's annoyance. Rooster grinned and offered her a cigar. Mildred looked at him in horror.

"Now, Sheriff Brown, you know good and well that I am not going to smoke a cigar. Land's sake, what kind of woman do you think I am?"

"Well, now, Mildred, I think you are one fine, upstanding woman," said Rooster, "even if you don't smoke cigars."

Rooster stepped gaily into his office and tossed the box of cigars onto his desk. He went and looked out the window down onto to the businesses lining the town square. It was a cold but sunny day and the wind whipped briskly down the streets, causing everyone to bundle up and trudge into the wind as they went about their business.

Rooster sat down, kicked his feet up onto his desk and lit a cigar. He leaned back in his chair, blowing smoke rings up over his head. He felt like the king of the world. Life couldn't get much better than this. This was heaven.

Harvey came in soon afterward, bundled up like an Eskimo. As he removed his coats and scarves and hats, he noticed Rooster smoking a big fat cigar. This struck Harvey as strange, and he froze in position while untying a scarf. He stared confusedly at Rooster for several seconds.

"What's the matter, Harvey? Ain't you ever seen a man smoking a cigar before?"

"Uh...yes."

"Well, come on in here and get one for yourself."

Harvey walked into Rooster's office slowly.

"Harvey, I'm going to be a daddy. Laurie's pregnant."

Harvey's eyes widened, and his jaw dropped, but he still said nothing. Mildred, overhearing this, put down her pen and came running into Rooster's office.

"Why, you sneaky devil, why didn't you say you were having a baby?"

"I just did."

"I mean, why didn't you tell me instead of trying to give me a cigar?"

"I don't know."

"Why, Rooster Brown, if that don't beat all," said Mildred as she walked around the desk to give him a hug. "I am so happy for you, for both of you."

Rooster looked up at Harvey, who was still staring at him slack-jawed.

"Dang, Harvey, if you can't think of nothing to say, at least plug that hole with one of these," said Rooster as he handed one of his stogies to Harvey.

Harvey took the cigar, put it in his mouth, and walked back into the main office shaking his head.

"When did you find out?" Mildred asked.

"We found out for sure yesterday, but Laurie had her suspicions a month ago."

"Well, of course, she did. She's a woman, and we don't really need doctors to tell us when we're pregnant. How far along is she?"

"Doc said about two months."

"My goodness. Well, Rooster, your life is about to change."

"I reckon I ought to be used to that by now."

Mildred went back to her writing, leaving Rooster to blow smoke rings and ponder the future. However, he couldn't sit still for very long, so he got up and grabbed his box of cigars and went off in search of people to tell the big news.

"Harvey, why don't you hold down the fort with Mildred. I'll be back shortly."

Harvey nodded his head as he warmed his hands over the small gas stove.

Rooster strode purposely along the hallways of the Loma Grande Courthouse offering a cigar to every man he met, and by the time he had covered the whole building, he was out of cigars and decided to go to the store to buy more. He walked out of the courthouse and across the street to one of the two grocery stores in town. He found another box of cigars and walked to the register when he saw something that stopped him in his tracks.

Standing at the cash register was a tall, slender, blond woman, perhaps the most beautiful woman he had ever seen in his life. She was counting out change to the clerk.

"Oh, dear," said the woman in an accent that Rooster quickly recognized. "I doan haf enough money. I vill put these one back."

Rooster knew a German accent when he heard one, and he quickly remembered what Mel had told him about the army officer's beautiful wife. He walked up to the counter.

"Wie viel brauchen Sie?" said Rooster.

The woman gasped and looked at him in shock. "Sie sprechen Deutsch?"

Rooster grinned. "Ein wenig – a little bit."

He offered his hand. "My name is Rooster Brown."

"Oh, you are de famous Shereef Brown," said the woman. She shook Rooster's hand. "I am Christine Cervenka. Pleased to meet vif you, Shereef Brown.

"I'm pleased to meet you, ma'am. You must be the one who's renting the small house from Mel Tucker."

"Oh, yes. How you know dees?"

"He's my father in law, and I used to live in that very same house."

"An whar you learn speak German?"

"Mostly around Stuttgart and Weisbaden. I was in the army there."

"Oh, make me so happy hear you speak German."

By now, a few people were beginning to line up behind them. The clerk cleared her throat and looked at Rooster expectantly.

Rooster set his box of cigars on the counter. "Just add whatever she is short to mine."

"Oh, you ahr so kind. I vill pay you back ven my husband sends me money."

"Don't worry about it. It was nice to meet you, Christine."

"You, too, Shereef Brown, an tank you so much."

"Please just call me Rooster. Everybody else does."

"Okay, Rooster. Tank you again."

Rooster stood there watching as she walked out onto the street. He was still standing there watching when the clerk cleared her throat again. He quickly fumbled around in his pockets and paid for the cigars and the extra for Christine. He walked out onto to the sidewalk and watched as she crossed the street.

Rooster shook his head and muttered under his breath, "Holy shit."

He was still watching Christine walk away when he stepped off the curb and fell down right in front of a car that was pulling in to park. His box of cigars went scattering, and his hat flew off his head. The car stopped with its bumper inches away from him. He quickly jumped up and saw old Mr. Hedgepeth grinning at him from behind the windshield.

"Dadgum, sheriff! You trying to give an old man a heart attack?" laughed Mr. Hedgepeth.

Rooster felt himself turn red. He dusted himself off, picked up his hat and looked around to see if anyone had witnessed him fall. Indeed, a few women stood watching, holding their hands to their mouths and trying not to laugh. Rooster muttered to himself and began picking up the cigars and putting them back into the box, carefully brushing off the ones that had dirt stuck to them. A few were broken and those he tossed back into the street. Once he had them all picked up, he stepped aside and motioned to Mr. Hedgepeth that he could now park his car.

He started walking back to the courthouse. His knee hurt, and he had scraped his hand on the pavement but other than wounded pride he was okay. It was very cold and that made his scrapes hurt even more. Instead of going back to the courthouse, he decided to get in his squad car and drive around. He peeled out and headed toward the gas station where he saw Christine walking past it and toward the little house in the trees. Obie and Kermit tipped their hats respectfully to her as she walked by. Rooster drove past them, watching her again as she walked away. He drove a few blocks, then turned around and went back to the station. Kermit and Obie came out to the squad car to meet him.

"What y'all think about that little fraulein?" he asked them.

"That is one fine looking woman," said Kermit.

"If only I was forty years younger," said Obie.

"If only what?" asked Rooster.

"Nothing," said Obie. "I just wish I was forty years younger."

"That's what I thought," laughed Rooster.

"What are you looking at, Mr. Married Man?" asked Kermit.

"Hell, I reckon I can still look, can't I?"

"Only a little bit, and when nobody else is paying any attention," said Obie.

"Well, I reckon it don't hurt to look, so I'm going to look all I want to," said Rooster.

"It might hurt you to look, especially if Laurie catches you," said Kermit.

"I guess I just won't let that happen then."

Two cars pulled in, and Obie and Kermit went to go wait on them, so Rooster pulled out of the driveway and slowly drove past his old home. She was already inside, so he turned and went back to the courthouse.

Rooster parked his squad car at the courthouse and walked over to Addis' office. As he got nearer, he noticed Mel's Cadillac out front, so he figured he could hand out two cigars in one trip. When he entered the office, Lacy was sitting at her desk typing. She smiled at Rooster.

"Good morning, Sheriff Brown. How are you today?"

"I'm doing real good, Lacy. How about yourself?"

"Just fine, and how is Mrs. Brown?"

"Mrs. Brown is with child," said Rooster, grinning.

"Oh, that is wonderful! Congratulations!"

The door to Addis' office opened, and Mel stuck his head out.

"I thought that sounded like you, Rooster. Come on in."

Rooster stepped into Addis' wood paneled office and extended his hand to both men.

"Congratulations, Sheriff. I hear you're going to be a father."

"That's right, Addis, we're real happy. Here, have a cigar."

Addis took a cigar then reached into his pocket and pulled out a Zippo lighter. He clanked open the lighter and lit Mel's cigar and then his own.

"It's been a hell of a year for you, eh, Rooster?" said Addis.

Rooster nodded his head. "Like a dream."

Mel chuckled. "Better than a dream. At least you won't wake up from this."

I hope that's true, thought Rooster.

They spent the next few minutes chitchatting idly about this and that. Rooster started to tell Mel that he had met the beautiful German woman but decided not to. Then he noticed that Addis' desk was covered with papers that he and Mel had obviously been poring over when he arrived. After a few minutes, Mel began looking at his watch.

"Thanks for the cigar, Rooster. Now, if you'll excuse us, we have a lot of things to go over here, and Addis is charging me by the hour," said Mel.

"Oh, sure, Mel, no problem. I just came in to hand out cigars, and I got a bunch more left, so I'll see y'all later."

Rooster closed the door behind him and tipped his hat at Lacy as he went out the front door.

After he left, Mel and Addis looked at each other knowingly and then returned to the business at hand.

24

The next few weeks were some of the happiest of Rooster's life. In anticipation of the baby, he began preparing a nursery in one of the bedrooms. He also fixed every little broken thing around the house so that it would be in immaculate condition to receive the infant child.

He and Laurie lay next to each other during the cold winter nights, snuggling and keeping each other warm. During those first days especially, they had some of the best sex they had ever experienced.

However, that happy scenario did not last long. As the pregnancy progressed, Laurie became increasingly sick, and it wasn't long before she lost all interest in sex. She was nauseous much of the time, her back hurt almost constantly, and she got hemorrhoids. She gained weight, her ankles swelled up, her face broke out, and not surprisingly, she was unhappy and very vocal about it. Rooster felt as if he were witnessing some transmogrification straight out of a movie. The sweet, pretty woman he loved with all his heart had turned into a wretched, harpy.

As if all that weren't enough, Mildred decided it was time to retire and catalogue the rhythms of the day at her leisure while at home. Rooster fretted that maybe his streak of good luck had run out and that his old miserable existence was coming back.

Rooster desperately needed to talk to someone about the hell he was going through at home. He complained to Harvey, who mostly just nodded his head and said "uh huh" to everything, and Mildred was too busy writing in her diary to be of any help. He even tried to bring it up to Mel but found that more difficult because, after all, Laurie was his daughter and the apple of his eye. However, he did find a sympathetic ear in Shirley, who had also had difficult pregnancies and who was an empathetic soul and could understand the hurt and confusion that Rooster was experiencing. She invited him over for coffee one morning to talk about it.

"More coffee?"

"Yes'm. Thanks, Shirley."

"Now, Rooster, you just have to keep reminding yourself that this is temporary, and once it's all over you will have your sweet wife back, and a new baby as well."

"I know, Shirley, I know. At least, that's what I keep telling myself, but dang it's hard. Just this morning, she yelled at me and started crying because I slammed a door too hard. It seems like everything I do annoys her, and she is constantly on me about one thing or another. It's like she's not even the same person anymore. I know it's just temporary, but Lord, it's hard."

Shirley sipped her coffee. "Well, believe it or not, I got even fatter than Laurie and my face looked just awful. One day, when I was really feeling sick, I jumped all over Mel about something—I don't even remember what it was now—but I was so mean that he actually slept in his car that night. I felt terrible about it later, but he got over it, and you will too."

"I guess so, Shirley. I guess I can hold out another few months, but that idea about sleeping in the car sounds pretty good. Thanks for the suggestion."

Rooster decided that the best strategy was just to stay the hell away from Laurie as much as possible until the baby was born, and besides, he had plenty to keep him busy anyway. Mildred had given her notice so they were planning a big retirement party for her, and he had to find another secretary to replace her. This concerned him because Mildred knew everything there was to know about running that office. Even with her copious notes, it would be difficult to replace her. Addis offered him the services of Lacy to help with official correspondence and bookkeeping duties, which would be a big help, but still, they needed someone to actually be there and answer the phones and such. Rooster placed an ad in The Merky Magpie and he told everyone he knew to ask around to see if anyone was looking for work.

A few applicants began to trickle in, and some of them seemed promising, but still Rooster didn't feel like he had found the right one. He sat at his desk one day, looking over the handful of applications, and he was leaning toward one woman in particular when he heard someone come into the main office.

"May I help you?" asked Mildred.

"Yah, I am here to apply for de job you haf in de paper."

Rooster recognized the voice instantly. It was Christine Cervenka, the beautiful German woman. He quickly got up from his desk and walked into the next room.

"Good morning, Christine."

"Oh, Shereef Brown, goot morning to you."

Mildred looked at Rooster through narrowed eyes.

"I met Mrs. Cervenka in the grocery store," Rooster quickly explained to Mildred. "I was stationed in Germany in the army, so when I heard her accent, I introduced myself."

"Yah, Shereef Brown can speak Deutsche, I mean, German, vary well."

"I'm sure Sheriff Brown can do many things I don't know about," said Mildred, handing Christine a job application and pen. "You will need to fill out this application. When you are finished, give it to me, and I will put it with the others."

"How long vill it be before you decide?" asked Christine.

"Oh, it shouldn't take too long," said Rooster. "We only have a few applications."

"I may haf anudder offer but dees sounds like better job. Do you tink you vill know by de end of de veek?"

"Oh, yes, ma'am. I will let you know as soon as I decide. Do you have a telephone?"

Christine's face fell. "No, ve don't haf a phone."

"That's all right. I know where you live. I'll just come by and tell you in person, okay?"

"Dat would be very nice of you, Shereef. Tank you very much."

Christine sat down to fill out the application and Rooster went back into his office. From his seat behind his desk, he could see her crossed legs. They were nice, long, slender legs, smooth and tan, just the way he liked them, and it had been a while since he had gotten laid, so he could feel Mr. Hard Dick starting to rouse from his imposed hibernation. Rooster shook his head and tried not to look, but he found it impossible. He stood up and looked out the window until he heard Christine speak to Mildred again.

"Here, ees finished."

"Okay, thank you."

Rooster stepped back out into the main office, "Thank you, Mrs. Cervenka. I will get in touch with you soon."

"Tank you very much, Shereef Brown."

Christine left, and Rooster stood there lost in thought once again until Mildred cleared her throat.

"Well, she seems nice, don't you think?" Rooster asked.

"I suppose so," said Mildred, still looking at Rooster suspiciously.

Rooster took the application from Mildred and carried it into his office. He closed the door and looked it over. He mostly just studied her handwriting and her name. He looked at it for several minutes. Then he gathered up all the other applications and tossed them in the trash.

That night, Rooster went home to find Laurie laid up in bed and crying. Shirley was there serving her soup and trying to care for her as best she could.

"The doctor said she has to be on bed rest from now until the baby is born, Rooster," said Shirley. "I'm going to have to stay here most of the time until then."

Rooster scratched his head. "That's fine, Shirley. I reckon we sure need the help. I hate to put you out though."

"Rooster, this is my only daughter we're talking about, and this will be my first grandchild. You couldn't keep me away from here if you tried."

"I'm so sorry, Rooster," said Laurie. "This is just awful. I've been so mean to you, and I know it."

"That's okay, darlin'. I know you don't feel well. Heck, maybe I should bunk over there with Mel and Kenneth for a while."

"You may do that if you like, Rooster, or you can stay down the hall in the spare bedroom. We have the telephone if we need anything, and I am going to have Mel grade a road directly between our houses so that we can go back and forth easily," said Shirley.

"Okay, that sounds like a good idea," said Rooster.

Rooster was ready to get the hell out of Dodge for a while anyway, so he went over to Mel's, and they grilled up some steaks and drank some of Mel's stash of beer and whiskey, and Rooster was enjoying himself the best he had in a long time.

Rooster had planned on telling Mel that he was going to hire Christine Cervenka as his secretary, but every time he was about to bring it up, Mel would start talking about something else, so he never did get around to saying anything.

The next morning, Rooster went back to his house to check on Laurie and Shirley. Laurie seemed to be feeling better now that her mother was tending to her, and this made Rooster feel better as well. After chatting with them both, he kissed Laurie on the forehead and drove into town. He went to the office early and puttered around before

Mildred or Harvey got there. He looked over the application again and noticed for the first time that Christine had put down her husband as a reference. He was a captain, and his name was Cyrus Cervenka. Rooster was a bit surprised to learn that her husband was an officer, but considering how beautiful his wife was, it made sense.

Once Mildred and Harvey arrived, Rooster decided to go tell Christine that she was hired. He didn't tell either of them where he was going, just that he would be back later. He drove slowly past the gas station where Joe and Obie were waiting on customers and then on to the little house in the trees. He turned onto the driveway for the first time in what seemed like a long while and parked under the trees. He sat there for a minute watching for any signs of activity. He looked at his watch, it was a little before nine. He figured she should be up by then, so he got out and went to the front door. His boots clumped along the front porch, and he paused for a second before rapping on the door. He waited and listened. He heard nothing, so he knocked again. Soon, he heard the sound of footsteps. Christine opened the door slightly, she was wearing a robe and looked as if she had just woken up. Rooster was a bit taken aback, he wasn't expecting her to still be in bed.

"Oh...uh...I'm sorry, Christine. I didn't mean to wake you."

"Oh, Shereef Brown...please excuse me. I vill be right back."

Rooster waited on the front porch, looking around at his old homestead. A couple of minutes later, Christine returned to the door. She was wearing slacks and a sweater, and she had combed her hair.

"Please come in, Shereef Brown."

Rooster took off his hat and stepped inside. He was surprised at how good everything looked, even better than when he and Laurie lived there.

"Goodness. The place looks really nice."

"Yah, tank you. Ve couldn't keep all our furniture here, but enough to make comfortable. Vould you like some coffee?"

"Yes, that sounds good. Thank you."

Christine went into the kitchen to put on a pot of coffee and came back.

"Did you make decision yet?" she asked a bit apprehensively.

"Yes, I did. I would like to offer you the job."

"Oh, Shereef Brown, tank you so much. Dat is vunderful."

"Well, you were the best candidate, and you don't have to call me sheriff. Everybody calls me Rooster."

"Okay, Rooster, I vill do dat. Oh, these is vary good news. My husband vill be so happy."

"Yes, I'm sure he will be. Where is your husband now?"

"He ees in Korea for few months. Eet has been so difficult wit out him. I vill be so happy when he come back."

"I'm sure he misses you too."

Christine brought in coffee, and they sat there sipping and making idle chitchat for several minutes. When they finished their coffee, Rooster looked at his watch.

"Well, I need to run. When can you start?"

"Ven you want me start?"

"How about tomorrow morning?"

"Yah, dat vill be goot. Tank you again, Rooster."

Rooster said good-bye and left. He could see her watching him through the window as he backed out the driveway. He shifted uncomfortably in his seat, trying to make room for the sudden erection that was making it difficult to sit comfortably. It occurred to him that he would have to learn to keep his mind on other things when she was around or he would not be able to walk while she was in the office.

Rooster decided to goof off for a while, so he rode around town, looking at this and that and generally killing time. Then, he drove out past the city limits, and soon he was turning onto the road to Bug Town. He really hadn't planned to go there, but it had been a while since he had seen Cletus and Alice so he decided to pay a social visit. When he was almost there, it occurred to him that he and Mel had just about drank all of Mel's booze, so it seemed only right to buy some more to replace it. He pulled into Cletus' place and rolled slowly up the rough drive to the shack. Cletus heard him and came out to see who it was. Rooster waved and pulled up under the tree. Cletus came up to greet him.

"Damn! I can't get used to seeing that police car pulling in here," said Cletus. "Every time I see it, I don't know whether to run or not."

Rooster chuckled. "Well, as long as I'm sheriff, you got nothing to worry about."

Rooster offered his hand to Cletus, and they shook.

"We're always honored to have the sheriff here," said Cletus. "What can I do for you today?"

"I mostly just came by to visit, but I probably ought to get some beer, and a jar of that whiskey. I need to replenish Mel's stock."

"And how the hell is ol' Mel Tucker these days?"

"You know Mel; he's always got something going on."

"I reckon that's so. He was just out here a week or so ago, seemed a little bothered about something but didn't say what it was."

"Knowing Mel, he probably lost a penny or something," Rooster laughed.

"That's possible. Usually the man that takes care of his pennies don't have to worry about his dollars."

Cletus hollered at Alice to come out. She limped out of the shack.

"Dang, Alice, what happened to you?" Rooster asked.

"Damn scorpion sting chit outta me," groaned Alice.

"You want something to drink now, Rooster?" asked Cletus.

"Nah, I better not. Finally learning my lesson, I guess. Just get me a case of beer and a jar of that moonshine of yours."

Cletus motioned at Alice, who went to fetch the booze.

Rooster and Cletus sat under the tree, which was now barren of leaves, and bullshitted while Alice brought up the liquor. Rooster paid Cletus, put everything in the trunk of the squad car, and then headed back to town.

When he got back to the office Mildred was furiously scribbling away in her notebook, having remembered some forgotten piece of information that she thought important. Harvey was counting the straws in the broom and neither of them paid much attention to him when he walked in the office. Rooster stood there for a few minutes, observing both of them. He cleared his throat. Both of them stopped what they were doing and looked at him expectantly.

"I just thought I'd let y'all know that I hired someone to replace Mildred."

Both Mildred and Harvey sat up straight in anticipation of the big news.

"Well, who is it, Rooster?" asked Mildred.

"Christine Cervenka, the German woman."

Both Harvey and Mildred's eyes grew wide.

"The German woman?" asked Mildred incredulously. "Rooster, she can barely speak English."

"Well now, Mildred, I reckon she can speak English good enough to answer the phone and sweep the floors and what all else needs to be done. This is just temporary until I can get a real professional secretary."

"Professional secretary? What was wrong with the other women that applied? Some of them had experience, and at least they can speak proper English."

"She speaks English just fine. What difference does it make if she has an accent?"

"Well, it just does. This is an important job, and it reflects on you and the whole department."

"Well, it's already done, it's my decision, and that's that," said Rooster angrily.

"Okay," said Mildred, shaking her head, and she resumed her writing.

Rooster looked over at Harvey. "Well, what do you think?"

"I think she's real pretty, Rooster, and I don't mind the way she talks."

Rooster nodded his head in agreement. "That's right, Harvey. She'll do just fine."

Rooster went into his office and sat in his chair. He looked in the desk drawer and found a cigar. He lit it and kicked his feet up on the desk. That's right, he said to himself, she'll do just fine.

On the way home, Rooster picked up another box of cigars to smoke with Mel while they were drinking their whiskey that night. He went and checked on Laurie and Shirley and found them both relatively calm and relaxed. Then, after he had visited with them for a while, he went over to Mel's house and unloaded his booze and smokes in the garage. Mel had a "secret" hiding place that everyone knew about, so it was just kind of an inside joke to refer to Mel's "secret" spot. This spot was in a crate covered by an old tarp underneath a stairwell in the garage. Rooster pulled back the tarp, opened the crate and saw that there was already some beer and a couple of jars of whiskey. He could tell that neither of them had come from Cletus and that puzzled him for a minute, but then he resumed hiding his stash, and by the time he covered it all back up, he had already forgotten about it.

Shirley made a big pot of stew earlier that day and had taken some over for her and Laurie, but there was still enough to feed Rooster,

Mel, and Kenneth. Once Shirley settled back in with Laurie, Rooster brought out the liquor and cigars.

"Well, don't this beat the band," said Mel.

"I reckon it don't get no better," said Rooster.

"We should make this permanent," said Kenneth, who was being allowed to drink and smoke while Shirley wasn't around.

The three men, or two men and a boy, all sat around the fire in front of Mel's fireplace sipping whiskey and smoking cigars and feeling like the titans of Merky. They made idle chitchat for a while; then, during a lull in the conversation, Rooster spoke up.

"I hired a new secretary today."

"Did you now? Who is she?" asked Mel, obviously interested.

"Your tenant, Christine Cervenka."

Mel sat upright abruptly and looked at Rooster.

"The German woman? Are you kidding me?"

"No, I'm not kidding. I hired her."

"You hired her to take Mildred's place?"

"That's right."

Mel just looked at Rooster for a few seconds without saying anything. Then, he slowly smiled and shook his head.

"Rooster, you do beat all sometimes."

Mel seemed content to let it drop, but Kenneth was excited to hear the news. Ever since the beautiful German woman had arrived in town, all the adolescent boys were in heat.

"Dang, Rooster! I'm going to come down to the courthouse every day now."

"That might not be a bad idea, Kenneth. You can help me run off all the rest of the hard dicks that are going to come around."

"Heh heh, maybe you should hire Kenneth as a deputy," said Mel.

"Hey, yeah, I'm almost finished with school," said Kenneth.

Rooster looked over at Kenneth as if for the first time.

"Maybe," he said.

"Really?" asked Kenneth.

"After you finish school, we can talk about it."

Kenneth jumped up with a whoop and ran around like he was chasing someone with a gun and making bang bang noises. He ran up the stairs and out of earshot. Rooster and Mel laughed at the boy's foolish energy. Then they settled back into drinking and smoking.

"You tell Laurie about your new secretary yet?" asked Mel.

"No, not yet."

"That should be interesting," said Mel.

"Ain't nothing for anybody to be worried about."

"Uh huh."

"Damn, Mel. I'd have to be a dumb ass to try something with that woman. Everybody in town would know about it."

"Lots of people are dumb asses, even some of the smart ones."

"Well, I'm not going to be one."

Mel exhaled and paused, as if trying to collect his thoughts.

"You know, Rooster, I haven't got anything against a man getting him something on the side every now and then. Hell, it's normal to want to do that. The thing is, a man's also got to know where home and hearth is, and stick by it. Just don't be stupid, that's all."

"I ain't going to do anything," said Rooster. "She's just a damn secretary."

"Okay," said Mel.

Kenneth came running back through the room, shooting his imaginary gun at his imaginary criminals, and they moved on to other topics.

The next morning, Rooster woke up late. He had slept on the couch downstairs, instead of the spare bed upstairs. His clothes were rumpled, his mouth dry, and he had a slight hangover. He got up and stumbled into the kitchen for something to drink. Mel was sitting at the kitchen table, drinking coffee.

"Damn, you really do look like a rooster with your hair sticking up like that," laughed Mel.

"Mmmph," Rooster grunted in response.

He drank a large glass of water then poured himself some coffee and sat down at the table with Mel. When he finally started to wake up, he realized that he would need to go back home to check on Laurie and change into some fresh clothes. Mel cooked up some breakfast, and after he ate he felt much better. He made the short drive over to his house. He walked in to the bedroom where Laurie and Shirley were talking quietly.

"Good morning," Rooster said, trying not to sound hung over.

Laurie glared at him. "So tell me about your new secretary."

By the time Rooster left for work, he was practically reaching around to feel how much of his ass Laurie had chewed off. She was furious with him and had let him have it with both barrels. He had protested and proclaimed his innocence, both in actions and intentions, but she would have none of it. Now he was worried that he would have to fire Christine and look like a jackass. When he got out to the highway, he turned on the lights and sirens, then floored the gas pedal and sped away from town. When he had put several miles behind him, he switched off the siren and lights and slowed down to the speed limit. He was upset, hung over, and angry, and he didn't know what to do. He turned around and headed into town, not sure of what he was going to do or say. He decided to lay low for a little bit until he calmed down. He drove around town until about nine and then went to the office. He was trying to figure out how he was going to tell Christine that she was already fired on her first day on the job.

When he walked into the office, he found Mildred, Harvey, and Christine, all sitting around Mildred's desk, laughing and carrying on. They all smiled at him cheerily when he came in the door.

"We were wondering if you were going to make it in today," said Mildred.

"Good morning, Rooster," said Christine happily.

"Morning, Rooster," said Harvey. "Christine is really nice, and she has some great stories to tell."

"That's nice," said Rooster, trying not to let them see he was upset.

"I jus tell dem about ven I vas a little girl and picking mushrooms in de forest."

"And about how they stole some poor farmer's clothes who was bathing in a creek," laughed Mildred.

"He deserved it. He vas always mean to de children and den it vas our turn to get even," said Christine.

They were all having such a good time that it brightened Rooster's mood a little. He didn't want to tell Christine she was fired just then and spoil it for everyone, so he decided to wait until the end of the day. That way, at least she could earn a day's pay for her trouble.

After Rooster settled in his office, Mildred went about explaining to Christine what her basic duties would be. Christine was taking notes, writing everything down, trying to keep up with what Mildred was telling her. Harvey seemed to be under Christine's spell also, for he took an unusual interest in Mildred's job description, and he added to it whenever he thought of something. They all seemed to be enjoying themselves, and Rooster just sat in his office, listening to their voices and trying not to think about what he would have to do later.

He was lost in thought when the phone rang, causing him to jump slightly. He picked up the receiver. It was Laurie.

"Rooster, I'm sorry about this morning. I was really mean to you, and I want to apologize."

Rooster sat there listening to Laurie's words, simultaneously feeling relief, anger, and disgust.

"It's all right, Laurie," was all he could muster to say.

"No, it's not. I shouldn't have treated you that way. It's just that I was up a lot last night, and I was so tired this morning. When I found out that you hired that woman, it upset me so much."

"Who told you that I hired her?"

Laurie demurred and didn't answer him. "It doesn't matter. I should trust you, and that's that."

Rooster got up and closed the door. "So do you want me to fire her or not?"

Laurie was silent for a few seconds. "Do what you think is best. She can't help it if she is beautiful."

"She needs a job. She's a long way from home with nobody here to help her, just like I was once."

Laurie sighed. "You're right, Rooster. You're so kind to want to help this woman. I should have realized that. I'm so horrible..." and then she began to cry.

"No, Laurie. No, you're not. You're just miserable and confused, and you don't feel good. I should have told you about it. I just didn't think it was that big of a deal."

Laurie sniffled. "Why don't you come home and stay the night tonight. I miss having you here."

"I miss being there. What about Shirley?"

"I think Momma would like to have a night in her own bed too."

"Okay, I'll see you later then."

Rooster hung up the phone and opened the door to see Mildred and Christine laughing as Harvey capered about. He closed the door and sat back down at this desk. He shook his head.

"What have I done?" he muttered to himself.

25

Mildred stayed on long enough to train Christine reasonably well, and she was impressed with how quickly Christine caught on, but finally the big day arrived, and all the Merky bigwigs and courthouse staff came out to see her off into retirement. The sheriff's office was decorated in red, white, and blue ribbons, and there was cake and punch and gifts, and people were milling around enjoying themselves. When finally it came time for Mildred to deliver her farewell speech, she of course cried, as did many others in attendance, even though everyone there knew they would probably see her the next day at the grocery store. Even Rooster had to blink back tears, and Harvey unashamedly wept. It was a lovely send off and one that Mildred would lovingly commemorate in her bulging notebook that night. After Mildred and all the guests departed, it was just Rooster, Harvey, and Christine remaining, the first time for the new staff to be on their own.

Even though Laurie had apologized to Rooster and told him he didn't have to fire Christine, she was none too happy about the situation either. Being acutely aware of this, Rooster made a point of checking in on her regularly and generally being more attentive. This seemed to work just fine, so long as Mildred was still on the job, but once she left Laurie began to fret again, even though she had never even seen Christine.

As the pregnancy progressed, Laurie's condition deteriorated until the doctor became concerned for her survival.

"We're going to have put you in the hospital until the baby is born," said the doctor to Laurie's wails of protest.

Both Laurie and Shirley burst into tears upon hearing this, and the combined force of their emotions made Rooster unsteady on his feet. He was scared too. He was actually fearful that he might lose his wife and unborn child. Yet somewhere in the darkest recesses of his mind, a little cheer went out, ever so slightly, so as not to offend the more noble parts of his brain. Whether he would admit it, acknowledge it, or even realize it, he was just a little bit happy to hear this unexpected bit of news. If his brain were unable or unwilling to admit to this shameful fact, at least one other part of his anatomy understood very well the potential of this situation. The subconscious mind can be a wonderful and mysterious thing, accepting that which the conscious mind rejects, and even embracing and constructing upon it elaborate schemes and trickery without so much as the conscious mind having a clue to what its brethren is up to. This was the case with one Rooster Brown, dutiful husband, comforting his distraught wife in the face of emotional chaos, with the slightest of smiles upon his face.

Laurie was ensconced in a hospital bed in the Merky General Hospital for the duration of the pregnancy. It was at this moment of crisis, that the call to arms was sent out to all the friends and family of the poor, moldering Laurie, and all of them, being good, noble-hearted creatures, answered the call with gusto. A small army of Laurie supporters was assembled and assigned shifts, so that the poor, miserable woman would never have to be alone, unless she chose to be so. Each of these angels of mercy was committed to see this through and to welcome a healthy baby into the world.

Perhaps the main beneficiary of all this benevolence was not so much Laurie, but rather the father to be. Rooster found himself more or less off the hook. Of course, he still had to appear every day at least two or three times to reassure Laurie that he had not fled with the beautiful German woman, and to represent himself to the others as the dutiful and faithful husband. This, he did gladly each day, and he did not have to pretend any whatsoever that he cared for her and loved her with all his heart. Still, it allowed him a great deal more freedom to come and go at will, especially at night when most everyone was in bed.

Meanwhile, with Mildred gone, it was now just the three of them staffing the sheriff's office. Rooster took to having Harvey spend most of his days on patrol. This was a change because before he had usually asked Harvey to stay in the office while he went and drove around in the patrol car, which he enjoyed immensely. Once Harvey was out of the office, Rooster would pretend to work and find every excuse he could to ask Christine to do this or the other.

He also took to speaking as much German as he could recall, and he tried his best to remember every German word and phrase he had learned. This delighted Christine, who was lonely and homesick, and it made her feel more at home. Every day she and Rooster would speak bits of German to each other, and Rooster was having her teach him more. This of course flattered and pleased her to no end. Rooster began to notice that she was appearing to become more at ease around him and had begun gently teasing him, often touching him on the arm or shoulder during playful moments. He often found himself looking at her and having thoughts about her, and he would have to try to clear his mind so that Mr. Hard Dick would go away and let him walk about the office undetected. One day he suspected that she saw him trying to arrange his parts so that he could walk about without a bulge in his britches but she pretended not to have noticed. He began to try to think of ways to approach her without seeming obvious, and he waited for his chance.

One day at noon, Rooster decided to close the office and take Harvey and Christine out to lunch at Mel's Truck Stop. When they got there, all the tables were taken and all that was left was a booth. There was an awkward pause before they sat down as Rooster and Christine both mentally calculated seating arrangements. This was important, for not only were they in a public place during the busiest time of day, but everyone there was watching them. Just as they were about to sit, a former classmate of Harvey's showed up. Her name was Claudette Weed, she was a recent divorcee, and she had always nurtured a crush on Harvey. She quickly joined them, and the seating dilemma was solved. Claudette sat next to Harvey, and Rooster and Christine slid into their side of the booth. Rooster knew that everyone was looking at them, and he knew they would talk, but at least he had some justification for sitting next to Christine.

They sat laughing and talking as they waited for the waitress. Claudette was quite a flirt, and Harvey fidgeted red faced next to her, clearly enjoying the attention, even if he didn't quite know what to do about it. Rooster and Christine had started out sitting far apart but slowly and almost imperceptibly were slowly creeping closer together. They didn't sit too close together, both fully aware of the many prying eyes surrounding them. However, soon Christine's right foot and Rooster's left foot were gently touching. Rooster was quite pleased to find himself sitting next to the most beautiful woman in town.

Wanda came up to take their order. She was more reserved than usual and did not engage in her usual banter. She took everyone's order and then it was Rooster's turn. She took his order without saying much, but before she left to turn in their order she asked Rooster pointedly, "How's your wife?"

As soon as she said it, Christine moved her foot and leaned away from Rooster. Rooster replied, "Fine," and the point was taken.

They enjoyed their lunch and headed back to the office. This time, Rooster left Harvey behind, and he went on patrol by himself. After he had made a few rounds through town, he decided to go to the hospital and check on Laurie. She was lying in bed, her hair a mess and clearly uncomfortable. Rooster was shocked at the sight of her. She was disgusting, and he found it difficult to look at her, but he tried not to show it, as he sat beside her, listening to her complain about one thing after another. He listened but heard little, his mind instead seeing pictures of himself making love to the beautiful Christine. When it was time to leave, he gave Laurie a tepid kiss and excused himself. As he walked down the hall, he wondered how he could ever bear to go home with her after the baby was born.

He also thought about what would happen if he didn't. He was where he was, precisely because of Mel and his position in the community. Rooster had no illusions about standing on his own. He was entirely dependent upon his connection to the Tucker family to maintain his now lofty place in the world. He knew that to throw that away would be stupid, yet it would also be stupid to let slip away an opportunity to seduce the beautiful Christine. He was only slightly swayed by common decency, and he immediately determined that he should give up neither. He was, after all, Sheriff Rooster Brown, the King of Merky.

However, another development also complicated the situation. Since he had hired Christine, the office had begun receiving more visitors than usual. These were mostly various members of Rooster's Posse and Kenneth and his schoolboy friends. He never knew when somebody was going to just drop in, and he was starting to become frustrated by the constant interruptions. He didn't say too much about it at first, but when it became obvious that this was turning into an ongoing thing, he decided to put a stop to it. He told everyone that unless they had good reason to be there, they were not to come by and loiter or interrupt official business. Everyone knew that this was a bunch of crap and that there was very little "official business" being transacted, so they cut back on their visits but did not stop them completely.

Even with the reduction in visitors, Rooster still found it a bit daunting to approach Christine. They joked and bantered all day, but it was in a good-natured sibling way, and he wasn't sure if she felt the same way that he did. He was also acutely aware that if he handled it too clumsily, he would come off looking like a cad and damage the relationship he had established. There was also the danger that, if offended, she might tell others about it and hurt his reputation, if not outright endanger his marriage. So he played it slow and easy, figuring that the best thing he could do was to continue to endear himself to her and wait for a sign or opening.

So it went, with Rooster nursing his hard-ons, acting like the good and noble sheriff and devoted husband, and all the while wallowing in lust and frustration and a pathetic self-pity. In the meantime, Laurie lay in her hospital bed, wallowing in her own misery and despair. She would often call him from the hospital, and he would listen to her, trying to conceal his impatience, and finding whatever excuse he could to end the call. This, of course, only upset her more and fed into her suffering so that it grew into an all-consuming state. However, Rooster knew that soon she would be coming home, and he would resume the amazing life that had landed in his lap. He had no desire to upset the status quo, but now that he understood what a bountiful place the world was, he was determined to get all that he could.

One day, as he and Christine were talking about this and that in the office, the subject of beer came up.

"Ah, Rooster, I never vas a big drinker, but I do enjoy a good beer sometimes. I doan know why, but I haf been missing it lately."

At this, Rooster's ears pricked up.

"I know where to get some beer."

Christine's eyes widened. "But vere? I tought it vas illegal here."

"It is, officially, at least, but all these do-gooders around here like a little drink too. There's a bootlegger in Bug Town that everybody gets their beer from, and whiskey too."

Christine lowered her voice and leaned toward Rooster. "Do you tink you can get me some?"

"I know I can. If you want, I'll take you there too."

"Oh, Rooster, dat would be vonderful."

"But I have to warn you, it's not German beer. It's mostly Mexican, but there's some American beer too. And if you like the hard stuff, we can get some whiskey that will knock your socks off."

"I tink I just vant a beer, but maybe a little of dat udder stuff too."

"Let's go after work tonight."

"Is dis okay? Vat about your wife?"

"Don't worry about that. She won't mind. I'll go to see her after work, and I'll come by to get you after it gets dark."

"Are you sure?"

"Yes, I'm sure."

They went on about their work, but Rooster was almost giddy at this unexpected bit of good fortune. It would give him some time with Christine away from the office and the chance to loosen her up a bit. He was having a hell of a time controlling Mr. Hard Dick at just the thought of it. When they left work that evening they agreed that Rooster would come by at about eight and pick her up, then they would go see Cletus.

When Rooster went by to see Laurie that afternoon, he was in a happy mood, and he doted on her and held her hand and stroked her head and told her that he loved her, and before long, she was the happiest she had been in days. He kept this up until about a quarter till eight when it was dark outside and almost time to pick up Christine. Rooster practically skipped down the hall on his way out and paused to stop in front of the window of the front door and admire his reflection. As he was checking to see if his hair was combed, he was startled by the face of Mel who had seen him from the outside and stuck his face up to the window. Mel laughed and pointed at him and then opened the door and came in.

"There you are, Rooster. I was hoping to run into you tonight."

"Why? What's going on, Mel?"

"Oh, nothing too much. I just need you to come over and help me move some stuff around tonight."

"Tonight? Can't it wait?" asked Rooster as his heart sank.

"Why? What else do you have to do?" asked Mel.

"Well...uh...I um...I need to go get some cigarettes."

"That can't take long. I'll wait for you."

"Well, I mean...that, and I also need to go back to the office for a minute too."

"Hell, I'll go with you."

"Oh...um...uh...okay, Mel."

Mel looked at Rooster suspiciously. He knew Rooster was lying, but he didn't know about what. He decided not to push it, and instead let it pass, but he made a note to observe how he acted and what he said.

Rooster fumed in silent exasperation. He couldn't believe that his big chance with Christine was being derailed by Mel at the last minute. He was worried that if he didn't show up, she would be hurt or angry. He also knew not to be acting too strangely around Mel. Reluctantly, he decided it was best to just go on out and help Mel with whatever it was he needed moved and hope that he could get back before too late to pick up Christine.

"You know what, I can wait on this other stuff. Let's just go on out and take care of your chores tonight," said Rooster, hoping that it was just going to be a couple of boxes and he could get on back to town quickly.

It turned out that Mel was clearing out his barn, the one with the bunkhouse where Rooster had stayed briefly when he was hiding from Bill Hickey and his deputies. There was all kinds of junk that Mel wanted moved, and Rooster's heart sank as he realized that it was not going to get done quickly or easily.

"Damn, Mel, why didn't you mention this sooner? We could have done this during the day."

"I figured you were busy during the day, and this is something I just decided I needed to do. You act like I'm keeping you from something."

"No, no. You're not keeping me from anything," said Rooster, and he decided it would be wise to just drop it and try to finish as quickly as possible.

Rooster wondered why Mel needed this space cleared out all of a sudden, but at this point, he felt it best to just keep his mouth shut. They worked for a couple of hours moving things around until a sizeable space had been cleared. By the time they were finished, it was past ten. Rooster wanted to go back into town and see if Christine was still up, but he knew that would look suspicious, so he just stayed home that night, sulking about his missed opportunity. He was so upset about it that he didn't sleep well, and he tossed and turned most of the night. He was not looking forward to seeing Christine and explaining why he stood her up.

When it was time to go to work, Rooster drove into town fretting the whole way. He got there earlier than usual, and when he walked into the office, Christine was already there sitting at her desk. She smiled at him, but it was a strained smile, and he could see that she was hurt. Unfortunately, Harvey was there also, so he was not able to immediately explain what had happened. He told Harvey to go out on patrol, so that they could have a few minutes together, and just as Harvey walked out the door, in walked Kenneth and a couple of his friends. Rooster felt his face flush in frustration.

"Kenneth, what the hell are you doing here? Don't you have school today?"

"Yeah, but not for another thirty minutes or so."

If that weren't bad enough, then a couple of local do-nothings came in to loiter and ogle Christine. Rooster felt his blood pressure starting to rise.

"Look, damn it! This ain't the coffee shop. This is a place of business, and if y'all are not here for business, then you need to get out."

Everyone grumbled and slunk away until finally it was just Rooster and Christine left. Rooster looked at Christine with a pained expression on his face.

"I'm sorry I didn't make it last night. Just as I was about to come over, Mel came by and asked me to help him move some stuff, and I couldn't get out of it."

"Dat's okay, Rooster. I probably doan need any beer any vay," sighed Christine.

"No, don't say that. I think it would be fun. I just couldn't say anything about it around Mel."

"Ya, dat's all right, Rooster. It's probably best if ve doan go."

"Dang it, Christine, I'm sorry. I really am. I just couldn't tell Mel, that's all."

"I doan vant to cause problems, Rooster. It's better dis way."

Rooster felt a slow rage welling up inside him. Goddamn that Mel. Why did he have to move those boxes right then anyway? Rooster wanted to go and tell him off, but he knew that would be stupid, so he just fumed in silence. But he wasn't beat yet damn it, not by a long shot. He would figure out how to do this if it killed him.

He decided to go out for a ride to cool off, and he left Christine in the office by herself. He took off and drove around town for a while before he headed down that familiar road to Bug Town. When he pulled up to the shack, Cletus was walking around in pair of long johns and wearing cowboy boots and a beat up old cowboy hat. Rooster smiled to himself as he got out of the car.

"Cletus, where you going all dressed up like that? You got a big society party tonight or something?"

"Why sure. You know it, Rooster. The bootlegger's ball is the big event of the year."

The two men sat down in their usual places under the trees. Alice fetched them some coffee, and they sat in the chilly breeze.

"Damn, Cletus, ain't you cold?" Rooster asked, looking at Cletus' sparse garb.

"Naw, it's always cold out here. You just get used to it."

"Alice don't look like she's used to it," said Rooster, pointing at Alice who was bundled up like a prairie squaw.

"That's the Meskin in her. She ain't used to cold weather," said Cletus.

"Eet nothing to do with no goddamn Meskin," said Alice. "That crazy bastard so drunk he doan feel cold."

"I reckon you may be right, Alice," laughed Rooster, "which reminds me..."

"How much you want?" grinned Cletus.

"Oh, a couple dozen bottles of beer and maybe a little bit of that whiskey ought to do it."

Cletus motioned to Alice, who scurried off to fetch the booze as Rooster and Cletus sat sipping their coffee. Later, Rooster cruised back into town, deep in thought. He had a trap to set.

26

Rooster said nothing about drinking to Christine for the rest of that day. He resumed just as he had before with gentle teasing and joking around in German, and before long, the awkwardness that had hung in the air faded, and things were just about back to normal.

That afternoon, Rooster made sure to go to the hospital to dote on Laurie and hold her hand and wipe her forehead for the benefit of the ever-present room sitters, all the while secretly lusting for the beautiful and exotic Christine. Rooster realized that he wasn't as smart as he liked to think he was, and if he had learned anything, it was to not rush out and do something stupid. He would bide his time, be patient and capture that which eluded him. Behind those lying brown eyes of his, the wheels of trickery and deceit and subterfuge were spinning like the blades of a windmill. The King of Merky would not be denied.

The next few days around the office, Rooster played it smooth and low key. He took Harvey and Christine out to eat one day and even let Harvey sit next to Christine much to Harvey's discomfort. Although Harvey was just as smitten with Christine as anyone else, there had been a new development around town: Harvey had a girlfriend. It was the divorcee Claudette Weed. Claudette's mother had refused to let her go out with Harvey when they were in school, but now that Claudette was out on her own, she was not so easily controlled. Claudette was a sales clerk at the dime store, and she rented a small apartment in an old rooming house. If she was bothered by the stigma of being a divorcee, she sure didn't show it. In fact, she seemed to relish her freedom much to her mother's consternation. Harvey also was unfazed by any possible damage to his reputation, and he was the happiest he had ever been in his life.

Harvey's mother did not approve at all, and she did her best to discourage this budding romance, but for the first time in his life, Harvey refused to obey her and declared his independence, even threatening to move out into his own place. Grudgingly, perhaps even deep down approvingly, Olivia Wells accepted this new development, but she refused to acknowledge it to anyone who asked.

Although Rooster had become increasingly strict with his ban against loiterers hanging out at the office, he made one exception, and that was for Claudette. Though her hours at the dime store limited her ability to come and go as she pleased, she would take every opportunity to visit Harvey, and because of this, she also became increasingly friendly with Christine. Rooster watched this new friendship carefully from the corner of his eye. Christine was happy to have found a female friend that was approximately her age, and even though they came from very different worlds, the two women hit it off well. Rooster would often let Christine take off for thirty minutes or so when things were slow, which was pretty much all the time, and she would go window-shopping along the square, and usually this meant dropping in to see Claudette at the dime store.

While all this was going on, the clock was steadily ticking, something Rooster was keenly aware of. Laurie had been in the hospital for over six weeks and had only another month left until her due date, but the doctor had said she could give birth at any time. Rooster knew that once the baby was born and Laurie returned home, his window of opportunity would close.

He had been slowly stockpiling a significant cache of booze the past several weeks. He had begun drinking almost every day, and whenever he went to see Cletus, which was now a few times a week, he would buy a little extra each time and hide it away at his home. Now he had enough to throw a small party.

When he felt the time was right, Rooster invited Harvey, Claudette, and Christine out to his house for some barbecue and beer. He made it sound like it was going to be a small party, but, in reality they were the only ones he invited. In fact, he made sure that Mel and everyone else who might come by were under the impression that he was not feeling well and that he was going to bed early that night.

He left work early enough to go by the hospital and pat poor Laurie on the head and perform his caring husband routine for the Laurie supporters. He also told them that he was not feeling well and was going to go home and turn in early that night. He made sure that Mel and Shirley were aware of this so that they wouldn't come by unannounced. Once he had everyone convinced that he was going home sick, he peeled out of the hospital parking lot and headed to his house.

Once there, he built a fire in the pit by the Butcher Creek overlook behind his house until he had a nice bed of glowing coals. He had the beer cooling in the refrigerator and a couple of jars of moonshine as well. He put some potatoes in the pit, salted some steaks and put them in the refrigerator, and waited for his guests to arrive.

A little after dark, Harvey, Claudette, and Christine arrived. It was the first time that Claudette and Christine had been to Rooster's house, and they were duly impressed as Rooster showed them around. Once they had taken the tour, Rooster took them all out back to the fire pit by the bluff, and they put on the steaks and sipped their beers.

"Rooster, vere are de udder guests?" Christine asked.

"I don't know. I only invited a couple of others, and I guess they're not going to make it."

"Oh, I tought dis vas going to be a big party or someting."

"Naw, just a few friends. I can't throw a big party while Laurie's away."

Christine just nodded her head thoughtfully, trying to reconcile her memory with what Rooster had just said.

Rooster made sure and kept an eye on everyone's beers, so that when one was empty, it was quickly replaced by another. Harvey, who was not used to drinking much at all soon went into the house to lie down, leaving just the three of them. Claudette, who had no such limitations on the amount of alcohol she could consume, happily drank one after another until she too had to go into the house to lie down. This left just Rooster and Christine sitting beside the fire with their beers, listening to the creek gurgle.

Christine obviously knew more about drinking than Harvey or Claudette for she paced herself, especially after catching on to Rooster's habit of quickly replacing one empty bottle with a full one. Rooster had downed several bottles before realizing that Christine was nursing her beers. He made a mental note to slow down lest he pass out too, as he was prone to do if he wasn't careful. He studied Christine from the corner of his eye and decided it was time to bring out the hard stuff.

He excused himself and went back to the house. He went through the sitting room and saw Harvey and Claudette happily snuggled together, asleep on the sofa. He smiled at the sight of them and went to the kitchen where he was keeping his jars of whiskey. He retrieved one and grabbed a couple of glasses and took them out back to where Christine sat, enraptured by the fire. He poured two large shots in each glass and handed one to Christine.

"Vat is dis, Rooster?"

"It's whiskey. I thought we could drink a little toast."

Christine sniffed the glass and drew back. "My Got. I doan tink I can drink dis, Rooster."

"It's really not that bad. Just slug it down. It will make you feel very warm and good inside."

Christine looked at Rooster with the flames from the campfire dancing in her eyes. For just a moment, Rooster thought he saw something that looked like passion, and his heart jumped a bit. He raised his glass toward her and waited for her to do the same. She clinked her glass against his, and they both emptied their glasses. Christine gagged and choked a bit, but she swallowed the whole thing and quickly chased it down with her beer. Rooster also washed his down with a beer. Even though he was accustomed to Cletus' hard liquor, it still warmed his throat all the way down to his gut. He felt a warm, relaxing sensation spread throughout his body. He smiled at Christine who was gasping for air.

"Oh, my Got! Dat is some strong stuff," Christine said, grimacing. She emptied her beer and asked Rooster for another to wash the taste from her mouth.

Rooster tossed another branch on the fire, and they sat back and watched as the flames rose from the pit. The dancing flames illuminated Christine's face and made her even more beautiful. She smiled at Rooster.

"Dis is nice, Rooster. Tank you for inviting me."

"I'm glad to do it. I know you miss your family. You need to get out and associate with people, so that you don't get too lonely."

"Yah, dis is true. I do feel lonely sometimes."

"Well, you shouldn't. You have friends here. Everybody likes you."

"I am very grateful for de job, Rooster. I cannot tank you enough."

"You don't have to thank me. You do a good job."

They both leaned back and watched the flames lick at the firewood as the whiskey began to creep from their bellies to their extremities in a slow, warm glow from within. Rooster felt his brain relax and a smile emerge upon his face. He looked over at Christine, and he could tell that she was feeling a similar, if not stronger, effect from the booze. She looked at him, her eyes partly vacant, yet warm and inviting.

"My got, I doan need any more of dat stuff, Rooster," she said, slurring her words ever so slightly.

"A little bit goes a long way," Rooster grinned.

"Yah, it feels goot."

Rooster got up to toss a stick on the fire, and when he sat down he scooted a little closer to Christine.

"It's a long time since I vas drunk," said Christine dreamily. "I need dis."

"It's hard to be so far from home, away from family and friends," said Rooster softly.

"Yah, you know about dis, Rooster. You vas away for a long time too," said Christine, patting Rooster's knee.

"Yeah except I didn't have any family to come home to, so I didn't have anyone to miss," said Rooster. "Still, I missed something."

"I miss my husband and my family back in Germany," said Christine.

Rooster winced ever so slightly at the mention of her husband.

"It's goot to have a man for a friend," said Christine, again patting Rooster's knee. "It make me not feel so alone."

Rooster scooted a little closer and put his hand on Christine's shoulder. "You've helped me too. It's nice to have a woman my age around, especially with Laurie in the hospital."

Christine looked slightly pained. She turned to look at Rooster.

"How is your vife? The baby vill come soon, yah?"

"Yes, soon."

Christine's skirt had risen up, exposing her thigh, but she seemed not to notice.

"You miss your vife, yah?"

Rooster smiled and nodded his head slightly.

Christine smiled at Rooster. Her words were becoming more slurred. She put her hand on his chest.

"You haf been wit out you wife's bed for a while now."

Rooster froze.

"I know how hard dat is. I haf not been wit my husband for many days now. I miss de sex," Christine laughed drunkenly.

Rooster ran his hand down her back.

"We ahr both in de same spot, Rooster..." Christine's voice trailed off, her eyes closed, and she slowly slumped over. She was out like a light. Yet another victim of Cletus' home brew, down for the count.

Rooster looked at her incredulously. She was obviously lonely, horny, and drunk, and now she was passed out cold. He could not believe his poor luck.

He sat there drinking by himself for another few minutes before picking Christine up in his arms and carrying her into the house. He laid her on the rug next to Harvey and Claudette, and he retrieved a pillow and an old quilt and covered her. He stood there looking at her for several seconds, and then suddenly he felt the essence of his grandfather coursing through his veins. The thought crossed his mind that he could probably take her into the bedroom and have his way with her and she would not even wake up. He thought about that for a minute and then he went to bed.

Sometime in the night, Harvey and Claudette woke up and left. They put a note for Rooster near Christine saying that they were unable to wake her and that he would have to take her home in the morning. Rooster slept past his usual time, and when he got up the next morning, he found Christine in the kitchen sipping coffee and cooking breakfast. Both of them were feeling hung over and neither of them felt the need to talk much. After breakfast, they got in the patrol car to go back to town.

As the car pulled away from the house and headed to the main road, Mel stood watching, hidden among a stand of trees. He turned and walked briskly back to his house and went to his telephone. He picked it up, dialed a number and waited patiently. After several rings, a voice answered on the other end.

"Addis, this is Mel..."

27

Rooster and Christine spoke little on the way into town. Twice, Rooster had to pull over to the side of the road to let her throw up, and by the time they arrived at the little house in the trees, it was obvious she was in no shape to go to work that day. Rooster told Christine she could have the day off, and she quietly agreed. He parked the car and helped her up the steps. They paused on the porch to say goodbye and Christine sheepishly gave Rooster a hug before turning and going inside. He got in the patrol car and rolled out to the main road. He was so distracted that he didn't notice a familiar car parked across the street. After he passed by the car, Addis rose up in the seat and wound the stem on his camera before he started his car and left.

When Rooster got to the office, Harvey was already there but looking pale and listless. Rooster tried to talk to him but got little in the way of intelligible conversation, so he told Harvey to go home also. In fact, he was not feeling well himself, but since he was more conditioned to drinking, it was just a minor annoyance to him, rather than the debilitating state that it was for Christine and Harvey. And the fact of the matter was, he just felt like being on his own today. He needed to think, and it was hard to do that in the presence of others. He sat at his desk and fished about in the drawer until he found a long lost cigar hiding in the back. He lit it up, kicked his feet up on the desk, and leaned back in his chair and blowing smoke rings contemplatively. He had come close to the prize last night, painfully close, but one more opportunity had slipped through his fingers.

As he was sitting there, mulling over last night's events, the phone on his desk rang. He just sat there and looked at it. He really didn't feel like answering it, so he let it ring. It rang several times before it occurred to him that it might actually be some type of emergency, so he picked it up.

"Sheriff's office," he said into the receiver.

"Rooster?" It was Laurie.

Rooster winced. He felt himself deflate even further, and he was angry at himself for answering the phone after all.

"Good morning, darling," he said, trying to sound upbeat.

"What took you so long to answer the phone?" asked Laurie.

"Well…um…Christine and Harvey are both out sick today, so I'm having to do everything by myself."

"They're both out sick? That's odd," said Laurie.

"Yeah, I guess so. Maybe they been doing some smooching and caught the same bug or something," said Rooster.

"What? Oh, Rooster, you don't really think that, do you?"

"Nah, I guess not. I don't think Harvey would know what to do anyway. Besides, he's in love with Claudette."

"Well, then why would you say that?"

"I don't know," said Rooster, getting a little flustered. "How are you feeling today?" he asked, trying to change the subject.

Laurie launched into a fresh litany of ailments as Rooster sat and glumly listened. When a member of the Posse finally poked their head in the door, he seized the moment.

"Listen, hon, somebody just walked in the office. I'll come by to see you later," he said and quickly hung up.

When the Posse member saw that Christine was out for the day, they didn't linger and left quickly. Rooster stubbed out the rest of the cigar and decided to go on patrol for a while. He figured he should go ahead and get one of his Laurie visits out of the way and so free up the rest of the morning.

When he got to the hospital, Shirley was just leaving.

"Are you feeling better, Rooster?" she asked as she gathered up her purse and other belongings.

"Yes'm, a good night's sleep did me wonders," said Rooster.

"Well, good. We'll see you later," Shirley said as she left.

"Do you have the same thing that Christine and Harvey have?" asked Laurie a bit suspiciously.

"No, they have upset stomachs. I just had a headache," said Rooster.

Rooster sat in the chair next to Laurie. It was just the two of them now. They made small talk for a few minutes, and then grew quiet. Finally, Laurie broke the silence "You don't really think there is anything going on between Harvey and Christine, do you?" she asked.

Rooster was about say no when it occurred to him that maybe it wouldn't be a bad idea to sew a little doubt so as to take some of the heat off himself.

"Well, I'm not sure," he said. "I don't want to spread gossip or anything."

"I just find that hard to believe," said Laurie.

"Well, Harvey is not as dumb as everybody makes him out to be. Sometimes those are the ones you got to watch out for. I don't know nothing for sure, so don't say anything to anybody else," said Rooster.

Laurie laughed and took Rooster's hand and they sat there talking quietly until a nurse came in to tend to Laurie, and Rooster took that as his cue to leave. As he was walking down the hall, he saw Mel coming from the other direction.

"Good morning there, sheriff. You feeling better today?" Mel asked cheerfully.

"Yes, Mel. I'm feeling much better now."

I just bet you are, Mel thought. "Good, glad to hear it," he said. "I'm going to go and check in on Laurie. I'll talk to you later."

"Okay, Mel. See you later."

Mel entered the room as the nurse was leaving and sat down beside Laurie. They engaged in idle talk for a few minutes before Laurie surprised Mel.

"Daddy, is there something going on between Harvey and Rooster's secretary? Rooster said he thinks there might be."

Mel looked at Laurie in disbelief. "What? That's the craziest thing I ever heard in my life!"

"I know!" Laurie laughed. "I don't where he comes up with this stuff sometimes."

Mel felt himself starting to flush with anger, and for a brief moment, he thought about telling Laurie what he had seen that morning, but as he looked at his poor, pitiful daughter lying there in her miserable state, he couldn't bear to bring further suffering upon her. He reached down and patted her hand.

"No, darling, I think Harvey is pretty well occupied with Claudette right now. Rooster must still be feeling poorly, he's not thinking straight."

As he sat there fuming, Mel resolved to keep a close eye on Rooster.

Meanwhile, Rooster went back to the office until it was lunchtime, and then he went over to Mel's Truck Stop and got a hamburger. Wanda was there, and she was friendlier to him since he was by himself today. He made a point to joke around with her until it seemed they were back on good terms, and once again she didn't charge him for his meal. After eating, he started to get drowsy and was thinking about going home to take a nap when he decided instead to go see Cletus. His hangover was still lingering, and he decided a little hair of the dog was just what the doctor ordered.

Over the past few weeks, Rooster had spent quite a bit of time going to see Cletus and Mexican Alice, and he had slowly developed a true friendship with them. For some reason, he felt more at ease around them than with the other citizens of Merky. Perhaps it was because they were outsiders, as he had been for most of his life. The loosening effect of alcohol no doubt contributed to this as well since it lowered inhibitions and facilitated conversation. Cletus and Alice were also completely unpretentious, something that Rooster found to be refreshing since he now had to deal with all sorts of big shot society types who clearly only associated with him because of his position in the community. It was a relief and a refuge to escape to Bug Town every now and then, and to be truthful, his craving for alcohol had increased substantially as well.

His timing turned out to be fortuitous today because Alice had made a large pot of menudo, well known among Mexicans to be an effective treatment for hangovers. As he sat underneath the trees, which were now sprouting a full canopy of leaves, eating his soup and drinking a beer, he felt good and at one with the rhythms of the universe, although he could not have expressed it as such. All would have been perfect had it not been for one certain German woman who had thrown a monkey wrench into everything. Perhaps, because of their newly formed bond, Cletus knew that something was bothering Rooster, but he also knew that, oftentimes, troublesome matters were best coaxed out gently rather than yanked out harshly, so he chose the former route and made easy conversation that might allow Rooster to speak his mind easily and naturally.

"Well, Rooster, I guess it must be hard to be the sheriff sometimes," said Cletus.

"Yeah, I reckon so," said Rooster blankly.

"I can tell something is bothering you, probably some criminal case, I suspect."

"Well, naw, it's just um...uh," Rooster hesitated as he glanced over at Alice.

Cletus, picking up on the cue, told Alice to go slop the hogs, which she did with only minimal fussing and cussing. Once she was out of earshot, Rooster loosened up a bit more.

"No, Cletus. It ain't got nothing to do with work. It's personal business."

"Hell, that's okay. You ain't got to tell me none of your personal problems, unless it's something I can help you with."

"I appreciate that, but it's just something I'm going to have to work out myself," said Rooster.

"That's okay, Rooster," said Cletus.

Neither of them said anything for a minute, then Cletus spoke up.

"How's that new secretary of yours working out?"

Rooster winced slightly, and Cletus knew he had hit a nerve.

"She's doing real well...just driving me and everybody around her crazy horny."

Cletus laughed. "Yes'm, I reckon I would be too if I had to see that good-looking thing every day. Sometimes, I'm glad I'm just a moonshiner. All I have to worry about is getting arrested."

Rooster put down his bowl and tossed the beer bottle in a nearby trash heap. "And I reckon you ain't got to worry about that too much any more. I got to go, Cletus. I'll talk to y'all later."

Rooster stood up and shouted to Alice, "Muchas gracias, Alice! Adios!" and he left.

As Rooster was driving away, Alice came back from the hog pen.

"Wat wrong wit Rooster?" she asked.

"Oh, he's just got a little woman problem, that's all."

"Woman? He married!"

"That's the problem," Cletus chuckled.

Rooster drove back to Merky and made sure he chewed some gum and smoked a cigarette to cover the beer on his breath. He went back to the office for a while then went over to see Laurie again before going home for the night. He was tired and ready for a good night's sleep. On the way home from the hospital, he drove by the little house in the trees, craning his neck to see if he could get catch a glimpse of Christine. He saw nothing of note and drove on home, muttering to himself quietly.

The next day, all three employees of the Loma Grande County Sheriff's Department made it to work in good health and in fine spirits. They were all recuperated from their big night of drinking and ready to resume their usual routine. Rooster especially was happy to see everyone back to normal.

"Did y'all have a good time the other night?" he asked jovially.

Oh, yah. It vas a lot of fun Rooster," said Christine.

"Yes, sir, me and Claudette both had a good time," said Harvey.

"Well, then we ought to do it again real soon," said Rooster.

"Oh, Rooster, I doan tink I want to drink again for a while. It vas fun, but I can do widout," said Christine, wrinkling her nose.

Harvey made a sour expression. "I don't like to drink very much."

Rooster was floored.

"What? Y'all both just said you had a good time."

"Ve did, but it vas too hard de next day. I only vant to drink occasionally, and dat was enough for a while."

"Yeah," Harvey agreed.

Rooster was disappointed, but he tried not to show it. He felt his chance to be with Christine was slipping away, and he felt a despairing sense of helplessness well up within him. He hoped that once the memory of the hangover faded and loneliness began to creep back in he could persuade her otherwise, but he decided the best option was to drop it for now. So he went back to his strategy of gentle teasing and flirting and hoped that opportunity would once again knock before the baby was born.

28

The next couple of weeks dragged along for Rooster, each day seemed as long as a month. Laurie's due date was getting closer and closer, and with each passing day, she grew more grotesque and more unpleasant to be around, so that even the Laurie supporters were praying for the baby to come as soon as possible. As she grew in size and repulsiveness, Rooster's love for her shrank relative to her wretchedness, and his desire for the beautiful Christine grew.

However, it seemed that Christine sensed this, and she realized that they had come dangerously close to a liaison the night of the party, and she was doing her best to avoid putting herself in that situation again. Rooster often suggested they get together for this or that, but she always declined. They still kept up the teasing and bantering, but Christine made sure to keep her distance, physically as well as emotionally.

Rooster figured if he couldn't get laid, he might as well get drunk, and so continued to make frequent trips to see Cletus. One day after work, and after he had visited Laurie in the hospital, he was craving a drink and hightailed it out to Bug Town. As he came to the center of the ragged, little village, he spotted something unusual. In the vacant lot across from the general store, a large tent had been erected, and the rag tag populace of Bug Town was milling about obviously roused from their usual lethargy and excited by this new development. Rooster slowed down and looked about to see if he could tell what was going on. Still unsure of what was happening, he pulled over in an empty part of the vacant lot and got out of his car. He could see people setting up benches, what appeared to be some kind of a dais, and an old upright piano. Suddenly, it hit him in a flash. Powerful memories of his childhood raced through his mind, and he knew what was happening—it was a tent revival, in the middle of Bug Town no less.

Little children were running about excitedly underneath the tent, this being as close to a circus as most of them would ever get. The adults also seemed to be caught up in the moment and were even helping to carry things about and arrange the chairs and so forth. A man spotted Rooster looking around and came up to greet him.

"Good afternoon, officer. Welcome to the Prosper Revival," said the man, extending his hand.

Rooster shook his hand. "Howdy. Are you the preacher?"

"I am indeed, sir, one of them, at least. My name is Odell Brock."

"Rooster Brown. I'm the sheriff here."

"We are honored to have you here, sir. Will you be staying for the service?"

"No, I was just passing through. I have other business to take care of tonight."

"I'm sorry to hear that," said Odell, obviously disappointed. "However, we will be here for a few days if you have time later."

"Okay, I'll keep that in mind," said Rooster.

Just as Rooster was about to leave, a man and a woman came up to them.

"Oh, Sheriff Brown, this is my wife, Addie Brock, and my associate minister, Eddie Stiflemire."

"Please to meet y'all," Rooster said.

"Will you be worshipping with us tonight, sheriff?" asked Addie, a pretty, blue-eyed brunette.

"I'm afraid not."

"The sheriff has other matters to attend to tonight," explained Odell.

"How did y'all come up with the name Prosper Revival?" asked Rooster. "I thought money was the root of all evil."

"We're from the town of Prosper," smiled Addie. "We get asked that all the time."

"And prospering doesn't necessarily just mean money," said Eddie. "You can have a prosperous life without being wealthy. If you are rich in spirit, then you are truly blessed."

Rooster was starting to get restless. "All right. Well, I need to go. Good luck with your revival."

"Thank you, sheriff. God bless you," said Addie.

Rooster got in his patrol car and drove slowly past as the evangelists returned to work. For the first time, he noticed two panel trucks with the words "Prosper Revival" painted on the side. He smiled and shook his head, and once he was past them, he gunned the engine and spun the tires, leaving a cloud of dust in his wake.

He went out to Cletus and Alice's place just in time for a plate of Alice's pork and beans. Rooster was so horny that even Alice was starting to look good to him. He had become accustomed to her lined face and her harsh mannerisms and could see the attractive woman she had once been. He had a couple of beers and headed home for the night. If there was anything good in his life, it was that the baby was literally due within days, and once that was over, hopefully Laurie would return to her old self, and life would become less of a struggle.

The next day, when Rooster got to work, he was surprised to see that Christine had not arrived yet. This was unusual because she was almost always the first to arrive. He didn't think much of it until a little time had passed and she still had not shown up. Thinking she might be sick or something, Rooster asked Harvey to go check on her. When Harvey came back he told Rooster that she did not answer the door, and as far as he could tell, she didn't appear to be home. That perplexed Rooster, and this time he went to her house himself. He knocked hard on the door, and when no one answered, he went in. All her things were there, but the place looked a bit messier than he remembered it. He went out back into the yard and called her name but got no response. Now he was really baffled and drove to the station where Kermit and Obie were on duty. He asked if they had seen her, and they hadn't, so he drove around town looking for her. He drove around for twenty or thirty minutes but had no luck, so he returned to the office.

He decided to wait awhile, and if they still hadn't heard from her, he would go out and look for her again. By noon, there was still no word, so he went by her house once again and still no one was there. Then, Rooster thought to go see if Claudette knew where she might be. He went to the dime store and was told that Claudette had the day off, so he went by her apartment, but she was not home either.

By the end of the day Rooster was very worried, and he wondered whether she had been kidnapped, or had run off without telling anyone, or even if she was dead. He decided to go see Laurie after work, and then afterward, he would mount a full-scale search if need be. When he got to the hospital, Laurie looked like a balloon about to burst. Her greasy hair was pulled back from her face, which had cleared up, and she was looking better. She was strangely serene, a welcome change, and she almost seemed her old self. She told Rooster that she thought the baby could come anytime. Rooster stayed as long as he could stand it, but every minute seemed as if it were an hour. Finally, when he had stayed long enough to satisfy the unspoken time requirement, he left.

It was getting dark as he rushed straight to the little house in the trees, and as soon as he turned into the long drive, he felt his heart flutter because there was a light on. She was home. He zoomed up the driveway and skidded to a stop underneath the trees. He paused for a moment to compose himself, and then got out and strolled to the door as if nothing were amiss. He knocked on the door and stepped back. He could hear someone stirring about. He waited another minute or so then knocked again. It sounded as if things were being knocked over, and he heard Christine's voice.

"Yoost a minute!"

After a couple more minutes, the door opened and Christine stood there in her nightgown, obviously having been asleep. Rooster could smell alcohol on her breath, and it was obvious that she had been drinking.

"Oh, Rooster..." she said weakly.

"Christine, are you all right? We've been worried to death," said Rooster.

"Oh, I'm sorry," she said, sounding half-asleep and confused.

"Yoost a minute. I vill be right back," she said and closed the door.

Rooster stood on the porch, confused and not knowing whether to be relieved, angry, or hurt. A couple of minutes later, Christine came back to the door wearing a robe. She appeared to have brushed her hair and perhaps washed her face. She seemed to be more awake now.

"Come in, Rooster," she said softly.

Rooster stepped in and removed his hat.

"Sit down," she said, pointing to the sofa.

"Christine, where have you been? We've been really worried about you," Rooster said, trying to conceal his irritation.

"Yah, I'm so sorry Rooster. It vas a bad day."

"Why? What happened?"

"Yesterday, I got de letter from my husband. He say he not coming home as soon as ve tought. I vas so hurt and upset dat I ran away for de day, and den I got some beer from Cletus."

"Cletus? But how did you get out there?"

"I got Claudette to take me. It vas her day off."

"We looked all over town for you."

"Yah, after ve got de beer, ve went and drove around out in de country and got drunk."

"You should have at least told me you weren't going to come in," said Rooster, his annoyance now clearly evident in his voice.

"I'm so sorry, Rooster. I know it vas wrong. I vas jus so upset, and I didn't vant to talk to anyone."

Rooster sat there, shaking and trying not to show his anger.

"You vant a beer, Rooster? I haf some in de refrigerator."

Rooster exhaled. "Yes. Yes, I do."

Christine went to the kitchen and brought back two beers. She set one in front of Rooster.

Christine sat next to him on the sofa and put her hand on his shoulder. "I'm so sorry, Rooster. You haf been so kind to me. I didn't mean to scare you."

Rooster slouched back on the sofa and took a long drink from the beer. It felt good going down his throat. He took a deep breath and exhaled through his mouth. He looked over at Christine. She was beautiful in the soft light of the living room. He noticed that she wasn't wearing a bra.

Christine took a drink from her beer.

"You vant some whiskey? I haf some of dat, too"

Rooster tried not to look at her. "That sounds good."

She got up, went into the kitchen again, and brought out a jar of home brew and a couple of glasses. She poured them both a generous shot and raised her glass. Rooster raised his glass, and they clinked them together.

"To goot friends," said Christine.

"To good friends," responded Rooster.

They both slugged down the whiskey in one shot and then chased it with a drink of beer. Rooster felt himself relax as the familiar warmth made its way down his throat and into his belly. Christine gagged slightly and took a couple of deep breaths.

"Dat is some strong stuff. Dat is what knocked me out today."

"It's not for sissies," said Rooster.

"Yah, dats for sure."

Christine drank a couple of big swallows of beer to wash the taste of the home brew from her mouth. She seemed to relax more now and lay back on the sofa. She put her feet up on the coffee table, showing her tanned legs. Rooster looked at them from the corner of his eyes. Christine put her hand on his arm.

"Yah, you know dat vas a lot of fun at your house. I'm sorry I passed out like dat."

"I understand. It's the home brew that does it."

"Yah, it's already making me feel drunk again. I doan tink I need any more tonight."

Christine took another sip of her beer and lay her head back. Her robe slipped away from her legs, showing a bit of her thighs. Rooster scooted over a bit closer to her.

"Yah, it's hell being away from home and being alone," said Christine, slurring her words ever so slightly. Rooster could tell she was getting drunk again.

"I know it is. It's hard to be alone," he replied.

"How did you deal wid it? You know, ven you vas overseas."

"I got drunk a lot, and sometimes I found somebody to be with, even if for just a night."

"Yah, sometimes dat is Okay. Does your vife know about dat?"

"No, there's things she doesn't know about."

"Yah, sometimes dat is de best. Ve are all human, right? Sometimes, ve do tings ve shouldn't."

"Have you done things that your husband doesn't know about?"

"Not really, not too much any vay. Is not a crime to tink tings, no?"

"No, it's not, and sometimes not to do them either. Sometimes, things just happen."

Rooster reached over and put his hand on Christine's leg. She looked away, as if her not seeing it somehow made it okay. She made no attempt to push him away. She lit a cigarette, turned and blew the smoke in Rooster's face.

"Rooster, you are a lucky man," she said teasingly.

"I reckon I am."

He ran his hand along the top of her thigh, feeling the sheer fabric of her nightgown and the warmth of her leg underneath it. It was smooth and warm, and it looked like the leg of a movie star the way her nightgown lay across it. Christine ran her fingers through his hair as he stroked her thigh. He gently pulled her toward him. They kissed, softly and sweetly at first, while caressing and exploring each other's bodies with their hands. The kisses quickly became more passionate as their breaths intermingled and their tongues darted in and out of each other's mouths. Rooster stroked her breasts, fondling her nipples until they became firm and erect. She kissed him more aggressively, rubbing her hand over his chest and belly, and then stroking the growing bulge in his pants. He fondled her breasts, working his way down to her crotch. He rubbed her crotch and she started grinding her hips slightly. He put his hand in her panties, down to her vagina, which was warm and wet. She spread her legs slightly and he stuck his middle finger into the opening of her vagina, working it around inside her and rubbing the wetness over her clitoris. She started grinding her hips even more and moaning softly.

Christine unbuckled his belt, then unfastened his pants and began tugging on them. He raised up from the sofa to allow her to pull them down, which she did quickly. Then, she opened his shirt, unsnapping it in a quick barrage of snaps. She leaned over and began kissing his chest and his nipples. She fondled his penis, which had quickly grown erect, then she dropped to her knees and began sucking it. Rooster gasped and stiffened. He grabbed the cushions of the sofa, bunching up the fabric in his fists and gripping it tightly. Christine slowly went up and down his penis, licking and sucking it, then quickly bobbing her head up and down as Rooster groaned in ecstasy. After a few minutes, she stood up and pulled down her panties and stepped out of them, then straddled Rooster sitting on the sofa. She lowered herself onto him and slowly began riding up and down on his now stiff penis. Rooster groaned in pleasure, his hands on her hips, guiding her up and down. She rode him like that for several minutes when suddenly she got off him and stood up.

"Let's go in dere," she said, pointing to the bedroom.

Rooster pulled off his cowboy boots and stood up, holding his pants up enough so that he could walk. He followed Christine into the bedroom, and they both sat on the edge of the bed and took off all their clothes. Christine climbed onto the bed and lay back and Rooster crawled over on top of her and stuck his dick inside her, and they began to copulate. Rooster looked down at the beautiful woman underneath him, and he started thrusting harder. Christine writhed beneath him, groaning in pleasure. They went like this for several minutes until Rooster could hold it back no more, and he unleashed a huge spasm inside her, causing her to shiver and groan. After he had expelled it all, they both lay there, out of breath and their hearts pounding. They stayed like that until their heartbeats and their breathing were almost back to normal.

Rooster was still inside her when his penis came back to life. He gained another erection and soon he was pumping again, and this time they both positioned themselves for the long haul. Rooster humped and pumped for what seemed like an hour until finally he released once again into her. Again, they collapsed into a panting, sweaty heap. This time, he rolled off of her and they both lapsed into a light slumber.

When Rooster awakened later, he wasn't sure how long he had been there or what time it was. He rustled about in the bed, waking Christine, who rubbed her forehead and got up to go to the bathroom. Rooster lay there, wondering what he should do next. Christine came back to the bedroom and sat on the bed.

"Rooster, you should go home," she said.

"Yeah, I know," he said.

He got up and dressed, and Christine put her robe back on and walked him to the front door. Neither of them said anything. Rooster paused at the front door, and Christine kissed him lightly on the lips and gently pushed him out the door. He passed through the largely deserted streets of Merky on his way home and went to bed. He was sleeping soundly when the phone rang. He got up out of bed, stumbled into the living room and picked up the receiver. It was Shirley.

"Rooster, Laurie's going into labor. You better come as soon as you can."

"Oh...oh...okay, Shirley, I'll be right there," he said.

He was a little more awake now, but still groggy and confused. He went to the kitchen and put on a pot of coffee then went to wash up and get dressed. It was 2:00 a.m. when he left for the hospital.

Laurie was in labor all right, but the baby was in no hurry to come, so Rooster, Shirley, Mel, and assorted Laurie supporters kept an exhausted and fitful vigil. This went on all day long. Rooster called the office and told Christine he was not sure when he would be coming in. She sounded a bit relieved to hear that.

"Yah, okay, Rooster. No problem. If anyting comes up, ve vill call you."

Rooster slept in fits and starts on a sofa in the hospital waiting room, and when evening came around, he finally went home with strict instructions that he be called if anything changed. He was sleeping soundly again, when the phone rang. It was Mel.

"The doc thinks this it, Rooster. Hurry up and get here as soon as you can."

It was a little after midnight. Once again, Rooster stumbled about trying to wake up and compose himself enough to get to the hospital.

This time, when he got there he was greeted by the sight of Laurie holding a freshly swaddled newborn in her arms. She looked better than she had in weeks, as if she had finally expelled the demon that possessed her. Rooster glimpsed the woman he had married what seemed like a very long time ago.

"It's a boy," she said wearily, but happily, as she handed it to him.

Rooster was exhausted and emotionally drained. He tried not to weep when the infant was placed in his arms. His mind was bouncing all over, and for just a second, he saw Christine's head bobbing up and down in his lap. He shook his head as if to shake the image out of his brain, shocked at the things his own mind would dredge up unexpectedly. The shadow of guilt lurked just out of reach for now, but was close enough to trouble him later when he was alone. He stayed with them until the sun was coming up and then left to go home for some rest. He decided to go by the office first. Harvey was there, but Christine had not made it in yet. Rooster was disappointed and a little surprised, she had been so punctual for so long. Rooster was wobbly and unsteady, and he knew he had to go home and sleep if he was going to be able to function. He got home a little after nine and collapsed into bed. He slept soundly until about two thirty in the afternoon. He opened his eyes briefly and was about to drift off back to sleep when he suddenly remembered—the baby!

He flung the covers back, ran to the kitchen and put on a pot of coffee, took a quick bath and raced back to the hospital. Laurie was nursing the baby when he got there, and she was looking more and more like her old self. The inherent sweetness he had fallen in love with was creeping back into her body, and he felt as if it had all been a long, strange dream. Rooster held his baby then suddenly remembered that he needed to name it soon. When it was time for the baby to nap again and Laurie was peacefully dozing, he went to the nurse's station and asked what he needed to do to name the baby. The nurse checked her records.

"Someone has already taken care of that," said the nurse.

"Oh, I guess Laurie did it already," said Rooster.

"No, it was Mr. Tucker."

That hit Rooster like a punch in the gut. He was speechless.

The nurse looked at her record book.

"We have the baby's name as William Melvin Brown," she said, looking up at Rooster.

Rooster just nodded his head and walked away. That was, in fact, the name that they had agreed upon if it were a boy. What bothered him was that he didn't even get the privilege of naming his own son, that son of a bitch Mel had stolen it from him. Rooster was too angry to return to see Laurie or the baby, so instead he left. He thought about going to the office, but instead, before he knew what was happening, he was on the way to Cletus' shack.

He drove through Bug Town where the Prosper Revival was now fully set up and in business. It was still early, so the tent was mostly empty, except for a few children playing about. Rooster passed on by and rolled slowly up the bumpy path to Cletus' shack.

Cletus saw him pulling in and gave him a big grin and a wave, which made Rooster smile a bit in spite of himself. He parked the car and got out.

"Howdy do, sheriff. What's the word on that baby?" Cletus asked cheerfully.

"It's a boy, eight pounds and seven ounces, with a hard head and big dick, just like his daddy," said Rooster.

"Hot damn! Congratulations, Rooster!" exclaimed Cletus. "Come on and have a drink. Let's celebrate."

The two men sat down in their usual chairs and clinked their beers together in a toast. Even grouchy ol' Mexican Alice came out and gave Rooster a hug. He was starting to relax and his anger at Mel was fading although it would be a sore spot with him for a while. Cletus brought out a jar of home brew and Rooster took a big drink and almost instantly regretted it, for he knew he was going to get drunker than he intended. He tried not to overindulge, but by the time he left he was drunk, and combined with his exhaustion and high-strung emotional condition, he was in an unsteady state.

He was too drunk to go to the office or the hospital, so he drove around for a bit before deciding to go see Christine and give her the good news. He spun the tires a little as he turned into the driveway and drove up to the little house in the trees. He hadn't even got to the door when it swung open and Christine greeted him.

"Rooster, congratulations! I hear you haf a son."

"That's right, his name is William Melvin Brown."

"Dat is vunderful. Come in."

Rooster sat down on the sofa, and Christine sat in a chair opposite him.

"I haf some goot news, too," said Christine excitedly.

"That's good," said Rooster, trying not to wobble. "What is it?"

"I got letter from my husband. Was mix up. He does not haf to stay in Korea. He is going to Germany, back vere I am from. I can go home now, and be wit my husband an wit my people."

Rooster watched as Christine spoke excitedly to him. He was captivated, in fact almost hypnotized by her. She was just so uncommonly pretty, and she was so beautiful in her happiness. He couldn't believe how pretty she was, and that he had just fucked the shit out of her not more than a couple of days ago. All of a sudden, something from deep inside him welled up, and a primal selfishness overtook him. It didn't matter if Laurie did return to normal, or that he had a son. There was no way he could let a beautiful woman like Christine slip away, no way in hell.

He was obviously drunk, exhausted, and not thinking clearly. He would realize that later.

"You don't have to go back to your husband. I'll go to Germany with you."

Christine looked at him, horrified.

"Vat? Vat are you saying?"

"I want to be with you. I'll go to Germany with you."

"Vat about you wife and you baby?" Christine's voice was rising.

"They'll be okay. Mel will take care of them," said Rooster dumbly.

"Vat? Vat? I can't believe what shit you are saying! Are you out you fucking mind? Oh, my Got! I can't believe what shit you say! You leaf you wife and new baby like dey are fucking nothing! You sorry bastard! Get out of here, you fucking bastard!"

"What?..wait...Christine, I just want to be with you..."

"Get de fuck out! I can't believe dis shit! I vas told you are bad person! I vas told! I should haf believe!"

"What? Who told you I'm a bad person?" Rooster said in surprise.

"Get de fuck out, bastard! That night was big mistake! That all! Big mistake! Doan come here no more! I'm not coming back to work! I quit!"

Christine pushed him out the door, onto the front porch, and slammed the door behind him.

Rooster stood there in shock and horror, not quite sure what had just happened, but certainly aware that he had just fucked up in a major way. He stood there, frozen, for a couple of seconds. Then, Christine opened the door again.

"You leaf me alone, or I tell everybody vat you did and vat you say! I doan care vat dey tink about me, I am leafing!" and she slammed the door again.

Rooster hurried back to his car and left quickly. He was really worried now. What if Christine did tell somebody what they had done, and what he said? His ass would be sunk, and he knew it. He was drunk, worried, and too scared to go any place where he might run into someone, so he raced home and drank some more until he passed out.

When he awoke the next morning, the first thing that popped into his mind was his new baby, and the second thing was the scene with Christine. He was both elated and scared to death, and fearful of his whole world collapsing. What the hell had he been thinking? He couldn't believe what words had come out of his own mouth. What an idiot he was. He'd had the whole world handed to him on a silver platter, and yet there he was about to screw it all up. He jumped out of bed, put on some coffee and began immediately pacing about the house, trying to figure out what he could do to make things right. He knew the first order of business was to go see Laurie and the baby and pretend like everything was okay. He hoped that Christine would quit like she said, but who knew what she might do. That was what worried him, what would she do now?

Rooster got to the hospital just as Laurie was nursing their baby boy, his own precious son. She looked like an angel, the epitome of motherhood and all that goes with it. All traces of the demon that had possessed her for the past few months were gone, and the sweet, pretty girl he had fallen in love with had returned. He felt deep shame at how he had acted and how he had been thinking these past several weeks. He had everything he could ever want, and yet he had been willing to throw it all away for a piece of ass, a beautiful piece of ass nonetheless, but one that, in truth, would have been a gamble at best. How could have he been willing to throw it all away? And for what? An ill-conceived lark to Germany? He had been to Germany, and when he really thought about it, he remembered that he had been mostly homesick the whole time. Rooster was scared now, scared of his own idiot brain and the questionable situations it might put him in if he wasn't careful.

Another unpleasant realization was also seeping into his mind. He was becoming just like his grandfather. Moreover, he realized why that had been happening: liquor. By most accounts, Devin Brown was a pleasant person as long as he was sober, but when he succumbed to the bottle, he gave in to his most base and selfish instincts. Rooster understood that he was slipping down that same path to disaster. He fretted that if he didn't do something soon he would lose everything in another stupid bought of drunkenness, which just caused him to crave alcohol even more.

He pretended all was well, and in fact, he was happy as he could be there with his wonderful wife and his precious newborn son. He was not eager to go to the office for fear that Christine might be there, waiting to light into him once again, this time within earshot of the governing body of Merky. The thought of that sent a shiver down his spine, so he was happy and relieved when Harvey came in to see them. They chatted for a bit, and then Rooster told Laurie that he needed to step out and talk to Harvey about some police business.

They went outside. Rooster lit a cigarette.

"Did Christine come in to work today?" Rooster asked, trying not to sound nervous.

"No, I haven't seen her yet."

"She came to work yesterday though, right?"

"Oh, yes. She was real excited, said she was going back to Germany soon."

"How soon, Harvey? Did she say when she was going back?"

"Uh...no, but it sounded like pretty soon."

That made Rooster feel better, if she would just move on then everything would be all right. He wished he could talk to her and find out more, but he didn't dare try to speak to her after what happened. If she told Claudette, or anyone else, about their affair, he was doomed, and that terrified him. If only she would just leave quickly and spare him.

"Okay. Listen, I need to take care of Laurie. Why don't you stay in the office today. Just hold down the fort, answer the phone, and let me know if you need anything."

Harvey shrugged. "Okay, whatever you say."

Rooster spent the day shuttling back and forth between the hospital and home and anywhere in town but the office, lest he run into Christine. He encountered plenty of well-wishers who wanted to shake his hand, pat his back, and congratulate him, which only reinforced the magnitude of what he stood to lose should the truth come out. At the end of the day, he reconnoitered with Harvey and learned that Christine had not come to work at all, which gave him some relief, but he still fretted about whether she would tell anyone, especially Claudette. He was just about sick with worry and could not take his mind off any number of disastrous scenarios that played out in his mind. He spent the evening with Laurie and the baby. Soon they would be leaving the hospital and coming home with him to begin their new life together. If only he could hold it together until the threat was over. When it was time to leave Laurie and the baby again, Rooster was too anxious to go home, and he thought about going to see Cletus.

However, he was torn between his cravings and his desire to do the right thing. He understood that ever since Laurie had gone into the hospital he had been drinking entirely too much, and he knew that he couldn't continue like that. He had to stop before it got out of hand, as it had when he was in the army. Still he was drawn toward Bug Town almost as if he had no control over it, and before he knew it, he was on his way there. This time, when he passed through the village, it was abuzz with excitement for the Prosper Revival was in full swing. He was going to just drive past, but for some reason, he decided to stop and watch the proceedings. He parked and walked to the tent. He stood just outside, peering in through an opening. Inside, it was full, and the people were clapping their hands to the music. Addie was playing the piano, and Odell and Eddie were leading the audience in a sing-a-long of upbeat gospel music. Rooster scanned the crowd and was shocked to see Cletus and Alice sitting in the middle of the crowd clapping their hands to the music and apparently enjoying themselves. He was also disappointed, for that meant they weren't home, and there would be no point in driving on out there.

He got in his patrol car and drove back to Merky. He wanted to drive past the little house in the trees and look for any sign of Christine, but he was fearful of being seen by her. He drove around town and decided to go the office. It was well past normal business hours, so he felt it would be somewhat safe to go inside. The courthouse was empty, and his footsteps echoed loudly in the hallway. He went to his office and unlocked the door. It was odd being there this late at night with no one else around, and he felt strange, as if he were intruding. He sat at his desk but could not relax, and he kept getting the strange feeling that he should leave lest he get caught. He had to remind himself that he was the sheriff and he had every right to be there. Of course, that caused him to reflect upon the fact that he *was* the sheriff and what an idiot he had been to jeopardize that. However, he just couldn't sit still, so he got up and left, walking back out to his car amid the echoing footsteps of the empty courthouse.

He decided to go back out to Bug Town and see what was happening out there. When he arrived, everything was proceeding along just as he left it. He parked again and went back to the tent. He spotted an empty chair along the back row and sat down. The crowd was still singing, but when the song was over, Odell came to the dais with a Bible in his hand and began to preach to the crowd.

"Praise Jesus! What a beautiful sight to see so many of God's people together in fellowship tonight," he said in a loud voice so that everyone in the crowd could hear him.

Everyone began to settle down and sit quietly in their seats to listen.

"Folks, the Lord has been speaking to me tonight, and he tells me that someone here in this very audience is troubled."

Rooster squirmed in his seat.

"For the Lord knows what is in your hearts. He knows the burdens you carry and the secrets you harbor. The Lord wants all his people to find peace, and the only way that is possible is to accept Jesus Christ into your heart and let him carry those burdens for you."

At this point, Addie began playing the piano softly in the background.

"Folks, in this very group tonight, someone is suffering. Someone is suffering from the sins they have committed."

Rooster crossed then uncrossed his legs and looked around the crowd as others began to fidget in their seats as well.

"Tonight, in this very group is someone who has been untruthful... tonight, in this very group, is someone who has taken that which does not belong to them...folks, tonight there is someone here who has lusted for that which belongs to someone else."

By now, virtually the entire audience had been implicated, and they were beginning to squirm accordingly.

"Folks, tonight, right here in this very group...is someone who has stolen...tonight, here in this very group is someone who has committed adultery..."

The audience was by now starting to collectively sweat. The preacher continued.

"...and folks, tonight, right here in this very place...is someone who has harbored murder in their heart..."

By now, Rooster was fidgeting more and a droplet of sweat was beginning to drip down his forehead. He wanted to get up and leave, but he felt that to do so would incriminate him, so he stayed put. Addie was singing softly along to her playing, keeping it low and in the background, so not overpower the words of Odell, yet loud enough to provide an emotional undercurrent to the preaching.

"Friends, if there is anyone here tonight who would like to turn their burden over to Jesus, please come forward and pray with us, so that you might have salvation."

At first call, no one stood, so Odell continued.

"Friends, if you are troubled by the life you have been living, then turn it over to Jesus. If the weight of your sins is becoming too much to carry then come forward and let Jesus carry them for you."

A young woman stood and began making her way to the front of the tent. An older man soon followed her, and then others. As they reached the altar, Eddie took them each by the hand, kneeled with them, and prayed with each one. Most of them were weeping.

"Praise Jesus!" shouted Odell. "Seek the power and the forgiveness of Jesus! Come forward all of you who have sinned and wish to repent!"

Once the first few people went to the altar to accept Jesus, then others began to follow. By now, many in the crowd had made their way to the front of the tent to pray and to accept Jesus. Odell continued, his passion and volume increasing with each word.

"For no one knows the day the Savior will return! It could be next year, next week, tomorrow, or it could be tonight! The choice you make will determine whether you spend eternity in paradise or in hell! Friends, Jesus wants you to make the right choice, but he can't make it for you. This could be your last chance to get right with the Lord!"

Rooster sat in the back row, literally quaking in his boots. First, he had jeopardized his position in the community, and now his eternal afterlife hung in the balance. He wanted to get up and go down to the front of the tent like the others had, but he held back. He was afraid of what the community would say about him if word got out that he had been saved at a Holy Roller camp, in Bug Town no less, yet he feared for his soul if he didn't. Religion in Merky followed the mainstream, and this type of religion was generally laughed at by the pillars of the community. Rooster fidgeted and fretted in the back row as one after another stepped forward into eternal salvation.

Finally, he could stand it no longer and he got up and walked briskly toward the front of the tent where Eddie was ministering to the congregants. Eddie reached out his hand and pulled Rooster forward and down to his knees. Eddie knelt with Rooster and began to pray.

"Father, please bless this man who has come forward in front of these witnesses to declare his faith and acceptance in your redeeming blood."

Then, he spoke directly to Rooster. "Do you accept Jesus Christ as your Lord and Savior?"

Rooster answered in barely a whisper, "Yes."

"Then pray with me," said Eddie. "Holy Father, please forgive this man his sins and grant him a new beginning in Jesus Christ. From this day forward, let him know thy love and salvation. Grant him peace of mind and remove the heaviness from his heart as he accepts you, Lord. Wash this man in the cleansing blood of Jesus as he begins this new journey in faith. We ask for salvation for this man and for all those who seek redemption in Jesus Christ. Amen."

Eddie hugged Rooster and shook his hand. Tears streamed down Rooster's face, and he got up and walked back to his seat at the rear of the tent. From the corner of his eye, he could see Cletus and Alice watching him somberly. When he got to his seat, he wanted to keep going and leave, but instead he sat down and tried to stop the tears from flowing. A man who was sitting next to him smiled and shook his hand and congratulated him. Rooster looked around to see if there was anyone else he knew in the crowd. As he was looking about, he was surprised to see both Cletus and Alice walking to the front of the tent to be saved. That made him feel a little better and not so conspicuous. He watched as they knelt and prayed with Eddie just as he had, and when they got up to return to their seats he could see they also were crying. Odell continued the altar call until virtually everyone there had come forward and accepted Jesus, and then when everyone had returned to their seats, Addie led the group singing "Amazing Grace," and it was over for the night.

As soon as the services were over, everyone began milling about to leave. Rooster got up and began walking to his patrol car, hoping to avoid talking to anyone. He was almost to his car when he heard someone calling his name.

"Sheriff Brown!"

He stopped in his tracks and turned to look. It was Addie Brock. He stopped and waited as she ran toward him.

"Sheriff Brown, I just wanted to congratulate you and thank you for coming."

"That's all right," Rooster mumbled.

"You are welcome to come back as often as you like. Once you accept the Lord, it is important to maintain fellowship with other Christians so that you establish a strong foundation of faith."

"Okay, I might do that, if I have time," said Rooster, looking about nervously.

Addie took his hand. "That was a beautiful thing you did tonight. A public profession of faith is the first and most important step toward salvation. God bless you."

"Thank you. Bless you too," said Rooster. "I have to go now. Good bye."

"Good bye, sheriff," said Addie.

He hadn't gone more than two more steps when he heard his name being called once again.

"Rooster!"

He knew almost even before he heard the voice that it was Cletus. He stopped but didn't turn around. Cletus came up to him and slapped him on the back.

"I wasn't expecting to see you here tonight," said Cletus.

"I reckon I can say the same thing about you."

"I guess that's right. Well, a little religion never hurt anybody. You might need it some time," said Cletus casually.

If Cletus had experienced a religious conversion that night, it didn't seem to have affected him too profoundly. He acted as if he had just left a barn dance. Rooster was relieved that he didn't seem to want to talk about what had just happened. Good ol' Cletus, he could always count on him to know how to handle a situation.

"Well, Rooster, we got to get going. Stop on by when you got some time to spare."

"I will. Good night."

Rooster took off for his car once again, this time at a fast clip before anyone else could stop him. He got in the car and headed back to Merky. He felt somewhat relieved, if the Lord came right now, he would be in good shape. However, he was still worried about what might transpire with Christine. When he got to his house, it was dark and empty and felt like a shell instead of a home. It had been like that ever since Laurie had gone into the hospital. Perhaps that was partly why it had been so easy to lust after Christine. Tomorrow, he would bring Laurie and the baby home. He hoped that once his family was here, it would start to feel like home again. Before Rooster went to sleep he knelt beside the bed and prayed with more intensity and sincerity than he had in years.

"Lord, I know I don't deserve any mercy, and I know I don't have any right to ask for it. But please, Lord, please don't let Laurie find out what I did. If you could please help me, Lord, I will be your faithful servant forever, and I will always try to do right. Thank you in Jesus' name. Amen."

Then he went to bed.

29

Rooster slept well that night, better than he had in days, and he awoke feeling rested. He said a little prayer of thanks before breakfast, and as he got ready to go bring Laurie and the baby home, he recalled the events of the night before. In spite of his reticence to make a public declaration of faith, he had, in fact, been very sincere in his acceptance of Christ, and he wanted to make good on this new phase of his life. He determined that he and Laurie and the baby would attend church regularly and lead good Christian lives. In fact, Laurie usually did go to church almost every Sunday, and Rooster went whenever the urge struck him, which was not often, but he deemed that would change. In particular, if the Lord granted his wish to spare him from the revelations of his affair with Christine, he would be forever indebted and would conduct his life in such a fashion as to be pleasing to the Heavenly Master. He was still worried about Christine tattling on him, but there was little he could do at this point except hope for the best. After he finished breakfast, he bathed and straightened up the house a little and set off for the hospital to bring his family home.

When he arrived at the hospital, Laurie was bathed, dressed, and ready to go. She looked prettier than she had in months. The baby, little William Melvin Brown, was swaddled in blankets and ready to be carried out to the car. Mel and Shirley were there to chaperone, and there was a happy and festive air about the place.

Rooster was still nervous about carrying the baby, it was so tiny, and he was so big and clumsy that he was afraid he would inadvertently harm it. They managed to get everyone and everything loaded and began a small convoy to the house. Besides Mel and Shirley, there were a few of Laurie's friends, such as Molly Muckelroy and Glenda Binkley, also accompanying them home. Rooster had the baby's room all set up and ready to go, so when they got home Laurie was able to put him to bed right away. They had a small impromptu party of sorts with the various relatives and friends helping the new family settle in. Laurie was so happy to be back in her own home with her baby and husband that she cried. She was pretty much back to her sweet old self, and Rooster was also very happy except for intense feelings of guilt which arose randomly at just about any time. Once the family was settled in, the visitors began to trickle away until it was just the little family of three enjoying their new life.

Rooster was in hog heaven, or he would have been, were it not for the nagging fear that his secret would come out, and everything would collapse around him. After dinner, he decided he should go into town and check in on the office. When he got to town, he decided to drive past the little house in the trees and see if there were any signs of Christine. He was surprised to see a couple of army trucks parked in front and some soldiers carrying out furniture and loading it into the trucks. He dared not stop but felt encouraged at what he had just seen. He raced on over to the courthouse and into his office where Harvey was napping quietly in a chair.

"I hope I'm not disturbing you there, deputy," Rooster said loudly.

Harvey started and jumped up. "Oh! Rooster..."

"Well, I guess everything must be all right here. I hope so anyway."

"Oh, yes, everything is fine," said Harvey.

Rooster looked around to make sure no one else was in the office.

"I saw somebody loading furniture over at Christine's," he said quietly.

"Yes, she came by and said she was quitting," said Harvey as he picked up an envelope from her desk. "She left this for you."

Rooster took the envelope and nervously opened it. It was a hand-written letter. It said:

Dear Sheriff Brown,

Thank you for hiring me. I enjoyed working for you, but I am resigning my job to go back to Germany to be with my husband and my family. I wish you well.

Sincerely,

Christine Cervenka

Rooster folded the letter and put it back in the envelope.

"Did she say anything else?" asked Rooster cautiously.

"Not too much. She said she liked working here but that she wanted to go home," replied Harvey.

"Did Claudette say anything?"

"Claudette? No, just that she would miss her."

"Okay."

Rooster was relieved, but he wouldn't feel entirely safe until Christine was gone for good. Suddenly, he realized that he would need to hire another secretary, and soon.

Rooster spent the next couple of hours in the office before he started getting antsy and decided to go out for a drive. Once again, he passed by the little house in the trees. One of the army trucks was gone, but now Mel's Cadillac was parked out front. That caused him some immediate concern that he wasn't out of the woods yet. He felt an immediate desire to go out to Cletus' for a drink, but quickly remembered that things were different now, and he couldn't just go out and have a drink whenever he pleased as he had for the past several months. Besides, he had an agreement with the Lord that he intended to honor, and if he was going to renege on any agreements, he knew he had better at least wait until Christine was gone.

Rooster spent the rest of the day patrolling town and then went home. When he got there, Laurie and Shirley were cooking supper. He kissed Laurie on the cheek, then went into the nursery and looked at his baby sleeping soundly. Then he went and waited in the living room for supper to be ready.

"Is that all he does, is sleep?" asked Rooster while the women were setting the table.

"No, he eats and messes his diapers too," said Shirley.

"If you want to find out, I'll be happy to let you feed and change him," laughed Laurie.

"That's okay, I believe you," said Rooster.

Just then, Mel pulled up in front of the house, right on time for supper. He clomped up the front porch and on into the living room.

"Well, howdy there, Poppa," he said when he spotted Rooster.

"Hello, Mel. How are you?" said Rooster.

"Oh, I'm doing all right. I just got through seeing my tenant get moved out."

"Which tenant moved?" asked Shirley.

"The German woman, Christine Cervenka."

"You mean Rooster's secretary?" asked Laurie, a hint of irritation in her voice.

"That's the one. She's moving back to Germany."

"She is? Rooster, you never mentioned that," said Laurie.

"Um, yeah, I guess with all the excitement about the baby I forgot to tell you."

"What are you going to do for a secretary now, Rooster?" asked Shirley.

"I don't know. I guess I need to run an ad. Maybe I can get Mildred to come in and help until I find a replacement."

Shirley put her finger to her cheek. "You know what? I bet I know someone who would be perfect. She has experience and is very dependable."

"That would be great," said Rooster.

"I'll talk to her and let you know," said Shirley.

While Shirley and Laurie finished getting supper ready, Rooster and Mel sat in the living room talking.

"Did Christine say when she was leaving for Germany?" asked Rooster, trying to sound nonchalant.

"Didn't she tell you?" asked Mel.

"Uh, no, I haven't had much chance to talk to her lately."

"She told me she would be catching a plane in a couple of days. She has a place to stay on the base until she leaves."

"So she is out of the house now?"

"Oh, yes."

Mel lowered his voice. "Kind of peculiar the way she just up and took off, don't you think, Rooster?"

"Um, I don't know. Sometimes that's the way it is in the military."

"Kind of strange how she didn't tell you too much about it either."

"Well, yeah, but I've been pretty busy with the baby and all."

Mel acted like he was going to say something else, but then let it drop. Rooster thought that Mel probably knew something had happened, but he hoped that with Christine now gone, he wouldn't make too big a deal about it.

When it was time to eat, Rooster surprised everyone by suggesting that he say grace before the meal.

"Why, Rooster, this is a little unusual," said Shirley.

"Well, I have a family now and a lot to be grateful for. I want to set a good example for my son. I want us to start going to church as a family too."

The rest of them looked at each other in disbelief, and then they all bowed their heads to pray. Rooster cleared his throat. Mel peeked out of the corner of one eye and watched as Rooster spoke.

"Heavenly father, we offer thanks for this meal that we are about to enjoy. We thank you for the newest addition to our family, William Melvin Brown. We are all very blessed, Father, especially me. I want to thank you for giving me this wonderful family, and I pray that you help me to strengthen the bond that holds us together. Amen."

Everyone repeated "Amen," and they began to eat. No one was quite sure what to think of Rooster offering to say grace, but it was regarded by Laurie and Shirley as a welcome development. Mel said little about it, but he seemed to be smiling to himself ever so slightly, as if in on a private joke.

After supper, Shirley and Mel went home, leaving the new family unit alone. Laurie was in a sweet mood, the baby was sleeping, and Rooster was immensely happy. It all seemed perfect when they went to bed that night. However, the peace was broken soon after Rooster and Laurie drifted off to sleep when the piercing wail of little William Melvin Brown awakened them with a start. He kept them both up much of the night with each taking turns tending to him. By dawn, he had worn himself out crying and was back to sleeping soundly. Rooster, on the other hand, was tired and his nerves were on edge. By the time he left for work, Laurie and the baby were sleeping peacefully. When he got to the office, he told Harvey to go out on patrol, and he locked the door to the office, positioned himself in his chair, and napped for a couple of hours. When he woke up later, he went out and patrolled for a bit then went over to the house in the trees. He parked out front and sat there for a few minutes, perhaps waiting to be sure that she was not still there. He got out, walked to the front door and pushed it open. The house was completely empty, and it felt strange to him. He walked from room to room, remembering when he had first moved in it and how thrilled he was to have a place of his own.

He thought about the first time he and Laurie had made love here and how they started their life together in this very place. And then, of course, he remembered the night he spent with Christine. So much had happened in this tiny little house. It would always be a special place to him.

When he got back to the office, Shirley was there with a woman he had never met before. She was an older lady, perhaps in her late fifties or sixties. She was obviously past menopause, had a dour wrinkled face, and wore eyeglasses with thick bottle cap lenses. Her hair was curled into a tight permanent and had a slight bluish tint to it.

"Rooster, this is Ethel Clapsaddle. She's the one I was telling you about," said Shirley.

Rooster looked at Shirley blankly.

"Remember, I told you I knew someone who would be perfect for the secretary job."

"Oooh, yes, I remember now. Pleased to meet you, ma'am," said Rooster.

"Pleased to meet you, sheriff. I have twenty years of secretarial experience, and I have also done payroll and just about any type of administrative duties you can think of," said Ethel.

"Well, that sounds terrific. We will certainly give you serious consideration. Of course, I will need you to fill out an application," said Rooster.

"Oh, Rooster, is that really necessary?" asked Shirley, a hint of irritation in her voice.

"Um, well, yes, everybody needs to fill out an application," said Rooster.

"He's right," said Ethel. "I don't mind. I can do it right now. Is there a desk I can use?"

"Why don't you use Rooster's desk. That way, we can close the door and give you some privacy," said Shirley.

Rooster got Ethel an application and showed her to his desk.

"Just come on out when you're finished," said Rooster.

Once he had closed the door, Shirley came over to him and placed her hand on his shoulder, squeezing it firmly.

"Rooster, Ethel is extremely qualified. I know this is your decision, but I don't see the point in interviewing a bunch of people," said Shirley, with a degree of seriousness in her voice that was unusual for her.

"I'm sure she's very qualified, but it's always good to have a large pool of applicants," said Rooster, trying to sound like he knew what he was talking about.

Shirley squeezed his shoulder even harder and looked intently into his eyes. "You don't need a large pool when you have the best candidate show up first in line. You don't want somebody who is going to leave again after a few months, and you especially don't want somebody who is going to cause problems in other ways."

Rooster started to respond, but he could tell by the look in Shirley's eye, her tone of voice, and the fact that she was squeezing his shoulder painfully hard that she wasn't going to back down. And with her remark about "causing problems in other ways" the message was unmistakable. Shirley rarely put her foot down about anything, but it was clear that this time Rooster had no choice, and he knew that she was probably right anyway.

"Okay, Shirley," he said, pulling away from her iron grip. "She's got the job."

When Ethel emerged with her completed application, Rooster hired her on the spot. His mother-in-law was happy, he had a skilled secretary, and there would be no chance of hanky panky this time around. He also knew that Laurie would be pleased, so that sealed the deal.

That night, the baby gave a repeat performance of the previous evening and kept them awake most of the night.

"Damn! Why can't he sleep at night?" Rooster asked Laurie in a fit of frustration.

"He will eventually. Sometimes, babies get their days and nights mixed up," she replied wearily.

This would be the routine for the next few weeks until they got the infant on a more or less normal schedule. In spite of the stresses of the new baby, this was a very happy period for all of them. As promised, Rooster began going to church every Sunday, family in tow, and he stopped drinking. He had a couple of slip-ups but nothing too serious. He missed the company of Cletus and Mexican Alice, but it was best not to tempt himself too much. He felt as if he were finally fulfilling the role he had been chosen for—sheriff, family man, and upstanding citizen. He wished his parents could see him now, especially his father. He didn't know why, but apparently God had chosen him for something he would not have dared to choose for himself, and God had granted him his request to keep his secret, so he would now honor his end of the bargain. Whenever he found himself tempted by one thing or another or having improper thoughts, he would remind himself of the bountiful blessings bestowed upon him and the agreement he had made with the Lord that night at the Prosper Revival. He was on the path of righteousness.

30

Not too long after the baby was born, Harvey and Claudette surprised everyone by going to the justice of the peace and getting married. Since both of their families were opposed to the marriage, and because Claudette had already been married, they decided a church wedding would be inappropriate. Rooster stood next to them and served as their witness. They moved into the little house in the trees which had been so important in Rooster's life.

Ethel Clapsaddle turned out to be an excellent secretary. She jumped in and immediately began correcting many things that Christine had done wrong, which Rooster had been completely unaware of. Moreover, she was good friends with Mildred, the original secretary, so if she had questions she could just call Mildred and get the answer she needed. In no time at all, she had the office humming along with an almost machine-like efficiency.

Rooster kept his word to the Lord and attended church almost every Sunday, and he prayed daily, seeking guidance and offering his thanks and gratitude for his bountiful existence. He even retrieved his father's Bible from his sock drawer and began reading it, although it was difficult for him. He made it through Genesis without too much difficulty, and he plodded through Exodus, but when he got to Leviticus, it started going downhill. Each day he would read less and less, then he started skipping a day, and before long, it was back in the sock drawer.

His initial enthusiasm for church was seen by many in the congregation as a willingness to become more involved in church activities, something he had no interest in. He was asked to join the choir, but was able to get out of that by demonstrating that he really could not sing at all. One of the more persistent members of the congregation convinced him to teach Sunday school. Reluctantly he agreed, figuring it would just be babysitting a bunch of young children.

However, it turned out to be more complicated than he had anticipated. He was supposed to follow a lesson plan and control a room full of energetic children, all the while explaining the Bible, something he struggled with himself. The children didn't always cooperate and they were easily distracted. Also, they would ask him questions he wasn't able to answer, simple things such as "if God created everything, then who created God?" and "why did God drown all the animals, were they wicked too?" and "why didn't God just kill Satan?" and so forth. It didn't take long before he quit.

Although he truly felt blessed in many ways, and he believed in a Creator, he found church boring and confusing, and he was annoyed at having to get up early on Sunday morning when he would rather sleep in and stay at home. However, he understood the social aspect of church attendance and he knew it could affect his reputation if he missed too much. He grudgingly accepted it as a price to pay for his position in the community; however, he often found it easy to come up with excuses to miss church and his zeal waned, much as it had previously when he had tried to embrace the religious life.

Overall, it was a period of happiness and stability for the people of Merky. The little community took on an aura of idyllic tranquility, and it seemed as if nothing could spoil their little Garden of Eden.

Then, one Saturday morning, Rooster got a call at home from the hospital. Two teenage boys had been brought in the night before with alcohol poisoning. They admitted to drinking moonshine but claimed they couldn't remember where they had gotten it. Rooster, of course, knew right away where it had come from. Selling moonshine was one thing, but selling bad moonshine was something altogether different. Rooster went to the hospital and told the doctor he would take care of the problem. He was about to leave for Bug Town to talk to Cletus, when the parents of the young men pulled him aside. Both boys were from prominent families, and the parents were intent on keeping this incident quiet. Rooster and the hospital staff agreed that they would not talk about it to anyone.

When he pulled in to Cletus' place, there was no one around. He honked the horn and got out of the car. Cletus emerged from the shack bleary eyed and half-asleep.

"Well, good morning, stranger. We haven't seen you in a while. What can I do for you this morning, Rooster?"

"Howdy, Cletus. I just need to talk to you for a bit," replied Rooster.

"Okay, sure. Come on and have a seat," said Cletus. "You want something to drink?"

Rooster felt a powerful urge for a shot of whiskey, but instead he said a silent prayer and suppressed the thought.

"No thanks, Cletus. The reason I came out this morning is that two boys got very sick from some moonshine last night and had to go to the hospital. If you are selling bad product, then you need to stop, and get rid of it."

Cletus looked puzzled. "As far as I know, my stuff is good, and I don't sell to boys anyway. My stuff is too strong for youngsters."

"I don't know where else it would have come from. It pretty much has to be you."

"Well...yeah...I guess so. Damn! I hate to pour it out but whatever you say, Rooster. I don't want to make anybody sick."

"You're a good man, Cletus. I knew you would understand," said Rooster. Then, the two men sat around talking about this and that and catching up on recent events. Alice got up and made them coffee and tacos, and it was a very pleasant visit.

The next week, Rooster got another call from the hospital. Two more boys showed up with alcohol poisoning, and just like the ones before them, they claimed to have no memory of where they got it. Rooster cursed under his breath as he once again drove out to see Cletus. This time, Cletus was insistent that it wasn't him.

"Rooster, I ain't sold nobody no home brew since you come out last weekend. I poured it all out, just like you said. You can go check for yourself."

Rooster did, in fact, look around. The still had apparently been sitting idle, and all he found was Mexican beer.

"Well, all right. Maybe it was something you had already sold. I don't know what to think either, just make sure you don't sell anymore of the home brew, just beer."

Cletus agreed, and Rooster went back to town, feeling confident that the issue was resolved. For the next couple of weeks, all was calm and then Rooster got a call at home in the middle of the night. It was the hospital again, only this time it was much more serious. Four boys were dead. Rooster went to the hospital where the boy's grieving families were gathered. One of the mothers confronted him angrily.

"You could have stopped this! You knew that Cletus Gross was selling poison! Now my boy is dead! What kind of sorry excuse for a lawman are you!?" the woman screamed in his face.

"Ma...ma'am, I'm sorry about your son...bu...but I did go out there, and I made Cletus pour it all out. I don't know what happened," stammered Rooster.

"You should have arrested him!" the woman screamed. "My boy is dead!"

A couple of the other parents also shouted at Rooster while others appeared as if in shock and a couple of the more composed ones tried to calm the frantic ones.

"Now, Nancy, it isn't the sheriff's fault. Our boys did something they shouldn't have," said one woman.

"If it's anyone's fault, it's that damn Cletus Gross and his ugly, old squaw," said a man.

"My boy...my boy..." moaned a man sitting quietly off to the side.

"I'll take care of it. I'll go pick him up first thing in the morning," said Rooster.

"You better, or we'll kill him ourselves," said another man.

Rooster broke away from the families and found the doctor.

"Are you sure it was the whiskey that killed them?" he asked the doctor, a young man not long out of medical school.

448

"There's no question. All the signs are there, and half a bottle of the whiskey was found with them. What else could have killed four healthy young men like that?"

"Damn!" Rooster exclaimed. "I can't believe this. I told him to pour it all out, and he said he did."

Rooster went back to the families and told them he would arrest Cletus at first sunlight and take him to the courthouse to be charged. Witnessing the depth of their anguish made him ill, and a deep anger arose in him. He looked at his watch; it was a little after 3:00 am. It was too late to go back to bed, and he didn't think he would sleep much anyway, so he went to the office instead. The courthouse was empty except for a night watchman, and it felt eerie to be there. He sat at his desk, and in spite of his distress, he fell asleep in his chair. He was dozing when the phone rang, startling him. He picked up the receiver.

"Sheriff's office," he said hoarsely into the phone.

"Sheriff Brown?" a voice asked.

"Yes, this is Sheriff Brown. Who's speaking?"

"I just thought you ought to know that a crowd of people are on their way to hang Cletus Gross and his woman. You better hurry on out there," said the voice and hung up.

Rooster jumped up from his desk, his heart suddenly racing. He grabbed a shotgun from the gun rack and ran out to his car. He raced up to the little house in the trees and skidded to a stop with the horn blaring.

"Harvey! Get dressed and grab a gun! Hurry!" he shouted at the bedroom window.

Harvey appeared at the window. "What's going on?" he yelled.

"Trouble out at Cletus' place! Get dressed and get your gun! Hurry!"

Harvey disappeared, but now Claudette was at the window.

"Rooster, what's happening!?" she screamed.

"I don't know. Some kind of trouble. We'll tell you later!" he shouted back as Harvey came racing outside, his shirttail flapping and belt a flailing unbuckled. When Harvey got in the car, Rooster peeled out, throwing dirt and pebbles all over. He had the lights flashing and the siren howling as Harvey tried to compose himself.

"What's going on, Rooster?" Harvey gasped. "What's wrong?"

"People going out to hang Cletus...bad whiskey killed some boys...got to hurry..." Rooster answered him in a breathless staccato manner, for he didn't know what exactly was going on himself, but he knew that it was probably going to be bad.

The sun was just coming up when they got there, and a crowd of perhaps twelve or fifteen people were already there. Cletus and Alice had already been beaten, they were bleeding and their clothes were ripped and torn. The crowd had just put ropes around their necks and were about to hang them from an oak tree when Rooster and Harvey skidded to a stop. Rooster jumped out of the car, grabbed his shotgun and pointed it at the crowd.

"Stop right now!" he shouted at the crowd.

"You just go on, sheriff, we're going to handle this," said someone from the crowd.

Rooster fired a shot into the air, causing the mob to turn and look at him.

"Look here, sheriff, this man and his squaw killed our boys, and they're going to pay for it. You knew he was selling bad whiskey, and you could have stopped him, so we ought to string your ass up too," said a man who apparently was one of the leaders of the mob.

Rooster pointed his shotgun directly at the man who was speaking. "You either stop, or you're going to be the next one that dies."

"You going to kill all of us?" the man sneered at Rooster.

"I'll kill as many as I have to."

The man just stood there, still holding the rope and not showing any inclination to leave.

"There's not going to be any hangings today," said Rooster firmly. "Go on home."

"You're just going to let them go free?" asked someone else.

"No, I'm not. I'm going to take them to jail just as soon y'all get out of here, and if the judge wants to hang them, then so be it, but it's going to have go through the court."

Everyone in the crowd was now unsure of what to do. They clearly wanted justice, but now that they had been prevented from carrying out their deed, some of them were apparently thinking things over. The two or three leaders of the mob had yet to be convinced. Rooster recognized this and spoke once again, this time directing his words to the leaders.

"I've already killed two son of a bitches in the act of committing a crime, and I'll do it again. Lynching is against the law, and I represent the law in this county. I'm not going to ask you again. Drop the ropes and leave—now!"

The man who appeared to be the main leader threw down the rope in disgust and walked away. The others then followed him. Some got in their cars right away and left, while others lingered to make sure that Rooster did, in fact, arrest Cletus and Alice.

Once Rooster felt the threat had passed, he told Harvey to watch the ones who remained behind, and he went over to attend to Cletus and Alice. They had both been beaten badly. Alice was sobbing, and Cletus seemed dazed. Rooster knelt down to where they were both sitting on the ground.

"Are y'all all right?" he asked softly. "Do you have any broken bones or anything?"

Cletus shook his head slowly. "I told 'em I didn't sell those boys that whiskey...I told 'em, but they wouldn't believe me..."

Alice just cried, unable to talk. Rooster felt a pang of sadness at the pitiful sight of his old friends. They were both beaten and bruised, and in that moment, the essence of their pathetic lives seemed especially pronounced. Rooster ascertained that they were both able to get up and walk to the patrol car, so he gently escorted them to the car and put them both in the back seat. He told Harvey to keep an eye on them and not let the remnants of the crowd approach. He went to their shacks and looked around to see if he could find any whiskey as evidence. He searched the whole place and all he found was beer. Cletus' still did not appear to have been used recently. He even went inside the shack that they lived in. In all the time he had known them, he had never gone inside their home. He felt as if he was intruding, but he went on in anyway. In one corner was a bed covered with a quilt and across from that was an old dresser, and on the other end was a washbasin, a rusty mirror, and a couple of chairs. He noticed some framed photographs on the dresser and leaned over to look at them. They were photos of Cletus and Alice in their youth, before they met each other. The photo of Cletus was when he was in the army and young, handsome, and clean cut—the picture of youth and health. The other photo was of a very pretty young woman. It shocked him to realize that the young woman in the photograph was Alice. He was struck how the circumstances of a person's life could take them from such a promising beginning to such a sorry ending. It caused him to reflect how fortunate he was not to be living in a shack such as this, especially considering his own contemptible behavior at times.

Satisfied that there was no moonshine to be found, Rooster went back to the car where Harvey was standing guard over the prisoners. He was about to get in and leave when he noticed that a few members of the mob were still hanging around. He went over to them and told them to leave in a very firm and demanding manner, and they obeyed him and left. That pleased him in a curious way. Once the last stragglers had driven out of sight, he got in the car and drove his prisoners to jail.

Along the way, both Alice and Cletus cried softly, which pained Rooster. He also was conflicted about having to arrest them and possibly send them to death row. He was truly fond of them, even Alice, and he never dreamed that he would be put in such a situation when he became sheriff. When he got to the jail, there was already a crowd waiting. Word had spread fast around Merky. The crowd was angry and hostile and they started booing and cursing at the suspects as soon as Rooster pulled up to the jail. Rooster got out of the car quickly and took control of the situation.

"I have two suspects here that are going to be put in jail. If anyone tries to harm them, they will be joining them in jail—if I don't shoot you first. Step away from the car and stay back!" Rooster shouted forcefully at the crowd.

They all obeyed him and backed away, but that didn't stop them from shouting and cursing when he took Cletus and Alice from the car. He quickly got them into the jail and locked the main door behind them. He instructed the jailer to keep the door locked until he had them safely in their cells and told Harvey to stay and guard the door. Rooster took the two of them upstairs and put them in the very same cell in which he had spent the night in what seemed like a lifetime ago. He went inside with them and sat down.

"Y'all know I don't want to have to do this. I'd give anything if it was somebody else, but I have to enforce the law," said Rooster.

Cletus sniffled and spoke haltingly, "Rooster...we didn't do nothing...I swear, I'm telling you as my friend. I did not sell those boys that whiskey, and I haven't sold any since you told me to stop. I've been making home brew for years and not once have I ever had anybody get sick from it."

"I know, Cletus, I believe you, but where else would they have gotten it? I've never heard of anybody else bootlegging around here, have you?"

Cletus just shook his head. "I didn't do it...I didn't do it..."

Alice wiped her eyes. "Rooster, we yoo friend. We no lie to yoo."

"I know, Alice, I know. This is real hard for me too."

"We doan tell nobody yoo was gone kill that woman. We doan tell nobody," said Alice.

Rooster gasped. Suddenly he was back in that truck stop parking lot on a dark night with murder in his heart. Vividly he saw himself spinning the cylinder of the gun, eagerly waiting to slaughter a woman. Then, he saw himself in his lowest moment of despair, pointing the barrel at his temple, mere seconds from eternity. A rush of emotions flooded his brain, paralyzing him with fear and dread. He struggled to respond.

"Now look...look here..." he gasped, "you need to watch what you say...I don't know what you're talking about. I'm the only friend you got right now, so don't go talking nonsense."

Alice nodded her head, wiped her eyes, and blew her nose. Cletus groaned softly as he dabbed at his eye, which was almost swollen shut.

"Lay down and get some rest. I'll see if I can get a doctor to look at you later and make sure you're not hurt too bad," said Rooster. "I'll be back later after I talk to the district attorney and the judge."

Rooster paused as he left the jail cell. "I'm sorry I have to be doing this."

Rooster went downstairs and gave the jailer strict instructions to keep the door locked at all times. He then went outside and told the crowd that Alice and Cletus were locked up, that there was nothing else to see, and for everyone to go home. Most of them did leave, but a few remained talking among themselves. As Rooster got into his patrol car, he realized he had no idea what to do next. He knew the suspects would have to go before a judge and he would have to contact the district attorney to file the charges. However, before he did anything, he decided he should contact Addis to get his advice first so that he didn't look like a total idiot. It was a Saturday, and Addis' office was closed, so Rooster went to his home instead.

It was a tranquil morning on Addis' street. The news of the deaths, and the arrest of suspects, had not made it to this part of town yet. Rooster knocked on the door, and after a few minutes, Addis appeared. He didn't appear to have been awake very long. He was obviously surprised to see Rooster.

"Rooster...what on earth?"

"Addis, I'm sorry to bother you so early in the morning, but I need some advice, if you don't mind. There's been some bad news overnight. Four boys are dead from drinking poison whiskey. I've already arrested the suspects, but I need to talk to you before I go to the D.A. and the judge."

Addis' eyes widened. "Bad whiskey? Where did they get it?"

"Who else? Cletus."

Addis exhaled. "Oh...yes...of course. Come in, Rooster."

They sat down and talked at Addis' kitchen table, and Addis told him what he needed to do. Rooster listened carefully, and he was grateful to have a friend who was so smart. He had just survived his first real crisis as sheriff. Maybe he wasn't so dumb after all.

Rooster left Addis and went to his office at the courthouse. He called Joe Grundy at home to tell him what had happened, however, Joe had already heard the news and was getting ready to go to his office to begin preparing the paperwork. Rooster called the jail, where Harvey was still standing guard, and asked him to come help him with the law book. Then he called Ethel at home and asked her to come in as well. He was going to need all the help he could get.

31

Little Merky rarely saw this type of tragedy, and the town was apoplectic and heartbroken in the days following the death of the four boys. This anger and grief ushered in an era of temperance the likes of which had not been seen since Prohibition. Churches held anti-liquor rallies, and no one could be found who would dare speak a word of defense for demon liquor. The hatred directed at Cletus and Mexican Alice was such that the jail was kept locked at all times, and the jailer carried a gun lest a crowd break in and lynch them on the town square, something that was suggested often. It only took one day after the death of the boys before someone burned down their shacks and slaughtered or stole their livestock. Their meager lives were reduced even more and all that they could claim as their own was their very souls and even that looked doubtful for the long haul.

The following Monday, they were brought before Judge Wilmer Kitchens for the arraignment, and District Attorney Joe Grundy presented his preliminary findings, which were based largely on circumstantial evidence since no one could prove that the poison liquor actually came from Cletus. However, you could not find so much as one person in the whole county who didn't think that they were guilty. This was a capital case, and Addis, being one of only two attorneys in town, was picked to defend the two bootleggers, something he reluctantly agreed to. Because of the animosity he knew would be directed at him, he tried to get Cletus and Alice to plead guilty, ostensibly to avoid the electric chair, but mostly to spare himself from having to defend them in court. However, they resolutely claimed their innocence, and so he was then forced to formulate some type of defense for the trial, a daunting task considering the mood of the town. The judge decided the evidence, such as it was, was adequate to begin court proceedings, and he gave the prosecutor a deadline to put together a case and seat a jury.

In the minds of practically every single person in Merky, their guilt was already determined, and all that remained was the formal sentencing and execution. If there was any doubt in the mind of anyone in town as to their actual guilt, it was in the mind of the person who arrested them. Although Rooster said little about it, he was bothered by Cletus and Alice's protestations of innocence. He knew them as well as anyone, and he couldn't help but believe them, even though he couldn't imagine who else would have been selling poison whiskey. It was these lingering doubts that troubled him and caused him to pray intently for guidance. If there was an injustice being played out, then he wanted to do the right thing. Although his enthusiasm for church had diminished, he still kept the faith. He felt he had a debt to repay and that he had somehow been called to carry out the Lord's work whenever possible. He was determined to do the right thing.

The boys who had been poisoned in the previous episodes all claimed they couldn't remember much of what happened, including where they had obtained their whiskey, something that most people thought plausible. Rooster, however, had his doubts. That seemed a bit too convenient to him, and he knew from personal experience that liquor made a handy excuse to forget things you would rather not remember. So he went to the hospital and got the names of all the boys who had been poisoned. He found out where they lived and what they looked like, and he began to watch for them. Sure enough, one evening he saw the two boys that were involved in the first incident out driving around. He followed them to the edge of town and then turned on his lights and siren and pulled them over.

The boys had been watching him from the rearview mirrors as he followed them, and they made sure they weren't speeding or breaking any laws. They were obviously perplexed and concerned when Rooster came striding up to the driver's door.

"Hello, sheriff. We weren't doing anything wrong, were we?" said the driver.

"Aren't you the boys that got poisoned off that bad whiskey?" Rooster asked gruffly.

"Uh, yes, sir, but we don't have any more. We quit drinking," said the boy.

"I need to talk to you boys. Get in my car, we're going for a ride."

The boys got into the car with Rooster, one in the front and one in the back, and he drove out of town for a couple more miles before pulling over. He turned sideways in his seat, so that he could make eye contact with both boys.

"I want to know where you got that whiskey that made you sick," he asked forcefully.

The boys both squirmed but said nothing.

"Damn it! I asked you where you got that whiskey!" Rooster shouted at them.

Both boys flinched. "We don't remember, sir," said one.

"We were too drunk. We can't remember," said the other.

"That's bullshit!" Rooster shouted at them again.

Rooster pointed at the boy in the back seat. "You! Get out now! Wait over there by that sign till I tell you to come back."

The boy quickly got out and ran over to a nearby road sign. Rooster glared at the boy sitting next to him in the front seat.

"Boy, if you lie to me again, I'm going to put your ass in jail. Do you understand?"

"Yes...yes, sir," stammered the boy.

"Now, I'm not going to listen to any more bullshit from you. I know where you got that whiskey because I've already talked to the other boys who got poisoned, so I'm going to know if you're lying. This is important for a criminal investigation. Now tell me where you got that whiskey," said Rooster.

The boy looked like he wanted to cry, "Billy Tatum. I got it from Billy Tatum. Please don't tell him I told you. He said he would kill us if we ratted on him."

"Well, all right then," said Rooster. Then he honked the horn at the other boy and waved him back to the car. He told the first boy to get out and stand by the sign like the other boy had. When the other boy came back to the car Rooster used the same ruse on him until that boy also confessed that they had gotten the whiskey from someone named Billy Tatum and that they had been threatened with retaliation if they revealed that to anyone.

Then, Rooster drove both boys back to their car, but before he let them out, he gave them a stern warning.

"Don't either one of you tell anyone what just happened tonight. If you do, I'll find out about it, and I'll come after you. You understand me?" he growled at them.

"Yes, sir," both boys stammered as they got out of the car.

Rooster was vaguely aware of Billy Tatum. He was a local farm laborer who preferred to spend most of his time in the country. He was a bit antisocial but generally well liked. Rooster figured that he must be related to his old nemesis, Joe, and he was going to find out what was going on. The next day, he pulled into the Texaco station and waited in his car at the pumps as Joe had once done to him. Kermit came out to wait on him.

"Howdy do, Sheriff Brown. How can we help you today?" drawled Kermit lazily.

"Hello, Kermit. Tell Joe to come out here. I want to talk to him."

Rooster watched as Kermit sauntered back to the station and talked to Joe. He could see the expression on Joe's face when Kermit spoke to him, and he knew Joe wasn't pleased about this request, but he came out to the car.

"Kermit said you wanted to talk to me," said Joe warily.

"That's right. Get in the car. We need to take a ride," said Rooster, dipping his head to the passenger seat.

"Uh...well, I can't do that, I'm on duty now," said Joe, frowning.

"I'm not asking you. I'm telling you. This is official police business. Get in the car now," said Rooster forcefully.

"Shit!" Joe said angrily as he wiped his hand on a red shop rag and walked around the car. He got in, and Rooster took off driving out of town. Once they passed the city limits, he stomped the gas pedal and turned on the siren. By the time they got to the Bug Town turnoff, they were going ninety miles an hour. Rooster hit the brakes and fishtailed onto the turnoff and down the dirt road to Bug Town.

"What the hell is going on?" asked Joe as he gripped the door handle.

Rooster said nothing as they went through Bug Town and out to Cletus' place. He turned up the car path, which was already beginning to grow over with weeds, and parked in front of the burned remains of Cletus' shacks. He turned off the motor and turned to Joe.

"Who is Billy Tatum?" asked Rooster.

Joe's brow furrowed. "What?"

"I said who is Billy Tatum?"

Joe looked out the window and said nothing. Rooster reached into his holster, pulled out his gun and pointed it at Joe.

"You know I haven't forgot how you treated me when you were the mighty lawman. That son of a bitch Hickey and his other asshole deputy acted like they were going to shoot me and throw me in a ditch. Well, the shoe is on the other foot now, and I might just shoot your ass and call it self-defense if you play games with me. Now tell me who Billy Tatum is."

"He's one of my cousins. Why? What did he do?"

"I didn't say he did anything. I just want to know who he is. Where can I find this cousin of yours?"

"I don't know. I think he left town."

"Left town? Where did he go?"

"I don't know. I ain't his keeper."

"Why did he leave?"

"I don't know."

"That's bullshit!"

"It's the truth. He's a grown man. I don't keep up with everything he does."

"The man just up and leaves town and doesn't tell anybody why or where he's going, not even his family. That sure sounds like bullshit to me."

"I don't know any more than that, Rooster, so if that's not good enough, then you'll just have to shoot me," said Joe defiantly.

Rooster studied Joe for a few seconds before putting his gun back in his holster and starting the car. Neither man said anything on the ride back to town until Rooster dropped off Joe.

"I'm not through with this yet, and you better not tell anybody what we talked about or you just might get a bullet in your ass after all," said Rooster as he pulled into the station. Joe said nothing as he got out of the car.

Rooster went back to his office and asked Ethel if she knew anything about the Tatums.

"Oh, Lord yes. They're almost as bad as the Blackwells, except for Joe. He's always been the best of the bunch," replied Ethel.

"I need to get some information on the Tatums. Can you get me the names and addresses of all the ones that live around here?" asked Rooster.

Ethel seemed surprised at the request. "Well, yes, I suppose I can. What did they do?"

"Oh, nothing that I know of. I'm just curious, and I would like to talk to some of them."

The next day, Rooster had just parked in front of the courthouse and gotten out of his car when Mel came racing up and pulled in next to him.

"Hey, Rooster, what's this I hear about you taking my employee off the job without my permission?" asked Mel, sounding irritated.

Rooster felt himself blush. "I had some questions for him about an investigation I'm working on."

"Then, you need to talk to him on his own time. Don't be pulling people off the job when they're on my clock," said Mel. "What the hell kind of investigation is it anyway?"

"It's official police business, damn it," said Rooster angrily.

Mel's eye's widened. "Oh, I see how it is now. You're Mr. Big Shot Sheriff and can just do whatever the hell you want. Well, just don't forget who helped put you where you are today, all right?"

"I haven't forgot, Mel, but I'm not your employee anymore. I had some questions for Joe, and I may need to talk to him again before I'm done."

"Talk to him about what? He hasn't done anything. The only people guilty of anything around here are sitting in jail now."

"Look, Mel, it's not anything you need to be worried about. If I want to talk to Joe again, then I'll wait till he's off duty, okay?"

Mel cursed under his breath and spun the tires as he left, leaving Rooster standing in a pale blue haze of burned rubber. Rooster felt his face burning. The last thing he needed was to argue with Mel about something that wasn't even his business in the first place. He went on in to the office where Ethel and Harvey were already sitting around talking.

"Morning, boss," said Harvey cheerfully. Ever since he had gotten married Harvey was even happier than usual, something that Rooster attributed to marital bliss and getting laid frequently.

"Rooster, I have those names and addresses you wanted," said Ethel. "There's just a few Tatums left around here anymore. I didn't realize that so many of them had left or died off."

She handed the list to Rooster. Joe was on it, and Billy, and a couple of other names as well, and that was it. The first thing Rooster noticed was that both Joe and Billy's last known address was at the same place, some house out in the country, which struck him as curious. He decided that he would go there and see if Billy Tatum had really moved away. He waited until he saw Joe working at the station, then drove out to the country and found the house. He parked in front of it and was immediately greeted by several barking and growling dogs. He sat there and honked the horn, but no one came out. He got out of the car, but one of the dogs came toward him aggressively, so he got back in and drove back to town. He went to the grocery store and bought a couple of packs of wieners, then went back to the house again. This time, he sat in his car with the window down and began feeding the dogs the wieners and talking to them soothingly. Once he thought he had earned their trust, he got out of the car, but with his gun drawn, just in case.

He went up onto the porch and knocked on the door. No one answered, so he opened it and went in. He walked through each room cautiously, uncertain whether someone might be there. After he had gone through the whole house and he was satisfied that there was no one there, he went out back and noticed a small barn. He decided to look around in there as well before leaving. It had not seen a coat of paint in decades, and the wood was weathered. It had the smell of dirt, hay, and manure lingering about in the air as well as something else that he couldn't quite put his finger on. The bottom of the door dragged through the dry dirt as he pushed it open. Rays of sunlight passed through cracks in the walls forming beams of light in the dust he had just stirred up. When his eyes adjusted to the dimness, he was surprised to see some type of contraption sitting in the middle of the barn. There was a metal drum and various other tubs and containers all connected by copper tubing. Rooster stood there gaping at it for several seconds before he finally realized what he was looking at. It was a still.

He looked over his shoulder to make sure no one was coming, and he stepped toward it gingerly. He walked around it slowly, carefully scrutinizing it in detail, and then noticing a door to another room, he entered it, and there he saw many cases of Mexican beer stacked about. Then he went back into the first room and looked around more thoroughly. There were several jars of clear liquid sitting on a shelf and, below that, a workbench with an assortment of parts, tools, and cans and various containers of unknown substances. He opened one of the jars and sniffed it. It was clearly some type of whiskey. For a moment, he felt an overpowering urge to drink some of it but then thought of the dead boys and put the lid back on it. There was also an old notebook lying off to the side. Nervously, he walked over and picked it up. The pages were filled in with some type of ledger entries. Each page was divided into columns and rows, which were filled in with numbers and letters. It appeared to be an accounting of something, and then it occurred to him that it must be to keep track of the whiskey produced in the still. He picked up the notebook and took it, along with the jar of whiskey, and crept out of the barn. He looked around to make sure no one was watching and walked past the now placated and friendly dogs and got in his car and left.

Once he got back to the courthouse, he closed the door to his office, opened the notebook and began trying to make sense of it. It had numbers and notes that seemed to do with supplies purchased and with units produced. It also had three sets of initials that appeared over and over: BT, JT, and MT. He quickly decided that BT was Billy Tatum, and that JT must stand for Joe Tatum, but he could not figure out who MT stood for. He assumed that MT was another member of the Tatum clan, someone he was unfamiliar with.

He flipped through the notebook until he came to a page with the initials MT and a couple of phone numbers written under them. Rooster rarely ever used the phone, so phone numbers meant little to him. Then it occurred to him to call the numbers and see who answered. He called the first number and no one answered, so he called the second one. It rang a few times before someone answered. Rooster said nothing but just listened to the voice on the other end of the line saying, "Hello...hello..." His eyes widened as he realized who the other person was. It was Shirley. He quickly hung up the phone and tried to make sense of what had just happened. He thought that maybe he had dialed the wrong number. He tried it again, and once again, Shirley answered, sounding annoyed this time. Rooster hung up again. Upon reflection, it occurred to him that it would not be unusual for Joe to have Mel's phone number written down somewhere since he worked for him. Then he tried the other number, and this time a man answered. It was Mel. The number was to his office. Rooster once again hung up the phone without saying anything. As he looked at the notepad, his eyes rested on the initials MT. Then, a thought entered his mind, a thought that he would soon wish had just lain dormant forever.

32

Rooster could not believe that the initials in the notebook stood for Mel Tucker. It had to be someone else with the same initials, and he would find out who that person was. In the meantime, he needed to get back out to the Joe's house and seize the still as evidence. He had a vague notion that he probably needed a search warrant but had no idea how to go about getting one. Harvey was little help, for although he could recite any law in the state backward and forward, he had no insight as to how the process actually worked. So Rooster decided to go and ask his mentor, Addis Thigpen. He went to Addis' office and was able to get in to see him right away.

"How can I help you today?" Addis asked cheerfully.

"I need to know how to go about getting a search warrant."

Addis looked at him quizzically. "What do you need one of those for?"

"I think I may have found who really made that poisoned whiskey. I might be able to get your clients off the hook," Rooster said proudly.

Addis frowned and leaned forward. "What do you mean?"

Rooster explained to him how he had questioned the boys and gotten the information from them and that he had gone out to Joe's house and already seen the still. He didn't tell him about the notebook or the jar of whiskey he took.

"Well, you have to be careful, Rooster. You've already broken the law by going out there and snooping around without the owner's permission. That will be a problem if you tell the judge that. You need to have probable cause. You can't just go and ask for a warrant because you think somebody is guilty."

"I could tell the judge that someone told me Billy Tatum sold them the whiskey, right?"

"That would probably work, but the judge may ask for the names of the person who told you that. If they decide not to testify later, it could work against you."

"Damn, I just need to get out there and seize the still. How long does it take to get a search warrant?"

"Usually not too long if the judge is available. Have you told anyone else about this, Rooster?" asked Addis, almost in a whisper.

"No," said Rooster proudly, "not a soul."

"That's good, Rooster. That's real good. Here's what you should do. It's already too late in the day to do anything and you don't want to disturb the judge tonight. Wait until first thing in the morning and then go to the judge. Tell him an informant told you something that leads you to believe that someone else may be making whiskey. Once you've got the warrant, then you can go out and legally seize the evidence."

Rooster got up to leave. "Thank you, Addis. I knew you would be the person to ask."

"My pleasure," said Addis as he walked him to the door. Once Rooster left, Addis went back to his office and closed the door. Then he picked up the telephone and started dialing.

Rooster was excited and a little proud of himself too. He felt like he was actually doing some real police work for the first time since becoming sheriff. It had taken him a while, but he had grown into the role, assuming the aura of authority and learning to use it when necessary, as he had proven by stopping the lynching of Cletus and Alice. He knew that he had stumbled onto something that could possibly free his friends and put the real perpetrator behind bars. He was going to serve justice. He was going to serve the Lord.

The next morning, Rooster nervously approached Judge Wilmer Kitchens in his chambers to request a search warrant. He explained that he had been told that the whiskey came from Billy Tatum and he wanted to search the house Billy was living in. Judge Kitchens agreed and signed the order. Rooster swelled up with pride and anticipation at yet one more step on his path to becoming a legitimate lawman.

This time he took Harvey with him, and they waited until they knew Joe would likely be home before going to the farmhouse. They pulled up in front of the house and honked the horn until Joe came outside to call off the dogs, which were decidedly more friendly this time anyway.

"What do you want?" Joe asked gruffly.

"We've got a search warrant," replied Rooster. "We're going to search your house and barn."

Joe just shrugged. "Suit yourself."

Rooster decided it would be better to go through the house first instead of straight to the barn so as not to tip Joe off that he knew something was in there. They put on a good show of it, slowly and methodically going through the entire house before turning to the barn. Rooster walked purposely out to the barn, grabbed the handle and pulled back on the door. It was later in the evening, and there was even less daylight this time, but as soon as his eyes adjusted to the light, his jaw dropped in surprise. The barn was completely empty.

Rooster rushed in and looked all about. There was nothing there. He charged into another room of the barn, still nothing. He went outside and looked all around. There was only a well house left, so he rushed over to look in it, but there was nothing inside but the pump. Rooster flushed with anger. He didn't know exactly what had happened, but he knew that somehow he had been tricked.

"Find what you were looking for yet?" smirked Joe.

Rooster said nothing to him. He had Harvey go and look under the house, and he went back inside to look for an opening to the attic. He found a scuttle hole and went to his car to get a flashlight. He stood on a chair and shined the flashlight all around the attic. There was nothing there either.

Rooster tried to control his anger and not let Joe see how upset he was. He got Harvey, and they left without saying anything else to Joe. On the way back into town, he pounded his fists on the steering wheel in anger.

"Damn it! There was a still there yesterday. I can't believe this," said Rooster, seething.

"Maybe somebody told him you were coming," said Harvey.

"Who? Who? Who could have told him? Not the judge, not Addis, they were the only two people who knew anything about this."

"Maybe somebody saw you go in and they moved it."

That was the only plausible explanation for Rooster. Someone must have been watching him from somewhere, over a ridge maybe, or hiding in a field. He should have looked around more when he was there before. What bothered him the most was that he felt like he had blown his chance at proving Cletus and Alice innocent. He had let his friends down, and worse, he was letting someone who was guilty get away. He berated himself for thinking he was a clever lawman, when clearly he was a nincompoop. He just wished he knew what had happened and how Joe had known to hide the still.

When they got back to the office, Ethel had a note from the judge requesting he report back to him. Rooster was not looking forward to that. He had gone in there acting like he knew what the hell he was doing and now he was going to have tell the judge that he found nothing. He decided it was better to get it over with so he went to the judge's chambers. He knocked lightly on the door. The judge was sitting at his desk, poring over various documents.

"How did your search go?" he asked Rooster.

"Not so good. I didn't find anything."

"That's often what happens on a search like this. Someone may have tipped them off. The important thing is to pursue these things when they come up. Do you have any other evidence you would like to follow up on?"

"I don't have anything off the top of my head, but I'm going to keep asking around and looking around. I honestly think something else is going on here and we just don't know everything yet."

"That's what law enforcement is all about, sheriff. It sounds like you're doing the right thing. If you need anything else, let me know.

If you need another search warrant, you may call me at home at any time of day or night. Sometimes it's important to act on these things right away."

"You don't mind being called at home or in the middle of the night?" asked Rooster, perplexed.

"Of course not, any good lawyer will tell you that prompt action is the most important thing during an investigation."

"They will?" asked Rooster.

"Absolutely."

Rooster thanked the judge and left. He was feeling very confused at that moment. He wished he could go somewhere and have a drink. He went back to his office and decided to try to figure out who MT was. If he could find that person, then he might be able to find the missing still as well. He got out a Merky phone book and started going through all the listings under 'T.' After just a couple of minutes his eyes were ready to cross, and he had barely made any progress. Then he realized that Harvey could probably help him quickly. He called him into the office.

"Harvey, I need you to go through this phone book and tell me how many people in Merky have the initials MT."

"Five," Harvey answered.

"You already know that?" asked Rooster.

"Yup."

By now Rooster knew better than to doubt Harvey about matters pertaining to raw data such as numbers, rules, names and the like so instead he just had Harvey write down the names on a sheet of paper for him.

One of the names on the list was Mary Turpin, the wife of a local minister. The Turpins were religious teetotalers, so he immediately knew to scratch her off the list. Two others on the list were elderly widows, and it was unlikely they were involved. The two remaining names were Merle Taylor and Mel Tucker.

"Who is Merle Taylor?" Rooster asked Harvey.

"Merle? He's a school teacher," replied Harvey.

Rooster felt a surge of excitement. If Merle Taylor was a teacher, he would be around teenage boys and could have sold them the bad whiskey.

"Where can I find Merle Taylor?"

"I think Colorado."

"What do you mean Colorado?"

"Merle takes off every summer and goes to Colorado while school is out."

Rooster looked at the list again, if he took off Merle's name that only left Mel. Something wasn't right. He couldn't believe that Mel had anything to do with this.

"Are you sure there's no one else here with the initials MT?"

"I'm pretty sure, unless it's somebody that just moved here that I don't know about."

That must be it, Rooster thought. There must be someone new in town with those initials. He decided to go find the boys again and get the information out of them. He wasn't beaten yet.

He went out to get in the patrol car and as he was pulling out Mel came pulling in. Mel waved at him to stop, so he pulled back in. Mel got out of his car and walked around to Rooster's car.

"What's this I hear about you going out and searching Joe's house?"

"What about it?"

"Why are you bothering Joe? He hasn't done anything. What are you trying to prove?"

"Why are you worried about it? It's none of your business."

"Bullshit it's not my business!" said Mel, his face turning red, "That's my employee you're harassing for no good reason."

"How the hell do you know it's no good reason? Why are you worried about it?"

"I just am. I don't like people going around stirring up shit. You're starting to act like goddamn Bill Hickey. That's the reason we got rid of that son of a bitch."

Now Rooster turned red. "That's right, we got rid of Hickey, and I'm the sheriff now!"

Rooster put the car in reverse and took off. He watched Mel in the rearview mirror as he hopped a curb and screeched his tires. His heart was beating fast, and he was breathing heavy. He was mad as hell at Mel for still trying to boss him around, and he wasn't going to take it, father-in-law or not. He couldn't understand why Mel was acting this way. For the second time that day, he really wanted a drink, but there was none to be had in Merky anymore.

Rooster was too upset to do much of anything just then, and it was almost lunchtime anyway so he went home to see Laurie and the baby. When he got there, Laurie was on the phone to Shirley.

"Okay, Mama. Well, with Daddy you never know. Rooster's here, so I have to go. Bye now."

"What's Shirley up to today?" asked Rooster.

"Oh, nothing, she's just mad at Daddy."

"Hmph, well I can't imagine anybody being upset with Mel," said Rooster sarcastically. "What did he do?"

"He was out running around till late last night."

"Doing what?"

"She doesn't know for sure, helping Joe move something or another."

Rooster froze in his tracks and stared at Laurie.

"What's wrong, Rooster?" she asked.

"Oh...nothing...I just remembered something I need to do at the office," said Rooster, turning away from her, "Is dinner ready yet?"

"It will be soon. Sit down and I'll let you know," said Laurie as she walked back into the kitchen.

Rooster was too anxious at that moment to sit down. Instead, he went outside onto the porch and lit up a cigarette. He was beginning to be sorry that he had ever tried to be a real lawman; he wished he had just let things be. He still didn't know for sure what was going on, but he didn't like the sound of what little was trickling his way.

Soon dinner was ready and he and Laurie sat at the kitchen table eating. Laurie babbled on about this or that that the baby had done while Rooster was mostly silent and just nodding his head in agreement. He was having difficulty focusing on what she was saying. His mind kept returning to the same thing, a terrible thing that he wished would just go away.

When they were finished eating and it was time for him to leave, he paused as he was walking out the door and turned to Laurie.

"Did Shirley say what Mel and Joe were moving last night, or where they moved it to?"

"No, just some kind of junk," said Laurie. "Oh, wait, I think she said they put it all in Daddy's bunkhouse. She wasn't too happy about that either. She said they have enough junk of their own without bringing in Joe's too."

Rooster nodded silently and went on his way. He wanted to just drop the whole thing and pretend none of this had ever happened. In hindsight, he decided that it probably was Cletus and Alice who had made the poison whiskey, and why was he worried about them anyway? Sometimes it was better to just let things be. Rooster decided that he wasn't going to pursue the matter any further and that he should try to patch things up with Mel. After all, he wouldn't be where he was today without Mel's help and support.

He drove over to Mel and Shirley's to see if Mel was home. He didn't see Mel's Cadillac, so he stopped and got out to talk to Shirley. He knocked on the door and then went on in. Shirley was cleaning house.

"Well, hello, Rooster. What are you up to today?" said Shirley.

"Oh, not much, Shirley, just fixing to go back to work. Is Mel around?"

"No, at least I don't think so. He might be over at the barn. Him and Joe were putting something in there last night. Like we don't have enough stuff of our own," said Shirley, sounding annoyed.

"Okay, well, maybe I'll go over and see if anyone's around. See you later, Shirley."

Rooster walked over to the barn with the little bunkhouse that he had stayed in when Hickey and his deputy were threatening him. He didn't see any sign of Mel or anyone else. He was about to leave when he decided to go look inside. He went to the door and was surprised to see it locked with a padlock. He tried to look in the window, but found that it was covered with cardboard from the inside. Once again, he decided he wasn't going to worry about it, and went on his way back to town. He would find Mel later and make things right.

When arrived at the office, Ethel told him that the jailer had requested he come to the jail. That puzzled Rooster, but since he didn't have anything else to do, he went there right away. When he got there, the jailer told him that Cletus wanted to talk to him. Rooster would have preferred not to talk to them just then, but not knowing what it was about, he decided he should just in case it pertained to their case. When Cletus and Alice saw him come in, their faces lit up, and they both stood up to greet him. Rooster smiled in spite of himself.

"Oh, Rooster, it's so good to see you," said Cletus.

"How are y'all doing today?" replied Rooster.

"Oh, as well as can be expected I reckon," said Cletus.

"I was told you wanted to talk to me."

"Yes, yes, we do. Why don't you sit for a spell?"

Rooster pulled up a stool next to the cell and sat down expectantly.

"Rooster...me and Alice know we ain't got a chance in hell of ever walking out of here free. Everybody thinks we poisoned those boys, but I swear on the Bible that we didn't. I guess it don't matter none. The town's done decided, and there ain't nothing we can do about it."

"Now, Cletus, you haven't even gone to trial yet. Things could turn out all right after all."

"You're just being nice, Rooster, and we appreciate that. That's why we called you here."

Rooster looked at them, slightly confused.

"You saved us from a surefire lynching. You kept the town's people from killing us, and you still been friendly to us, even after all this happened." Cletus' voice was starting to crack with emotion. "You treated us like human beings even after ever body else was ready to cut our throats and dump us in the trash."

Alice dabbed at her eyes with her sleeve and smiled at Rooster.

"We want you to have our place, Rooster," said Cletus. "We won't ever get to go home, not alive anyways. It ain't much, but maybe you can sell it and use the money to raise that boy of yours."

"Cletus...I...I don't know what to say," said Rooster.

"It was Alice's idea. She was the one what thought it up, and I thought it was a damn good idea."

"Yoo doan treat us like trash, yoo still friend," said Alice.

Rooster was flabbergasted. He didn't know what to say.

"Alice...I...," his voice trailed off.

"If you could get that lawyer fellow Mr. Thigpen to write up a will for us, we'd be happy to sign it. Ain't much else we can do sitting in this cell," said Cletus.

"All right...I'll talk to him," said Rooster weakly.

Cletus and Alice both reached through the bars to shake his hand and thanked him for all that he had done for them. Rooster turned and left with a lump in his throat.

Rooster wished he had not gone there, for now he was starting to feel unsure of himself again. He reminded himself that he had no real proof of their innocence, and at this point it was mostly out of his hands. He was going to go back to the office, but he decided to stop by the gas station first and get a pack of cigarettes. As he went inside to the counter, Joe came in from the mechanics bay, wiping his hands with a red shop rag.

"Well, there's Sherlock Holmes," Joe smirked, "How can I help you, detective?"

"What did you say?" Rooster snarled at him.

"I said, 'How can I help you, sir?'" Joe smiled at him.

Rooster got his cigarettes and slammed the money down on the counter and left. That goddamn Joe really had a way of getting his goat. Despite his attempts to rationalize accepting things as they were, it bothered him to think that Joe might really be the one who poisoned those boys. If Mel was involved or was covering for Joe, then that complicated things quite a bit, but at this point he really had no idea what was going on. It was the possibility of Mel's involvement that put the brakes on the whole thing. So Rooster did what he usually did in such situations: he took the coward's way out. Rooster truly liked Cletus and Alice, but there was no way in hell he was going to jeopardize his family life by going after his father-in-law. It was settled.

Rooster went back to the courthouse and happened to see Addis. Rooster had a suspicion that Addis had given him some bum advice about the search warrant, and he was a little angry about that, but in light of what he had learned since then, he decided it may have been for the best after all. He went over to Addis to talk.

"Hey, Addis, I just came from the jail."

"Oh?" said Addis, peering over his glasses.

"Yeah, I just spoke to Cletus and Alice and they want to talk to you."

"About what?" asked Addis, sounding slightly annoyed.

"They want you to write a will for them."

"A will?" said Addis, smiling slightly.

"They want to leave their land to somebody."

"Who?"

"Um...me."

Upon hearing this, Addis broke into a wide grin. "I see. All right, that should be no problem. I'll try to get over there soon."

Addis and Rooster went their separate ways, and the days continued to tick off until the trial.

That Sunday, Rooster, Laurie, and baby boy William Melvin went to church. The minister gave a blistering sermon about Judas betraying Jesus for thirty pieces of silver. Rooster sat through it as well as he could, but as soon as it was over, he was ready to head for the door. Although Rooster felt bad for his friends, it was a necessary sacrifice to serve the greater good, much as Jesus' sacrifice was. If he was a Judas, then so be it. However, that night he had trouble going to sleep and was bothered by bad dreams.

The date of the trial was approaching and excitement was beginning to build in the tiny burg of Merky, for soon, justice would be served, the perpetrators would be punished, and all would be right with the world. Rooster quit pursuing his suspicions about Mel and Joe. He still went to go visit Cletus and Alice in jail regularly, partly to be a friend and to comfort them, partly to ensure his potential inheritance, and partly to make sure there was no more mention of Rooster's intention to kill Jeanine. The outcome seemed predestined, but there were still many nights when Rooster did not sleep well.

However, all that certainty was shattered in the blink of an eye. One weekend, two boys raced their car through downtown Merky and crashed into the courthouse, and it happened early enough in the night to attract a large crowd. There were several bottles of beer in the car as well as a jar of home brew whiskey. Had the incident happened on a country lane, it could have been swept aside with hardly anyone knowing about it, but because it took place in the middle of town with many reliable witnesses, there could be no doubt: demon liquor was back in town, and the only known moonshiners had been locked away for a while now. It was as if the corpse of a falsehood had

risen from the grave and marched down Main Street in broad daylight, and even those who didn't believe in ghosts could not deny they
had seen it.

This troubling development turned little Merky on its head and
cast that which had been deemed as certain as the sunrise into total
uncertainty and chaos. Most people didn't want to admit it, and many
did not accept it, but this incident meant that, just possibly, the two
people who were sitting in jail may, in fact, be innocent. Many were
willing to ignore this possibility, but for others, this would not stand,
and it meant that a thorough investigation had to take place, and the
only person authorized to conduct such an investigation was none
other than Rooster Brown himself.

Judge Kitchens called Rooster and Joe Grundy into his office to discuss the recent developments.

"Sheriff, you had information that led you to believe someone else
was selling the poison whiskey, have you uncovered any more evidence?" asked the judge.

Rooster shifted in his chair. "No, sir, Your Honor. I guess I hit a dead
end." Rooster did not want to tell them anything that would implicate
Mel, so he kept what little information he had to himself.

"What about you, Mr. Grundy? How is your case proceeding?"

Joe frowned. "The case is all circumstantial. It's mostly testimony
from various citizens who are willing to admit publicly that they have
bought home brew whiskey from Cletus and Alice at various times.
The boys involved still claim they can't remember who they bought
the alcohol from."

"Gentleman, in light of recent developments, I think it prudent to
delay the trial so as to allow further investigation into the matter. I

will put the trial on hold. Sheriff, please make this your top priority and report back to the district attorney daily on any new findings you may have."

With that, the judge set them on their way, and Rooster found himself in the unhappy predicament of looking for evidence that could possibly implicate his own father-in-law. At that moment, he wished he had just stayed at the gas station. Damn that Mel! It was his idea to run for sheriff, and now he was one of the prime suspects, although no one else knew it yet. An unpleasant reality began to settle in Rooster's mind, he couldn't just ignore this and hope it went away. He would have to play an active role in determining who went to prison and who went free, regardless of who was innocent and who was guilty.

To complicate matters further, somehow word got out (Harvey) that the Tatums were possible suspects in this matter. Tongues were flapping, gossip was flying from ear to ear all over town, and it was apparent there would not be an easy way out of this for Sheriff Rooster Brown. Everyone was talking about it, including Laurie and Shirley, and they asked Rooster about it every chance they got. Rooster tried to be coy, but one evening, in a moment of weakness, when the weight of it was particularly heavy, Rooster admitted to Laurie that he thought Mel might be involved.

"What? Rooster, you can't be serious!" Laurie practically shrieked at him.

"I don't know anything for certain, okay? But I saw a still in Joe's barn, and I saw a notebook with the initials MT in it, and it had Mel's phone number in it too." Rooster still had not told anyone about the notebook and the jar of whiskey he had taken.

"That doesn't prove anything!" Laurie shouted.

"I know it doesn't, but how come the still disappeared right at the time Mel was helping Joe move stuff out of his barn?"

"Daddy is a kind, helpful person, that's how. If he helped Joe move something, it was because he didn't know what it was, all right? I can't believe what I'm hearing. After all Daddy has done for you, and now you accuse him of being involved in this..." and at that Laurie burst into tears and ran into the bedroom sobbing.

Rooster was shaken, but he was also relieved to have told someone. He didn't want to do anything to hurt Mel, but he was in a tough situation. At least by telling Laurie, maybe she could help him figure out what to do. He really wanted to go and look in Mel's barn to see if the still was there, but he was afraid of what he might find and so did nothing.

Of course whatever alit upon Laurie's ears would soon flit like a hummingbird to Shirley's ears, and then ultimately to the one himself—Mel Tucker. Things had been a little tense and frosty between Mel and Rooster ever since Rooster started treating Joe as a suspect and especially since that day outside the courthouse when Mel confronted him. Mel wasn't used to taking backtalk from too many people, especially those who worked for him, or who he had helped in some way or another. When he heard that Rooster suspected he was involved in the whiskey poisonings, he wasted no time in challenging him.

The next morning, when Rooster was driving to work, he heard a car horn honking and looked in his rearview mirror to see Mel following him in his Cadillac. Instantly, he knew what had happened, and his heart began pounding. He would have preferred to keep driving, perhaps to Mexico and beyond, but he knew couldn't run for long, so he pulled over. Mel hopped out of his car and strode purposefully to Rooster's car door.

"So what's this shit I hear that you're out to get me?" Mel said, huffing angrily.

Rooster felt himself turn a deep shade of red. "Mel, I..."

"Let me tell you something, big shot. You don't know a goddamn thing. I don't need my own son-in-law stabbing me in the back. If it wasn't for me, you'd still be shoveling shit out on that ranch. You'd still be a goddamn nothing if it weren't for me, so you just make sure you remember that, all right?"

"Look, Mel. You're right, I don't know nothing. You're right that I wouldn't be sheriff if it weren't for you. But, if it weren't for me, your daughter would have got the shit raped out of her by those fucking Blackwell boys. Now why don't you listen to me for just a minute, okay?"

Mel stood there red faced, huffing and puffing, with his hands on his hips.

"Look, I saw that goddamn still in Joe's barn and the next day the damn thing disappears, and then I hear you was helping him move shit into your barn."

"I can put anything in my goddamn barn I want to. You don't know what's in there," said Mel.

"That's right, I don't know what's in there, but listen to me, damn it. If that still is in your barn, then get rid of it. I don't want to know anything about it, but the goddamn judge is asking me to investigate this shit some more. Just get rid of the thing, okay?"

"You don't tell me what to do, boy. I'll keep whatever the hell I want in my own damn barn. I don't need some nitwit like you bossing me around."

"I'm not bossing you around, goddamn it! I'm trying to help you, you dumb-ass."

Mel shook his head. "No...no...you don't' tell me anything. You just stay off my property, and you stay out of my business."

Mel stomped off, got in his car and peeled out throwing rocks and dirt all over Rooster's squad car. Rooster could only sit there, his hands shaking and sweat dripping down his forehead. He felt like he was going to wet his pants. He opened the car door, leaned out and retched.

He didn't really want to go to work, nor did he want to go home and tell Laurie what had just happened, so he drove around for thirty minutes or so until he felt calm enough to go into the office. As soon as he walked in, Mildred looked at him funny.

"Rooster, do you feel all right?" she asked, obviously concerned.

"Uh...yeah...I'm okay."

"You look a little pale, and maybe feverish too," Mildred said.

Rooster just then realized that the armpits of his shirt were wet, and he had a few stains of bile down his shirtfront as well.

"Maybe, I should go home..." he muttered.

"Well, before you do, the judge and the district attorney want to see you."

Rooster groaned then went to go see the judge. He went down the hallway to the courtroom and knocked lightly on the judge's chamber door. Judge Kitchens and Joe Grundy both looked at him curiously when he entered, but said nothing about his sweaty armpits or stained shirt.

"Sheriff, have you uncovered any more evidence yet?"

"Um, no, sir, Your Honor, I haven't."

"Have you talked to those boys again?"

"Uh, well, no."

The judge looked at the district attorney silently, then turned to Rooster. "Why don't you bring them into court? We'll swear them in and take statements from them as a preliminary hearing. We need to move ahead on this thing."

"Okay..."

Rooster got up and left, wishing he had stayed in bed with the covers pulled over his head, but it was too late now. What a day this was shaping up to be. He went back to his office and instructed Harvey to go and bring two of the boys back and he would go find the other two. Within an hour, they had all the boys and they took them to the courtroom to be questioned by the district attorney. Addis was also called in as a witness and to advise the boys if they so desired. All of the boys insisted that they could not remember anything at all prior to their poisoning incidents, including where they purchased the whiskey. Rooster was called to the stand and questioned as well and gave a contradictory statement that the boys had, in fact, told him that they bought the whiskey from Billy Tatum. Truth to be told, if he had not already requested a search warrant and told the judge that the boys had implicated Billy, he also would have preferred to simply state he couldn't remember. He wished he had just let things be. Why the hell did he have to try and be a lawman anyway? As much as he was fond of Cletus and Alice, he was ready to throw them to the wolves and get back to his normal life as soon as possible.

However, the district attorney and the judge were not buying the boys' claims of amnesia, and they were charged with possession of an illegal substance and failure to cooperate with a court of law. The judge ordered them jailed. Rooster was about to take the boys away when the judge waved him over to the bench.

"Oh, sheriff, one more thing."

Rooster walked over and looked at him expectantly.

"Make sure you put them all in a cell next to Cletus and Alice. We want them to have someone to talk to while they're there."

Rooster knew what the judge was up to.

"Yes, sir," he said.

When they arrived at the jail, Cletus and Alice sat up on their bunks to watch the boys being escorted in. Cletus smiled happily at the notion of having someone new to talk to. As Rooster was leaving, he could hear Cletus talking to the boys in a friendly manner.

"What are y'all in for?"

While the boys were left to simmer in jail, word had gotten out that there was a new push to the investigation under way. The town was buzzing with speculation and the Tatum name was mentioned frequently. There was a feeling in the air that something big was about to go down.

And, if all that weren't enough, the Tucker clan was furious at Rooster for admitting that he suspected Mel was involved. Rooster came home to find a note from Laurie that said she and the baby had moved in with Mel and Shirley and that he was to stay away from them until he apologized. Once again, Rooster found himself alone, and without the family he had come to love and depend upon. He realized how much his world was built around them. And try as he might, he was unable to find help or solace from his relationship with the Lord. He had been praying constantly since all this had happened, continuously seeking guidance and answers, pleading for a sign, and receiving nothing but silence in response.

That night, he walked out into the yard of his empty home and looked skyward.

"Are you there?" he said softly as he gazed upon the stars.

The next morning, Rooster got a telephone call at the office. It was Mel.

"Rooster, you and me need to talk. In private."

The two men agreed to meet in Rooster's office that afternoon, after Mildred had gone home for the day. Rooster was a bundle of nerves the whole day, fearing and dreading what might happen. It seemed like the day dragged on forever. Finally, it was time, and Rooster sat waiting nervously at his desk. At a little after five, he heard footsteps coming down the hall then the door to the main office creaked open. He got up and waved Mel into his private office.

Mel was carrying a large brown envelope, which he tossed onto Rooster's desk as he sat down.

"What's this?" asked Rooster.

"Open it and look," replied Mel.

Rooster opened the envelope and pulled out several large photographs. They were photographs of him and Christine hugging on the front porch of the little house in the trees. Rooster felt his stomach tighten as he looked at them.

"Hell of a thing, ain't it, Rooster? What kind of man would cheat on his wife while she's on death's doorstep carrying his baby? What kind of man does something like that? What do you reckon the people of Merky would think about that?" Mel leaned forward and looked Rooster in the eye. "What do you reckon Laurie would think about that?"

Rooster could feel his face burning.

"How..." His voice trailed off.

"Oh, I have my ways, Rooster. I have my ways. I got plenty more copies of those too."

Rooster looked at the photos in disbelief, but there was no denying what he was looking at.

"I saw you and her leaving your house that morning. I should have told Laurie what was going on then, but I didn't have the heart to do it, not with her in the shape she was in. Plus, I knew you were going through a hard time, and I guess I wanted to give you the benefit of the doubt, but now I know better."

Rooster set the photos down and rubbed his temples as he groped for words.

"Mel...I'm sorry. I was stupid, real stupid. The last thing I want to do is hurt Laurie."

"You know, Rooster, I might have given you a break and just let things be, but now you're going around sticking your nose where it don't belong, and I can't stand for that."

"What do you mean 'where it don't belong'? I'm the goddamn sheriff."

"When you start coming after me, then you're sticking your nose where it don't belong."

"I wasn't coming after you, damn it. I was investigating Billy and Joe and all this other shit started coming up that makes it look like you were involved in it too."

"Well, you need to just stop investigating, or I'm going to have to give Laurie some of these pictures, and while I'm at it, maybe I'll give some to Arlen too. Bet they'd look real good on the front page of the paper."

"Goddamn it, Mel, it's too late to stop it now. The judge and DA are involved. Why are you so damn worried about Joe? Since when do you give a shit about Joe?"

"I got my reasons."

"What reasons? Are you mixed up in this shit too?"

"Well, Rooster, you know ol' Mel likes to have his fingers in all the pies."

"What? Why would get mixed up in this? Don't you have enough already?"

"It's not always about having enough, Rooster. Sometimes, it's about keeping what you got."

"What do you mean?"

"Even Mel Tucker fucks up every now and then, son. I made some investments that didn't work out too well, and I needed to make up the difference. I didn't know that stupid fuck Billy was going to poison those boys."

"God..." Rooster cradled his head in his hands.

"But the main business at hand is that you need to stop this shit now."

"I haven't done anything to help them since I figured out you were involved, but the judge and the DA know there's something else going on, and they're pushing me."

"Then I guess you're not going to be married much longer. Probably won't be sheriff much longer either after everybody sees these photos."

"Look, Mel, I'll do what I can to stop this shit. I'll get up and swear on the Bible that it was Cletus and Alice that sold the whiskey. I'll lie and do whatever I can, but I can't guarantee anything."

Mel glared at Rooster. "You really make me sick. You wouldn't have amounted to anything if it weren't for me. You'd still be on that ranch shoveling shit if it weren't for me. I should have just let you rot in jail. Well, I'm not going to be the only one that suffers, you can bet on that. I'm going to make sure Laurie sees these photos and sees what her husband is really like."

"What good is it going to do to show her that? It's not going to stop this investigation."

"Sometimes, it doesn't matter if anything does any good. Sometimes, it just feels good to watch a man pay for his sins."

"Look, damn it, leave Laurie out of this."

"Leave her out of it? You sorry bastard, you should have thought of that before you started fucking around on her."

Rooster stared at Mel, his chest heaving and his heart racing. Months of resentment from kissing Mel's ass and the humiliation of his insults welled up, and then suddenly he remembered something.

"You're not the only one that's got dirt on somebody, Mel."

"You think you got something on me? That's a good one," Mel laughed.

"I got something to hang your ass with right now. I got the goddamn ledger that Joe had with your name and phone number in it that shows you was involved in this shit."

"Bullshit. You're lying."

"No, I'm not. That stupid ass left it laying around, and I picked it up when I was searching his house. It's got your name and phone number all over it."

"So? That doesn't prove anything."

"It does if those boys decide to testify. It does if I testify. I'm not fucking around, Mel. If you show Laurie those pictures, then I'll come after your ass with everything I got, and we'll both pay for our sins."

Mel frowned, and he glanced around the room.

"Don't bother looking here, I got it hid where you won't find it," said Rooster.

Mel glared at Rooster, and then he smiled slightly.

"I guess it's a draw...for now. You just better figure out how to stop this investigation," he said, and he got up and left.

The next few days were extremely difficult for Rooster. He languished alone in his empty house, abandoned by his family and, seemingly, his God as well. Prayers for help went unanswered and sleep did not come.

Meanwhile, in the jailhouse, the boys were suffering under the weight of their own conscious as Cletus and Alice did their best to befriend their new cellmates. However, unbeknownst to anyone else, messages had been passed to the boys making it clear that they would be dealt with severely if they revealed the source of the poisoned moonshine, so all they could do was wallow in their shame and guilt.

Even though the standoff with the Tucker family was almost unbearable for Rooster, he still held out hope. If no other evidence or witnesses surfaced, then it was likely that Cletus and Alice would be prosecuted for the death of the boys, and life could get back to normal.

Then, one afternoon, a call came into the sheriff's office that there was a herd of cattle loose on a country road. There had been a minor accident, and they needed some help clearing the road and rounding up the livestock. The call came just as Rooster had been called in to speak with the judge and DA again. Rooster decided that Harvey could probably handle this, at least until he could get away and go out there himself. Harvey was always excited and eager to respond to any type of call, so he happily took off to fulfill his role of deputy.

Rooster dreaded meeting with the judge and DA for he knew what they wanted.

"Sheriff, how has your investigation been coming along?" asked Joe Grundy.

"Well, not so good. I can't seem to find anybody that knows anything or that is willing to talk," responded Rooster.

The judge frowned. "I have been thinking about this. Since moonshine is involved, we could probably call and ask the Texas Rangers to assist in the investigation."

Rooster sat upright in his seat. "The Texas Rangers?"

"Yes, sheriff, I think that you need some assistance if we are ever going to get to the bottom of any of this. I have some contacts, so I will see if I can get someone assigned to this case," said the judge, barely concealing his displeasure.

"I agree," said Joe Grundy. "No offense, sheriff, but we probably need someone with more experience and expertise."

Rooster felt his stomach tightening into a knot. He had thought that if he stalled long enough then things would just die down and that would be the end of any more investigating.

"Well, I don't know..." said Rooster.

"I do. I will put in a call to them tomorrow," said the judge, and he turned his back to Rooster to resume his work.

Rooster got up and left, feeling embarrassed, alarmed, and weak in the knees. He went back to his office and sat at his desk, holding his head in his hands. He was fretting like this when Ethel came and knocked on his door.

"Rooster, I'm sorry to disturb you, but the dispatcher hasn't been able to contact Harvey."

Rooster shook his head in anger. That damn Harvey couldn't do anything without someone to hold his hand. He got up and put on his hat.

"Okay, Ethel, I'll go out and check up on him."

Rooster drove out to where the cows were supposed to be loose, but he didn't see so much as a single cow anywhere. He drove on down the road a bit and saw Harvey's car sitting just off the road in an open pasture. He pulled in next to it and got out. Harvey was nowhere to be seen. He shouted his name several times but got no response.

This struck him as very strange, and he walked around Harvey's car looking for any sign of the deputy. Then he looked inside the car and noticed what looked like blood on the seats. He ran his finger through it and sniffed it. It was clearly blood. He looked around some more, scanning in all directions but saw nothing. Then he looked back in the car and noticed the car keys lying on the floorboard. He didn't know exactly why, but for some reason, he took the keys and walked around to the rear of the car. He looked at the trunk and all at once was overcome with an overpowering feeling of fear and dread. He stared at the key slot for a few seconds with his heart pounding before shakily putting the key in the keyhole and opening the trunk. He raised the trunk lid, and as he saw inside it, he gasped loudly and stumbled backward. He whimpered for a second and then dropped to his knees and cried out loudly, for in the trunk of the car lay the bloodied body of Harvey Wells.

33

Rooster rose from his knees, trembling, his heart pounding.

"Harvey..." he gasped, "Oh, Harvey..."

Harvey lay motionless, his pallid face contrasting with the red stain on the front of his shirt.

Rooster just stood there, paralyzed with fear and anguish, until Harvey moaned softly.

"Oh, God, you're alive! You're alive, oh thank God, you're alive," Rooster said breathlessly.

Harvey gasped for air and then moaned again. Rooster reached in the trunk of the car, lifted him out and quickly put him in the backseat of his patrol car. He pulled back Harvey's shirt and saw what appeared to be a bullet hole in his chest. There was also a wound on his head, but he didn't seem to be bleeding heavily in either spot.

Rooster switched on the lights and siren and spun his tires for a hundred and fifty feet down the road, stirring up a huge cloud of dust. He raced back into town as fast as he could go, all the while pleading with Harvey not to die.

He sped through town, running every light and almost crashing into two other cars. He careened into the hospital parking lot and came to a stop with a screech. He lifted Harvey out of the back seat and ran into the hospital yelling for help the whole time.

A nurse met him at the door, holding it open as he ran in shouting for a doctor. Suddenly, there were more nurses and a doctor, and Harvey was put on a gurney and rushed into the emergency room. A nurse told Rooster to stay in the waiting room and as soon as they had some information they would come talk to him.

Rooster paced back and forth in waiting room, smoking one cigarette after another. Soon, a nurse came out and told him that Harvey had been shot in the chest and the bullet had exited through his back. Miraculously, it missed his heart and any major arteries, so there was minimal bleeding. He had also been struck on the head with something, which caused the gash in his scalp. The nurse told Rooster that Harvey was very fortunate and that unless there were complications he would most likely survive.

Rooster closed his eyes and exhaled deeply then said a silent prayer of thanks. He thanked the nurse and collapsed into a chair. As he sat there rubbing his temples, the thought occurred to him that he should notify Claudette and Harvey's mother; however, another more compelling thought soon entered his mind, and he rose up and strode out of the hospital and got in his patrol car.

He screeched his tires on the pavement as he raced toward the town square. By now, most businesses were closed, but he knew that Mel often worked late in his office in the rear of the Western Auto store. He whipped into the alley behind the Western Auto and parked his car. He marched determinedly to the back door that led directly to Mel's office.

He kicked the door open with a boom that caused Mel to leap up from his chair behind his desk. Rooster crossed the room in two steps and grabbed Mel by the lapels of his suit. He lifted him off the floor and pinned him against the wall. He thrust his face inches from Mel's, then slowly lowered him back to the floor, released his grip, and stepped back.

Mel leaned against the wall, wide eyed and gasping for air.

Rooster stood glaring at him. Then he pulled out his gun and waved it in the air before laying it on Mel's desk.

"Leave Harvey out of this! If you want to shoot somebody, there it is. Go ahead. I deserve it. Just don't hurt anybody else."

Mel, still trying to catch his breath, said nothing. He grasped at his desk chair and pulled it toward him, easing into it cautiously. He sat there for a few seconds before speaking.

"What the hell is the matter with you? What are you talking about?"

"I'm talking about Harvey Wells with a bullet hole in his chest goddamit!"

"What...?"

"Like you don't know nothing about it. Bullshit!"

"I...I...don't know what you're talking about..."

Rooster sat there, silently studying Mel.

"Somebody tried to kill Harvey, and he's goddamn lucky to be alive."

"Rooster...I..."

"This is too much, Mel. You win. You're right, I'm a sorry piece of shit. I don't deserve any of what I have, especially...Laurie," Rooster's voice cracked. "If you think I'm not sorry for what I did, you're wrong. I think about it every day. I kick myself every day for it..." At this point, Rooster was overcome with emotion, and the tears began to flow down his cheeks, and he was unable to speak.

Mel's expression softened as he watched the big man in his despair.

Rooster inhaled deeply and wiped his eyes. "I have that ledger I took from Joe in my office. I'll give it to you, and you can burn it. Nobody else knows about it, not even Harvey. I won't tell anyone about it. I just want all this to stop."

Mel paused, "Oh...okay, Rooster, I...I appreciate that. When can I get it?"

Rooster was about to respond when suddenly his eyes widened. "Oh, shit! I have to go tell Claudette and Harvey's mother about this. Meet me at my office in an hour."

Rooster turned quickly and ran to his car, leaving Mel alone to contemplate what had just happened. Mel looked down at his hands, which were trembling. He glanced at the clock on the wall, then got up and locked the door.

When an hour had passed, Mel unlocked the door to his office and cautiously peered outside. He walked to his car, looking around as he went. When he arrived at Rooster's office, it was a hive of activity. Arlen Moore, Joe Grundy, Judge Kitchens, Ethel, and many others were there.

It seemed as if everyone was talking and doing something all at the same time. Rooster was talking to Arlen who was busily scribbling notes. Ethel was on the telephone, and the judge and the district attorney were talking animatedly.

"I just got off the phone with the capitol, and they said the Texas Rangers will be here tomorrow morning. You can rest assured that when they get here not one stone will go unturned, and anyone who was involved in this will be found out and sent to the electric chair," said Judge Kitchens.

Mel flinched at the judge's words. He quietly walked up next to Rooster and put his hand on his shoulder.

Rooster, completely unaware that Mel had entered the room, glanced at him distractedly then turned back and resumed talking to Arlen. Mel looked around at the others in the room, none of whom was paying any attention to him. Mel tapped Rooster's shoulder once again.

Rooster turned toward him. "Mel, I'm sorry, but I'm busy right now. What do you want?"

"Well...Rooster, I'm here about what we talked about earlier, remember?"

Rooster looked annoyed. "I don't have time right now, Mel."

From the other side of the room, Mel could hear the judge still talking about the Texas Rangers. "Yes, sir, they are the finest lawmen in the state. You can bet they will search every square inch of this town, every square inch of this courthouse if necessary, until they find whoever may have been involved in this. I would not want to be that individual, for their time on this earth is short."

Mel looked about nervously, wondering where the ledger could be. If he could just find it himself, then he could slip out with it without anyone noticing. He looked around, trying not to appear suspicious, but with all the activity in the room, he was afraid to try anything.

Then he thought of something that he could use as an inducement. This time, he went up to Rooster and grabbed his arm forcefully. Rooster turned, his eyes flashing. "What is it, Mel?"

"Rooster, I need to tell you something important. It will just take a minute, please," he said as he pulled Rooster away from the group. He beckoned Rooster in close to him.

"Listen, Rooster, I appreciate that you're going to give me that book, and it's only fair that I do something for you as well. I'll give you all the photos I have of you and Christine, all of them, and the negatives too. We'll burn all of it together. Just bring that book home with you tonight. I'll meet you at your house, okay? Okay Rooster?"

Rooster looked at Mel intently. "Okay. It may be late before I get home, but I'll bring it. Make sure you don't forget your part."

"I won't. I'll be waiting for you."

Mel turned and hurried away, and Rooster went back to join the others, a slight smile on his face.

When all the excitement at the courthouse died down, Rooster went back to the hospital to check on Harvey. Claudette and Mrs. Wells were at his bedside keeping vigil. Although he had stabilized, he was still unconscious, and the doctor was unable to give any kind of prognosis as to when he might awaken. A steady stream of visitors and well-wishers came and went to check on the beloved town oddball.

It was dark when Rooster finally got home. He was surprised to see the lights on in his house, even though he was expecting Mel to be waiting for him. He was eager to see if Mel would have the incriminating photographs as he had promised. He had offered the ledger to Mel on impulse, out of despair and hopelessness, and perhaps a subconscious desire to stop hiding from the truth. However, when Mel offered the photos to him, he realized he had a bargaining chip that he should use to his advantage, and he determined that he would not give up the ledger without receiving the photos in return. As a precaution, he had put the ledger in a paper sack and locked it in the trunk of his patrol car before leaving the courthouse.

Mel was pacing back and forth in the living room when he entered. He looked both relieved and worried to see Rooster. There was a large brown envelope lying on the coffee table.

"Hello, Mel."

"Hello, Rooster."

Neither man seemed to know what else to say at first.

"Is that the photos?" asked Rooster, pointing toward the envelope.

"Yes," said Mel, "do you have the ledger?"

"It's in my car."

"Go ahead and bring it in and we'll do this at the same time."

"Okay."

Rooster went out to his car and retrieved the ledger from the trunk. He paused by the car and ran his fingers along the handle of his gun before going back into the house.

Mel was sitting on the sofa holding the envelope in his hands when Rooster returned.

"Take them out of the envelope and put them on the table, so I can see them," said Rooster.

Mel frowned slightly and opened the envelope letting the photos slide out onto the table. Then he shook the envelope until the negatives fell out as well.

Mel looked at Rooster expectantly. Rooster held up the ledger so that he could see it, but did not hand it to him.

"We're you trying to have me killed?"

"No, Rooster. I had nothing to do with that, I swear."

"How do I know you're not lying? You've got a lot at stake."

"I'm not a violent man, Rooster, you know that."

"I'm not sure what I know anymore."

"Is Harvey okay?"

"They think he's going to live."

Mel took a deep breath. "I hope they can say the same for you and me."

"What does that mean?"

"You know they were looking for you instead."

"Yes, I figured that. What does that have to do with you?"

"I know too much."

"Weren't you a part of it? Why would they come after you?"

"I'm a rich man. That makes me everyone's enemy."

"Well, why the hell did you get mixed up in this in the first place? That's what I don't understand."

Mel shook his head in disgust. "I lost money on some bad investments, and ol' Mel don't like losing. I should have just sucked it up. I could have made it back...eventually. But my pride wouldn't let me do that, I had to get it back now. I had heard that Joe and Billy knew how to make home brew, and it seemed like an easy way to make money. All I did was finance the operation. I bought the supplies and had them bring in beer from Mexico, just like Cletus. I didn't know they were going to sell to kids, or I wouldn't have had anything to do with it. Apparently, Billy didn't want to infringe on Cletus' business, and I guess it's easier to intimidate kids to keep them from talking. I should have known that Joe resented me for how I treated him at the station. When things started going bad, they threatened to take me down with them. Then they started threatening to go after Shirley, and Kenneth...and Laurie."

Rooster listened silently to Mel. Then, he slowly turned his head from side to side, listening for any sounds that might be coming from outside.

"And there's something else I need to tell you, Rooster. Another stupid thing I did, years ago."

Rooster said nothing.

"When I was much younger and finally starting to achieve some success in business, I let it go to my head. I did something very bad.

I betrayed my wife, much as you did. She never found out, thank goodness, but her father, that same old man that helped me get started, did, and he kicked my ass. I deserved every bit of it, and I never complained or resented him for it. In fact, I was grateful to him for teaching me a lesson, and for sparing Shirley. As much as I hated you for what you did to Laurie, I understood how it can happen. I don't want Laurie to ever see these photos, no matter what happens. We're both idiots, Rooster. God help us."

Rooster sat down on the sofa next to Mel. He looked at the photos of him and Christine on the porch of the little house in the trees, and both shame and fear rose up inside him. He handed the ledger over to Mel.

"Here's your book. Let's just burn all this shit right now."

"Okay, Rooster. Let's do it before somebody else finds out about it."

Mel offered his hand to Rooster and the two men shook firmly. Then, they built a small fire out back by the creek and watched as the flames consumed the evidence. Neither man said anything as the fire did its work. After everything was reduced to ashes, Rooster broke the silence.

"What about that still, Mel? Is it in your barn?"

"Yes..."

"Well, goddamn, let's go get rid of it before the fucking Texas Rangers get here."

The two men made sure all the papers were completely burned and they stirred the ashes well before dousing the remaining embers. It was late and they didn't want to alert Shirley or Laurie to what was happening, so they took the path that Mel had graded between the houses during Laurie's pregnancy and walked in the dark to Mel's barn. They each took an armful and carried it back to Rooster's place.

Then they faced another dilemma—what to do with it. They discussed various options: throwing it in Butcher Creek, dumping it alongside the road, hauling it out to Cletus and Alice's place, hiding it in Rooster's attic, hiding it along the creek bottom on either place, or taking it to the town dump.

Finally, Rooster decided the best solution was to bury it on his property. He and Mel cut apart and flattened out the tubs and drums as best they could, then they dug a pit and buried everything, and then piled firewood on top of it. By the time they did all this, it was well past midnight, and both men were exhausted.

Before Mel left to go home, he and Rooster had one final talk.

"Rooster, I'll talk to Laurie and tell her we worked things out and that you were only trying to do the right thing. She and the baby will be back home tomorrow."

"I appreciate it, Mel. I'm sorry all this shit happened..." Rooster's voice broke with emotion. "I'm sorry for what I did..."

"I know you are, son, I know you are. The important thing is that we stick together from here on out."

Rooster nodded his head and they clasped hands once again before heading to their respective homes.

Tired as he was, Rooster found it difficult to sleep. He was worried about Harvey, worried about what the Texas Rangers might uncover, and worried about what Joe and Billy would say if they were caught.

However, for once, he was not worried about Laurie discovering his affair with Christine. Now that Mel had confessed to his own indiscretion and they had burned the evidence he felt like he was safe. However, he was burdened with guilt and fears of cosmic retribution, and in the dark of night, these things enter the mind and do not leave until daylight.

34

Rooster got up well before the alarm went off and made coffee. He was nervous and intimidated by the thought of having to meet with the Texas Rangers. He was worried that he might slip up and say something to implicate Mel, but mostly he was afraid that they would see him for the ignoramus that he was. He knew he was in over his head, which was not a disqualifier in the small community of Merky, but now he would be dealing with real lawmen.

He thought back to his debate training and decided that his best course of action was to formulate one version of events, stick to that version, and pretend to be confident and competent.

He made breakfast, bathed and put on his best clothing so as to, at least, look professional. He looked in the mirror and tried his best to prepare himself for what lay ahead, and then he got in his patrol car and drove to the courthouse.

It was still dark when he got there, and other than a night watchman and dispatcher, there was no one else around, for which he was grateful. He went to his office and reviewed the scant notes he had compiled about the case, making sure there were no references that would tie it to Mel. He mentally rehearsed what he would say to the Texas Rangers about what he knew, and he said a silent prayer.

It didn't take long for concerned citizens to trickle in to the sheriff's office, and then the trickle turned into a torrent. The entire town was outraged about what had happened to their beloved Harvey and hell-bent on revenge. This only heightened Rooster's anxiety for he realized that he would be dealing with an event that far surpassed his abilities, and that he had no control over the eventual outcome. He could only hope and pray that he and Mel survived it unscathed.

It was around midmorning when two men made their way through the crowds and into the sheriff's office. There was no doubt that these men were Texas Rangers. The first was tall and robust, with graying hair and sharp blue eyes. The second was a bit smaller and younger, with dark hair and brown eyes. They were both dressed in slacks, western shirts with ties, badges over their hearts, white felt cowboy hats, and each carried a gleaming pistol in the holsters around their waists.

The older man introduced himself first, "Sheriff Brown, we're with the Texas Rangers. I'm Harold Clary and this is my partner, Clyde Blackburn."

Rooster shook both men's hands and offered them each a chair in his office.

"Thank you, sheriff. We have a lot to go over, but first we need to ask these people to leave the area so we can speak privately," said Harold.

"Yes, sir," said Rooster, and he went into the lobby and in a loud voice told everyone to leave. Then, he had Ethel move a chair into the hallway, so she could sit there and keep people from entering.

When everyone was out of the lobby, Rooster closed the doors to his office and sat down at his desk across from the two men. Clyde pulled a notepad and pen from his pocket.

"How is Deputy Wells doing?" asked Harold.

"He's alive and stable but still not able to talk," said Rooster.

"Tell us what happened."

Rooster took a deep breath and relayed the story of how they received a call about loose cattle on a rural road and the events that followed.

"Was Deputy Wells able to speak when you found him? Were you able to get any information about the assailants?"

"No, sir, he was unconscious when I found him."

"Do you have any idea who may have done this? We were told there is an ongoing investigation into some deaths related to a moonshine operation. Do you think there is a connection to that investigation?"

"Yes, that's possible, but I don't know for certain."

"Have you secured the crime scene?"

Rooster felt himself flush, "Um...no sir, I had to rush Harvey to the hospital, and with all the excitement, I haven't had a chance to go back out there."

The two Rangers glanced at each other while Rooster fidgeted in his chair.

"Then we need to go there right away. Hopefully, nothing has been tampered with. We'll follow you in our car."

Rooster led the Rangers out of his office, through the crowded hallway, past the assembled gawkers, and out to the parking area. He felt the eyes of everyone on him, but he pretended not to notice.

On the way to the crime scene, Rooster looked in the rear view mirror at the dark sedan following him. He cursed himself for not having had the sense to have someone guard Harvey's patrol car from curiosity seekers, but it had not even entered his mind to do so. He had been so concerned about meeting with Mel and disposing of all the evidence that could incriminate them both that it had not occurred to him that he should secure the site.

Oh, well, he thought. It's probably okay. It's unlikely that anyone messed with the car.

When they arrived at the shooting site, Rooster's heart sank, for there must have been a dozen cars parked along the roadside. People were milling about the area, and some were even sitting in Harvey's patrol car.

Rooster pulled up near them and began honking his horn and yelling at everyone to leave the area immediately. Most of them seemed shocked at this sudden intrusion to what had otherwise been something of a picnic. A few jumped up and ran toward their vehicles, while others seemed confused and reluctant to leave.

Rooster quickly got out of his vehicle and began shouting until all of them began walking toward their cars. The Rangers pulled in behind him and Clyde got out and asked everyone to wait by their vehicles in case they needed to speak to them.

Harold opened the trunk of his car and retrieved various items with which he would use to inspect the patrol car. Fortunately, he was quickly able to find a couple of bloody fingerprints. Unfortunately, so many people had been in and around the vehicle that most other potential evidence was compromised. After the Rangers were satisfied that they had gotten most of the usable evidence they began questioning the onlookers. One of them had picked up a bullet shell from the ground, which they handed over to the Rangers. After the questioning was over, the Rangers told everyone to go home.

"Well, sheriff, it could have been worse. We were able to get a couple of good prints and a shell casing. If you have the keys to this car, then we can drive it into town now and impound it for further investigation later. Then, we'll have more questions about the moonshine case you've been working on."

Rooster nodded and handed the keys to Clyde. He was still feeling like a fool but grateful that they had found something useful. He was nervous about discussing the moonshine investigation and on the way into town he went over what he might say to the Rangers.

They secured Harvey's car in a fenced area near the jail and went back to the courthouse. They went back to the sheriff's office, and the Rangers questioned him intensely for what seemed like hours to Rooster. He went over the entire sequence of events beginning with the first incident and up until the shooting of Harvey. He told them how he found the still and how it was gone when he returned. He told them what the young men had relayed to him and how they had refused to talk since then.

The Rangers decided to break for a late lunch, and after that, they would question the boys at the jail. All in all, it went well, and Rooster congratulated himself for not incriminating Mel in any way.

After lunch, Rooster took the Rangers to the jail. They went up the stairs to the second floor cells where the boys were being held. When the Rangers walked up to their cell and peered in at them, all the boys sat up wide-eyed on their bunks. They had no idea who these two men were, but they knew they were important. In the cell next to them, Cletus and Alice also watched slack-jawed at what was unfolding.

The jailer unlocked the cell door, and the Rangers entered and then closed the door behind them.

Harold put his foot up on one of the bunks and studied the boys intently as they squirmed silently.

"I'm Lieutenant Clary, and this is Sergeant Blackburn. We're with the Texas Rangers, and we're here to ask you some questions. We expect your full cooperation. Do you understand?"

The boys all nodded their heads and said, "Yes, sir."

"I want you to understand the importance of what we're doing here. This is a serious criminal investigation. I also want you to understand that we are here to protect you, but you must be completely honest with us."

Harold pointed toward Cletus and Alice in the next cell. "Did you buy the tainted alcohol from either of those two individuals?"

"No, sir," was the answer from each of the boys.

"Who sold that bad moonshine to you? Tell me the truth."

The boys unanimously implicated Billy Tatum.

Next, the Rangers questioned Cletus and Alice, who made no attempt to hide the fact that they were long-time moonshiners and were proud of it as well. Although they freely admitted to breaking the law for years, they absolutely denied any part in making the bad home brew.

Their lack of pretense and openness seemed to win the confidence of the Rangers. Their questioning was over quickly.

The results of the investigation so far left little doubt that Billy and Joe were the prime suspects in the moonshine poisoning, and probably the shooting of Harvey as well. Neither of them had been seen recently. Joe had been scheduled off work the day of the shooting and he didn't show up the next day. Billy rarely came into town. At that point, no one knew where they were.

The judge issued an arrest warrant for Joe and Billy at the Rangers' request, and they and Rooster drove out to their house in the country looking for them. Rooster was nervous, both at the prospect of a gun battle, and at the possibility that, if taken alive, the Tatums would finger Mel.

However, that was not to be, for all they found was an empty house. The Rangers told Rooster that they would stay for a couple more days for further investigation and then, if nothing else turned up, they would return to Austin.

When Rooster got home that evening, Laurie and the baby were back, just as Mel had promised. However, she was still upset, and it was apparent that Rooster would have to do some serious groveling before things returned to normal, which he was more than happy to do. However, his overtures were met with cold indifference. After being rebuffed several times, Rooster tried a different approach and picked up the baby. He carried him around the house, cooing to him and kissing him, and even changed his diaper, something he rarely did.

Soon, Laurie began to loosen up, smiling at the sight of the two of them. Rooster then tried the indirect approach by talking to the baby, telling him how much he missed him and his mommy and how much he loved them. Laurie puttered around the house, straightening up here and there while Rooster played with the baby. Finally, she came and sat down in the living room with them.

"It seems like he has grown a lot, just in a few days," said Rooster.

Laurie smiled softly, but said nothing.

"I don't know what I would do without him. I never realized how much family meant till I had one," Rooster said softly.

Laurie still said nothing.

"I never knew how much my in-laws could mean either. As much as Mel can drive me crazy, I love him like my own father. I wasn't trying to hurt him, Laurie. I was trying to protect him. I know it sounds crazy, but I was scared. I would never do anything to harm our family, never. I'm sorry."

Laurie eyes misted, and she nodded her head silently.

"I guess I'll go fix supper now," she said as she got up and went into the kitchen.

Rooster put the baby down on the sofa and followed her. He gently took her by the arm and pulled her to him, and they embraced. Laurie began to weep.

"I'm sorry, Laurie. I'm just a big dummy."

They stood there in each other's arms for several minutes until Laurie pulled away and began taking out pots and pans to make supper with.

Rooster went outside to have a smoke. He lit a cigarette and inhaled deeply, then tilted his head back and exhaled upward. His relief was immense. He knew it would still take a little while to smooth things over, but they had taken the first step. Everything would be all right.

As he smoked, he watched the clouds blowing across the blue sky. He looked across the fields that lie between his house and the road. He looked around in all directions. He wondered where Joe and Billy were.

35

That night Rooster made love to his wife. Afterward he lay awake in bed, listening to the night sounds coming in through the bedroom window. For some reason, tired as he was, sleep would not come, so he got up and walked softly about the house in the dark to check on everything. Then he went out on the front porch in his underwear to have a smoke.

There was enough moonlight so that he could make out the basic lay of the land and the shape of objects and so forth. He thought back to what Mel had said the night they burned the ledger and the photographs: that he hoped they would live, and how Joe and Billy were his enemies. He listened carefully for any unusual sounds. He wondered if he or Laurie even had a key to the house since they never locked the doors. He sat there for a while until he started feeling drowsy and then he went back to bed.

He slept soundly for a few hours. He had strange dreams off and on during the night, but they faded away soon after he awoke, leaving him feeling unsettled, but with no actual memory of what caused the feelings. He was surprised to see that it had rained while he slept, and as he got ready for work more clouds blew in and the rain increased.

When he got to work, the courthouse was quiet, in strange contrast to the crowds that had been there yesterday. It was dark and wet, and it seemed as if it were still night with the glow of the lights emanating from inside the courthouse. Ethel had not yet arrived, odd but understandable because of the rain. Rooster sat in his office and waited.

It wasn't long before Ethel made it in, carrying a dripping umbrella with her, and soon afterward, the Rangers also came in, the brims of their hats dripping on the floor.

Harold and Clyde got to work right away. They requested the names, addresses, telephone numbers, and employers of any associates of the Tatums. Ethel provided them with all the information she had, and they took off in the rain.

Rooster waited until they were gone, and then he went to the hospital. When he arrived at Harvey's room, he was surprised to see him awake and talking. He smiled when Rooster walked into the room, and Rooster couldn't help but break into a big grin at the sight of his buddy. He walked over and put his hand on Harvey's shoulder.

"Good to see you, my friend. I was afraid you might not make it," said Rooster.

Harvey nodded. "I have had the strangest dreams."

"I bet. I've had some of those myself."

They chatted amiably for several minutes, catching up as two old friends who hadn't seen each in some time might do.

"Do you remember what happened?" asked Rooster.

"Some," said Harvey.

"Well, there are two Texas Rangers here who will want to talk to you soon, so try to remember as much as you can."

Harvey's eyes widened. "Okay, I'll try real hard."

Just then, Claudette walked into the room, and at the sight of Harvey, she burst into tears, ran over and threw her arms around him. Rooster blinked back his own tears before saying goodbye and leaving.

It was raining even harder when he stepped outside, so he ran to his car, splashing through puddles along the way. He drove through town, his windshield wipers on high, watching the water rushing through the gutters and the glow of the shop lights in the rain.

He drove around for a bit and then went back to the courthouse. When he got to his office, the Rangers were back and going over their notes again. They had only been able to talk to a couple of people who had little information to give them.

"Good morning again, sheriff," said Harold.

"It's a wet one," replied Rooster.

"Have you heard how Deputy Wells is doing?" asked Clyde.

"Yes, I just went to go see him. He's awake and able to talk now."

"Were you able to question him about the attack?" asked Harold.

"No, his wife got there just as I did. I told him you were here and that you would want to talk to him. He said he would try to remember as much as he could."

"Excellent. Then, let's go there now," said Harold.

The Rangers followed Rooster to the hospital. By now, Harvey's mother was there as well. After a few minutes of introductions and small talk, the Rangers asked Claudette and Mrs. Wells to step outside while they questioned Harvey.

"Deputy Wells, I want you to tell us everything that happened, as much as you can remember. Start from when you left the sheriff's office," said Clyde.

Harvey began recounting every detail from the moment he left until he arrived. The Rangers, who were unaware of Harvey's penchant for excruciatingly mundane details, soon began to grow frustrated. Finally, Harold interrupted him.

"Okay, deputy, just start from when you first arrived at the place where you were shot."

"Okay. I never did see any cows running loose, but I kept on driving and I came upon a pickup parked alongside the road. There were two people sitting in it. The driver stuck his arm out and waved a red bandana, and the one on the passenger side pointed toward an open field. I pulled over in the field, and that's when both men got out of the truck and came toward me. One was carrying a baseball bat, and the other one had a gun. They both had bandanas over their faces. And that's all I remember."

"Could you see enough of their faces to tell who they were?" asked Clyde.

"No, I couldn't see much. They were wearing hats too."

"Did they say anything? Did you recognize a voice?"

"No," said Harvey.

"What about the vehicle? Can you describe it?"

"No, just the license plate."

"You can remember the license plate but not the vehicle?" asked Harold, his brow furrowing.

"Well, sure."

Rooster spoke up, "Take his word for it. I'll explain later."

The Rangers took the license plate number from Harvey and went back to the courthouse to try to look up who it belonged to. It was registered to Billy Tatum. The Rangers called headquarters in Austin, and an all-points bulletin for the arrest of Joe and Billy was issued.

The Rangers stayed for a couple of more days. They questioned more people and searched other possible places where they thought Billy and Joe might be hiding but turned up nothing. They met one more time with Rooster before leaving.

"Sheriff, if you uncover any more information or you need to contact us for any reason at all, you can reach us at this phone number," said Clyde as he handed Rooster a scrap of paper.

"Okay, thanks. I'll let you know if I need anything."

"One more thing, you might want to consider deputizing a couple of trustworthy citizens until Deputy Wells is able to return to duty," said Harold. "You never know where the suspects may be. They could be hiding around here somewhere. It's best to be cautious until we know for sure."

"Oh, okay," replied Rooster. "That's probably a good idea."

After the Rangers left, Rooster sat in his office, trying to think of who he could recruit to be his deputies. Then suddenly, an idea popped into his head, and he excitedly picked up the phone and began dialing. After a few rings, someone picked up the phone.

"Hello, Mel?" said Rooster.

36

The next morning, Rooster swore in both Mel and Kenneth as his deputies. Kenneth was now eighteen and finished with high school and still undecided between joining the circus or enlisting in the marines, so he was more than happy to sign on as a deputy. Mel, pragmatic as always, decided it was in his best interest to be on this side of the law, instead of a suspect. Laurie and Shirley were there to witness the swearing in, but neither of them were too thrilled about it.

"I think one lawman in the family is enough," said Laurie, frowning.

"That's right. You all need to be careful, especially until those awful Tatum boys are caught," said Shirley.

Kenneth was especially excited about the prospect of being a deputy. He was constantly using his shirtsleeve to polish the badge that he prominently displayed on his chest, and around his waist, he wore a gleaming pistol.

Mel, who was already used to being a big shot, took it more in stride, but he was quickly growing more and more enamored of the idea. Afterward, they all went out for lunch at the truck stop where they were treated with even more deference than usual. With all the recent goings on, and the fact that the Tatum boys were still on the loose, the townsfolk were all a bit on edge, and many citizens had taken to carrying guns as well.

Kenneth took Harvey's patrol car and began driving all over town in it, relishing this unexpected treat. Mel preferred his Cadillac, which was just as well since they only had two patrol cars, but he seemed to enjoy wearing a gun belt and badge.

However, this new arrangement was not to last long. Carrying the gun on his hip caused Mel to throw out his back, and soon he was laid up in bed and unable to do much of anything. Kenneth, in his youthful zeal, shot himself in the foot practicing quick draw techniques. Within two days, Rooster was back to being the lone lawman in Loma Grande County, and Joe and Billy were still nowhere to be found.

On the third day, Rooster received a phone call from Harold Clary.

"Good morning, sheriff. We have some news for you."

"Good morning. I hope that means you caught them."

"Not exactly, but it was close. They were pulled over by a highway patrol near Fort Worth and got into a gunfight. Billy was killed, but Joe got away. The trooper was shot too, but it was a minor wound and he should be all right."

"I see. Well, that's one down. Hopefully, it won't take long to get Joe."

"Yes, hopefully. We'd like to take him alive. That way, we can question him and maybe find out more about your moonshine operation down there."

Rooster grimaced, "Yes, that would be great, but it doesn't sound like he's going to surrender."

"You never know. Once someone is actually facing the barrel of a gun, they often change their mind. At any rate, we don't know where he is now, but be extra vigilant in case he decides to head back your way."

"He wouldn't come back here, would he?"

"It's possible. Sometimes people have unfinished business they want to take care of, especially if they think their time is short."

"Okay, I'll keep an eye out, just in case."

"Did you find a couple of citizens to swear in as deputies?"

"Oh um, yes, I did."

"Good, then you're not on your own, that's the main thing."

"Right, right. Well, thanks for letting me know what's going on."

"You're welcome. Just let us know if we can be of assistance."

Rooster hung up the phone and exhaled deeply. It didn't take long for word of the shootout with the highway patrol to make the rounds in Merky. Speculation about the whereabouts and intents of Joe were running rampant. A rumor quickly took root that he was on his way back to Merky to take revenge on all those who had wronged him: namely Rooster and Mel.

However, pretty much everyone who had ever had a run-in with Joe were also nervously looking over their shoulders and the local merchants were selling shotgun shells in unusually high numbers. Although he tried not to show it, Rooster was also on edge and worried about his family. He decided that it would be best for Laurie and the baby to move back in with Mel and Shirley temporarily. Although they were alone out in the country, Kenneth could still handle a gun even though he was homebound and using a cane until his foot healed. Rooster also took Laurie and Shirley out to the creek bottom and showed them how to use a handgun. Mel found a smaller pistol that he could carry without hurting his back and then pretty much the entire Tucker and Brown families, with the exception of baby William Melvin, were armed to the teeth.

Then, they learned that there had been an armed robbery of a bank in San Antonio and the bandit fit Joe's description. There were also reports of several vehicles stolen all the way from Fort Worth to San Antonio. To Rooster, it was clear that Joe was on his way back to Merky to extract his final revenge before being killed in a hail of bullets.

Rooster deemed it time to recruit more volunteers so he deputized a few local men and they took up positions on the main roads to check every vehicle coming into town. Others took it upon themselves to patrol the community, and a de facto vigilante police force took shape. With all the armed citizens running about it felt like a small military force had taken over the town.

Harvey was now out of the hospital, but still weak and in no condition to be of any assistance. Besides that, Claudette and his mother were terrified to let him back on the force. His days as a member of the Merky Sheriff's Department were over; henceforth, he would be a civilian. This put even more pressure on Rooster, which was more psychological than anything. Harvey had been little more than a mascot in a sense, but he was a comforting presence to Rooster, who now felt the weight and responsibility of his position very acutely.

For now, Rooster focused on protecting his family and capturing Joe. He patrolled both his and Mel's houses at night, and he stayed alone in his house while the rest of the family kept vigil in Mel's.

After a week had passed and there was still no sign of Joe, people began to relax a bit. Then, another week went by, and things were pretty much back to normal. There was still an occasional sighting or rumor floating about, but for the most part, people had come to the conclusion that Joe had moved on to parts unknown.

Laurie was ready to move back into her own home and pestering Rooster about it constantly. He finally gave in and told her it was probably safe to move back in. Laurie was ecstatic and said she would be back by the time he got off work that day.

Then Rooster received another phone call from Harold Clary.

"Sheriff, we think Joe Tatum may be heading back to Merky."

Rooster felt a knot in his gut. "How do you know that?"

"A gun shop was broken into in San Antonio, and we matched finger-prints from the scene to those on Deputy Well's car. Also, a relative in San Antonio said she was contacted by him, that he knows his time is short, and that he wants go out with a bang."

"Oh, damn..."

"We advise you to be very careful and be on the lookout. We have also contacted law enforcement from some other communities in your area, and they have offered to help."

"Okay, that's probably a good idea. Any help would be appreciated."

Rooster had barely hung up with Harold when his phone rang again. This time, it was Laurie.

"When did you start drinking again?" Laurie asked, her disappointment and aggravation apparent in her voice.

"What are you talking about? I haven't drank anything in months."

"Well, there's a beer bottle sitting on the kitchen table."

A jolt of fear and panic flashed through Rooster's body.

"Laurie, get out of there now right now! Go back to Mel's and lock the doors! Hurry! Go now!"

Laurie gasped, "Okay, I'm going."

Rooster slammed down the receiver and ran out into the lobby.

"Ethel! Call all the deputies and tell them to go my house as fast as they can get there!"

Ethel blanched and picked up the phone. Rooster ran back into his office and took a shotgun and rifle from the gun cabinet, and then he ran to his patrol car. Rooster sped as fast as he could go toward his home. He did not have his siren on because he did not want Joe to hear him coming.

When he got to his house, his heart sank, for Laurie's car was still sitting in front. Rooster slowed down and rolled up next to Laurie's car, mentally evaluating the situation and trying to think how best to act. He paused for a moment, then got out of his car and walked softly to the house. When he stepped up on the front porch, he had to tip toe to keep his boots from making too much noise. He pulled his pistol from the holster and crept toward the front door. He eased it open, grimacing as it creaked. He peered around the open door but saw nothing. He stepped inside then was jolted by a familiar voice.

"Hello, sheriff."

Rooster turned toward the voice. It was Joe. He was sitting in the living room, pointing a pistol at Laurie, who was sitting next to him, tears streaming down her cheeks.

"Oh, Rooster, I'm so sorry," Laurie sobbed.

"Oh, now, darling, no need to be sorry. Not yet anyway," smirked Joe.

Rooster stood motionless and silent.

"You need to put that gun down now, or I'll shoot your wife," said Joe. "Put it on the coffee table nice and slow. Don't try to be a hero."

Rooster slowly put the pistol down on the table.

"Okay, good. Maybe you're not so dumb after all. Now you go sit over there," said Joe, motioning toward a chair on the other side of the room.

Rooster eased into the chair.

"Well, this is nice, real nice. I like reunions. But we're missing somebody. We need Mel Tucker here."

Rooster and Laurie said nothing.

"Little missy, why don't you go get on that telephone and call Mel for me."

Laurie sobbed quietly.

"I said call Mel—now!"

Laurie went to the telephone and began dialing. After a couple of rings, someone picked up on the other end. She tried to talk but could only cry. Joe got up, keeping his gun pointed at Rooster, and took the receiver from Laurie.

Rooster could hear Mel's voice on the other end. "Laurie? What's wrong?"

"Hello, Mel. This is your old business partner, remember me?" said Joe, smiling.

"We're having us a nice little get together over here at Rooster's place, but it just ain't complete without you. You need to come on over here right now. Make sure you don't bring a gun with you or anything sneaky like that, and if you're not here in fifteen minutes, then I guess I'll have to shoot somebody, maybe your daughter. You understand me? Okay then."

Joe hung up the phone and sat down.

"You know what? I'm hungry. Why don't you go in the kitchen and fix me something to eat," Joe said to Laurie.

Rooster looked at Laurie and nodded, and she got up and went into the kitchen.

"Now don't get any ideas about running off or anything, Laurie," said Joe as she walked into the kitchen.

"Well, Rooster, how does it feel knowing today will be your last? I guess that might give a man something to think about, a reason to reflect on the bad things he's done in his life."

Rooster said nothing, but in fact, he was thinking about some of the bad things he had done in his life: planning a murder, cheating on his wife, allowing his innocent friends to take a manslaughter rap, letting everyone think he was a hero when he was anything but one.

He had tried to live a righteous life after his religious experience at the revival, but his enthusiasm for it had waned as it always had, and he had slowly drifted back to his normal mindset. According to his father's religion, he would go to Heaven because of the words he had professed, not for what he had done, but somehow he found little comfort in that. He just hoped that whatever came after death was not too bad, and he hoped that death itself would not be too painful.

Laurie brought the breakfast in and set it in front of Joe. He apparently hadn't eaten recently because he wolfed it down quickly.

"That was good," he said as he set his fork down and wiped his mouth.

Then they all heard the sound of a car pulling up in front of the house.

Joe pointed his gun at Rooster. "Laurie, go look and see who that is."

Laurie got up and looked out the window. "It's Daddy..."

"Good. Now sit back down."

They all sat waiting expectantly until Mel came walking slowly in. He was still nursing a sore back.

"Good morning, Mr. Tucker. Come right in," said Joe, obviously pleased. "Have a seat."

Mel eased down into a chair, looking worried.

"Well, this is just real nice. Just like old times, except now I'm the big boss man. Who'd a thought?" Joe laughed. "How's life been treating you, partner? I guess the moonshine business is pretty slow right now."

Joe looked at Laurie. "Did your daddy ever tell you about our moonshining operation?"

Laurie said nothing.

"I asked you a question," Joe said, frowning. "Did he ever tell you he was part of our moonshine business?"

"No..." replied Laurie weakly.

"I guess I should have known. Why would he when he can pin it all on me and Billy?" said Joe, his voice rising in anger. "That's how Mel Tucker operates, just use people up and then shit on them when he's done. Why don't you tell Laurie about it, Mel?"

Mel sighed, "It's the truth, Laurie. I was partners with Joe and Billy."

Laurie looked down at her lap.

"And I don't blame Joe for hating me. I don't blame him one bit," said Mel. "I don't blame a lot of people for not liking me, but that doesn't have anything to do with Laurie. She didn't know anything about that. You've got what you want, Joe. You've got me and Rooster. Would you please let Laurie leave? She has a baby that needs her," said Mel. "You can do what you want with us, but she's innocent."

"You know what, Mel? I guess that's right. I don't have any quarrel with Laurie, and she's going to have it hard enough raising that baby on her own. So, go ahead, Laurie. Get on out of here."

Laurie looked about the room, wide-eyed.

"Go on, Laurie. Get out of here," said Mel.

"Laurie, please go," added Rooster.

Laurie got up with tears streaming down her cheeks and walked quickly out the door.

Meanwhile, out by the main road, the recently appointed deputies were watching through binoculars.

"Somebody's leaving. It's Laurie."

"Thank goodness."

The men stood around discussing what they should do. Some wanted to charge the place, while others were concerned about provoking a shooting.

Then, a police car came down the road and pulled up beside them. It had the markings of the Rio Sueño Police Department on the door. The man inside rolled down the window.

"Well, I'll be damned," said one of the deputies.

37

"Well, fellows, it's been fun. I guess the only thing left is to decide which one of you dies first," said Joe. "I guess I could just flip a coin, but I sort of hate for it to be over with so quick. I kind of want to enjoy this a little more."

Mel wiped his brow nervously.

Rooster looked about the room, trying very hard to think of some way out. Then, he noticed the beer bottle sitting on the table.

"You know, I wouldn't mind a beer before I die. Why don't we all have one?" said Rooster.

Joe looked at Rooster disgustedly. "Why should I let you have a beer after all the crap you put me through? I should just shoot you and be done with it."

"Hell, man, even people going to the electric chair get a last meal," replied Rooster.

Joe looked at Rooster thoughtfully for a moment and then smiled slightly. "Okay, I guess a beer sounds good. There's some in the refrigerator. Go bring us each one, but don't try anything stupid."

Rooster got up and slowly walked into the kitchen. As he was taking the beers out of the refrigerator, he thought he heard something out in front of the house.

When he walked back into the kitchen, Joe was standing next to the window looking outside.

"What the hell's going on out there?" Joe muttered to himself.

In that instant, reflexively and without thought, Rooster once again became the ace pitcher of his youth, and hurled one of the beers at Joe's head. Joe turned just in time for the bottle to smack him squarely in the forehead.

"Run, Mel!" Rooster shouted.

As Joe stumbled backward, Mel took off running for the door. Rooster launched another beer at Joe, missing his head narrowly, and then he threw the third and final beer, once again hitting Joe in the head and knocking him down.

Rooster lunged for his pistol, which was still lying on the coffee table, but before he could get off a shot Joe managed to rise up from the floor and shoot. Rooster felt a sting in his side and he knew he had been hit. He pointed his gun at Joe and fired, then turned and ran toward the back door. He leaped out the door then stumbled and fell, dropping his gun in the process.

Before Rooster could get to his gun, Joe staggered out the back door, blood running from his forehead into his eyes. He stood unsteadily on his feet and pointed his gun at Rooster.

"You bastard!" he shouted. "You're going to die, but first I'm going to make you suffer."

Joe took aim and fired. Rooster felt a pain in his leg, and he howled in agony.

"How's that feel, asshole?" Joe shouted and then he took aim again. He fired once more, this time into Rooster's left arm. Once again, Rooster cried out.

"Okay, you son of a bitch, I'm through playing. Prepare to meet your maker," said Joe as he raised his pistol and took aim at Rooster's head.

Rooster closed his eyes and waited for the final shot. He heard it and flinched, but felt nothing this time. He opened his eyes and saw Joe standing wide-eyed and clasping his chest. Joe gasped and stumbled forward and fell to the ground. When Joe fell, Rooster saw someone standing behind him, someone who looked strangely familiar. Rooster lay back down on the ground, grimacing in pain.

The man walked over to Rooster and knelt down beside him.

Rooster looked up at him, uncertain of whether he was dreaming or hallucinating. The man was none other than his old nemesis Bill Hickey.

"Hickey...what...," Rooster stammered, but he was growing weaker with each second.

Hickey knelt down beside him and examined his wounds.

"You might want to pray, son. If you got anything you want to say, you better say it now," said Hickey solemnly.

Rooster felt himself fading in and out. He looked up at Hickey, and his mind flashed back to his childhood, and he saw his whole life passing before his eyes, but one moment in particular stood out. He looked into Hickey's eyes.

"Tha...that night...at the truck stop...you were right...I was going to kill her..." and then he wavered for a few more seconds and passed out.

Rooster regained consciousness briefly in the ambulance on the way to the hospital; a medic was sitting next to him, watching him grimly.

"Hang in there, sheriff," said the medic. Then, everything faded to darkness once again.

The next time Rooster woke up, he was in a hospital room. Laurie was sitting by his bedside, dozing in a chair. He looked around without saying anything for a couple of minutes. Then he tried to move and pain shot through his body, causing him to cry out, which woke Laurie.

"Oh, sweetie," Laurie said, choking back tears.

"Uhhh..." was all Rooster could muster before blacking out again.

He lapsed in and out of consciousness throughout the day and night, and each time he opened his eyes there was someone different in the room. Then, he lapsed into a fever and went into a coma. It was during this time that he had a vivid dream.

A giant being with a long, flowing beard and wrapped in robes appeared before him. This being was so large that he reached down and picked up Rooster, who was a large strapping man, and cradled him in his arms like a small child. He lay there in the being's embrace and felt loved and protected as never before. Rooster's entire life appeared before him, and with incredible insight, he saw how everything he had ever done, or said, or even thought, affected everyone around him in profound ways. Rooster felt a deep shame come upon himself, yet he felt no judgment from the being. With amazing clarity, he realized how intertwined everyone in the world was with each other and how his own thoughts, words, and deeds radiated out into the present, the future, and even the past. He understood that he had the power to influence not only his own circumstances, but also those of the people in his life, and even people he would never meet, and how the power of one's actions could carry on far into the future. Then, he felt the presence of his mother and father. Instead of disappointment, he felt love and understanding from them, and he understood that although the past could not be changed, the future was still his to create.

Then, Rooster felt them all leaving him, and he went back into the darkness. When he awoke, his fever had broken, and he felt clear headed and refreshed. He opened his eyes, and the first thing he saw was Bill Hickey sitting beside him in his hospital room. The memory of the dream was still fresh with him, and as soon as he saw Hickey he no longer considered him an adversary, but someone who had been part of his life for a reason. Although he was still weak and his throat was dry, Rooster did not hesitate before speaking.

"I'm sorry..."

Hickey looked at him perplexedly.

"I'm sorry...I lied...that night...If I just...told truth...then..." Rooster struggled to speak.

Hickey's expression softened, and he smiled ever so slightly.

"If you would have just admitted it, I would have let you go. You can't arrest man for thinking about committing a crime, or we'd all be in jail."

Rooster said nothing.

Hickey continued, "In a strange way, you did me a favor...I moved on with my life, and it turned out better than I ever would have guessed." He looked at Rooster. "You're the one who paid the price...and almost the ultimate price at that."

"I deserved to pay a price...I deserved worse than I got..."

"Oh, I don't know," said Hickey. "You're overlooking the good that you did. You stopped a robbery in progress, and you saved a young woman from a very bad experience. Sometimes, things take on a life of their own, and all you can do is just go along for the ride. Don't be so hard on yourself. We all live lies in one way or another. It seems like you've learned something from it, that's the main thing."

They chatted for quite a while. Rooster learned that, after Hickey had moved to Rio Sueño, he joined the police force there and was moving up the ranks. He and his family liked it better there, and they were happy with the change.

"I didn't think so at the time, but losing that election taught me some things that I needed to learn, how to treat people, how to earn respect instead of demanding it. I learned that I don't know as much as I thought I did and that failure is a part of life. But sometimes failure is exactly what you need to grow. I would never have learned that if I had won that election. My wife and kids are happier. I'm happier. Who would have guessed? Yes, it's true that I hated you with a passion for a long time, but I don't any more. You taught me humility, something I needed to learn. No, Rooster, you don't need to fret about that night anymore. You may have gone there with bad intent, but you didn't follow through with it. Even if the Blackwell boys hadn't shown up when they did, you still may not have been able to do it. I don't think you would have. You were just a lonely, sad person, overcome with your own worries. You're not that person anymore. That's over with. You did what anyone else would have done in those circumstances; you saved your own ass. That's the basis of survival—save yourself first."

When it was time for him to leave, Bill Hickey and Rooster shook hands, and Hickey said he would stay in touch.

Perhaps it was the lingering effects of his dream, or of the painkillers, but after Bill Hickey left, Rooster became swept up in the idea of being completely truthful about everything, all the time. He decided that he would confess to Laurie about his affair with Christine, and about his sordid past with the whores of Europe and Asia. Fortunately, Mel came in to visit Rooster first, before he was able to carry out his plan, and Mel set him straight.

"Now, Rooster, a little religion is fine and all, but goddamn, don't be stupid son."

Rooster, jolted back to reality by Mel's words, came to his senses and, once again, found himself indebted to Mel for his prudent advice.

It would take a while for Rooster to recover completely from his wounds, but because of his overall good health and strength, he was able to leave the hospital within a few days and resume light duty as sheriff.

While his body was mending, he went to his workshop in the barn and began tinkering. He dug around until he found some old lumber scraps, which he fashioned into a box with a hinged top and a hasp. Into the box, he placed his grandfather's gun and his father's Bible. He put a small lock through the hasp and then put the box away in the attic. Although those things were important to him, he no longer needed them in his daily life. He bought his own gun, one without the deeds of his grandfather notched into the handle. The Bible, although a sentimental reminder of his father, was not necessary for him to chart his course in life. He was his own man now, living his own life, the past was part of who he was, but it would no longer have any power over his future.

Cletus and Alice, having no place to go after being declared innocent, continued to stay at the jail for a while, albeit with the freedom to come and go as they pleased. The townspeople, feeling guilty for their treatment of the two moonshiners, took up donations to help them rebuild their lives. A significant amount of cash was raised and presented to them with sincere and humble apologies. The pair graciously accepted the money with benevolent forgiveness and gratitude, and then promptly left for Mexico to begin anew.

As luck would have it, a personable young man, just returned from the army, and with military police experience, applied for the job of deputy and Rooster hired him on the spot.

Harvey had also undergone a change after his injury. Although he seemed like the same gentle soul, he had somehow matured, became more of an adult, and lost most of his ability to memorize vast amounts of data and trivia. He acquired more common sense than he ever had before. He was hired as a teller at the bank, and Claudette became pregnant.

After some time had passed, and things were mostly back to normal, Rooster and Laurie threw a party for family and friends. There was no special occasion to mark. It was more of an unspoken acknowledgment that a rough period had passed, and a celebration of that mysterious thing called life.

The day of the party was near perfect, neither too hot nor too cold, and sunny and clear. Everyone who was important in their lives was there, in good spirits, and happy to be alive and in each other's company. Rooster made the rounds, spending time with each and every one, not from any sense of obligation on the part of the host, but rather a deep and loving connection with everyone present.

Laurie was radiant and beautiful, with a new bulge in her belly, and the glow of motherhood upon her face, evidence of a much easier pregnancy this time around.

As Rooster walked about, carrying his baby boy, and visiting with friends and family, one thought kept entering his mind again and again:

Rooster Brown, you are one lucky fool.

ABOUT THE AUTHOR

Tom Pointer graduated from Saint Edward's University with a bachelor of arts. He lives in a 600-square-foot house in the thriving, creative metropolis of Austin, Texas. One of his favorite activities is cycling the hike-and-bike trail around the city's Lady Bird Lake.

As a writer, Pointer likes to tackle universal themes such as the struggle to overcome your family history, which he addresses in his contemporary western novel, One Lucky Fool.

www.ingramcontent.com/pod-product-compliance
Lightning Source LLC
Chambersburg PA
CBHW051931020726
47501CB00001B/68